FRENCH BRED

GROWING UP PROVINCIAL IN A BYGONE FRANCE

Paul Bruthiaux

Published by New Generation Publishing in 2012

Copyright © Paul Bruthiaux 2012

First Edition

www.newgeneration-publishing.com

 New Generation Publishing

A frog he would a-wooing go,
Whether his mother would let him or no.

English folk song

CONTENTS

PREFACE

In the narrative that follows, I have been mostly truthful. But I confess that on occasion, I had to reconstruct when memory failed. I took care to spare everyone's blushes by changing the names of all those involved except for members of my immediate family, who will recognise themselves anyway provided they belong to the tiny subset of those who are still of this world *and* fluent in English. As for everyone else, though many of the protagonists are no longer in a position to sue for defamation, it is difficult to predict which of their descendants might take umbrage. I may have lionised some to excess and painted others blacker than they deserved. If they get to read these pages, those in the first group will not mind, and I hope that those in the second will accept my apology. To find out which group they fall into, some will have to borrow the book from the Great Lending Library in the Sky.

In the details, I may also be guilty of embellishing. But as every narrator knows, a central tenet of storytelling is never to let an awkward fact get in the way of a good yarn. And since no less a figure than Voltaire could argue that writers should aim to be interesting rather than exact, I am in good company. If it worked for Voltaire, it works for me.

I am grateful to Darin Jewell of Inspira Group for venturing where others feared to tread and agreeing to act as my agent. I also wish to thank Daniel Cooke of New Generation Publishing for his ingenuity and efficiency in bringing the book to life. Heartfelt thanks go to Diane Henneton for her moral support and especially her expert guidance on some of the finer points of contemporary French language and culture, on which four decades of residence outside France have left me with somewhat hazy notions. I especially wish to thank William Gibson for running a critical eye over the manuscript and for pointing out the innumerable flaws in it, for being unsparing in his criticisms of the worst ones, and for offering detailed suggestions about how I might put them right. Above all, I wish to thank all those who over the formative years I describe in the book provided the human dimension: family members, school friends, teachers, and countless holders of bit parts in this narrative. Thank you all for the nurturing, the friendships, the enlightenment, the entertainment, the foibles, the strengths, the values, the aspirations, the inspirations. Thank you for being there and for being who you were.

CHAPTER ONE: CITY LIMITS

Is the small town a place, truly, of the world, or is it no
more than something out of a boy's dreaming?

William Saroyan (1908-1981)

I was born in Lure, Haute-Saône. It would not have
been my first choice of birthplace, but I was not
consulted in the matter.

Deep in the heart of eastern *France profonde*, much
closer to the German border than to Paris and closer
still to Switzerland, Lure was then a town of some
6,000 inhabitants, tucked away in a part of the country
few travellers ever saw and where even fewer lingered.

At first glance, things looked promising. The natural
setting was charming. The name Haute-Saône itself
suggested pastoral loveliness. Most French
départements were labelled by their revolutionary
creators after rivers and mountains. If the rivers were
too long or the mountains too high, *départements* were
named according to whether they lay on the upper or
lower reaches of the river or higher or lower up the
mountain in question. Our *département* was named
after the languid Saône River, and its upper reaches,
where we lived, were designated as *Haute*. In my
youthful insecurity, I took pride in this stroke of
administrative good fortune.

Initially, I imagined that our *Haute* status would
make us immune to ridicule. But the delusion did not
last. One day when I was about eight or nine, our
primary school teacher introduced a new classmate who
had grown up in Parisian splendour and whose father
had just been sentenced by a vengeful employer to a
stretch of provincial exile. Lure, Haute-Saône, this
seasoned observer opined, was the tiniest town in the
whole world. I knew it was small, of course. On family

9

outings, I had sized up the competition: Vesoul (pop. 10,000) to the west, and especially Belfort (pop. 35,000) to the east, and I had marvelled at the urban sprawl. Vesoul was almost twice as large as Lure and had not one but two Catholic churches and Belfort had a couple of traffic lights and even a department store. It staggered the imagination! I was all too aware that my home town was insignificant, but I did not enjoy having my nose rubbed in it.

Then another classmate dropped a bombshell: to everyone in France except us, it seemed, Haute-Saône was known as *Haute-Patate*. I never discovered where the potato slur had originated. As I rode my bike through the countryside, I could see that many of the villages were wretched and that this was not much of a cash economy. But in summer the wheat grew tall, the cows looked plump, and no one went hungry. Perhaps there had been a string of poor harvests in days of yore and potatoes had offered the only escape from famine. In our century, there were few signs of the tuber except in shops and markets. But the label had stuck and Haute-Saône remained the butt of jokes, a kind of French Ireland, treated by Parisians with the amused contempt Londoners long reserved for the Emerald Isle and its benighted residents.

Though the slur endures, a modest turnaround is under way, most visibly on a number of websites of the 'Haute-Saône.com' type, which attempt to turn the tables on the mockers. Perhaps this was inspired by the fine American state of Idaho, which has long made a virtue out of growing potatoes, lots of potatoes, and even advertises the fact on its car number plates. Today, enterprising *Hauts-Saônois*, as the locals are called, are turning the obvious deficiencies of their *département* to their advantage by advertising it as the ideal destination for get-away-from-it-all holidays.

Some go for the New Zealand approach and proudly announce that Haute-Saône cows outnumber Haute-Saône people by a ratio of six to one. Others push snappy slogans such as 'You don't want to see anybody? Come to Haute-Saône' or 'You don't need anything? We've got plenty of that!'

But at the time, the positive thinkers were in the closet and the jibes flew. A favourite target of metropolitan humourists was language. Like all regional variants, Haute-Saône French has its peculiarities and these were picked on relentlessly by outsiders and treated as evidence not only of social backwardness and educational deprivation but of something close to mental retardation. What else would explain the fact that local speech reversed the standard French word order in *j'ai personne vu* (I nobody saw), for example, or pronounced *vingt* (twenty) with the final t sounded even when it was not followed by another word? Another obvious sign that this *département* was peopled by subhuman wretches was the local habit of duplicating verbs as in *regarde voir* (look see), as used when drawing someone's attention to something really interesting, like a cow or a potato. To Parisians, the way French was spoken the further they went from Paris, in Brittany or Provence, for example, and especially in Belgium or Switzerland was mildly comical. But our version of French was hilarious!

For me personally, further humiliation (if any were needed) came from my growing love of cars. All French *départements* are numbered in alphabetical order. Saône (Haute) comes in at number 70. The system makes it easy to identify where each car comes from. But it is also made for getting drivers dirty looks (and worse) when they find themselves lost and slowing the traffic in another *département* and especially in a metropolis such as Belfort, the nearby town with the traffic lights and the department store. The system also allows anyone to calculate the age of a car to within a few months, which means that, for the young and car-loving, it can cause untold anguish if one's dad is known to drive the oldest car of all the cars all the other dads in one's social circle drive.

The system is simple. Each set of 999 cars is assigned a letter combination such as AA. The next set gets AB, then AC, and so on. When all the combinations in the AZ set have been allotted, the car registration bureaucrats move on to BA, then BB, then BC, and so forth. But because the system was introduced centrally and on the same day throughout the country, it is easy to see which *départements* are racing ahead in car sales and which lag behind. Not surprisingly, Paris (75) has long been in the lead, followed at a respectful distance by *départements* with large cities at their heart: Lyon (69), or Marseille (13), for example. This reflects much higher populations but also economic vitality. In my days, consumer credit was unheard of so buying a car took serious cash and, as I mentioned, there was not a lot of that in Haute-Saône. So Haute-Saône lagged far behind. As richer, more urban *départements* were racing ahead into the K's and L's, Haute-Saône was stuck in the mid-B's. Nobody in Haute-Saône seemed to be buying cars. So chips on the shoulders of the young and car-loving grew larger and heavier. True, the neurosis seemed to afflict only boys, especially my younger brother Pierre and myself. Girls seemed to be immune. But girls were strange creatures. They had curious preoccupations, like skipping ropes and gazing at their damask cheeks in mirrors for hours. Girls did not care about cars, it seemed. Luckily, girls did not register much on our radar at the time. But cars, now *that* was worth losing sleep over!

As an insecure soul growing up in provincial obscurity, as soon as I was old enough to trade up from fairy tales and then comics to proper books, I searched history for any aspect of my surroundings I might pride in. It did not take long for me to realise that Haute-Saône had never produced anybody really famous: not one athlete, not one fearless explorer, not one plump dignitary of the Church, not one heroic general, not one notorious criminal, not even a notorious politician. The closest Haute-Saône had come to fame, my father's encyclopaedia informed me, was a Vesoul-born nineteenth-century painter named Gérome, who had produced a string of representations of classical myths that had sold well internationally. But by the turn of the twentieth century, pictures of Socrates finding Alcibiades in the house of Aspasia had ceased to thrill and Haute-Saône was left without anyone or, for that matter, anything to boast about.

In the early 1950s, the Swiss-born architect Le Corbusier came to the rescue by proposing a revolutionary design for a church to be built on a hilltop overlooking the nearby town of Ronchamp. The church was to grace an ancient pilgrimage site devoted to the Virgin Mary and replace a neo-Gothic eyesore that had mercifully been blown to smithereens in the fighting that took place in those hills towards the end of World War II.

Le Corbusier's sleek design features a soaring roof that seems to float atop asymmetrical walls made of thick white concrete. The walls are pierced by deep, narrow portholes that let in a gentle, meditation-inducing light. Not surprisingly, the project met with vehement opposition from an unholy alliance of Catholic luminaries and secular reactionaries, who knew a church when they saw one and had no time for this new-fangled abomination. But over the months, I watched from our kitchen window as the speck on the hill grew larger and more clearly distinguishable, until over the years it started drawing in pilgrims and attracting hyperactive teenagers on bikes in search of a destination and a challenge. The short ride from Lure, Haute-Saône to Ronchamp itself was flat and most of the climb was manageable. But a steep stretch halfway up was known to floor lesser athletes and sort the men from the boys. Negotiating it without dismounting and pushing was incontrovertible evidence that manhood had been attained at last.

Le Corbusier put up some dreadful buildings in his day, but his design for that little church on the hill at Ronchamp was truly inspired. Today, devotees of the Virgin Mary are a fast-disappearing breed, and judging by the few cars parked by the church on an average day, lovers of architectural innovation are mostly German or Swiss. How they find the place is something of a mystery. The *Lonely Planet* guide to France, as good a gauge of popular destinations as any, does not devote as much as a sentence to it or to anything else in Haute-Saône, for that matter.

In fact, the most ardent champion of the little church I ever met, much later, was the young American doctor who sewed me back together in a run-down public hospital in Manhattan after I was mugged one dark and stormy night at the end of my first and otherwise hugely enjoyable trip to America in my early twenties. In my distress, I noticed that he had a large colour poster of the church on his wall, and we came to discuss its aesthetic merits. The little church at Ronchamp was one of the most graceful buildings in the world, he said. Through freshly stitched lips, I concurred.

But for the most part, the French public and

especially the local population remained indifferent to the beauty of the Ronchamp church. Haute-Saône had a gem in its midst but few seemed to care. And once the Virgin Mary started to lose her grip on the public imagination, the people of Haute-Saône stayed away in droves. What was it that was stopping them from priding in this treasure? Why was it so difficult to develop a sense of self-worth in Haute-Saône?

In truth, our *département* had managed to produce a minor celebrity, and what is more, one born in Lure itself. His name was Georges Colomb, the author of late nineteenth-century classics he published under the pseudonym of Christophe, presumably because he felt this bit of whimsy complemented his family name nicely.

Colomb was the son of a principal of the secondary school where my father was to teach and where my siblings and I were to study almost a century later. He graduated in mathematics and later earned a doctorate in biology. He taught in eminent Paris institutions and at one time numbered Marcel Proust among his students. In between, he moonlighted as a writer and illustrator. Published in the last decade of the nineteenth century, his books were hugely innovative because they consisted of framed drawings accompanied by short stretches of text. In brief, Colomb was a pioneer of the modern comic strip.

One of his publishing successes, the aptly misspelt *Sapeur Camember* tells of the travails of an exceptionally dim, Lure-born army recruit who struggles through situations he barely understands and controls even less. He responds with a string of malapropisms and he is constantly reminded of his lowly social status by army superiors even dimmer than himself. In one episode, he is ordered to dig a hole and then a second hole in which to dump the content of the first hole only to be immediately carpeted by his commanding officer for not digging the second hole large enough to accommodate the content of both holes. This never failed to get a chuckle out of my father, who harboured deep contempt for the French military and insisted that a soldier's life really *was* like that.

Once he had achieved professional and social success in Paris, Colomb found the capital's intelligentsia more to his taste and turned his back on his provincial origins. He depicts his birthplace as just the kind of swampy backwater that would bring forth a barely literate yokel such as *Camember*. Today, his fame has grown: his books are available in the French original and there have been attempts to bring them to the screen. In fact, the secondary school my siblings and I attended is now known as *Lycée Georges Colomb*. But in my time, the man and his output were ignored except by a handful of *aficionados* such as my father. Colomb had been right: Lure, Haute-Saône *was* a backwater and its people seemed happy to keep it that way.

*

We lived in Lure, Haute-Saône because my father had landed a school-teaching job there on being released from five years in a POW camp during World War II. The town was about halfway between his birthplace near Dijon to the southwest and my mother's near Epinal to the north, so it made it easy to keep in touch with both sides of the family. The town was small, but this suited my father, who disliked cities and loved open spaces. It offered all the basic amenities of urban life: a secondary school, a hospital, a railway station, most of the shops we could possibly need, and of course a Catholic church. There was rarely any need to travel to one of the larger towns nearby. If we passed through one, it was only as a way station to the great outdoors on a Sunday afternoon family drive.

Even though German-speaking Alsace was not far away, our corner of the world was French-speaking. It was only later, once I was old enough to ride my bike further afield, that I began to sense that possession of the French language may not after all be a universal requirement for a fulfilling life. Evidence for this astonishing discovery could be discerned at the invisible line just east of Belfort, where village names as quintessentially French as Courtelevant and Foussemagne suddenly gave way to Retzwiller and Wolfersdorf. Although the Paris-led assault on regional languages including Alsatian German was already well under way, the linguistic divide remained stark, on the map at least. But we lived far enough to the west of that line not to notice it in everyday life. Needless to say, it was impressed upon us from an early age in school that we should feel grateful to the generations of French kings, presidents, and military strategists that had kept us on the lucky side of the divide.

Our town was founded in the early seventh century by an Irish monk, one of a fearless band of clerics who had fanned out across Western Europe in an effort to spread Christianity. They did this by founding a string of monasteries that later became small market towns, and their success was still evident almost a millennium and a half later. The medieval origins of the town could be seen in the concentric street pattern at its heart. Virtually everything of importance could be found within this historic core except for the hospital, the imposing army barracks on the southern edge of town, and a handful of ailing factories dotted around the outskirts.

A major feature of the town was the railway that

split it into two roughly equal halves. When the tracks were laid in the mid-nineteenth century, the area surrounding the urban core consisted entirely of farmland, so the route sensibly skirted what was then the entire town. But over the decades, even sleepy Lure, Haute-Saône had expanded and the tracks began to serve as a social divider: the urban sophisticates to the north, the semi-rural unwashed to the south. But the unfashionable side, where we lived, appealed to my father because rents were lower and our flat was spacious and the rent included a small garden where he could relax by tending his tomatoes, peas, and carrots.

Another advantage of living on the far side of the tracks was that they provided free entertainment. The railway connected Paris to Belfort and the Swiss city of Basel beyond. Traffic was heavy and trips across town were frequently interrupted as a clunky red and white barrier was lowered manually by a man-and-wife team who lived in a shack next to the railway crossing and who shuffled out, day or night, rain or shine as a bell signalled that a train was coming. If the barrier was down, a narrow side gate allowed pedestrians in a hurry to beat the train. If the train was pulling out of the station a few hundred metres away, there was plenty of time to do this safely. But if it was heading towards the station from the opposite direction, there was only a short stretch of straight track to scan. Beyond that was a bend, and there lurked danger. Anyone in a rush had only their ears to rely on.

This was serious business. A sign showing a man being dismembered by a train was displayed prominently on the gate, and from a young age my siblings and I were shown the picture and warned against even thinking about using the shortcut. The message was driven home one day when a young and popular priest who had only recently joined the parish was mowed down by a train as he tried his luck and miscalculated. To lose a man, a woman, or a child to a train would have been unfortunate, but to lose a priest was catastrophic. But for Catholic parents, the tragedy provided the logical element they needed to knock railway sense into their children: if even a man of God could be so easily dispatched by a passing train, what chance could mere children possibly have? So Catholic children such as myself duly stopped at the barrier, waited, and watched as the great machines rolled by.

One reason for my early fascination with trains was the observation that they emitted one sound as they approached and another as they sped away. But me, the main source of juvenile awe was the gigantic black locomotives, which spewed steam and smoke and soot and all manner of wonderful substances and made noises that filled me with exquisite dread as they hissed and spluttered through my little world. Local passenger trains, known as *autorail*, were more like large buses on wheels and sounded more like tractors than trains. If travel plans involved nothing more adventurous than visiting a moneyed aunt in Vesoul or consulting a medical specialist in Belfort, these contraptions were convenient as well as folksy. They came in cheerful red and yellow and stopped at every tiny station along the way. But with either destination only about thirty kilometres away, there were not all that many tiny stations to stop at. For travellers headed for a metropolis such as Paris or even Nancy, the only option was a real train hauled by a hissing, belching steam locomotive, not some smoke-free underpowered bus substitute.

Steam locomotives produce a lot of heat. In the winter cold, as I brought my bike to a halt at the railway crossing and waited for the red and white barrier to go up and I felt like an ice cube on wheels, the slow-moving locomotives produced a blast of warm air that brought me back to life. For a few seconds, I basked in the warmth and forgot the bitter cold. If the train driver determined that there was not much to stop for in Lure, Haute-Saône and raced through at top speed, even a short puff of warm air was a life-giver.

Trains were for dreaming. They took people places, or at least suggested places where they might one day take them. Trains, I imagined, went to bustling cities with lots of traffic lights and department stores and streets wider even than those of Belfort, my main gauge of urban sophistication at the time. It would be many years before I took my first hesitant steps onto the wide boulevards of anything much larger. Meanwhile, dreams of long-distance travel were sustained by the metal plates that hung on the side of each carriage and announced that this awesome sight, this mighty train, was the legendary *Paris-Bâle*. This proved that many of the passengers on the train had been to the French capital or were headed that way and were therefore certified globe-trotters, as I would surely be one day.

Today, many of those baby-boomers who witnessed the passing of the steam age insist that the main reason for their longevity and rude health is that they grew strong on lungfuls of coal dust flying off steam locomotives, not on daily intakes of omega three fatty acid as is the sad lot of today's over-protected and under-stimulated children. In fact, the real enthusiasts among the baby-boomers routinely pay for the privilege of suffering all manner of indignities and discomforts just to ride the steam train from Porthmadog to Blaenau Ffestiniog in Wales, for example, or from Sighisoara to Cluj Napoca in Transylvania. I am with them all the way. Nothing beats a steam train.

By the early 1960s, two new reasons for me to time my bike rides across town to a nicety so that the red and white barrier would be down had emerged. One was the introduction of the diesel locomotive, a soot-free, almost noiseless invention that brought to Lure, Haute-Saône fleeting visions of modernity and ushered in the demise of the steam locomotives. The other was the daily appearance of the Peugeot car transporter.

Car ownership was growing fast across France and the local manufacturer, Peugeot, was expanding its plant in nearby Montbéliard, cranking out boxy 403 and 404 models as fast as the paint could dry. Gradually, more and more of my classmates' dads gave up local factory jobs and climbed on a Peugeot company bus each day to earn a wage far above what the town's ageing textile factories and grimy foundries could offer. Some dads even worked something called a 'night shift', a startling innovation at the time. The town was on the up.

Every day in the late afternoon, the red and white barrier came down to let through a freight train of a type never seen before. It consisted of purpose-built wagons with no sides or roof, each carrying two tiers of gleaming new cars. The train rumbled through, taking the day's output to showrooms all over France and beyond as the Peugeot brand gained international recognition. To older residents, this was an astonishing development as the Peugeot family firm was remembered primarily as a humble bicycle manufacturer. At long last, we had a local success story to pride in, so local in fact that one year a quiet boy named Peugeot turned up in my class. But children are as unimpressed by commercial success as they are merciless. His presence among us was a fresh chance to make mischief, and each time his name was called, the class broke out into a chorus of *vroom, vroom* noises, which we took to be the height of wit. I hope the Peugeot boy had the last laugh and became company

CEO.

*

Navigating the streets of Lure, Haute-Saône was not difficult. There were two routes across the railway tracks and through town. For most purposes, the obvious choice was the High Street, or *Grand Rue* (not *Grande Rue* despite *Rue* being feminine). Officially, the street was called *Avenue de la République*, but nobody called it anything so pompous. It ran straight through the heart of the town, pulling in passing traffic at one end and pushing it out at the other. Heading in from the direction of Paris and Vesoul to the west, the road veered south down a steep hill as it entered the town and took visitors past the sights: the Catholic church, most of the essential shops, the post office, the red and white barrier at the railway crossing, the hospital, and the army barracks. At the southern end, the road veered east again and went over a bridge that spanned the Ognon River, a pleasant waterway but one cursed with a name only an incorrigibly rustic place such as Haute-Saône could have got itself stuck with. The name differs only marginally from the spelling of the French word for the humble onion. But the two words share a common pronunciation and this provided sneering outsiders with yet another source of mirth as if cow and potato jokes were not enough. Once over the bridge, it was a clear run past the Le Corbusier church at Ronchamp, through Belfort and its two traffic lights, and on to the German border and what I imagined to be the untamed vastness beyond.

For anyone wanting to see and be seen, the *Grand Rue* was the route to take. The alternative, the road less travelled by, took in a splendid cluster of eighteenth-century buildings that had risen out of the wealth accumulated by the original monastery. Some of these structures served as the elegant homes of the great and the good: lawyers, doctors, dentists. But this upper stratum also included a generous helping of government functionaries headquartered in the largest and most magnificent of these buildings, which functioned as the *sous-préfecture* for the eastern half of the *département*. Not surprisingly given the monastic origins of these buildings, one of them housed the vicarage. Its splendid parkland was a pleasure to bike through whenever I had business with the priests, which during my years as an altar boy of exemplary dedication to duty, I frequently did.

Just past the abodes of the rich and the godly was an attractive pond said to connect with an underground stream and to be very deep indeed. The water was black as night so the story was probably true. It was lined with drooping willows and ringed by a path that pulled in boys on bikes by day and – it was said – courting couples after dark. The pond was also home to a pair of belligerent swans. At the time, it was not entirely clear to me how courting couples amused themselves in isolated places after dark but their activities must have been safe from interference by the swans, which were known to favour an early-to-bed-and-early-to-rise approach to healthy living. Boys passing by in the daytime were another matter as the swans regarded anything in short trousers and on a bike as a trespasser and reacted accordingly and without warning. A swan on the war path can be very scary.

Incongruously, an entire side of this charming setting was occupied by a gaol. More stately homes and resident dentists followed, after which it was all downhill, socially speaking. The street ran past the back of our secondary school and on to the railway station, a structure so modest that some trains seemed not to recognise it for what it was and whistled right through. The route then followed a bleak side street and went over a narrow railway crossing from where travellers late for their train or simply broke could slip into the station along the tracks and straight onto the platform without first calling at the ticket counter. Travel to distant parts was not yet on my agenda but buzzing aimlessly about town often was, and for me, the major attraction of this route was the *frisson* invariably generated by biking past the little *café* that served as Rest & Recreation headquarters for the army garrison. Admittedly, the Rest & Recreation concept was as hazy in my young head as what courting couples got up to by the pond after the swans had turned in for the night. But I knew that this little *café* was not a place to be seen gawking at for too long.

Every day from early afternoon, two or three army Jeeps could be seen parked in front of the *café*. Then the preferred mode of conveyance of the French soldiery, these American-made jalopies had survived an Atlantic crossing, a Normandy landing, a trek across the Rhine, and a storming of half of Germany before being handed over to a grateful French army, which had never had anything quite as nifty in its arsenal. In the peaceful 1950s, one of the strategic functions of these Jeeps was to deposit men in uniform in front of the *café*, scoop them up as they staggered out a few hours later, and return them to store. Rumour had it that this joint offered more than *café au lait* and *croissants* or even *pastis*. No one ever elaborated but everyone knew that this was a place of no good. That was all growing boys on bikes needed to know to be fascinated by it.

Beyond the railway crossing, the route meandered through increasingly insalubrious tenements before returning to comparative gentility and linking with the main route through town close to where we lived. But as most locals on their errands preferred to take in the major sights, the road less travelled by stayed that way. Very little ever happened in Lure, Haute-Saône and even less ever changed. For many, even that was too much commotion. I suffered from a different condition: for me, change could not come soon enough.

CHAPTER TWO: HOME TRUTHS

The great advantage of living in a large family is that early lesson in life's essential unfairness.

Nancy Mitford (1904-1973)

I was born, or so I was informed, early one exceptionally cold December morning two and a half years after the end of World War II. My mother liked to tell the story of how, when the momentous event could no longer be postponed, she and my father had to trudge uphill through knee-deep snow to make it to the hospital on schedule. At the time, my father did not yet own a car, the town was too small to have a bus service, and ordering a taxi would have required a phone, which neither my parents nor any of their neighbours possessed, even assuming that the town's few taxis had not been laid low by post-war petrol rationing. So they had no choice but to hike through the bitter winter weather to the hospital, which is where my story begins.

Once of this world and just as now largely deprived of hair, I was parked in a cot near a window that kept being blown open by the icy winter gale, dumping snow on my bald pate. Fearing for her progeny, my mother summoned the indomitable ward nurse, who gave the recalcitrant window a critical look, sized up the technical challenge, marched off, and quickly marched back in again wielding a hammer with which she proceeded to bash the window into submission. The window-and-hammer routine went on for several days until mother and child were pronounced fit to trudge back downhill through the snow to what was to be my first home.

In post-World War II France, adequate housing was a serious problem. Although our town had suffered only limited bomb damage, reconstruction efforts across the country focused on seaports, railways, roads, and especially bridges so there was little money for replacing – let alone expanding – the housing stock especially in outposts such as Lure, Haute-Saône. With a million baby-boomers born every minute or so, the housing shortage was acute. For the first three years of my life, we lived in what was only one step above a slum. Our accommodation consisted of just two rooms on the upper floor of a crumbling house, with an outhouse at the back and washing facilities confined to the kitchen sink. But at least we had running water, a luxury denied to many of my contemporaries.

The front door opened into an alleyway – I would not call it a street – with a name that included the French words for both 'ditch' (*fossé*) and 'moat' (*douve*) because it marked what had been the outer boundary of the medieval town. My earliest memory of my young life has me climbing on a chair to watch the rubbish collection down below. The star of the show was a shaggy brown horse pulling a wooden cart. Rubbish collection was motorised everywhere else in town, but the alleyway was too narrow and the bend at one end too tight to let the municipal dumpster through. On the opposite side of the alleyway were the back doors to the mansions that lined the relatively chic *Rue de la Gare*, which led from the railway station to the post office at the heart of the town and offered travellers their first glimpse of urban polish, Lure, Haute-Saône style.

*

When I was about three, as my parents kept amassing babies and the housing shortage was beginning to ease, the family moved into much larger accommodation on the upper floor of a substantial house on the far side of town.

The house stood on one side of a large yard on a quiet street. In grander times, access to the front door had been up an imposing stone staircase that we were not allowed to use, the family being restricted to a side door that in more prosperous times had been the tradesmen's entrance. The yard was largely unattended and left to go to weed and the house cried out for a coat of paint. Inside and out, urgent repairs were required to almost all of its essential features. The place had decline written all over it. But like most houses, it had a story to tell.

It had been built almost a century earlier by a family of *emigré* industrialists who had made the move west at the end of the Franco-Prussian war of 1870-71. One of the consequences of the cessation of hostilities was that the good people of Alsace went to bed French one night and woke up German in the morning. Naturally, this was a state of affairs no patriotic Alsatian could tolerate. Those of elastic allegiances stayed behind German lines and cut a deal. True patriots – the vast majority as this was represented to us in school – gathered their children and what belongings they could carry and headed west. Lure, Haute-Saône was along the route, the population was low, land was plentiful, and the location kept new arrivals within reach of their original base in case things improved and opportunities for cross-border commerce arose. So the town suddenly acquired new residents with German-sounding names along with the capital and the know-how to start businesses, build factories, and create jobs.

Our home owed its existence to this twist of fate and the industrious Alsatian family it had sent westward. The house was substantial so it must have been designed to impress as well as provide shelter for an affluent family. Facing it was a clump of tall fir trees, higher and more majestic than anything neighbouring properties could boast. To one side was a dilapidated building that had once housed coaches and horses. In one musty corner lived a clutch of rabbits that no one in particular seemed to own. For my siblings and I, barred as we were from keeping pets at home by parents who explained that the upkeep of six children kept them busy enough, feeding the creatures vegetable rejects from our kitchen was a popular source of entertainment. Just beyond that was the original engine of prosperity, the foundry that had once generated the means to pay for the now fading opulence.

The foundry was still operating but it was hardly at the vanguard of technology. Six days a week, the workers, all of them men, rode in on their bikes, went home for lunch at the blast of the municipal siren that could be heard all over town on the stroke of twelve noon, and then repeated the procedure in the afternoon. Occasionally, a lorry drove into the yard and around the fir trees, dumped some crates or a bundle of metal rods at the foundry gate, and trundled off to its next assignment. The foundry produced odd-shaped chunks of metal destined to become parts of unidentified machines. It belched smoke, churned up coal dust, and clanged away all day. But the fir trees provided an effective screen and the disturbance was manageable. Those Alsatian patriots had planned things well.

Being taken on a tour of the foundry in full swing as a small child was an unforgettable experience. The smells, the noise, the heat, the sight of red-hot metal being poured into moulds from huge vats hanging from the roof on massive chains was breathtaking. High above my head, power was transmitted to mighty machines via long leather belts that looped around enormous wheels. Men in overalls the colour of soot hammered away at things. Sparks flew. Instructions were shouted. Some of the men seemed to find young children's presence entertaining and inaudible comments were exchanged. The only difference between this Satanic mill and the originals was that children were taken there to look, not to work.

Our living quarters consisted of a large flat that filled the entire upper floor of the house across the yard from the foundry. The flat was reached via a wide indoor staircase that smelled of wood polish and everyone's cooking. It was flanked by a broad flat bannister obviously designed for children in a hurry to slide down. The practice was wildly popular but it was regularly quashed by our parents, who feared not for our safety but for the prospect of another sermon from our grandmother, who had by then come to live with us and who had strong views on what was and was not proper behaviour on the part of God-fearing children. Apparently, sliding down bannisters was not. Every weekday, the first sibling home from school picked up the mail left at the bottom of the bannister by Madame Brossard, our all-seeing, all-knowing resident landlady after she had rifled through the stack and added fresh data to her encyclopaedic mental record of who had written to us in the preceding months, a subject on which she frequently commented to my grandmother, who seemed curiously awed by Madame Brossard and her affectation of gentility.

The flat was sliced in half by a long hallway that ran from the kitchen at one end to what my father called his 'study' at the other. As money became more plentiful, the kitchen first acquired an electric cooker, with four rings of various diameters and a cavernous oven, all of which had become prerequisites for a family that by the mid-1950s consisted of a grandmother, two parents, and no fewer than six children, all demanding to be fed at frequent intervals. Then, as the task of doing the family laundry by hand became overwhelming even for a mother-grandmother team, the next item on the shopping list had to be a washing machine. This state-of-the-art item featured a set of horizontal rubber-coated rollers at the back through which the damp laundry could be forced by cranking a handle so that most of the remaining water could be wrung out. This was man's work and my father gladly obliged since laundry days were scheduled to coincide with his presence at home.

Eventually, when I was about eight or nine, a refrigerator completed the set of labour-saving devices. This was no slim-line affair. Insulation was provided by thick sides and a massive door that only grown-ups and older siblings could hope to open. Its electric motor came on intermittently with a loud roar. But crude as it was, it did the job and it beat one of us having to run downstairs to fetch or store essential ingredients my mother had until then kept in a larder in a cool and relatively salubrious corner of the basement two floors below.

Ever the inventive sort, I soon devised an additional use for the refrigerator. Once a month or so, I stood with my back flush against its door, drew a line on it with a pencil just above my head. I then extrapolated based on recent progress how long it would be before I equalled and then surpassed the refrigerator in height. Beating the refrigerator became a major ambition and achieving it around the age of twelve or thirteen gave me a huge psychological boost. Manhood could not be far away.

The living room consisted of a vast space divided into two zones by strategically-placed furniture: one half for the adults, the other for the children. Meals were taken in the adults' section, but my siblings and I spent most of our time in our own section since this was also where we did our homework. Periodically, one of us announced that he or she had finally managed to memorise a Latin declension or a few more lines of La Fontaine or Corneille and was ready to recite to any willing adult. The young scholar then shuffled over to the other side, recited away, shuffled back, and sat down to address the next educational challenge on the list.

The rest of the living accommodation consisted of four large bedrooms. The most imposing and the only one with a fireplace was reserved for my grandmother. Once a year, my siblings and I were allowed inside to pick up the Christmas presents that had supposedly wafted down the chimney. On every other day, the bedroom was strictly out of bounds. In truth, for a good half of the year, it would have been as unwelcoming as it was magical on that special occasion. My grandmother was a staunch believer in the power of fresh air to cure most ills. Every morning in all weathers, she opened her window wide and in winter made a major contribution to keeping the entire flat frigid. My parents had their own bedroom. A third bedroom housed all four of my sisters: Odile, Bernadette, Madeleine, and Marie-Jeanne, in descending order of age, despite the fact that they ranged in age from two to seventeen when they were first corralled together.

The fourth bedroom was divided into a sleeping area my younger brother Pierre and I shared and a partitioned-off section that functioned as the family bathroom even if the only built-in amenity was a washbasin. Pride of place went to the enamel bucket that served as our communal toilet. Each day, one of my mother's chores was to take the bucket down to the flush toilet on the half-landing below, which for reasons of stalled negotiations between my father and Madame Brossard, our money-grasping landlady, the family was not permitted to use. But in a display of generosity about which she bragged to all her other tenants, Madame Brossard allowed my mother to pass through its portals once a day to empty the bucket. She then poured in a generous measure of bleach, put the lid back on, and returned the bucket to its rightful location. The partition was made of wood so thin that it rattled every time the door opened or closed, and as it stopped well short of the ceiling, the lavatorial experience could be shared with my brother and myself or anyone else who happened to be in the room.

If any of us had constipation problems, the cause would not have been hard to diagnose. Children are not fussy when it comes to calls of nature and the combination of bleach and lid was surprisingly effective in taking care of the smell. But how my brother and I managed to fall asleep to the sound of family bowels being emptied and the content plopping into the bleach at the bottom of the bucket is more than I can now imagine. Further negotiations involving additional cash transfers from my father to Madame Brossard must have followed because the toilet on the half-landing eventually became part of our domain. Only then did I shed the acute embarrassment that had forced me to make up excuses for never inviting any of my friends to my home. One or two years later, a tiny shower was added to the bathroom. We were on our way to a life of ease.

At the very top of the house was a large attic where my mother dried the family washing. In winter, it was so cold up there that the damp laundry froze on the line. At one end was a storage room where the usual family *bric-à-brac* was stored: a dismantled bed frame, a stack of battered suitcases that had – literally – been in the wars, several hat boxes that my grandmother no longer had any use for but that could not bring herself to discard and used instead for storing ancient letters and family photos and even stacks of Russian railway share certificates made worthless by the bolshevik default on Tsarist debts in 1917. Soon after my father bought his first car, a corner was cleared to make room for the camping gear that awaited the next summer jaunt. Standing forlornly in a corner was the blue high chair that had held the six of us once we were strong enough to sit upright and partake of family meals. A more recent addition was a rusty tricycle that had been handed down from sibling to sibling and then retired once my youngest sister Marie-Jeanne was old enough to ride a real bike. All this was covered in a thick layer of dust, with a large selection of spiders in attendance.

Next to that was a room occupied by Mademoiselle Lomballe, a friendly lady who in Victorian days in England would have been known as a 'distressed gentlewoman'. Though relatively well-off in her younger days, she had suffered the indignity of needing a job later in life to cope with reduced circumstances. She worked in a small shop that specialised in knitting and sewing supplies and my siblings and I occasionally stopped by to pick up an order from my mother for needles, wool, or thread. Despite her misfortunes, Mademoiselle Lomballe was kindly and good-humoured and my mother often encouraged us to run upstairs and ask whether there were errands we could run for her.

*

If decline was written all over the house, it did not prevent Madame Brossard our landlady from perpetuating time-honoured middle-class rituals. In fact, it probably encouraged it because this was the only way she could deal gracefully with the decline. This involved socialising regularly with peers, some of them in equally dire straits. Every now and then, haughty couples I knew from their regular attendance in church drove up to the house, parked their cars under the fir trees, spent the evening playing bridge, and then drove home. The exodus took place far too late for me to be still up and in a position to witness it. But by morning, the cars were gone.

The gracious hosts for these elegant evenings were Madame Brossard herself and her grown-up son, André. She was the daughter of the Alsatian patriot who had built and operated the foundry before it passed out of family hands. She had married a doctor and, it was rumoured up and down our street, driven him to the bottle and an early grave through a combination of relentless nagging and an elastic interpretation of her marriage vows. For all I knew, the passing years may have dimmed the lady's extra-marital ardour but her capacity for nagging was undiminished, this time with children as the target. We sensed that she hated us and we in turn hated her. Even my father, normally a mild-mannered man whom I never once heard swear, was unsparing in his denunciations.

Madame Brossard navigated genteel decline by collecting rents from the new foundry owners and as many tenants as she could cram into her crumbling house. Her take on the economics of renting was simple: spend nothing whatsoever on maintenance and use any pretext to raise the rents. Every few months, my father climbed the stairs fuming and launched into a diatribe against the woman's absolute gall at announcing yet another rent increase. He then sat down at his desk and penned a sarcastic letter explaining that he would gladly pay up as soon as she would attend to a long list of maintenance issues: a broken lock, a leaky corner of the roof, or the defunct electrics in the dank basement where he stored his coal, my mother kept her winter stock of potatoes, and all of us parked our bikes. When we were older and deemed capable of understanding that some people were nicer than others and that it was important to learn to tell the difference and sometimes necessary to discuss it openly, he read out these letters before pushing them under Madame Brossard's door. The readings had us in stitches but they drove my grandmother close to apoplexy. Herself the issue of stolid middle-class stock and of impeccable Catholic lineage, she considered the performance in poor taste and a shameless assault on Christian charity. My father had a good line in sarcasm. We looked forward to announcements of rent increases and the comedy this provided. The proposed increase was then shelved for a few months until Madame Brossard tried her luck once again and, once in a while, succeeded.

But even successful rent increases could not dim Madame Brossard's love of nagging or her detestation of children and the happy home life they represented. We shared a common hallway on the lower floor of the house, where she roosted. All day long, her door was kept ajar and she could be glimpsed sitting by her stove catching up on death notices and car crashes in *Les Affiches de la Haute-Saône*, the local weekly newspaper, as she waited for a young victim to ambush. As soon as she spotted one of us creeping past her door, she called out and the admonition started. We were always in the wrong place doing the wrong thing at the wrong time. There was a way of coming down the stairs that made absolutely no noise, apparently. How long would it be before we learned it? If we went in or out through one door, we should have gone in or out through another door. If we rode our bikes around the

36

fir trees one way, we should have ridden them the other way. Her *bête noire* was whistling, which we loved and practiced assiduously. Whistling made Jesus weep, apparently, which our parents reassured us was nonsense, though I later came to wonder how each school of thought could possibly know that.

Madame Brossard was never satisfied. Our parents were well aware of this but the neighbourhood was pleasant, the rent affordable despite the periodic increases, and the accommodation spacious enough for a large family living on a schoolteacher's income, and younger members of the family had access to outdoor space in which to play safely. So we all learned to live with it and we found solace in poking fun at Madame Brossard's son André instead.

André was older than my eldest sister Odile by about ten years and already an adult, hence the fun since he hardly fitted our mental picture of how a grown man should occupy his time. He had been one of my father's earliest students in the immediate post-war years and had gone on to study law in at the University of Nancy. After graduating, he came home and set about applying for positions that might befit his qualifications and especially his mother's inflated sense of her own worth and her special talent for turning a blind eye to the inexorable slump it was suffering.

Except for the corner of her kitchen we glimpsed as we hurried by, the scene in Madame Brossard's living quarters was a closed book to us children. But it was described to us in details by my grandmother, a regular visitor in part because the two were close in age and in social background but also because of my grandmother's curiously misplaced respect for someone whose behaviour hardly matched her own high moral principles. According to her, one of the significant features of this elegant interior was an upright piano of fine manufacture, proof positive surely that this was the home of persons of distinction.

Day after day, André sat in his mother's drawing room and wrote application letters to law firms and government departments. He relaxed from his toils by playing his mother's piano, tolerably well in fact, as we knew since we could hear every note wafting up through some loose floorboards. In clement weather, he did a bit of pruning on the rhododendron bushes in the front yard. On social nights, he graced his mother's bridge parties as the resident intellectual who had sat at the feet of learned law professors. In between, André devoted his life to the worship of God.

Every evening, about an hour before dinner time, my siblings and I took a break from our homework and watched as he wheeled his bike out of the basement, tucked his trousers inside his socks, and rode off to church. He rarely missed a service, rain or shine. There he was, on his knees, prayer book in hand, a look of beatific devotion on his face. I know this because from the age of about ten or eleven, I was there almost as often as he was but on the other side of the counter – so to speak – assisting the priests by carrying consecrated objects hither and thither, ringing bells at strategic moments, and generally making myself useful in the service of the Lord.

There was not an ounce of malice in André. If anything, that was his problem. He was an affable man who did not have it in him to say that enough was enough and walk out on his ghastly mother. Soon after she died (and, I hope, a wooden stake was driven through her heart just in case), André suddenly landed a legal position in the burgeoning Common Market bureaucracy. With indecent haste, he packed his bags, consigned his bike to the dark basement, and took the first train north to Brussels. In an instant, he was lost to bridge, the piano, and the worship of God.

*

In our immediate neighbourhood, three locations stood out, in ascending order of social prestige. At the unfashionable end of the street was a lowly *café*. On lethargic summer afternoons and for want of anything better to do, my brother and I sometimes walked over and watched the bowling: not *pétanque*, the game played with heavy steel bowls on any available piece of real estate but traditional bowling, which involved pins and large wooden bowls. The game was played along one side of the *café* on a dusty wooden launch pad, with a clutch of unstable wooden pins at one end and a *pastis*-fuelled covey of equally dusty and unstable locals at the other. The spectacle was hardly edifying but as long as we stood on the outside of the fence for the sole purpose of watching the bowling, our presence there was sanctioned by our parents.

Moving up the social ladder was the impressive house of our immediate neighbours, Monsieur and Madame Gautier and their two daughters, Françoise and Josiane. The sisters were lively friendly girls. True, Françoise was a tad bossy but so was my older sister Bernadette so the two of them kept each other in check. For my brother and myself, a more vexing problem was that they were girls and therefore incapable of taking an intelligent interest in cars or steam locomotives. But beggars couldn't be choosers as my philosophical brother often remarked though perhaps not in such elaborate terms and obviously not in English.

Monsieur Gautier had made his pile in insurance. When my siblings and I visited during school holidays, the family was invariably hospitable and the house was free of censorious grandmothers and nagging landladies. Their attic was filled with old clothes so afternoon games consisted of putting on guises as the mood took us or rather as the mood took Françoise and Bernadette who between them planned the events, worked out the procedures, and gave the orders. Boys were not consulted. I shudder to think what dressing up as princes and prancing about in flowing robes so that the girls could pretend to be princesses might have done to our nascent masculinities. But neither brother, I am happy to report, was harmed by the experience and our masculinities came through unimpaired. When the make-believe was over, we were invited to the family kitchen for a slice of cake and a glass of lemonade and occasionally into the living room, which featured the only television set in the entire street. But exactly what French television programming consisted of in the late 1950s I could not say as the television was never switched on. Difficult though this may be for many and especially for Americans of similar ages to believe, Françoise and Josiane showed not the slightest interest in television. I suppose it had been acquired as a kind of fashion accessory. Though visibly wealthier than we were, the Gautier family was open, unpretentious, and much more welcoming than the income gap between our two families would have predicted. Monsieur and Madame Gautier and my parents remained friends for many years.

Moving up as high as it was possible to climb in our neighbourhood was the house of a childless couple of Alsatian origin, Monsieur and Madame Lederbacher. These people were so grand that they never once acknowledged our existence in all the years we lived there despite the fact that our living room windows faced directly into theirs. They owned and operated another smoke-belching factory right behind the foundry next to our house. I never quite understood what that factory churned out but judging by the ritzy cars the Lederbacher couple drove and how often they traded them in, it must have had a ready market. Much later, as I reflected on the nature of second languages and what trying to learn one can do to one's self-confidence, I came to wonder whether the main reason for their aloofness was not perhaps the fact that they remained primarily German speakers and never really became comfortable with French, at least not to the point where their rhetorical flourishes might match their money and their inclination to flaunt it.

*

Beyond our immediate neighbourhood, sources of entertainment in Lure, Haute-Saône were few but not entirely lacking. Once a year, gentler times were evoked when a Punch and Judy show came to town. The puppet masters consisted of a father-and-son team who answered to the unusual name of Xolliax and who toured eastern France in search of young audiences and a living. The father, an artistic-looking older gentleman, with a flowing white mane, round glasses, and a friendly grin was a life-long friend of my grandmother's. Each year, she dipped into her meagre savings and took the juvenile element to see the show. We loved those puppets and we shrieked with laughter as they argued in squeaky voices and hit each other over the head with cudgels. Sadly, age eventually took its toll on the patriarch and the show went the way of all insubstantial pageants.

Theatre of sorts was also available outdoors. When I was still very young, the municipal council decided to make us modern by upgrading the sewers in the centre of town. One morning, huge yellow diggers and earth-movers rolled in and started tearing the street apart. My favourite, which I watched until I had to be dragged away, had wheels the size of small houses, or so it seemed to me at the time. The driver was perched high up and could switch between sitting on the right or the left of the monster depending on which side he had to watch most closely to prevent the beast from toppling into the hole it had just dug. For weeks, nearby streets ran with mud and smelled like an overflowing latrine. But this was street theatre of the highest order and I resolved to devote my professional life, when the time came, to operating diggers and earth-movers, until some other fantasy took over.

Martial displays came to town too. Army parades punctuated the calendar especially during commemorations of World Wars I and II. Presumably, Bastille Day on July 14 witnessed an even grander affair but we were never there to witness it because this was when we were away on our annual camping trip or partaking of country life in my father's ancestral village in Burgundy. But I did not mind: in my eyes, military displays paled in comparison with building sand castles on Atlantic beaches or pushing siblings and cousins into haystacks in an effort to help rural relatives bring in the harvest before the weather turned.

On the occasions I did witness, the parades featured a line of green lorries filled with joking, smoking conscripts who did not look as if they had it in them to hold the enemy at bay for very long. Next came odd-looking American hybrids recycled from World War II and known in French as *un half-track*. Bringing up the rear were whatever Jeeps could be spared from Rest & Recreation duty at the *louche* establishment by the railway station. I was never discouraged from watching these parades. But my father, who knew his *Sapeur Camember* practically by heart, warned me not to be over-impressed. This was the French army all over: all puffed up but behind the curve, ineffective, and wasteful.

These parades brought brief flashes of colour to our small town routines. But for sheer excitement, we had to wait for the travelling circus that came to town once a year. As the date approached, anticipation built up. Suddenly, posters advertising the event appeared on walls of uncertain ownership, usually next to an older notice warning that putting up posters on the wall was strictly prohibited and would incur crippling fines. The posters came in garish colours and featured as many of the upcoming attractions as could be crammed in: clowns, trapeze artists, lion tamers, and lions and other beasts seemingly quite beyond taming. None of us ever attended a performance because the cost was prohibitive for a large family and any attempt at sorting the academically deserving from the undeserving among siblings each year would have set off internecine ructions too ugly to contemplate. The circus also had the irksome habit of visiting on weekdays and as performances took place at night, this interfered with school the next morning. But my siblings and I were free to visit the travelling *ménagerie*: lions, panthers, leopards pacing angrily inside cramped cages but also hippos and rhinos penned inside tiny spaces and lying disconsolately on a thin layer of filthy straw. Cruelty to animals was not a concern.

For children prevented by circumstances from enjoying the fun inside the tent at night, a riveting part of the event consisting of watching how the entire set-up rose from nothing and just as quickly vanished into thin air. On circus morning, I made a point of setting off to school early to allow time for the necessary detour and for spending a few minutes watching the spectacle before heading to my classes.

As soon as the entire caravan reached the town early

43

in the morning, crews set to work and within a few frantic hours they had erected a massive tent, bolted together rows of terraced seats, and fed, watered, and displayed the animals. They even found time to drive an elephant show through the town in the afternoon. The performance must have required not just skill and discipline but also extraordinary energy. The moment it ended and the charmed spectators fanned out into the night on their way home, the tent was dismantled, the seats taken down, and the animals returned to their trailers. I was never there to witness it but this is what must have happened because by the time I passed by on my way to school the next morning, everything was gone, leaving not even rubbish behind. This was impressive. I presume they caught up on their sleep in their trailers as the caravan moved on to the next town, leaving ours to reminisce and await its return.

For anyone growing up in Lure, Haute-Saône and interested in creatures great and small, the ultimate ambition was to be taken to the Basel zoo. By convention, this privilege was tied to scholastic success. But as I will relate shortly, my academic career was destined to be less than scintillating and trips to the Basel zoo never included me so the annual visit by the travelling circus offered the only chance to learn about every creeping thing after its kind and now they might be related. Biology lessons never mentioned evolution not for ideological reasons, I suspect, but because the concept probably seemed too novel to the curriculum designers. Besides, unlike Latin and French poetry, both of which formed central planks of French education, there was not a lot that could be memorised about evolution.

*

All my siblings and classmates admitted to being thrilled by the circus. But for car-loving boys such as my brother and myself, as street theatre went, nothing could beat the Monte Carlo rally. Each January, crews raced towards the French Riviera along one of several roughly equivalent routes starting from cities dotted around the edges of the known universe: Lisbon, Oslo, Glasgow, Naples, Belgrade. The event is now confined to the French Alps and is a shadow of its former self. But at the time, for a boy already obsessed not only with cars but also with travel and exotic locations, it was a treat.

For some reason, routes starting from points north invariably took in our home town. As long-suffering residents of Lure, Haute-Saône, we were used to being ignored on a good day and mocked on all the other days, so we were thrilled though I could not help wondering why we were being so honoured. Perhaps the local byways were rough and winding enough to provide the right degree of challenge on the way to the perilous slopes of the Alps further south. Or perhaps, since our *département* was not exactly teeming with humanity, it was easy to trace a route through quiet villages and small towns without ever going near a busy city.

The frenzy over the rally was fed by the specialised magazines my brother and I shared and discussed at length. Over the weeks leading up to the event, we read accounts of past rallies and the prognostications of experts for the upcoming event. We compared the specifications of participating cars and struggled to pronounce the drivers' names, especially those with so many *umlauts* that we concluded they must be German or perhaps even Finnish. We consulted maps and compared the pros and cons of each route.

Once the rally was under way, we devoured daily

newspaper reports on its progress and read and reread accounts of motorised derring-do in the remotest corners of Europe. If the story of the day reported that a car had slid off the road on an icy patch or plunged down a ravine on a treacherous mountain curve, we empathised with the hapless drivers as if we knew them personally. On the day the rally was due to pass through town, we stood on a wind-swept corner, enjoying a rare permission to be late for lunch though definitely not for school. Our vantage point was the top of the hill by the hospital, where we had a sweeping view of the approach.

Suddenly, waves of Mini Coopers and Alfa-Romeos with large numbers in a white circle on their doors bounced over the railway crossing and roared up the hill past a small gathering of chilled enthusiasts and off into the distance. Through mud-splattered windscreens, we glimpsed helmeted crews peering at the road ahead or poring over maps: Swedes, Italians, Spaniards, our magazines informed us, even Finns, a nationality few of our classmates even knew existed. Though the winter cold made it difficult to hold a pen in a gloved hand, one of us ticked each passing car on a list we had torn out of one of our magazines. As the last car on the list roared past on its way to the bridge over the Ognon River and points beyond, we were left to imagine the road ahead and dream of one day driving that route in our very own car. Then, much too soon, preoccupations switched from the exotic back to the parochial and life resumed its leisurely course for another long year.

*

Clearly, there was stimulation to be had in Lure, Haute-Saône. But finding the place fulfilling beyond the ages of fourteen or fifteen called for an outlook that I, for one, did not possess and never acquired. To do this, I would first have to develop the ability to ignore the mockers, especially the sneering Parisians. I would have to see value in the notion that what you don't know you don't miss and ignore the urge to look beyond, especially at the remote and the exotic. I would have to regard the passing Monte Carlo rally as nothing more than a noisy smelly inconvenience. This would mean watching Mini-driving Finns and Scots in action and never feeling like stopping them to ask what Finland or Scotland were like, which, incidentally, would surely involve becoming fluent in languages other than French. In brief, I would have to be content with what was there. And throughout, I would have to deal with the pressure to conform imposed by the combined forces of two intolerant hierarchies, the French State and the Catholic Church and their fearsome powers of coercion, on which more later.

For better or worse, none of the above was in my nature and it would not be long before I started feeling restless in Lure, Haute-Saône. The place had undeniable charm but this was no country for young men. I would have to move on. But first, there was a lot more growing up to do.

CHAPTER THREE: FAMILY SECRETS

It isn't necessary to have relatives in Kansas City in order to be unhappy.

Groucho Marx (1890-1977)

Even by the Catholic standards of the times, ours was a large family so bear with me while I enumerate.

Nine people lived under one roof. My widowed maternal grandmother had joined the household when I was about three as creeping arthritis began to make her independent existence precarious. At the time, my father and mother were forty and thirty-six, respectively. They had married in 1938. Their first-born daughter, Odile, was left without siblings for the first seven years of her life after my father was sent to stand guard on the Maginot line in 1939 as part of the quixotic French attempt to block the advancing German army and did not return from captivity until 1945. On his return, a second daughter, Bernadette, soon emerged followed by your humble narrator little more than a year and a half later. Then at roughly two-year intervals, we were joined by my third sister Madeleine, my brother Pierre, and my youngest sister Marie-Jeanne. By 1954, the full set was in place.

I know very little of my paternal grandparents. I cannot even recall their first names. My father never talked about them. What little I picked up was from my mother. For the five long years of my father's captivity during World War II, daughter-in-law and mother-in-law did their best to comfort each other through visits and exchanges of his rare letters home. After my grandfather died, my grandmother remained on the ancestral family farm on the fringes of eastern

Burgundy where she raised a few chickens and grew the staples of traditional French cooking: cabbages, potatoes, carrots, onions, lettuce. For my mother, visiting her mother-in-law during those war years had the added advantage of giving her access to the essential produce that was so difficult to obtain even in small towns.

A single surviving portrait of my paternal family is a photo taken around the start of World War I. It shows my grandmother seated at the centre. Her husband is standing behind her, sporting a spiky moustache and wearing an ill-fitting army uniform. Next to him is their eldest daughter Marthe, a strikingly beautiful young woman who despite the matrimonial potential suggested by her looks became a nun. Her younger sister Marguerite stands next to her. Both girls are attired in the same austere style as their mother, each wearing a black dress of stiff material suggesting that life was not meant to be fun. Jean, my father's older brother stands to one side. Both brothers are wearing black suits brightened only by a broad white collar, presumably their Sunday best. The state of their shoes suggests that they had to trudge along muddy lanes to get to the photographer's studio. The only light touch in the family portrait is provided by the pretty dress worn by their younger sister Catherine, then aged two.

No one in the photo smiles. All three older women have the square jaw and the determined look of those who know what needs to be done and how to get it done. Even the two-year old shows an early hint of steel. My father's older brother looks immensely pleased with himself. In fact, all four siblings show signs of the single-minded attitude to life and its challenges that had only become more apparent when I knew them several decades after the photo was taken. Only the faces of my grandfather and my father hint at introspection, even diffidence. The look in their eyes suggests listeners and questioners, not leaders of men.

My father never spoke about his family because in a sense he never had one. At the end of World War I, his parents left Champdôtre, the ancestral Burgundy village close to the Saône River, for a life of service with a wealthy couple who lived in the northern French Alps, practically another planet by the parochial standards of the time. My grandmother took care of household matters while my grandfather tended the grounds and did odd jobs about the house. This seemed a curious move on their part given that the male population of the country had just been decimated and farming must have required more hands than were available. But over time, hints by various family members suggested that my grandparents' motivation may not have been purely economic. To my sensitive young antennas, it sounded as if they had jumped at a chance to escape the strictures of village life.

There had been at least one precedent. In the 1970s, a distant cousin of my father's unearthed a letter written over one hundred years earlier by a common ancestor who had swapped the immutability of rural Burgundy for the unpredictability of the Mexican high *sierra*. For impoverished but plucky Frenchmen, a chance had come to travel with the expeditionary force sent there in 1861 by Napoleon III, a ruler as vainglorious as he was cynical. Thinly disguised as retribution for Mexico's recent default on its debts, the move was in reality designed to assert France's colonial ambitions by subverting Mexican independence and, for good measure, grab a slice of its mineral riches while the Americans were too busy dealing with fratricidal turmoil at home to be in a position to object. A mere six months later, the adventure came to an inglorious halt as the French expeditionary force was routed at the

Battle of Puebla, which Mexicans commemorate whole-heartedly and raucously each year as *Cinco de Mayo*, an event on which my French history textbooks had been strangely muted.

Although the French recovered and went on to capture Mexico City and install a puppet emperor along with all the trappings of the office, the dream of a French colonisation of Latin America soon unravelled. In 1867, the defeated and demoralised French withdrew and began to devise ingenious ways of gaining a foothold in Africa instead.

Evidently, for many of the survivors, the prospect of life in the tropics must have seemed vastly preferable to an ignominious return home, and many stayed behind and started a new life in Mexico. Today, the Puebla phone book is still replete with French names as is the *Cementerio Francés*, the corner of the city's vast cemetery reserved exclusively for families of French ancestry.

In his letter, this ancestor did not explain whether he had been conscripted into the expeditionary force or joined it voluntarily or even followed in its wake in the hope of adventure and riches: presumably his intended reader, his sister, already knew this. He had written to her to commiserate with her over the death of their beloved mother, the news of which had taken months to reach him. In surprisingly elaborate French and neat handwriting (which may or may not have been his own), he expressed his regrets at the sorrow he had caused his mother on his departure and gave details of his new life.

He worked a silver mine near the small Mixtec town of Tlapa, deep in a remote valley halfway between Mexico City and Acapulco. The mine was barely productive, life was hard, and he sorely missed his family. The letter makes no mention of a wife or children and it hints at a succession of unspecified misfortunes that had befallen him since his arrival in his adoptive land. But divine providence would prevail, he was certain, and something would turn up.

Nothing was ever heard of him again.

Perhaps this brave ancestor's foray into alien territory and my own grandparents' trek south in search of a better life and a degree of emancipation found an echo in my own urge some four or five decades later to free myself from small-town rigidities. Unfortunately, I was never able to verify my hunch since both of my grandparents were dead by the time I was born. My grandfather died in his early sixties while my grandmother just scraped into her seventies. Life expectancy was low and neither was considered to have died especially young. My grandparents could not have imagined that their eldest daughter would make it to just short of a century and that their second daughter would beat that by almost a decade.

The working couple sent back what money they could and as a result of this enforced estrangement, their five children, my father included, were brought up by aunts.

By the time he turned eight, my father, their fourth child, had been spotted as a bright boy by the village schoolteacher and the village priest. Soon, he became a boarder in a remote Catholic seminary at the opposite end of Burgundy, where he was drilled in Latin and Greek and of course Catholic dogma. When some four decades later it was his own children's turn to ponder the mysteries of Latin (though mercifully not those of Greek), my father remembered his Latin as if it was yesterday and he clearly enjoyed reliving the experience as he helped us with our homework. By comparison, his love of the Catholic dogma seemed tepid. The bargain the Catholic Church struck was that it would educate poor boys at its own expense in the hope that some would stay on and train for the priesthood. The bet must have paid off because every tiny village in France had its own priest. But my father never gave the slightest hint that he had ever considered the priesthood as a career option.

Luckily for him, Catholic dogma did not get in the way of a love of scholarship. After completing his secondary education, he signed up for a degree course in history and geography at the University of Dijon. The plan was to become a schoolteacher, which would propel him far beyond what anyone in his family had ever achieved. He would not only command respect, he would also secure for himself and his future family a coveted position as a civil servant of the French State with all attendant perquisites including tenure and pension rights.

This preoccupation with job security may seem unambitious in a man in his early twenties. But my father had experienced rural poverty first hand. When we visited his surviving aunts and uncles four decades later, living conditions in the village seemed primitive even by the lowly standards of Lure, Haute-Saône. The main object of farming was still to feed large families, not to supply distant markets. Manure was stacked high in every farmyard, chickens wandered freely in and out of the living accommodation, children played outdoors in a rich mixture of dust and animal droppings, and not one of the farmhouses we visited had running water. I can only imagine how much worse conditions must have been a generation earlier, when the extended family did not include a single government job holder who could be relied upon to spread a little cash around and provide a modicum of comfort.

As if this social background was not difficult enough, my father entered university just as stock markets were crashing and the Great Depression was setting in. This was no time to take risks and strike out as an entrepreneur even if he had talent in that direction. So he struck another bargain and entered the service of a community of Jesuit priests who ran a secondary school in Dôle, a pretty town with a rich ecclesiastical past in an area of eastern France where the flat expanses of the Saône valley give way to the undulating foothills of the Jura mountains. He taught Latin and Greek, naturally, but also history and geography and just about anything else the Jesuits considered essential to the academic development of their charges. On his free days, he travelled to Dijon to take his university classes. Three years later, he had achieved an extraordinary distinction for someone of his social origins: he had become a university graduate.

Apart from books, dictionaries, and encyclopaedias from his student days, a revealing document survives: his accounts book. Each week, he meticulously recorded his petty expenses. These were modest, to say the least. Board and lodging was provided by the Jesuits, and his earthly needs consisted of a daily newspaper, a weekly train ticket to Dijon, and a supply of tobacco and cigarette paper. All through those years, he seems to have bought no new clothes or shoes let alone treated himself to a cinema ticket. Every last cent of spare cash must have gone on buying books though such major expenses must have been too infrequent to be recorded in his accounts.

In principle, a teaching job in a government school could be expected to provide the combination of prestige and security many young men though as yet few young women aspired to. But even a university education did not guarantee this happy outcome. In fact, a new graduate might wait years for an appointment. So my father soldiered on in the service of the Jesuits. In the process, he developed a talent for disputation that stayed with him all his life. Except perhaps for the hard sciences, which his Catholic education had taught him little of, there was no subject he would not debate. To him, debating meant having the last word not by wearing down opponents through convoluted disquisitions but by calmly lining up the evidence he gleaned from his voracious reading. Like any Jesuit – or any lawyer, for that matter – he meant to win through force of argument. He was quite capable of arguing one day against the viewpoint he had effectively defended the previous day in different company.

Successive photos show him seated in his study, slightly on the corpulent side, pale-skinned, and balding, his tortoiseshell glasses halfway down his nose, working his way through the newspapers and magazines that accumulated on his desk and the books that filled an entire wall.

My father gave only the sparsest of responses to our questions about his school years. He was slightly more voluble about his undergraduate days and more still about his early teaching experience with the Jesuits. But when a glint in his eyes and a hint of a smile indicated that he felt a story coming on, we knew that it was going to be about the war. These story-telling moments were rare so they were treasured. We gathered around, anxious not to miss a thing.

In June 1940, he had got himself tangled up with the advancing Germans, who had cunningly rounded the undefended western end of the Maginot line, the spot where the chain of fortified bunkers petered out hundreds of kilometres short of the English Channel, which should have been the obvious end point for these fortifications. But for fear of offending the plucky Belgians and to save expense, the French high command and its political masters had opted not to extend the defences westward beyond Luxembourg, which left the long land border between Belgium and France wide open. So the moment the 'phoney war' was over and the German advance began in earnest, to no one's surprise, German tanks rolled right through Belgium with the obvious intention of veering east once they were over the French border and getting behind the French lines. Soon, it became clear to my father that the odds were stacked against his side and that flight was his only option: purloining bikes, pleading for food at farmhouses, lying low all day and moving only at night, he slowly made his way south in the hope of rejoining his young wife and baby daughter in her parents' home on the edge of the Vosges mountains. But none of this saved him and thousands like him from capture. He and his comrades were first locked up in French barracks the German army had just taken over then packed into cattle trains and carted away to POW camps. Little did he know that his destination was a remote region of Central Europe close to the Austrian-Hungarian border, where he was to endure five years of separation from his young family.

In my father's opinion, no rational person in a position to exercise freewill should have anything to do with the French army. He was no pacifist. Armies were necessary in extremities. But they had to be good, and the French army, in his view, was not. Its grandiloquent ineptitude had cost him and countless others five years of freedom. He had immense respect and affection for his fellow foot soldiers. But to hear him tell it, the French army as a force was an ill-trained rabble, led – if that was the word – by obtuse autocrats and incompetent braggarts.

He described how French prisoners, when ordered

by their German minders to line up and march, showed their disrespect for their captors by deliberately sabotaging the parade and turning it into a chaotic farce. Instead, the British, the Australians, and the New Zealanders opted to show national pride through faultless choreography. The Germans stood and watched, clearly impressed, perhaps conceding privately that they had met their match and that the ability to make martial displays go like clockwork did not after all reside exclusively in the genes of the master race.

When the Americans finally entered the camp in the spring of 1945, my father's immediate reaction was one of deep gratitude since this meant the sudden appearance of nutritious food and especially the prospect of heading home at last. But he was also hugely impressed by the logistics of the US army and its ability to get what was left of the railways working again in days and throwing bridges over major waterways in mere hours.

My father loved to mention the war. It was almost as if he had enjoyed the experience. For most of his captivity, POWs in his camp were free to go outside during the day as long as they came back at night. If not, severe punishments were imposed on those left behind. The inmates helped local families with farming work in return for a square meal, a glass of wine, and a chance to barter the content of packages from home or the Red Cross: tobacco for potatoes, for example, or any other items they may not need personally but that could always be traded inside the camp. In his more voluble moments, when we were older and my mother was not listening, my father hinted that more than tobacco or potatoes were bartered on occasion, especially if the local family in question happened to include a pretty daughter or a lonely wife left behind by

57

a husband busy advancing the Nazi agenda on the Russian front. Understandably, his accounts of that side of bartering were short on the specifics.

A photo dated from the early years of the war shows him and two friends standing in a field in front of a haystack. All three grin broadly and look healthy. In fact, my father looks quite the man-about-town in white shirt, tie, and natty plus-fours. This is not the look of a distressed man. Always a realist, he had adapted to circumstances. He had spent most of his life in the company of men so he was in his element and male camaraderie came naturally to him.

One of his best stories concerned a theatrical Frenchman who liked nothing better than antagonising his German captors through gestures he knew they disapproved of but that were unlikely to lead to harsh consequences. The moment word reached the camp that the Americans had landed in Normandy and were steadily moving eastward, the Frenchman swore that he would not shave again until the camp was liberated. Weeks later, his beard had reached luxuriant proportions. In a vermin-infested camp, this must have taken exceptional fortitude. One day, a rumour began to spread that the Americans had beaten the Russians to the camp and would be marching through the front gate in a matter of hours. True to his word, the Frenchman took his razor to the growth and started pruning. But rumours swirl freely in the fog of war. Soon, counter-information reached the camp: the Americans were much further than initially reported and it would be several days before they could send the Germans packing. So the Frenchman downed tools in mid-shave. When the Americans finally showed up, they found him with months of shaggy growth on one side of his face and mere stubble on the other. No matter how many times my father went over this tale, it was several minutes before we could stop laughing and he could move on to his next yarn.

In more rueful moments, my father conceded that as the war dragged on conditions became harsher, the gruel thinner, and the huts colder. Surprisingly, the mail kept flowing between the camps and the prisoners' homes and my father managed to communicate with my mother, however sporadically. When we were older and my mother shared with us some of his letters, I realised that camp life had been much worse than his stories suggested and that the pain of separation had been intense. Because he had spent so much of his childhood away from his family, my father valued the one he had just started above all else and no amount of good-humoured fraternising with comrades could make up for the loss.

My mother often went over the reasons why he had never tried to escape. After all, some did and some even made it home. But POW camps were scattered all across Germany and his was at the far end of Austria, an integral part of the *Reich* at the time. Even if he had made it to the Swiss border at the opposite end of the country, the Swiss had a reputation for favouring expediency over principle: if they picked him up, they were more likely to push him back over the German border than to ease his passage across Switzerland and on to France. For a prisoner's wife, having a husband known to have escaped from a German POW camp was a badge of honour even if he had been caught because it showed what a brave man she had married. That bragging opportunity was not open to her. I sensed that she felt uncomfortable about this but even as an adolescent I knew better than to probe.

Once home after the war and settled as a schoolteacher and family man in Lure, Haute-Saône, my father helped to found the local association of former POWs and became its treasurer and major mover and shaker. The association met once a month. Tales of sorrow and joy were retold, many of which he later shared with us, and news of mutual acquaintances swapped. Central to the deliberations was the refreshment provided by Monsieur Sagret, the town's wine merchant and a pivotal member of the association. According to my mother, who let out this tidbit when we were older, my father came home from these gatherings in the wee hours and a very happy man indeed. He devoted a lot of time and energy to the association, which offered a chance to relive war-time camaraderie but also to provide for needy POW families: coal or potatoes for the winter, a leg of ham at Christmas, help with funeral expenses, or relief from hardship in its many forms.

But before funds could be disbursed, they had to be generated. To this end, a fun fair was held over a mid-August weekend each year on the edge of the town. We awaited the fun fair with trepidation and we never failed to attend.

Shepherded by my mother, my siblings and I set off after dinner on one of our rare nights out and walked excitedly to this remote spot along unlit lanes. Once there, our first duty was to make our presence known to my father, who seemed uncommonly happy to see us. Clearly, my father was having fun among good friends. Only with the greater depth of perception that a few more years allowed did it occur to me that one reason for this benevolence was that the wine merchant had once again provided of his plenty. Even with a thousand things to attend to if the event was to go smoothly, my father and his comrades made time for draining a bottle or two. My mother was the tolerant sort. She knew how important this event was to my father and to his happiness and she never gave the slightest hint that she thought he was behaving reprehensibly.

All the ingredients of small-town merriment were there. For the juvenile market, there was a merry-go-round featuring wooden horses painted in garish colours. Each horse was impaled on a vertical pole that slid up and down and that riders gripped tightly when young but learned to let go of in a show of 'look, no hands' as they grew older and more adventurous. As the wheezy machinery slowed but before the creaky contrivance came to a complete standstill, the previous contingent of merry-makers jumped off, some to be reunited with watchful parents, others racing off to the next attraction. This was our cue to climb on, stake a claim to the nearest unoccupied horse, and hand our ticket to the attendant.

Once I had outgrown the charms of the wooden steeds and was tall enough to see over the counter of the shooting gallery and strong enough to hold a rifle, I stood side by side with army recruits on leave from the town's barracks and unwilling or financially unable to spend quality time at the military Rest & Recreation headquarters by the railway station. The contest was unequal. Without doubt, these men in uniform must be deadly snipers so I watched and learned as they scooped up the lion's share of the prizes including the bottle of bubbly of questionable vintage awarded for hitting a bull's eye and that they presumably regarded as more commensurate with their professional status than a mangy teddy bear.

Once I was up a few more notches on the maturity scale, as soon as I reached the fair, I jumped into bumper cars and practiced the subtle art of picking a target and sideswiping it to force it to spin a full half-circle. Lurid lights flashed, music boomed out of massive speakers, and the summer air filled with the sound of cars crashing into each other with a thud and the screech of the hooked blades perched high on the masts attached to the back of each car and designed to pick up power by scraping against the electric grid overhead.

Though a good deal less sedate than the merry-go-round, this racetrack from hell attracted boys and girls equally. To the extent my limited means allowed, I took full advantage of this happy combination of genders as it gave me a chance to come into relatively close contact with girls under conditions that given the chaos and the din could not possibly have been policed by adults. As my car zigzagged from side to side, the moment I spotted in one of the cars a girl from school whose interest I hoped to attract, I made a beeline for her vehicle and sideswiped it with consummate skill. Seen from a grown man's vantage point, trying to make an impression on a girl by dislodging several of her vertebrae seems a curious way to go about seduction. But in their confused search for a mate, growing boys have few cards to play. At least, the strategy is a step up on pulling the girl's hair.

For the older and newly muscular male element, the lake around which the fair was built provided a rare route to romance as rowing boats could be hired by the hour. For a teenage boy of means who had failed to win a girl's heart by maiming her on the bumper cars the previous summer, the hope was that a year later she would have had her spine straightened out and forgiven if not forgotten the assault. If so, she might be persuaded to step into the boat and allow herself to be rowed noiselessly towards an unlit and unpopulated shore. Some boys claimed repeated success over the weekend the fair lasted, and not necessarily with the same girl, they were careful to add. But as the funds at my disposal never ran to boat rides let alone to the little treats a girl in love might expect, I only have the reports of boastful friends to go on. It is probably safe to dismiss these claims as so much testosterone-fuelled fabrication.

For all visitors regardless of age or romantic disposition though probably not for love-struck boys in rowing boats, who would presumably have preferred the remote corners of the lake to remain unlit, the highlight of the fun fair was the Sunday night fireworks show that marked the end of the event. The fireworks were set off from a small island in the middle of the lake, and this doubled the magic as the glittering display could be enjoyed up above as well as through its reflection on the water.

For two days each August, the fun fair was the happiest place on earth. When it ended, like the Punch and Judy show, the travelling circus, and the Monte Carlo rally, I was left with memories and the thin air they had vanished into.

Except for one important detail.

A hugely popular attraction of the fun fair was the balloon launch because it had repercussions that prolonged the fun for several more weeks. For a small sum, visitors to the fair could buy a balloon and take part in the collective launch. Each balloon carried a bright pink postcard from which a numbered counterfoil could be torn off and kept as a claim. The postcard contained instructions on how to return it if found. The prevailing winds blew eastward so the instructions were printed in German as well as French as surviving postcards were likely to be found in Switzerland or Germany though a few were occasionally returned from as far afield as Austria, hundreds of kilometres away. Finders were asked to indicate the location where they had picked up the postcard before dropping it in the mail. Postage was paid on arrival at a reduced rate secured by another member of the POW association who knew which strings to pull inside the post office. Eventually, the stack of weather-beaten postcards ended up on my father's desk. Ever the geography teacher, he took out one of his many maps, located tiny villages most residents of Switzerland, Germany, or Austria had probably never heard of and calculated to the nearest half-kilometre the distance between these places and Lure, Haute-Saône. The lucky owner of the postcard that had travelled furthest received a bottle of whatever was left in the wine merchant's cellars.

My father was a complex man. He could be difficult and prone to occasional flashes of anger especially when dealing with academic failure on the part of his progeny, typically my own. He was a disciplinarian though not consistently. He loved his family but verbalising this love or even uttering words of encouragement seemed beyond him. He had hardly known his parents and in the Catholic seminary that had substituted for a family, the priests' idea of encouragement was to set the bar high, pass judgment, and then set it higher still in readiness for the next attempt. No wonder he knew no better.

He died of natural causes at 83. As my mother, relatives, friends, and my siblings and I were walking away from the cemetery where he had just been buried, I recall experiencing an overwhelming surge of affection towards him. As the chill of the May evening descended, I felt that we were being unforgivably cruel in leaving him alone in the cold earth as we prepared to return to the warmth of his former home. I had an irrational urge to run back to the grave and keep him warm by hugging him for the first and last time, an impulse that still occasionally emerges in dreams.

What remains of him in my mind is a sense of

admiration for a man who had emerged from rural poverty and reached then unheard-of educational heights. Another key part of his legacy is a shared detestation of demagoguery and unchallenged truths. For my father, the appropriate response to attempts by opportunists to appropriate minds was education, which he understood as the development of an inquisitive and sceptical intellect. Obviously, access to information was key and anyone or anything standing between an inquisitive and sceptical intellect and information was hateful. My father would have loved the Internet. Sadly, he missed it by a couple of years. Having had a ringside seat at displays of fatuous self-importance by the Nazis and their many supporters in pre-war France, he detested all attempts at putting people, and especially young people, in uniforms and marching them up and down. I disagreed with my father on many subjects but never on this one.

*

My paternal grandmother and my maternal grandfather died within weeks of each other about six months before I was born. In their more cruel moments, my two older sisters, Odile and Bernadette, were fond of suggesting that the pair knew something my parents did not and felt such foreboding at the prospect of my emergence on stage that they independently decided to bail out while they had a chance. I knew that life and death did not quite work that way and that this was said in jest. But of all my sisters' jokes, this was not my favourite.

My mother had great affection for her father, a man she represented as warm and caring and with a flair for making children feel comfortable, a quality that, as we children knew all too well from her daily admonitions, his wife, our grandmother, distinctly lacked. When my mother needed parental affection and support, she looked to her father. Years later, she had fond tales of his life with which to delight her own children. We never tired of hearing these stories, which, to a background of slices of buttered *pain d'épices* and even – a rare treat in France – cups of tea, she told and retold on winter Sunday afternoons when outside temperatures were too low or the snow too thick to permit the much-loved Sunday afternoon drive.

My grandfather's name was Paul and as the first-born son I was named after him. He came from a family of small landowners whose acres were perched high above Corravillers, a tiny village on the edge of the Vosges mountains but on the southern and sunnier Haute-Saône side. Most of the land was too steep to support intensive farming but it provided good pasture, much of which was rented out to local farmers. The low-lying land had been sold to industrialists keen to build textile factories next to the fast-flowing streams. By local standards, the family was relatively well-off but its modest wealth was in real estate. In any case, there was very little on which to spend available cash. If my grandfather walked down the mountain to school and back up again each day, it was not because the family was short of money but because there was no other way to get there.

Both of his parents had died when he was very young and he was brought up by an aunt, Tante Julie. An obese and notoriously shiftless woman, Tante Julie was said to keep mature *munster* cheese, a local favourite, by her bedside in case she woke up hungry in the middle of the night and could not be bothered to get out of bed and amble over to the larder. Needless to say, no husband had ever shared that bed and been forced to shut out of his mind the whiff of runny *munster* as he went about the unenviable task of begetting issue.

By contrast, Tante Marie, my grandfather's sister and my mother's favourite relative, was an industrious and generous soul who ran a successful dress-making business in Monthureux-sur-Saône, a village close to where the Saône river has its source in the western foothills of the Vosges mountains. As her business expanded, she acquired modern dress-making machinery, much of which was made in Germany. At regular intervals, a German technician passed through the village, tweaked the equipment, replaced faulty parts, and promoted the latest offerings of German sewing technology. In the process, love blossomed and Tante Marie married the technician much to the consternation of my grandmother, her sister-in-law, who would sooner have welcomed a Bolshevik serial murderer to the bosom of the family than a German. Everyone in his new wife's family called him – though presumably not to his face – *Oncle Boche*, using the derogatory epithet hurled at all persons and all things German since World War I. If my mother knew his real name, she never revealed it.

Each summer, my mother spent part of her school holidays in Tante Marie's house. She revelled in the nurturing her own mother was not renowned for providing. But stories from her childhood also spoke of the gradual and to her painful estrangement of the couple, who ended up living at opposite ends of the house and barely spoke. Tante Marie died suddenly of the pneumonia she contracted while washing her latest *couture* in the Saône River one particularly cold winter morning. A few weeks later, on the appointed day, *Oncle Boche* and my grandfather met in the family lawyer's office to be informed that Tante Marie had bequeathed all her worldly goods to *Oncle Boche* himself as if her devoted brother, my grandfather, and her beloved niece, my mother, did not exist. Clearly, skulduggery had taken place but there was nothing my grandfather could do about it. This was only one of my mother's many tales of missed inheritances, fraudulently snatched at the wire by unscrupulous relatives aided and abetted by rapacious lawyers. The wealth may have flowed into undeserving pockets but we delighted in these stories. Among my mother's many strong points, one was her ability to turn misfortunes into entertainment material.

My grandfather was an entrepreneur at heart. He had trained with a local property wheeler and dealer and learned the legal side of real estate transactions and especially how to tell a promising deal from a dud. Already forty years old at the start of World War I, he had served as a lorry driver, ferrying supplies to the front and carrying the wounded back to where they could be stitched up. The war left him with a love of all things motorised. The moment he came home, he bought a car and his love affair with the combustion engine was only brought to an end by the Great Depression and personal financial collapse.

His business ventures included opening around 1920 the first cinema in Remiremont, the small town in the southern Vosges mountains where the family lived and my mother grew up. Like Dôle, where my father had cut his pedagogical teeth in the service of the Jesuits, Remiremont had a rich ecclesiastical past. The town was thick with churches, monasteries, and convents and was therefore not given to frivolity. But my grandfather was interested not in devotion but in business innovation and he went ahead with his cinema venture regardless. Though the investment was successful and profitable, it incurred the wrath of my grandmother, who whole-heartedly approved of devotion and abhorred frivolity. To her, the cinema was an abomination and the work of Beelzebub, designed to tempt weaker souls away from religion with images of men and women not married to each other dancing cheek to cheek and perhaps even stealing the occasional on-screen kiss.

By the mid-1920s, my grandfather had spotted the connection between rising car ownership and the scenic charms of the Vosges mountains. He bought an unprepossessing building at one end of a lake near the picturesque town of Gérardmer and turned it into a flourishing hotel. But soon, clouds began gathering on his business horizon closer to home, with the cinema at the centre of the financial storm. With the talkies now pulling in growing audiences, a competitor sniffed an opportunity and opened a rival cinema. With few films on offer and little difference between them, this ingenious entrepreneur soon concluded that since he could not win on content he would instead sabotage the competition by bribing the railway stationmaster into pretending that my grandfather's reels had not arrived. It did not take many cancelled performances for the fortunes of my grandfather's cinema to decline. The Great Depression did the rest. Debtors stopped paying, the bank called in loans, and my grandfather's business ventures went under one after the other.

The shock was immense. The family's living standards dived. But the most traumatic aspect of the disaster was the loss of self-respect. My grandfather was familiar with the ups and downs of business life but my grandmother valued respectability and social stability above all else and her world had crumbled. My mother described bailiffs loading family heirlooms into vans and salivating at the prospect of lucre while her mother sat in a corner on one of the remaining chairs, weeping quietly. Under French law and in French culture, bankruptcy was not simply the bump in the financial road it is to Americans. It was a blot on an entrepreneur's record, a sign of public failure, and incontrovertible evidence of incompetence if not of a deep character flaw. No one recovered from bankruptcy financially or psychologically. In France, no one was meant to.

On his deathbed, my grandfather asked his wife for forgiveness for the pain he had caused her during their four decades of marriage. Two things troubled him. One was his arms' length attitude to her Catholicism, which he knew had caused her deep anguish. But his greater concern was the shame he had inflicted on the family through his bankruptcy. At the end of her own life almost six decades later, my mother remained deeply troubled by it, still blaming predatory lawyers for her parents' misfortunes and for cynically enriching themselves in the process. If someone had asked for volunteers to kill all the lawyers, my mother would have been first in line.

*

My grandfather's financial tribulations left the family with no assets and very little income. So three years after his death, my grandmother moved in with us in Lure, Haute-Saône. Her name was Marie but we invariably called her *Grand-mère*. Though she was gradually becoming physically impaired by arthritis, she did what she could to help my parents raise their six children. Her strong views on religion and morality, her fatalistic acceptance of suffering as a way of life, and her stated preference for hard work at the expense of fun loomed large over the household.

She had inherited from her father the conviction that discipline mattered above all else both in personal life and in bringing up children. An imposing bewhiskered figure, he looks in photos as if he could quell mutinies with a mere glare. This was a man who knew right from wrong. For his wife and two daughters in particular this meant following orders: *his* orders. He ruled with an iron fist, laying down the law in every aspect of family members' lives.

Though he had a farming background, he was no tiller of the soil. He operated a dairy farm some twenty kilometres north of Nancy, an elegant city that was growing fast in the immediate aftermath of the Franco-Prussian war of 1870-71 when it found itself uncomfortably close to the newly-relocated German border but now the largest urban centre in all of eastern France. My mother, ever the story teller, recalled how on her annual visits to her beloved grandmother, the bewhiskered man's long-suffering wife, she watched rows of milkmaids on the production line soon after dawn. She then rode in the horse-drawn cart down to the railway station in the Moselle valley below the village, where the milk was loaded onto a train, to be delivered to breakfast tables in Nancy. Her grandfather was modestly successful so he determined that his two daughters would marry well. He, of course, would be the matchmaker. At times of his own choosing, he married off first his eldest daughter, whom we knew as *Tante Nini* (short for Eugénie) to a successful poultry dealer and a few years later his youngest, my grandmother, to a real estate dealer with prospects. Not overly ambitious but slightly higher than his own station in both cases. He must have felt very pleased with himself.

His son, Charles, the youngest of his three children, went one better and then one worse. A brilliant student, he gained a place in one of France's prestigious *Grandes Ecoles* and became a civil engineer. As

71

opportunities opened up worldwide and in part, I suspect, to escape his father's towering presence, he spent two decades building railways in Brazil. On his return to France, he had with him a mulatto beauty of Caribbean origin, a woman of ample personality and bosom and quite the antithesis of the family's idea of an appropriate helpmeet. In a photo, dressed in a richly embroidered white gown, a large flower jauntily adorning her flowing hair and a grin on her face a mile wide and about a mile wider than most other family members ever managed, she looks as if she is taking a break from shooting a rum commercial. Not surprisingly, this cheerful lady was not popular among her in-laws. Sensibly, the couple set up home close to the Spanish border at the opposite end of the country, where the weather reminded them of sunnier climes and where censorious relatives from frigid, quasi-Germanic Lorraine were not likely to come a-calling. Charles died young of an infectious disease he had contracted in the tropics. As I listened to my grandmother as she recounted her brother's exploits in embarrassed tones, I regretted not having known him. Already harbouring a yearning to find out what was over the horizon, I sensed that *Oncle* Charles would have been a fascinating person to get to know.

As befitted the daughters of an upwardly-mobile family, my grandmother and her slightly older sister was sent to Nancy to be inducted into the ways of the middle class by a local community of nuns who specialised in transmogrifying farmers' daughters into ladies. The institution was a kind of primary, lower secondary, and finishing school rolled into one. Catholicism played a central part in the process and the academic content was slender. What really mattered was that the ladies of tomorrow should learn how to conduct themselves in polite society, where they were destined to operate: how to serve food, how to eat it, how to speak, how to listen, how to write letters, how to respond to letters, how to walk, even how to sit. Almost to the end of her life, when creeping arthritis affected every joint in her body, my grandmother sat upright without her spine coming into contact with the back of the chair just as she had been instructed by the nuns under threat of having her knuckles rapped if she slouched.

As she went about the house doing what she could to help my parents cope with their brood, *Grand-mère* saw her role as that of duty-bound enforcer. She valued order and in her view, girls fitted into her scheme of things whereas boys did not and she made no secret of her preference. Girls were well-behaved and obedient while boys were by nature rebellious and destructive. In fact, she often acted as if my brother Pierre and I were planning to commit pillage and arson the moment her back was turned. We responded with displays of fear and submission that varied in authenticity depending on how close the physical threat she posed happened to be on each occasion. Given the effort she put into playing a full part in our upbringing, I do not feel proud today that we gave her so little credit at the time.

Policing the mayhem that six children living in a confined space are bound to generate from time to time formed a major part of her contribution. On schooldays, our beds were made by my mother after we jumped on our bikes and headed to our morning classes. But during school holidays, with nothing to do all day other than loafing around town with friends, we were required to make our own beds. This was not popular but girls could be trusted to do the job unsupervised. Boys were another matter. To ensure that we made our beds without setting them on fire, my grandmother stationed herself in the doorway of the bedroom my brother and I shared and glared at us throughout. Bed making is tedious at the best of times and two boys on holiday are in no mood to attend to pointless preoccupations with orderliness. But we were in no position to argue so we sabotaged the operation instead. Banter flew as did the occasional pillow. My grandmother's approach to restoring order was to raise the walking stick she never went anywhere without and then bring it down on the nearest miscreant. But because my brother's bed was nearest the door, he was invariably the one who got whacked. He took it in good humour as he took most things. When she died, when we were sixteen and thirteen, respectively, he asked to inherit the walking stick, which graces a prominent corner of his living room to this day.

My grandmother helped in other ways too. Her forte was cleaning, not cooking, the exact reverse of my mother, so the division of labour worked well. She read stories to preschoolers and tested older siblings on multiplication tables and French conjugations and later on Latin declensions. She knew how to deal with children even if shows of authority came to her more naturally than displays of affection. She was convinced that order was paramount in preparing children for the vale of tears that awaited them in this life. Her role was to inculcate and maintain that order, for our own good as she often insisted, a refrain my siblings and I came to mimic cruelly. Her rigidity was easy to mock and respect for her common sense and honest intentions came to me only later once I was old enough to value these more elusive qualities especially when they are exercised stoically amidst the ailments that come with ageing.

She came from a culture deeply marked by a very Catholic sense of all-pervading fatalism. This was a world in which we had been put not to enjoy ourselves but to suffer, just as our Saviour had. To drive her theme home, she wore mostly black or grey with a touch of purple on days when nothing in the Catholic calendar ruled out gaiety and specified repentance. To buttress her thesis of doom with the written word, she scoured the daily newspaper for evidence of natural disasters, car crashes, untimely deaths, and other scourges of humanity. She valued continuity in death as in life. As a case in point, she cited the example of how her father, the bewhiskered dairy farmer, had breathed his last in the exact same armchair and in the exact same room as his own father. To her, this was a positive in an existence that offered very few. In a culture obsessed with suffering and death and replete with Catholic symbols for both, when, where, and how the devout might die was something to which they devoted a great deal of thought. She was convinced that she would not make it past seventy simply because her own mother had died at that age. The day she reached that milestone, she stopped buying clothes or any other personal items for fear of wasting them on what little remained of her mortal coil. She surprised everyone and not least herself by living to almost eighty-five, a ripe old age in the 1960s.

In a different epoch, my grandmother would have made an efficient manager instead of a reluctant housewife. But women of her generation, born some four decades before the relative emancipation that followed World War I, were not given options. Decisions were made for them. No wonder they chafed.

*

Like her own mother's education, my mother's was entrusted from childhood in the early 1920s to the Catholic Church, specifically to another community of nuns who ran a school for young ladies in the very Catholic town of Remiremont. The curriculum was a little more academic than the one that had made a lady of her mother but the pedagogical approach rarely ventured beyond rote learning. Recitation was how the girls learned French grammar and spelling, history, geography, and even maths especially since the tortuous ratiocinations of algebra were not on the syllabus. Naturally, Catholic dogma and related practices framed the school day. According to my mother, the only reference the nuns ever made to modernity was when they railed against secularism and its blasphemous insistence on the strict separation of church and state and then led prayers for the spread of Catholic values throughout French society.

Foreign languages played no part in the nuns' educational outlook even though teaching talent of sorts was available in the form of an Irish nun kept by the school on sufferance and known to my mother and her classmates as *la* Miss. No one knew or said what accident had left the poor woman stranded in such an unlikely spot. If it was ever heard, English must have sounded especially alien in this remote corner of 1920s France. British tourists spoke English but they took their pleasures in Biarritz or Monte Carlo, not in rainy Remiremont. The Americans spoke English, after a fashion, and even the French conceded that the Americans had been helpful in pushing back the Germans and bringing World War I to an end. But by the time my mother went to school, the Americans were long gone. Charles Lindbergh, the superstar of the day, was American, of course. But anyone could learn all about his aerial exploits from French newspapers. Having the Irish nun teach English was simply a way for the school to keep her busy since there was apparently nothing else she could teach. In the end, her valiant efforts were spectacularly unsuccessful. Even when my parents visited me in London after I moved there in my late teens, I never heard my mother utter one word of English: she could not count to ten, say the alphabet, or greet or thank someone in even the simplest terms in the language.

My mother may have had a tin ear for foreign languages but she knew a thing or two about the expressive potential of her own. She was a repository of French idioms. After a night of carousing, your hair hurt *(avoir mal aux cheveux)*. If you were after the impossible, you were looking for midday at two o'clock *(chercher midi à quatorze heures)*. If the food on your plate tasted particularly good, you licked all five of your fingers plus your thumb *(se lécher les cinq doigts et le pouce)*. If you seemed stupid to her, you hadn't invented gunpowder *(ne pas avoir inventé la poudre)*. And so on. Almost regardless of topic, she peppered her speech with these images for the amusement of the gallery and especially of her children. Just as my grandmother would have made a fine manager in circumstances more generous to women, my mother would have made a fine entertainer. But being so good at it herself, she could not see the point of paying someone to do it and she never set foot inside a cinema. She occasionally allowed us to join our friends in one as long as the offerings had not been blacklisted by the Vatican but she never permitted my father to buy a television. Her antagonism towards all forms of filmed entertainment must have been due in part to the fact that the medium revived painful memories of the demise of her father's cinema and his subsequent bankruptcy. But whatever the cause, on the one occasion when she reported having watched television, it was clear that she was in the final stages of decline.

She spent the last year of her life in a retirement

home in a comfortable room fitted, as is the expectation, with a television set. But even in moments of loneliness as the friends she had made in the home were rapidly being lost to the reaper, she refused to learn how to operate a remote control. So when she announced one day in an almost inaudible voice to my younger sister Madeleine, who lived nearby and attended to her loyally in her final years, that she had seen my father, dead for sixteen years, on television, Madeleine knew that her mother's mind was going. Sensing at almost 95 that she did not have long to live, she may have been entertaining hopes of reunion in the afterlife. But for these to have been triggered by staring at a television screen for the first time in her life was so inconceivable that she could only have been hallucinating. She died peacefully a few days later.

*

Turning the clock back somewhat, my mother turned sixteen just as the Great Depression – and family bankruptcy – hit. So an inexpensive (or preferably free) route to further education had to be found. The solution was another Catholic institution, this time run by nuns devoted to turning Catholic girls into Catholic wives, mothers, and homemakers. As with my father's schooling by priests, the rationale was that this would not only shore up the Catholic faith against attacks by devil-worshiping secularists but also yield a generous supply of future soldiers of Christ, in this case, more nuns.

The school was in Dijon, a few hours away to the southwest of Remiremont by train. Nothing a wife and mother would need to know was left off the curriculum. Cooking lessons covered every base. There was not a cut of meat these young women were not taught to marinate, not a sauce they were not taught to mix, not a cake they were not taught to bake. The girls were not wealthy so there was no expectation that they would employ servants. They would do it all themselves and never grumble. They learned not only how to dress and cook a chicken but how to first slaughter, pluck, and gut it. They learned the finer points of ironing and dress-making, do-it-yourself repairs about the house, gardening, even nursing.

Through hints my mother dropped here and there in her stories, I guessed that the only significant aspect of Catholic motherhood left untouched by these thorough educators was sexuality. Presumably, the nuns believed that none of this would matter to those among their charges destined to become nuns and that for the rest, older students could be relied upon to inform younger ones informally. The system worked. Neither my mother nor most of the classmates she remained in contact with seem to have had any difficulty figuring out how to make babies.

My mother spent ten happy years in that school, first as a student and later as an instructor. Just as my father repaid the Jesuits for their help by teaching for pocket money while he studied for his degree, my mother stayed on at a nominal salary and taught what she had learnt until matrimony beckoned, once again in ways over which women in her social position had little control.

One of the instructors hailed from a nearby village. She had a brother, a practicing Catholic who had recently risen to the exalted status of university graduate and had excellent prospects of becoming a schoolteacher. The matchmaker in question was my father's eldest sister, whom we later came to know and love as Tante Marthe.

My mother never revealed how the introductions

were made but an engagement and then a wedding were announced. She was twenty-four, my father twenty-eight.

True to family tradition, discord soon emerged. The wedding photo shows the newly-weds, my mothers' parents, and her nearest relatives. But the only representatives from my father's side are his brother and his wife. His father was dead, but there is no sign of his mother or any of his three sisters, not even of the matchmaker herself. According to my mother, the moment the wedding was announced, ill feeling was stirred by Tante Marguerite, my father's second older sister, who could not abide the fact that her brother, a full ten years younger than her, was about to walk up the aisle while she remained on the shelf. Exactly nine months and two days later, a daughter was born and named Odile. A little more than a year after that, World War II broke out and my father and the military threat he presented to Nazism were neutralised when he was spirited out of French soil for five years.

In the rush south that followed the French capitulation in June 1940, the notorious *débacle*, my mother, her parents, and her baby daughter settled close to *Tante Nini*, my grandmother's sister, and her generous poultry-dealing family on the southern fringes of Burgundy. Where the green waters of the Doubs River meet the grey waters of the Saône River stands the tiny town of Verdun, a place happy to remain inconspicuous until German military minds determined, in their wisdom, that it had strategic importance.

From 1940 to 1942, German occupation affected only the northern half of the country plus a thin sliver of land that ran the entire length of France's Atlantic coast to guard against potential sea-borne invasions. The rest of the country, mendaciously labelled 'Free France', passed under the control of the pro-Nazi Vichy regime until the Germans had no option but to occupy all of the country as an Allied attack from across the Mediterranean became increasingly likely. But over those two early years of the war, my mother and her parents, whose windows overlooked the confluence of the two rivers and the occupied zone to the north, had to run the gauntlet of the German soldiery each time they cycled over the bridge in search of produce to supplement their meagre diet.

Like my father, my mother had the knack of making wartime stories sound fun. This reflected her resilience and optimism. But not all her stories could hide the anguish of separation and the uncertainty over when or even whether she might ever see her husband again. She had harrowing tales to tell, too. Her descriptions of the treatment meted out by advancing Free French fighters, many indecently recent converts to the cause, to local women accused of having consorted with German soldiers were deeply disturbing. Once guilt had been confirmed by a kangaroo court, the women were stripped naked, their heads were shaved, and they were tarred and feathered and paraded through the streets before being taken away to be shot. My mother could do tragedy as effectively as she could have us rolling in the aisles. As I said, she could have been a professional entertainer.

Once reunited, my parents set about living peacefully and adding to their progeny. A few months later, they moved to Lure, Haute-Saône when my father was appointed to his first formal teaching position. In all the years of their marriage I witnessed, I never heard them raise their voice against each other or even utter a swear word.

Like my father, my mother was slightly on the corpulent side. She had suffered some hair loss to paratyphoid fever as a child, but she made no attempt at beautifying herself artificially in compensation. She was naturally jovial and openly nurturing, and her smile and unaffectedly warm manner more than made up for this superficial defect. By contrast, my father found expressing emotions of all kinds difficult and displays of open affection between the two of them were rare. But this was par for the course. The closest couples came to showing intimacy in public was when they walked arm in arm along the street. Their conversations ended in 'Good-bye!', not 'Love you!'

*

My mother was an only child. On the paternal side of the family, even though my father's eldest sister became a nun, her four siblings managed to produce fifteen children between them, so we were richly supplied with cousins, many of them roughly our age. Family reunions were infrequent but correspondingly festive. Because they invariably marked some key event in the Catholic calendar, they were always held on Sundays. The extended family met in church and then trooped back to the house for lunch, which lasted the best part of the afternoon. The adults sat around one of two long dining tables at one end of the vast living room and made occasional sorties to the other half to defuse squabbles among cousins.

Planning these events took weeks. As very few family members owned a phone, invitations went out by mail and written responses were eagerly awaited. In extremities, telegrams could be sent. But these were expensive and so reserved for announcing major events, especially deaths in the family. No one looked forward to the appearance on their doorstep of the man from the post office, with one hand on the handlebar of his bike and a telegram in the other. Phone calls were possible, to announce a major delay in arriving at a family function, for example. But this required the cooperation of Monsieur Gagney, a trusted neighbour, stalwart member of the POW association my father set such store by, and the owner of the only phone we knew of in our street. The procedure involved Monsieur or Madame Gagney first begging the caller to hold despite the exorbitant cost of long-distance calls and then dispatching the most fleet-footed of their children to our house to summon one of our parents to the phone. Unlike telegrams, phone calls were exciting. They heralded the unexpected. We talked about them and relived the drama for weeks.

For better or worse, my parents' procreational enthusiasm did not rub off on their own children. Of the six of us, only three (Odile, Bernadette, and Pierre) had children and the grand total came to a measly seven. So far, the next generation is doing better, with the most recent family census already returning seven descendants, most of them girls. My family can be blamed for many things but not for overpopulating the planet.

True to my father's deeply-held belief in the benevolence of the State, all my siblings opted for government jobs: two as librarians (Pierre and Marie-Jeanne), one as a nurse (Bernadette), and one as a schoolteacher (Madeleine). So far, every one of my nephews and nieces has followed in their footsteps. My grandfather, he of the trail-blazing cinema and hotel ventures, must be turning in his grave.

*

Including my father's five years of captivity, my parents shared a total of fifty-five years of married life. Towards the end of their lives, both confided in their grown children that they had been happy. They had also managed to live through though not forget the greatest tragedy of their years together.

The only occasions when I saw my mother cry were after an argument she had with her own mother over how to handle our problematic eldest sister Odile. She was already six years old when my father returned from captivity in 1945. She had known no father, he had no idea how to relate to a child, and she took badly to having to share with him the exclusive maternal attention she had enjoyed during those early years.

At first, she showed every sign of being a promising student, with a special talent for Latin and even Greek. Trouble started in her late teens when family life began to be punctuated by her epileptic fits.

The fits started with no warning with Odile suddenly rolling her eyes uncontrollably, then shaking violently, and finally dropping to the floor where she lay writhing for what seemed like an eternity. From a young age, we all learned that intervention could do nothing for her and that forbearance was the only option until the fit burned itself out. After long, agonising minutes, the shaking began to diminish in intensity and her body relaxed until she lay flat on her back and an eerily peaceful smile illuminated her face. Looking back, it is not hard to understand why in less informed times, similarly helpless onlookers convinced themselves that the victim's body had been temporarily invaded by some incubus and that the fit was what the victim had to go through in order to expel it and consign it back to the hell from which it had emerged. But such an outlandish explanation would not have been countenanced by a rationalist such as my father. So we dealt with these inexplicable events by repressing the emotional turmoil we had just experienced and that we knew we would almost certainly experience again before long.

It is difficult to assess what inner scars the recurrent horror may have left in us, especially in my older siblings and myself, who when the fits were at their most frequent and most violent were old enough to sense that a tragedy of uncommon proportion was unfolding, especially as it appeared to have no solution. The private shame was intense. But in a town where everyone knew everyone else and where my father was a prominent figure, the public shame of having not just a disabled sister but one who was liable at any moment to go into a fit in a classroom, a shop, or even in the street dug even deeper.

On one especially traumatic occasion, Odile was brought home one afternoon in an unfamiliar car driven by a kindly gentleman, a distant acquaintance of my parents, who was familiar with her predicament and knew where she lived. Her face, hands, arms, and legs were all bandaged up and there were patches of dried blood on her face and in her hair. It was obvious that she had just been through a particularly violent fit somewhere in town. From other witnesses, we learned that as the fit started, she had fallen headfirst on the sharp edge of a solid granite kerb the municipality of Lure, Haute-Saône had recently installed along major streets in an effort to beautify the town. For several days, she lay in bed recovering and gradually regaining full use of her hands and facial muscles as the ugly scars healed. This was no longer a private tragedy. There was no hiding. The sense of helpless horror lingers to this day.

As the fits became more frequent, she had to be pulled out of school and tutored at home though she could still venture outside. Then, as the fits got worse, she was confined to the flat and restricted to helping with housework. Visits to eminent men of medical science in a grim hospital in Mulhouse made no difference. My parents tried to treat her normally and to make as few allowances as possible. But their approach was often undermined by my grandmother, who took pity on her ailing granddaughter and often helped her to cut corners. Clearly an intelligent girl, Odile quickly realised the potential this friction offered and learned to manipulate my grandmother to her advantage. Hence the arguments and the tears, which my siblings and I could only witness helplessly as taking sides would only have made matters worse.

Odile died at forty, in circumstances seemingly as tragic as those in which she had lived. I say seemingly because my parents never revealed the exact cause of her death, if they knew it. By the time she was about twenty-five, the fits were tapering off and she was beginning to live a more independent life. She moved to the French Alps, where under the supervision of the local social services, she earned a modest living doing menial jobs, mostly cleaning government offices. There she met an older man of North-African descent, lived with him for several years, and gave birth to a daughter. For the next ten years or so, there was no direct contact between her and my parents as my father could not bring himself to believe that she might have changed for the better and could be acting out of unselfish intentions even when she offered to visit and acquaint my parents with their first grandchild. To his last breath, he remained adamantly opposed to a reunion on the grounds that she had caused enough grief in the past and that he would not expose himself or my mother to the risk that she might cause more. Only after his death almost twenty years later did my mother feel free to communicate with her granddaughter, do what she could to atone for my father's unforgiving stance, help her with her studies, and offer her a belated sense that she had a family after all. Odile's daughter is now in her mid-thirties, well-adjusted, happily married, and with two delightful children of her own. Her mother probably never imagined such a positive outcome.

*

My mother outlived my father by sixteen years. Long after she had become reconciled with having to live alone, she confided that shortly before he died my father cast doubt on her deeply-held belief that they would be reunited in an afterlife. This confession troubled her though I suspect it did not entirely surprise her. Over the years, her gradual emancipation from Catholic certainties had run a steady course and she needed little encouragement to launch into a diatribe against the Pope, his covey of misogynistic cardinals, and the reactionary organisation these gentlemen mislead.

Understandably, she clung to parts of her Catholicism to the end. At her funeral, a particularly enlightened priest whom she had come to know as he visited the sick while she was hospitalised for pneumonia a few years earlier, gave a moving address – to call it a sermon would be a misnomer. Surprisingly given the dogmatic leanings of the church that employs him, he made a point of referring specifically to all the creeds, lapsed creeds, and non-creeds he assumed were represented among the mourners. If anyone has it in their power to turn this decrepit church around or at least mitigate its worst instincts, it will be men and women of inclusion and tolerance such as this remarkable priest.

My parents now lie as they planned it, side by side in the cemetery in Corravillers, my maternal grandfather's ancestral village. They share the grave with my maternal grandparents and several of my grandfather's ancestors whose birth dates, carved into the gravestone made of local granite, go back to the 1840s. The surroundings are tranquil. On two sides are steep meadows dotted with placid cows apparently impervious to the laws of gravity. Just below is the village church, its tower capped with a pretty pattern of red and yellow tiles. If you are passing, drop by and say hello. Turn left just past the church. The grave is the last but one in the far left corner. My parents were the gregarious sort and this is a lonely spot. They will be glad to see you.

CHAPTER FOUR: CLASS STRUGGLE

What we want is to see the child in pursuit of knowledge, not knowledge in pursuit of the child.

George Bernard Shaw (1856-1950)

School started early: early in the day as for all French schoolchildren, but for my siblings and myself, early in life too. My father was determined that his children would start their education a year ahead of their cohort. His thinking was that there was always a risk of being held back by illness or academic failure and having to repeat a grade so giving us an early start in our education was an insurance policy. Another reason was that for him, the ultimate aspiration was a government job and the pension that would eventually come with it so starting work a year earlier meant that the extra year spent in employment would convert into a slightly higher pension. Given my father's life trajectory from rural poverty to academic success quickly followed by the Great Depression, this outlook was entirely understandable.

For me, this early start was not such a good idea. Because I was born near the end of the year, I was almost two years younger than my oldest classmates and at such a young age a single year – let alone two – amounts to a lot of missed development. Looking back, part of my later academic failures, which caused my father such anguish, can be put down to mere immaturity. That said, three of my classmates were even younger and two of them – Pascal and Jean – went on to become distinguished engineers. The third, Philippe, shared my preference for goofing around at the back of the class over solving scientific problems such as how long it would take for a bathtub filled with so many litres of water to empty if there was a hole at the bottom so many millimetres in diameter. Wouldn't it be much quicker and easier, Philippe and I reasoned, to plug the hole with a bit of chewing gum? In fact, why not stop having baths altogether? After all, we were living in France, a country where sweatiness was seen as next to godliness and bathing was considered injurious to the epidermis. The logic seemed impeccable. Needless to say, neither Philippe nor I became engineers, distinguished or otherwise.

Initially, all went well with my education. Each morning from the age of four, my mother hoisted me onto the back of her bicycle and delivered me to Sainte Anne, the Catholic school at the far end of town. My parents and especially my father were no fans of faith-based education, but this was the only institution of learning in town that offered a preschool option. The school was run by nuns who worked and lived in a large building on two sides of a shady courtyard where we gathered and played under ancient lime trees. These were happy, carefree days.

Except for one thing.

Early that summer, a school pageant was organised with cowboys and indians as the theme. I was not yet the devotee of *Tintin en Amérique* I was later to become but perhaps the nuns were. In any event, this pageant sounded fun. But for some reason, something went wrong in the casting as the assembled forces consisted entirely of indians with not a cowboy in sight. So my mother turned to the sartorial challenge of turning me into a credible impersonation of a Sioux.

She often spent her afternoons seated at her sewing machine making the clothes that she could not afford to buy. So she set to work and fashioned some impressive headgear from unclaimed pigeon feathers I found lying around the house. She added a colourful shirt that anthropologists specialising in Sioux *couture* would undoubtedly have certified as authentic. But what still rankles is that she saw it fit to complete the verisimilitude by making me wear pyjama bottoms in the middle of the afternoon and in front of sniggering classmates and busloads of siblings, parents, grandparents, and cousins twice removed, not to mention a clutch of Church dignitaries and the entire content of the convent. The indignity of it was almost too much to bear!

In a photo taken that ignominious day, three little indians are standing in the sunshine. That's me in the middle. Throughout my life, I have never enjoyed being photographed. I feel awkward and I stare inanely or I look daggers at the photographer. But in this photo, I do not just look fatuous or crabby. I look outright homicidal. It is obvious I am contemplating serious blood-letting. Somehow, I recovered from this sartorial torment and moved on. But my ability to smile in photographs was irreparably compromised from that day forward.

*

I was barely five when I started primary school. That was not old enough to ride a bike there and back but old enough to walk all the way unaccompanied by a parent. So with shining morning faces, my older sister Bernadette – the bossy one – and I walked to school hand in hand. There was nothing unusual in this. In those pre-soccer-mum, pre-SUV days, all children in Lure, Haute-Saône walked to school. In fact, the children of Lure, Haute-Saône did more than just walk there and back. They walked there and back and then there and back all over again. This being France, everyone including five-year olds went home for lunch at noon precisely and then back to school exactly two hours later for another three hours of instruction. Getting a primary education in France used up twice as much shoe leather as anywhere else on earth.

The school seemed very far and the hike interminable. But once we were a little older, the trek was made more bearable if we were entrusted with the task of dropping by the bakery on the way home for lunch and picking up the day's supply of fresh bread. This was not just the chance of a whiff of fragrant *baguette* straight out of the oven. It meant having a head start on lunch, gnawing away at one end of the *baguette* and then starting at the other while resisting the temptation to stop only when the two ends met in the middle and there was nothing left to bring home. Like Marcel Proust and his *madeleines*, I vividly recall the feel of the warm crust in my hands and the appetising fragrance that wafted from the white interior as I broke off chunks of edible size. But even in a family where the rules were the rules and it did not take much to earn a parental earful, the *baguette* gnawing caused only indulgent smiles. After all, as our pious grandmother used to say to all who would listen, bread was God's food and it would have been churlish to reprimand children for doing what they could to stave off hunger while getting an education and adhering to the divine plan simultaneously.

Another reason why we walked to school and back without protest despite the distance was the wealth of experiences that could be enjoyed along the way. As our appreciation of the virtues of cash grew with age, much of our commuting time was spent scanning the pavement for mislaid bullion we might pick up and spend on something sweet and sticky in the corner shop near our house. The shop was richer than Aladdin's cave. The top of the counter – or what I could see of it if I stood tiptoe – was end-to-end glass jars filled with sweets wrapped in brightly coloured paper and that if chewed long enough stuck to my teeth in a most satisfying manner. The downside was having to face Madame Vitolle, the shop owner and a notorious harpy.

As my sister Bernadette and I walked in gingerly and the tinkle of the little bell on the door alerted her to the prospect of lucre, Madame Vitolle eyed us narrowly as if she suspected us of having counterfeited the coin we were about to push across her counter or of planning to make off with the day's takings at gunpoint. Admittedly, this was always a somewhat furtive operation as our parents held firm views on the uses and abuses of sugary substances and we were young and Catholic and therefore easily moved to guilt. Later, we discovered the real reason why Madame Vitolle was so unwelcoming despite our honest attempts to make her independently wealthy: she knew us as the children of parents who shunned her establishment on grounds of overcharging and of being run by a miserable old hag to boot. Not our parents' exact words perhaps but the gist was clear.

The walk to school was long and tiring but never dull. The route took us past one of the few farms on the edges of town that still worked a horse. But even more fascinating than occasional sightings of the massive beast was the fact that like most farmers, the horse's owner adorned the front of his house with a generous heap of steaming manure that oozed a brownish trickle across the pavement and down the street. Four daily chances to leap over the trickle and occasionally miscalculating and landing short made walking to school worthwhile all by itself.

Next was the large compound where Monsieur Segrat, the town's wine merchant and pivotal member of its POW association, stored his vintages. Periodically, Monsieur Segrat and his assistants could be glimpsed rolling out huge vats into the front yard and then flushing out the dregs with a powerful hose. To our delight, the product of the flushing trickled across the pavement, over the kerb, and down the street where it mingled with the ooze from the manure heap to form a subtle blend of crimson and gold. Before we could catch our breath from the thrill of it all, there was the heavenly smell of petrol being pumped at the Esso station opposite the hospital. And next to the school building was a dairy that sold all manner of fragrant cheeses but also fresh milk, naturally. The milk was stored in tall metal containers that like the wine merchant's vats had to be flushed out preferably right around the time school opened and closed. This released a pleasing, whitish liquid that gushed across the pavement and once again over the kerb and along the street right past the school door.

*

In France as in most countries, children go through primary school being taught by very few teachers so it is normally easy to recall these formative figures. A particular favourite of mine was Madame Voignard, a vivacious lady who unfortunately was with us for only a year. I call her a lady because she seemed grand and slightly out of place in homespun Lure, Haute-Saône. A key give-away was that she spoke in an accent that reminded me of the voices I heard on the radio, which came all the way from Paris, I was informed. Late in the school day, Madame Voignard held us spellbound with tales of how she had travelled the world and lived in Montevideo, the capital of Uruguay. To hear her tell it – and who were we to question her account? – Montevideo was a vast and magnificent city in a country of unparalleled bounty. To get there, she said, you had to sail the high seas for days on end on a ship bigger than a house, bigger than the whole school, even. How was this possible, I wondered, my imagination running wild.

Whatever else she taught me, this delightful lady turned out to be a major inspiration for my later globe-trotting and in particular for my otherwise irrational fascination with South America. When more than two decades later I managed to save enough to realise the dream, on my first night on the continent – in Caracas, Venezuela to be precise – I gazed in disbelief at the building across the street from my hotel – a bank, I think – on which a large neon sign displayed the magic words: *América del Sur*. Later, as I explored the vastness between Panama and Tierra del Fuego and back up again, Uruguay would turn out to be the flattest country and Montevideo the dullest capital city in the entire continent. But no matter: I was there at last.

In another of my years of primary schooling, our teacher was that educational rarity in our town: a man. This teacher made so little impression on me that I cannot even recall his name. He stuck to basics with as much grim determination as Madame Voignard had relied on her natural effervescence to keep us on side. Every day, he wore the same grey overalls, which added to his air of permanent gloom. He did not seem to enjoy his job very much. But one of the long-term benefits I derived from his efforts is an intimate knowledge of *La Marseillaise*, complete with its rousing tune and idiotic call to the citizenry to flood France's furrows with the impure blood of its enemies. He drilled this xenophobic nonsense into us by standing at the front of the class looking depressed and waving a ruler and occasionally tapping it on his desk to keep our ear-piercing attempts at patriotism more or less synchronised.

For three of my five years in primary school, our teacher was Mademoiselle Larroz, a young woman with a reputation as an innovator. This included the then unheard-of practice of discussing her students' progress with their parents. What an odd idea this must have seemed! What could parents know about their children's development that the Ministry of Education in Paris had not anticipated? But despite her revolutionary approach, even this paragon of educational virtue never managed to teach me how to write legibly.

We sat in immutable rows behind sloping desks, and with a few more years to go before the adoption of the ball-point pen, learning to write meant gradually mastering the volatile combination of pen and ink. At the time, a pen was in effect a thin stick made of soft wood. This was useful when lunch or even a nibble of the daily *baguette* on the way to lunch seemed several interminable hours away. As the stomach rumbled, the pen tasted good. Putting it to work as intended was another matter.

At the non-edible end, I pushed in a nib carefully selected from my personal collection, which I kept in a small metal box that never left my presence. I then picked an appropriate spot on the stick where to position my fingers, not too high or the thing would keel over as soon as pen made contact with paper but not too low or my fingertips would end up covered in ink. For some reason, sticking my tongue out of one side of my mouth, right or left, was a key factor in ensuring success. Once most of us had all of that more or less under control, we were deemed ready to start writing gripping accounts of what we as a family did last Sunday afternoon or how we had spent our recent holidays.

But to get this far, we first had to master the art of

connecting pen and ink. The ink was stored in round pots made of white ceramic and inserted into holes in the top right corner of each desk. If you were left-handed, too bad: that would have to change. Early each morning, the school *concierge* and general factotum, whose name I cannot recall because no one in the school ever called him anything other than *le concierge* and his wife *la femme du concierge* shuffled from classroom to classroom refilling the ink pots out of an industrial-sized bottle. I was never around that early of course but I knew he did because I occasionally watched him unloading fresh supplies from a lorry at the back of the school and the ink pots never ran dry.

An early lesson was that there's many a slip 'twixt ink pot and paper. Typically, motor-control in a child learning the basics of handwriting is a little shaky and nibs tended to leak generously so opportunities for spilling ink on the desk, the page, fingers, hands, knees, and especially clean shirts were endless. The result was that novice writing tended to consist of a string of smudges occasionally broken up by recognisable letters. In my case, I have as evidence a card I created from scratch for my mother's birthday. The card is dated so I know I wrote this when I was ten and already being inducted into the mysteries of secondary education including Latin. The card reads, in French in the original:

My dear Mummy: I promise to be good during the whole year and not to hurt you anymore. I will try to work hard in school to make you happy and Daddy too.

I suspect that this uncharacteristic outpouring of good intentions came in the aftermath of yet another disastrous school report. But the telling features of this artefact are the uneven writing, the smudges, the spelling errors, and the missing letters inserted later in the appropriate spots above the words. Given my father's low tolerance for disastrous school reports, he must have been the force behind this act of contrition. The writing clearly bears the marks of heavy editing on someone's part: his, surely. I never cracked the finer points of handwriting. Had I known that someone would eventually invent the laptop computer, I would not even have tried.

*

In an effort to identify scapegoats for my failure to scale the educational peaks my father kept pointing out to me, I blame three factors.

When I was about eight, my teacher suggested to my parents that the root cause of my learning difficulties and especially of my abysmal handwriting may well be poor eyesight. Never one to pass up a chance to help one of his children acquire an education, my father decided to make the substantial investment that having me fitted with glasses would represent. The problem was that there was no ophthalmologist practicing in Lure, Haute-Saône. For most needs, the medical talent on offer was adequate but it tended to stick to diagnosing flu and treating outbursts of *crise de foie*, that mysterious condition of the liver that seems to afflict only the French especially at festive times. But even in a genuine crisis, expert care was at hand. On one near-tragic occasion, our family physician, Docteur Magraix, won my parents' eternal gratitude by spotting early and treating promptly a potentially lethal case of diphtheria in my very young sister Marie-Jeanne. But obviously, it was not within the power of even this fine physician to prescribe glasses that might improve my eyesight and hopefully my school results.

So one afternoon when school was out, my father

drove me the thirty kilometres to Vesoul, the metropolis to the west where several ophthalmologists competed for business. My eyes were tested, corrective lenses were pronounced necessary, and I was measured for frames. But putting lenses and frame together would take a few hours, so my father and I got back in the car and went for a drive through some of the neighbouring villages. I remember the trip vividly including the names of the villages we passed: Echenoz, Montigny, Andelarre and its even tinier twin Andelarrot. These villages were hardly beauty spots. Most were wretched, little more than clusters of crumbling farmhouses. But what mattered was that I was in the car with my father and no one else. In a large family, this was a rare treat. I felt special as if I had grown by years in the space of mere hours.

Back at the ophthalmologist's, we picked up my new glasses and my father was assured that this would only be a temporary palliative: my eyesight would correct itself and I would soon be able to discard the thick lenses, write legibly, and stop looking so nerdy. Unfortunately, the prediction proved wide off the mark. Checkup after checkup, year after year, the prescription was ratcheted up and it has never shown the slightest sign of going into reverse. More than five decades later, I still look nerdy, only in a slightly more dignified sort of way.

*

The second contributing factor behind educational foundering on my part was the decision by an unusually public-spirited French government in the mid-1950s to provide every primary student up and down the land with free milk at the end of the school day. A few minutes before we were due to rush out and head home, two burly ladies in pink overalls came lumbering out of the school kitchens carrying a huge pot filled with hot milk, a pair of long ladles, and a large bag filled with cups made of a revolutionary new material called 'plastic'. They then went from classroom to classroom ladling out the milk and making it clear that they did not have all day and would we please stop whining about the milk being too hot and drink up so they could collect the cups and go home.

The policy may have had an entire laudable nutritional aim on the part of the government of the time. Or perhaps government experts had noticed that French kids were short and weedy compared to German kids, and with the end of World War II barely a decade past and the Common Market already at the planning stages, the gap had to be closed in a hurry if the French were to look their troublesome neighbours in the eye at last. And since there was no humane way to make the German kids shorter and weedier, the only option was to pump bone-strengthening calcium into the French kids instead. For reasons unknown, the milk experiment lasted only one year, though the unintended consequences of the torture linger in my personal tastes in hot drinks.

For the milk to be drinkable and cause no intestinal damage, it had to be boiled, and with one stove and one pot and one set of plastic cups and one pair of burly ladies and a full curriculum to go through and the school bell about to go, the entire process had to be squeezed into a time frame no young mouth could withstand. Normally, that time of day should have been one of anticipation of an imminent chance to leap over the rivulets from the manure heap all over again. What I got instead was ordeal by hot milk and the terrifying sense that my tongue was about to catch fire. I hated hot milk. Even today I cannot bear the smell let alone the taste of the stuff. An indirect consequence of the milk experiment was that the thought began to form in my mind that there must be a million places where I would rather be beside school. And it would be many years before I had cause to change my mind.

*

The third source of early educational trauma was the schoolyard and the perils that lurked therein. Two factors were at play. One was that even by French standards, I was very much on the short and weedy side as well as very young for my cohort. The other was that Lure, Haute-Saône was so small that a single building could comfortably house both our primary school and the entire content of the secondary school, or *lycée*. And since my father was the only history and geography teacher in the school, every secondary student in town passed through his classes. The result was that at break times, the schoolyard was teeming with history and geography haters. There is only so much public ridicule an average history and geography hater can take from a teacher for stating that the battle of Austerlitz was named after a railway station in Paris or for holding the map of France upside down in full view of sniggering classmates. But while the malcontents could not retaliate against the source of the ridicule directly, his short and weedy son presented little threat: he would do nicely.

As soon as I was sighted in the schoolyard, the schemers surrounded me in numbers and taunted me by questioning my father's moral character or the exact nature of my lineage on my mother's side. They made fun of my age, my size, my new glasses, the gaps between my teeth, everything. Sneers flew and guffaws followed. Invariably, the *pièce de résistance* consisted of punning on my family name and reducing it to *Brute*, which the thugs seemed to regard as a witticism of the highest order and that never failed to convulse them with laughter. Eventually, they got bored and went off in search of someone else to victimise. To their credit, especially in contrast to the atmosphere of real menace that plagues many twenty-first century schoolyards, these juvenile delinquents never laid a finger on me. But at the time, knowing that I had to run that gauntlet and face the verbal assault on a regular basis did little to boost my love of school.

On most days, avoiding the bullies was not difficult. Primary and secondary students shared the schoolyard but breaks were staggered so that the little kids were indoors when the big kids were outdoors and vice versa. But on occasion, calls of nature required a response that could not be put off. And at the age of eight or nine, the urge comes fast and furious and gives the sufferer very little time to consider his options.

The school was housed in a former monastery that had been expropriated by revolutionary enthusiasts and turned over to the edification of *la crème de* Lure, Haute-Saône along secular lines. The school buildings lined two sides of the schoolyard. A third featured a vegetable garden that provided the boarders with their daily vitamins and the Principal and his family, for whom access to this blessed plot was a perk of the job, with a chance to limber up and save on the food bills. The fourth side consisted of dark and mysterious storage spaces flanked by an outhouse so filthy that it defies the modern imagination.

A decade or so later, after I had lived in London long enough to make sense of lavatorial euphemisms in English, I learned that the British held what they called 'French plumbing' in contempt, and in truth, they had a point. The school outhouse was dark, dank, sooty, and it stank to high heaven. Days-old urine lingered in stagnant pools. There were ancient yellowish streaks of vomit on the walls. I cannot tell whether the girls faced similar horrors on their side of the divide. But even if their section was cleaner, which I doubt, it is hard to imagine how they could ignore the smell. Even by the standards of filth-tolerant children growing up in sub-hygienic post-war France, the place was nauseating.

The reason the outhouse was smelly is self-evident. But the reason it was sooty was that one of its side walls propped up the school's stack of coal. Each winter morning, once he was done with his ink-related duties, the *concierge* shovelled some of the black stuff into a wheelbarrow, carted it across the schoolyard and into each classroom, and stoked up the stove that stood in a corner. We approved of this policy and of the man's dedication to duty. We liked coal. Coal kept us warm. Most of us had similar stoves at home. In ours, each winter morning and evening, my father went through a similar routine with the difference that his involved hauling the stuff up three flights of stairs in a scuttle instead of across the schoolyard in a wheelbarrow. By the time we went to school, we knew enough about the natural world to appreciate the link between coal and not freezing to death.

The downside of coal, as anyone from the Welsh valleys or West Virginia will attest, is that it comes with a lot of fine black dust: too flimsy to produce much heat when burned in a stove, too fine to be picked up with a shovel, and too volatile to be carted across a windswept schoolyard in a wheelbarrow but perfect for creating a smooth surface on which boys can play marbles. And because we were boys and therefore uniquely equipped to live with filth and scatology, we had the run of that sooty, smelly corner of the schoolyard. Girls seemed to be averse to playing

103

marbles in coal dust next to the stinking outhouse or anywhere else for that matter and the teachers were even more fastidious. So girls and teachers left us alone and we were free to enjoy our games with no one around to find fault with our strategies or the language we resorted to when disputes arose. If the wind had picked up and the dust had drifted during the night or if the playing surface had become uneven and rocky, we simply kicked in a little more coal dust from the bottom of the stack, danced on it awhile, and then patted it down with our bare hands to restore the playing surface to competition standards. It was hard work but the result was smooth as silk.

At lesson times, the only reason to be in that corner of the schoolyard was to attend to calls of nature we had neglected to deal with during the break because we were too busy playing marbles. And at the age of seven or eight, sudden reminders of the limitations of a young bladder were frequent and led to a lone dash across the schoolyard where in all likelihood the thugs would be out on their break and lying in ambush.

For me, facing the hoodlums was a terrifying prospect. They looked twice my size and made ten times as much noise as all my classmates and I could manage even in our most feral moments. So as the pressure on my bladder grew, I delayed and delayed and usually got away with it *in extremis*. But one fateful day, as the afternoon was drawing to a close and there was only the ordeal by hot milk to go through before the dash for freedom, Mademoiselle Larroz decided to call me to the front of the class. Perhaps she was feeling the strain and needed moral support. Or she had spotted me shifting in my seat and concluded that giving me a chance to demonstrate my superior understanding of some key component of the curriculum or other would take my mind off the torment I seemed to be going through.

So there I was, chalk in hand, challenging conventional multiplication theory or something of that nature. Keeping a young bladder under control is difficult at the best of times. But it is especially tricky if the owner of the bladder happens to be standing as opposed to sitting with legs crossed. And on that occasion, bladder control suddenly failed and the sluices opened. At first, the warm fluid simply trickled down my bare legs and into my socks and shoes. Then as my shoes began to overflow, a puddle appeared around my feet and grew to a flood of biblical proportions. Fingers were pointed, observations whispered, and giggles suppressed until it became clear that this was the real thing and not a game. The mob loved it. They squealed, they howled, they fell about. Despicable little beasts!

Luckily for me, the clammy discomfort and the unspeakable mortification did not last long. Mademoiselle Larroz – bless her – reacted in a heartbeat. Having no doubt seen it all before, she knew exactly what to do and she dealt with the inundation like a trooper. She shushed the mob. She ordered a pair of boys who could not get much dirtier than they already were to locate bucket and mop and clean up the mess. She put the most fearsome-looking girl in the class in control and commanded her to use any means at hand to quell mutinies in her absence. Then she took me by the hand and walked me over to the Principal's quarters next to the vegetable garden, where Madame Boittard, the Principal's ample and kindly wife, who doubled as school nurse and agony aunt to young souls in distress restored me to respectability as best she could. I think she even gave me a little hug. Come to think of it, it must have been a big hug: Madame Boittard was not built for little hugs.

I hope the fearsome-looking girl smacked a few of my stupid classmates on the side of their stupid heads while Mademoiselle Larroz, Madame Boittard, and I were otherwise engaged. Mademoiselle Larroz was a pearl among pedagogues. I worshiped the woman. And Madame Boittard was not far behind in my personal pantheon.

*

Obviously, much more took place inside that school beside games of marbles, run-ins with thugs, and the occasional case of youthful incontinence.

Once we were safely past the seeping manure, the wine dregs, and the milk effluvia that made the hike to school such an adventure, we lined up in front of our respective classrooms. Once inside and seated, we were ready to start memorising whatever the curriculum planners in Paris had determined was essential to our intellectual development. Multiplication tables were high on the list. And as any proselytiser will confirm, the best way to get children to learn foundational information is to have them chant it. So we chanted and we chanted. To this day, more than five decades later, I can still chant the entire set of multiplication tables in French.

Long hours were also spent memorising French conjugations of varying degrees of perversity. Why we had to memorise this was not clear since we all started school knowing French already. Presumably, the aim was to help us learn the spellings, which are even more baroque than the conjugations themselves.

Once we had this pat, we moved on to another curricular favourite: lists of irregular plurals. So we chanted and we chanted and eventually accepted that several skins should be *peaux* and not *peaus*, as regular spelling rules would suggest, and several desks should be *bureaux* and not *bureaus*. Obviously, these idiosyncrasies were carved in stone and youthful experimentation was ruthlessly snuffed out. The point was driven home one day when I asked candidly why my family name was not included in this list of irregular plurals since it too ended in *-aux* just as much as *peaux* or *bureaux* and there were definitely more than one of us especially once I factored in all my siblings and our many cousins. The loud derision whipped up among my classmates by the teacher's dismissal of my honest attempt at seeing patterns left me feeling humiliated for days.

Another curricular highlight was the list of the largest cities in France. As with deadly sins, Catholic sacraments, and Disney's dwarves, for some reason, the list stopped at seven. I give it here in full from memory and in descending order just as we chanted it: Paris, Marseille, Lyon, Toulouse, Bordeaux, Nice *et* Nantes.

Memorising this made no practical sense. Not one of these cities was located near us in eastern France. Very few of us had ever been to any of them, not even Paris, an unconscionable 400 kilometres away. Nor were we as a family likely to visit any of these cities. We had no relatives in or even near any of them and in any case my father detested urban concentrations of more than a couple of thousand inhabitants so it was always highly unlikely that he would find himself driving the family through one of the magnificent seven. But it was in the curriculum so our teacher taught it and we chanted it.

It could have been worse. Towards the end of her life, my mother could still recite the list of French *départements* she had memorised some eight decades earlier complete with *préfecture* and every *sous-préfecture* in each one. With around ninety departments and an average of three or four *sous-préfectures* each, the list ran to well over three hundred: Ain: Bourg-en-Bresse, Belley, Gex, Nantua; Aisne: Laon, Château-Thierry, Saint-Quentin, Soissons, Vervins; Allier: Moulins, Montluçon, Vichy. And on and on and on, from A to Z. She could also recite the list of *comptoirs*, the trading posts the French had set up along the coasts of India in the eighteenth century and were still French possessions in her youth: Chandernagor, Karikal, Mahé, Pondichéry *et* Yanaon. According to my mother, her teachers did not appear to care where India was let alone what role – if any – these outposts played in contemporary French life. But knowing the list by heart was shared knowledge: it was part of what made you French. So it had to be learnt.

Definitions came next. Admittedly, definitions are a step up from lists in terms of cognitive challenge. But it is perfectly possible to learn a definition without understanding a word of it. Take the metre, for example. Now, the metric system is a central pillar of most educational systems – America's excepted – and a vast improvement on having to get one's young head around the difference between fluid ounces and the plain-vanilla variety or to figure out the British stone, which consists of fourteen pounds and for some reason is always 'stone' and never 'stones' even if, as most people do, you weigh more than one.

Understanding and then remembering the seductive logic of the metric system makes a lot of sense. But what was the point of chanting that a metre was a metre because somebody had cut two notches in a slab of platinum and iridium alloy and decided that the distance between the notches would henceforth be known as a 'metre' and then had the thing kept under lock and key in a building in an obscure Paris suburb, the *Pavillon de Breteuil* in Sèvres, to be exact? I can recite all this in French to this day.

The trouble with this approach is that it explained nothing. For naturally inquisitive children, this was a cardinal sin. Even in an eight-year-old, the rote memorisation approach raised a raft of questions: Who put those notches in the slab of platinum and iridium alloy? On whose authority? Why there and not somewhere else on the slab or on some other slab? What on earth were platinum and iridium anyway? And why did it matter that the thing was kept in that building and not in some other building? Had we been invited to ask, we would probably have been told that it was that way and not some other way because the textbook said so and the textbook was written by knowledgeable people in Paris with our own good in mind.

What made all this especially shameful was that the French educational authorities of the time did not even have the excuse of large classes to justify the mass delivery of useless snippets of information. Lure, Haute Saône was not exactly bursting at the seams with humanity. In fact, the main policy issue of the time was which school was likely to be axed in the next economy drive precisely because classes were too small. All this would soon go into reverse as the baby-boomers were beginning to march into schools in their thousands. But at the time, for schools and teachers alike, what mattered was survival, a concern that does not encourage experimentation or risk-taking in education or anything else. Though none of this was clear to me at the time, I sensed that school was there in part to stifle inquisitiveness and advance conformity. No wonder I spent the next decade searching for alternative sources of enlightenment.

CHAPTER FIVE: TESTING TIMES

It is important that students bring a certain ragamuffin, barefoot irreverence to their studies.

Jacob Bronowski (1908-1974)

Transitioning from primary to secondary school was not difficult. Many things stayed the same. A few classmates left, a few new ones came in, but most moved up as a cohort. Since primary school and secondary school shared the same space, there was little new to discover. The school building itself was where it had been for centuries and the schoolyard, the vegetable garden, the effluvia from the dairy next door, and the stinking outhouse were all there waiting for us at the end of the long, idyllic summer break.

Some important aspects of school life did change, and these had a major effect on my activities and perceptions. I was now allowed to ride my bike to school and no longer just up and down our street or around the fir trees in front of our house. The sense of power and freedom this created was exhilarating. Suddenly, I could be anywhere that mattered in minutes as opposed to what had seemed like hours. I could explore streets I only knew by name and parts of the town I barely knew existed. True, there was always the risk that if I explored too widely and fearsomely, I might come home late for lunch or dinner, both pivotal events in French family life that followed a sacrosanct schedule. But the adventure was worth the gamble.

Most of these voyages of discovery were entirely innocent. Once I had the benefit of mobility and speed, I was asked to run all sorts of family errands. Or I might be asked to pass critical information back and forth between families without a phone, which meant just about every family we knew. This made me feel useful and competent, almost adult. I was no longer just observing, absorbing, and imitating. I was contributing. In brief, I felt older, which was just how I wanted to feel at that age.

But wheels made detours around the margins of family law possible too. For me, being able to choose my route and make quick getaways if I was where I should not be and I noticed I was being observed brought all sorts of thrills within range. Now was my chance to ride very slowly past the one and only lingerie shop in town or leer at photos of a semi-nude Brigitte Bardot outside the *Rex* cinema. True, at the age of ten or eleven, I was still a little confused in the matter of semi-nude women. But an interest was emerging. If I felt especially daring, I might even go for broke and ride past the army Rest & Recreation headquarters in the grungy alleyway by the railway station and conjecture about what might be going on inside.

Another upside of having the freedom of the streets was that on my free afternoons, I could explore those twilight zones where town gave way to country and cows began to outnumber people. I might even ride across the bridge over the Ognon River and survey the great beyond including the Le Corbusier church at Ronchamp, just visible on the horizon. Or I might drop in on a classmate whose family lived on the outer fringes of town and witness different family rituals and taste unfamiliar foods. On a good day, if I timed my visit right, I might even catch older sisters at their homework and peek at bare legs swinging under desks and expanding chests resting on open textbooks.

*

An additional bonus of entering secondary school was

that I could now wear long trousers. In fact, in winter, it was not so much a matter of being allowed to wear long trousers as *not* being allowed out of the house *unless* I wore long trousers – lots of them, all at the same time: long trousers and long johns, at the very least. Quite why the same logic had not applied in primary school and continued not to apply to girls was not entirely clear to me. But the switch suggested oncoming manhood and I welcomed the symbolism as much as the protection against the winter gales.

Being hundreds of kilometres from the nearest seaboard and therefore subject to a continental climate, Lure, Haute-Saône had sharply contrasting seasons. Spring and autumn were mild and summer brought hot and sunny periods punctuated by gradual build-ups of stifling humidity that culminated in powerful thunderstorms. But summer coincided with school holidays and to a boy on the cusp of adolescence and motivated by the urge to spend those precious months out and about whenever possible, the summer weather seemed perfect, always, year after year. It was never too hot. It never rained. Or if it did, the rain was warm and dried the moment it landed on me. But winters could be brutal.

One winter in the early 1960s, it got so cold and stayed so cold for so long that water pipes froze all over town and the municipal authorities had to unplug ancient wells that even the older generation of residents had forgotten existed so everyone could lower a bucket and get their supply of drinking water for the day. At home, it was so cold in the unheated bedrooms that window panes remained covered in pretty ice patterns for weeks – on the inside!

Matters were not helped by the French habit of fitting wooden shutters to windows, the idea being that these help keep the heat in and the cold out. A fine energy-saving move in principle, decades ahead of its time in fact. The trouble was that French shutters were – and still are – invariably fitted to the *outside* of windows. So for the energy-saving policy to work as intended, every window in the house has to be opened when it is time to close the shutters at night and to open them again in the morning. And when it is -20°C outside, the windows do not have to be left open for very long before the temperature inside starts plummeting towards freezing and the stove has to be stoked up, thereby ruining the energy-saving policy. But to break that habit in a French home and leave the shutters alone in the fiercest of winters would have been as unthinkable as serving *kimchi* with the *soufflé* or eating dessert before the cheese.

At bedtime, we quickly shed some (but not all) of our clothes, threw on pyjamas that had been warming all evening by the stove in the living room, pushed our discarded clothes under the blankets to keep them warm and relatively easy to put back on in the morning, and dived into bed. Showers were out of the question.

In school that winter, we were allowed to keep our overcoats on all day. Maths lessons were a particular ordeal and not just because of the maths. By tradition, these lessons were always held in the largest classroom in the school, a corner room with ill-fitting windows that posed no obstacle to raging winter gales. That winter, instead of sitting in rows as we normally did, we huddled together around the ancient stove in the centre of the room and tried to catch some of the heat it managed to exude. The upside was that this gave me and my fellow dunces the perfect excuse for not understanding maths because, we argued, we were sitting too far from the blackboard.

Regardless of season, secondary school ushered in some exciting novelties. Gone were those pesky pens, nibs, and ink-pots and in were ball-point pens, the new rage. Each subject was taught by a different teacher so a new challenge was keeping tabs on which textbooks to pick at night for the next day's lessons. My mother saw to it that this was never left till morning, and for good reason. We did not have lessons in all subjects each day so the time horizon had to expand and homework had to be planned over several days, an eternity at the age of ten or eleven. But once I got the hang of it, being ahead of schedule with my homework gave me a glowing feeling. The added bonus was that once mastered, the practice left me free to devote my attention to whatever juvenile pursuit was really motivating me at the time, like running errands, exploring the town, or cleaning my bike.

Teachers were assigned one classroom each and we all fitted in snugly. Primary classes were held in downstairs rooms, a wise move on the part of the Principal given the sudden predicaments that can afflict those possessed of a young bladder, as I knew all too well. It would have made no sense to add the long descent of the stairs to the dash to the stinking outhouse on the other side of the schoolyard. But once in secondary school and therefore deemed to have achieved full control of our respective bladders, the issue of the dash to the outhouse no longer mattered and most secondary teachers could be safely assigned upstairs classrooms.

German was in Room Twelve. My father taught history and geography in Room Thirteen. English was in Room Fourteen, and maths in cavernous, frigid Room Fifteen. Latin classes were held in Room Sixteen, a cosy little nook up a few creaky stairs to one side of the building. The room was small but sufficient because Latin was by then becoming a *boutique* option and only about half of us took it. One exception was the classroom where Monsieur Morand, the physics and chemistry teacher and father of fellow-dunce Philippe, officiated. A balding, bespectacled man with a reputation as a humourist but whose jokes I never understood, Monsieur Morand operated in a remote classroom overlooking the vegetable garden on the far side of the schoolyard, rather like a hijacked aircraft parked in a far-flung corner of an airport. This, I now surmise, was no accident but a sensible precaution. The risk was that while Monsieur Morand was having himself a smoke outside with his good friend my father during a break, inquisitive young minds might decide to experiment and take bets on what might happen if they mixed the green content of this glass jar over here with the pink content of that glass jar over there and engulf the entire school and its human content in chemical Armageddon.

Back in the main building, we climbed to our classrooms via a majestic staircase that was strictly out-of-bounds to the primary school infants down below. Flanked by a splendid handrail made of wrought iron, the steps consisted of long slabs of local stone so worn down by generations of students that they sagged in the middle.

One protagonist whose role I chronicled earlier but whose function gained in importance once we were admitted to the heady world of secondary education was our faithful school *concierge*. He and his wife were the first persons we met as we went in through the school portals because the pair of them operated out of a poky service flat just inside the front door.

His wife was a thin little woman who wore the same black dress, day in and day out, summer or winter. She looked even older than my grandmother, if that was possible, but without any of her dignity. Gaunt, with sallow skin and grey hair, she was a scary crone. I dreaded being sent there on errands, to pick up a classroom key or report a mess that needed cleaning up. I knocked on the door, looked for a place to hide and found none, stood quaking as the door creaked open, and stammered out my message. Granted, she never raised her voice or threatened anyone in any way, but she did not have to: all she had to do was open the door and manifest herself. All that was missing for our worst nightmare to come true was a glimpse of her broomstick.

I suspect that being married to a mere *concierge* and not to some dashing *fonctionnaire* in city hall or the tax office had contributed to her jaundiced outlook on life, the universe, and all schoolchildren therein. Her husband was a flabby, slow, weary-looking man. Even to callow adolescents, his permanently red nose suggested that the embrace of his wife was not his primary source of comfort once the day's work was done. During all my years in that school, I never once saw him wearing anything other than standard French working-class dungarees, which must once have come in a fetching shade of blue but that were by then severely discoloured and gave alarmingly at the seat. Apart from refilling the ink pots and keeping us from freezing to death by stoking up the stoves in winter, his main contribution to our education was to alert us, however unwittingly, to the perils of the demon *vin rouge*.

In primary school, the same teacher taught us everything we needed to know in the same classroom for the entire year. But in secondary school, switching from French to maths, for example, in under five minutes involved major logistics as platoons of hyperactive students poured into the hallways, crossed paths, swapped pleasantries, and poked each other with pens. If the destination was a physics or chemistry lesson, the migration took even longer as it meant climbing down the majestic staircase in the main building, trudging across the schoolyard regardless of climatic conditions, and climbing the much less majestic wooden staircase at the other end.

In a building that had once been a monastery, the obvious way to choreograph the operation was by means of bell ringing. All the technology that was needed was a bell bolted to the wall above one of the arches of the pre-revolutionary cloisters, a chain, and a handle that rested on a hook high up on the arch so that none but the taller among the fun-seeking element in the school could reach it and ring the bell in amusing ways.

The routine consisted of the *concierge* ringing the bell at five minutes to the hour, rolling himself a cigarette, puffing away at it, then flicking the butt into the schoolyard and ringing the bell again on the hour. His dedication to duty ensured that all classes complied with the Ministry of Education requirement that instruction in each subject last fifty-five minutes and not a second more or less in all schools across the land. The task was hardly onerous. The *concierge* did not look as if he held the Haute-Saône record for IQ, but this was hardly rocket science, he had years of practice behind him, and creativity was out of the question. What could go wrong?

Periodically, something did. As everyone except perhaps the primary school infants knew, the *concierge* was partial to the bottle and once in a while, in his cups, he lost all sense of time and cast the bell-ringing timetable to the four winds. He came shuffling out of the conjugal lair in his house slippers, unhooked the chain, and rang the bell to his heart's content regardless of time of day or Ministry of Education edicts. In an instant, every classroom in the school was thrown into confusion. Eyes turned to the teacher for an official reaction, whispers were exchanged, giggles were suppressed. The wealthier students, who owned a watch, had a long look at it, held it to their ear to make sure it was ticking normally, wound it up a bit to be on the safe side, and then held their arm up and jabbed the dial with the index finger of their free hand to confirm to the class and especially to the teacher that something had gone awry with the bell-ringing.

In most cases, the teacher made a quick personal time check and chose to ignore the commotion. We were instructed not to let the *concierge*'s antics disrupt our concentration and swiftly brought back to whatever educational challenge we happened to be addressing. But on occasion, a mischievous teacher, or a bored one, or perhaps one who was new to the school and had not been forewarned of the *concierge*'s personal take on the passing of time let us out into the schoolyard as soon as the clanging started. The *concierge* was a sight: even more ruddy-nosed than usual, glassy-eyed and with an inane smile on his face, holding on to the bell chain for support and swaying this way and that.

This made our day. Fun on this scale made up for all the miseries and frustrations of acquiring a secondary education.

*

A major component of secondary education was the study periods that punctuated the week whenever there was a gap in the timetable. These took place in a dedicated classroom known as *étude*, so named because studying as opposed to teaching is what took place there. The room was also where the boarders were corralled between the last class of the afternoon and dinner time and where difficult townies such as myself, with a home to go to but no permission to go there quite yet, were sent for detention. Over time, this classroom had held generations of young scholars as they reflected on the lofty aims of French education, the key role Corneille's orotund output played in the advancement of France's *mission civilisatrice*, and the futility of resistance.

The classroom was especially intimidating, which must have been the original intention. The invigilators, known as *surveillants*, were not selected for their benevolent disposition. Their predecessors had been hired as *répétiteurs* and charged with drilling the students in Greek, Latin, and German grammar. But by the time we fell into the clutches of their successors, their role had shrunk to maintaining order at all times. In fact, these fiends were there precisely because they had been born with the rare ability to keep a roomful of subversive adolescents quiescent for hours simply by staring at them.

This echoing barn of a classroom was even larger than the one with the draughty windows where maths was taught. Judging by the state of the furniture, the room had been the nerve centre of secondary education in Lure, Haute-Saône for a very long time indeed. Near the front were rows of low desks for the younger students. At the back were much higher desks reserved for the older, taller generation. These desks were magnificent beasts, made of a single slab of ancient oak. Over time, their surface had been polished to such a sheen that the older students could look at their reflection and pop their pimples as effectively as if they had been standing in front of the mirror in their own bathroom, assuming they had a mirror or even a bathroom, which in French homes at the time was no certainty.

While exploring the byways of Latin, Greek, and

German grammar, generations of students had found the time to adorn the desks with elaborate artwork. Some of the artefacts were simply holes that went right through the desk. Anyone tall enough to reach up this high up and look down could see their shoes through them. These holes must have taken months to bore. In between were elaborate carvings that consisted of dates – hence the evidence of ancient study – and the usual combination of initials, hearts, and arrows, each suggesting an unrequited passion linking a young scholar and some girl glimpsed at vespers, perhaps.

Since I was too short to scale the benches at the back in a dignified manner during official study periods, how did I come to know all this? The answer is that I was best friends with a boy who had unfettered access to every corner of the school. His name was Daniel, and throughout primary and secondary school, we were inseparable. Daniel had the freedom of the school because his father had recently been promoted from Philosophy and Latin teacher to succeed Monsieur Boittard, the retiring Principal, he of the ample and kindly wife who had attended so soothingly to my incontinence problem a few years earlier.

Daniel and his parents lived in a large flat in a separate section of the school building. His father, Monsieur Françaix, was a warm, witty man who at an early age had developed a debilitating skeletal condition that had left him with a misshapen spine and made him much shorter than he would otherwise have been. But despite his respiratory and mobility difficulties and no matter what administrative, financial, or political tribulations his functions presumably inflicted on him, Monsieur Françaix was invariably cheerful. His specialty was deadpan humour, with his colleagues' children as his favourite target.

The routine never changed. As he met me in a

hallway, he stopped me and spun some yarn that sounded highly unlikely but not absolutely impossible. My mother had just phoned to say that lunch would be served late, for example. Now, I did have a mother, of course, but when I left home that morning she did not have a phone. Besides, I knew that the lunch hour was sacrosanct. But Monsieur Fronçaix looked so grave as he delivered his message. Who was I to gainsay his statements to his face?

He then waited as I calculated the odds that he may be telling the truth after all and simply stood there, watching my reaction and eventually allowing himself a wry smirk when he decided that the fun had lasted long enough. It could easily have been cruel, especially given the position of authority he was in. But he had a way of signalling with that smirk that this was playtime and I soon learned not to become alarmed by his outlandish statements.

Madame Fronçaix, Daniel's mother, was just as warm as her husband but much easier to read. During the long summer holidays, Daniel, myself, and a select inner core of friends, including my younger brother Pierre once he was old enough to talk intelligently about bikes and ride one as fast as we could, spent part our afternoons together loafing around the school building. Much of that time was spent in the schoolyard or even inside classrooms, including the dreaded *étude*, especially after the school acquired a television, only the second such marvel I had seen up close. At first, Daniel, I, and any member of our inner core that happened to be present that day watched whatever France's lone State channel saw fit to broadcast. But with games of badminton and Monopoly and discussions of the key characteristics of bikes (and later of girls) requiring our attention, we soon tired of staring at flickering images of interminable sporting events and inane variety shows. Once the novelty palled, we did not give the television another look, just as our friendly neighbours and playmates Françoise and Josiane had ignored theirs when we visited their house a few years earlier.

Whatever was keeping us busy around the school, there was always a slice of cake and a cool drink waiting for us when we needed a break. In fact, I had my very first taste of beer in Madame Fronçaix's kitchen when I was about thirteen or fourteen. It tasted bitter and unpleasant but beer was something men drank so it had to be tried at least once. Summer after summer, I found myself drifting towards Daniel's home. Gradually – and I still feel a little guilty about this – it struck me that I liked his home better than my own. Daniel was an only child so he got lots of attention as did all of us when we visited. All summer long, thanks to Daniel and his welcoming parents, we had the run of the school.

My mother and Madame Fronçaix were similar in nature. My mother was no slouch when it came to treating visitors to a slice of home-made cake and a refreshing drink. The two of them were fast friends and remained so for many years. But my father did not have Monsieur Fronçaix's equanimity except when he could escape outdoors: rambling, gardening, or camping, at which point he became a different person. He smiled, he laughed, he radiated *bonhomie* and infinite patience with noisy children. The noisier the better, it seemed, as long as he was outdoors. But when the weather kept us indoors, his mood turned sullen. In the background was a permanent fear of Madame Brossard, our crotchety landlady, who lived downstairs and never missed an opportunity to complain to my parents and especially to my grandmother, who shared her dislike of small, lively creatures, of the unbearable racket we were supposedly making upstairs. This cramped our style and made it more likely that we would jump on our bikes at every opportunity and seek freedom.

Monsieur Françaix was a little younger than my father so he retired a few years later. Within months, he was dead of a heart attack most likely caused by his lifelong disability. Life can be very unfair and death even more so. Monsieur Françaix was universally liked, it seems. His funeral drew a crowd of mourners larger than had been see in Lure, Haute-Saône for many years.

*

For me, maths, physics, chemistry, and biology were disaster areas from the start. Maths always struck me as utterly pointless. I could handle abstraction as long as what was being abstracted was the world I knew. But to me, maths abstracted for the sake of abstracting. Chemistry was nearly as bad, not because my world was not full of things chemical but because I could never see for myself how the pieces of the chemical world fitted together. Our school had no labs so I had to rely on the textbooks and the teacher's word and accept information I could never verify for myself. This was irksome.

Maths and chemistry were so alien to me that biology, or the 'natural sciences' as the subject was – and still is – called in French schools should have been a step up. But biology lessons were so dull that even cuddly animals and pretty flowers left me entirely cold. Had Mademoiselle Simard, our biology teacher, had the courage to tackle the topic I longed to hear about, namely the human ontogenesis, or in twelve-year-olds' parlance where babies come from, she would have taken instant possession of my pre-adolescent heart and mind. But no, enzymes and osmosis and things of that nature it had to be.

Physics was tough but it had some redeeming features. As I understood it, physics was about things that could be fitted together with a screwdriver and taken apart and then put back together again, usually with great difficulty. In that sense of the word, I had been studying physics ever since I acquired my very first toy car and was tall enough to reach into the drawer where my father kept his screwdriver. Later, the joy of physics consisted of making models of machines out of my Meccano set.

Meccano was a construction kit of British origin and consisting of blue metal sheets with holes in them, rods of varying lengths, and wheels of many sizes, which could be bolted together and turned into models of just about anything but especially of cars and lorries and even cranes. I got my first Meccano set when I was about eight. The set was small and unsophisticated at first, but successive Christmases and birthdays added functionality to the set. Soon I was able to put together machines that fascinated me because they suggested both power and mobility, two key elements of growing up.

One of my early attempts at studying physics via Meccano consisted of replicating my father's electric shaver. I bolted together several pieces into something rectangular I could hold in my hand. At one end, I added a revolving segment that would serve as the blade. At the other, I attached a length of thread purloined from my mother's sewing kit. I connected the thread to an element about the size of an electrical plug and added two short pins spaced exactly as power outlets required.

I picked my moment, a down time one afternoon when the house was quiet. I selected the spot, a messy corner of the bedroom my brother Pierre and I shared and where our parents feared to tread. Secure in the belief that there were few mysteries in the universe that could not be cracked by an inquisitive eight-year-old with a Meccano set, I pushed the plug into the power outlet, fully expecting the blade to start spinning.

I can still see the pyrotechnics. Suddenly, a flame of brilliant white shot out of the wall. The air filled with a loud, crackling noise. The electric shock knocked me sideways. I was too traumatised to cry and I remained prostrate on the floor until my brain could begin to make sense of what had just happened. As I recovered, my heartbeat slowed and animated adult voices began to be heard.

Identifying the terrorist who had just knocked out all the electrical appliances in the house cannot have been difficult because I must have looked as shaken as I felt. My parents were very good about it. My father climbed on a chair and replaced the defunct fuses while my mother gathered her children around her and explained that although power outlets had many virtues, the ability to double as toys was not one of them. We all nodded sagely. That fateful day, I reached two important conclusions. One was that although parents could be significant impediments to a happy and fulfilling life, generally speaking, they tended to be better informed than I was. The other was that my career path was unlikely to lead to electrical engineering.

To be worth studying, the physical world had to be tangible as well as familiar. This meant that, as far as I was concerned, the scope of physics ran to two things: the steam engine and its internal combustion cousin. I suppose I could have added bikes but bikes were too simple. There was not a lot of physics in bikes. But steam locomotives and cars were something else.

No one growing up in the 1950s in a small town cut in half by a railway and living as we did on the far side of the tracks could help learning about the physics of steam. By the time I started studying physics formally, I had watched hundreds of steam locomotives at the railway crossing in the middle of town. I knew the timetable of all the passenger trains, and even some of the freight trains made predictable appearances. Some sailed straight through without giving the place another look, but most made a brief stop. Those heading into town came in belching and hissing, their brakes squealing as they slowed. Those heading out crawled along like monstrous caterpillars as they struggled to gather speed. Some of the trains were so heavy that the huge wheels of the locomotive spun on the rails, sending a shower of sparks in every direction. At night, the effect was magical.

Back in school, learning how the coal heated the water and turned it into steam and how the steam was sent down to the pistons, in through one valve while the other closed and out again as the valves reversed roles, was pure pleasure. Drawing diagrams of the entire operation was even better especially if I was lucky enough to be asked to the front of the class to enlighten my more scientifically-challenged classmates.

When I was done with the steam engine but hungry for more science, there was the physics of the internal combustion engine to crack. The best thing about the internal combustion engine apart from the chance it gave me to learn really clever words like 'combustion' was that it alerted me to the wonderful interconnectedness of things. In effect, the internal combustion engine was a variant of the steam engine: it too had pistons and valves and it too made something inert move.

The physics of cars was so riveting that I devoted

entire afternoons to experimenting with my Meccano set. My early efforts involved nothing more ambitious than bolting together square boxes and attaching a wheel to each corner. I then pushed the thing one way, picked it up, turned it around, and then pushed it the other way. I could not steer these creations, but they were perfect for crashing into the pile of bricks my youngest sister Marie-Jeanne was lovingly assembling on the floor of the living room or for being launched to the far end of the hallway, where my father had his study. Not that he welcomed the presence of a small person crawling under his desk looking for an errant invention. But at least this was less likely to lead to punitive action than if my sister Marie-Jeanne decided that she could not see the funny side of her pile of bricks crashing down and sat squealing among the ruins until a vengeful parent rushed in and administered summary justice by smacking me on the side of the head.

As I learned more about physics, my creations acquired a proper steering wheel fitted into the structure and connected under the floor to the front wheels via a clever mechanism of my own devising that would have done the Peugeot family proud. Even my father was impressed when I showed him my invention. He was never likely to put such emotion into words, but I caught a look in his eyes. There was hope for me yet, that look seemed to be saying. Once the novelty of steering started to fade, I turned my fevered brain to the challenge of constructing a gearbox. But I never cracked that one. Maybe this was beyond the capabilities of my Meccano set, or my brain. Or perhaps working out the physics of steering and u-joints had taken me so long that by the time I was ready to explore the mysteries of variable transmission speeds, I had discovered girls, and was lost to mechanical engineering.

*

To my father's often expressed chagrin, my progress through secondary school was undistinguished, to say the least. I was not too bad at French, Latin, German, and English but my scores in scientific subjects were so poor that they lowered my average dangerously. This led to annual threats that I might have to repeat a year of school. I strongly suspect that year after year, our Principal Monsieur Fronçaix and my teachers massaged the numbers and nudged my average over the bar to save my father, their colleague and friend, the ignominy of seeing one of his children held back a year.

Soon, boredom and an almost permanent sense that I wanted to be somewhere else led to indiscipline. Over my seven years of secondary school, I had a wide variety of maths teachers. Maths teachers did not do well in Lure, Haute-Saône. They did not put down roots. Perhaps they took one look at us and decided that so few of us were scientist material that they would not bother to unpack and left town at the earliest opportunity.

One maths teacher who stuck around for a few years and must have come to regret it was Monsieur Blanc. This mild-mannered, absent-minded man, who always wore a scientist's white coat while teaching, could not have been more other-worldly and out of touch with the adolescent maelstrom around him. He seemed oblivious to our presence in the classroom and in particular to the plots we were permanently hatching to bring about his discomfiture.

We had it on the authority of students a year ahead of us that it was not difficult to drop things into the

128

pockets of his white coat as he paced up and down the aisle, soliloquising about logarithmic derivatives or quadratic integers or whatever. So we looked for things that cost nothing, could safely be brought into the classroom from outside, and could be relied upon to cause hilarity when Monsieur Blanc eventually realised that one of his pockets had become home to some slimy foreign object. Fresh apple cores and blobs of blotting paper soaked in spit were great favourites. Once the time bomb was in place, all we had to do was take bets on how long it would take Monsieur Blanc to dip his hand into his pocket and notice that something repulsive had infiltrated it. But Monsieur Blanc had seen it all before. He simply fished the slimy object out of his pocket and dropped it into the nearest rubbish bin and the soliloquising resumed.

Most of us learned very little maths in Monsieur Blanc's classes, though a select few obviously did since they went on to shine in scientific professions, in particular my friends Pascal and Jean, the two youngest boys in the class. Clearly, Monsieur Blanc knew his maths. But as often happens in a centrally-administered system where the Ministry of Education picks teachers largely on the basis of their academic prowess and only secondarily – if at all – for their pedagogic potential, poor Monsieur Blanc was hopelessly miscast. But he was such a nice man and such an easy target that at times I felt almost guilty for taking advantage of his good nature so mercilessly. Monsieur Blanc, if you are reading this, please forgive me.

*

I did much better at history and especially geography. This must have had something to do with my father's profession, but there was never any pressure. As long as we shared his passion for education and excelled at something, he did not particularly care what we excelled at.

History was interesting. It was about real people and how they managed their affairs, just like modern people except a long time ago. True, we mostly learned about kings, their armies, and their victories, especially French ones. But I knew that armies were made of real people with real problems and real needs. I had plenty of corroborating evidence. Lure, Haute-Saône was a garrison town and I had seen the Jeeps parked outside the Rest & Recreation headquarters by the railway station. Away from school, my knowledge of history was supplemented by stories of my father languishing in a POW camp and my mother holding the fort and beating the shortages by making purses out of sows' ears and creating gastronomic wonders from turnips and a little chicken fat. There was also my war-weary grandmother and her regular reminders of how the goose-stepping hordes had marched into her house one day, said they liked the feel of the place and would be staying awhile, and then proceeded to drink the cellar dry except for the bottles of *eau-de-vie* my grandfather had the good sense to bury in the garden as the prospect of having to share the house with uninvited guests became increasingly likely.

I was good at history but I had to work at it. Geography, on the other hand, was pure pleasure. I never studied, at least not in the conventional sense. I read the textbooks, pored over maps, thought about it, asked my father questions, and in it went. Geography textbooks were easy for me to come by. As a senior schoolteacher, my father regularly received inspection copies of new titles produced by publishers in response to frequent curricular changes. When the mail of the day included a new textbook, my father opened the package and quickly thumbed through the content before sitting down to lunch. Further evidence that he had educational hope for me yet was when he allowed and later even invited me to open these packages and leaf through the content before he did.

I knew the geography textbook for my school year by heart so I read the textbook for the year above instead. At the start of each academic year, I knew it all. I re-read the textbook to be sure that I had not forgotten anything important over the summer holidays and semester after semester, in test after test, I was top of the class. If by accident I came second, I was so mortified that I spent the following semester reading the textbook twice as often and asking my father twice as many questions.

There were no field trips. I imagine that these would have been regarded as a dangerous distraction from real learning, which took place in classrooms with desks and textbooks in them. But life offered other opportunities to learn new things and to learn them in ways classrooms and textbooks could never permit, at least for those lucky enough to have a father who could drive – no mother I knew was in that position – and who loved the outdoors as much as my father did. For him, the drive was only a means to an end, which was to spend as much time as possible out in the open as opposed to being cooped up indoors listening to his children's bickering and living in dread of what Madame Brossard, our child-hating landlady downstairs, would find to collar him about in the morning.

But even if the aim was always to park the car, get out, and walk, the drives themselves offered learning opportunities. As he drove, my father pointed out features of the landscape that were not always obvious to school children already wedded to the idea that valuable information could only come from deciphering words on a page. Flat landscapes were interesting but difficult to interpret. But mountains were full of salient features, so learning was easy.

One of my favourite drives took the family to the edge of the Jura mountains to the south of Lure, Haute-Saône. The hillsides consisted of layers of rock of various colours and consistencies, which made it obvious that the place had taken eons to acquire its present form as floods and other natural cataclysms shaped and re-shaped the landscape. As we drove around one last bend in the road, an especially spectacular chunk of hillside came into view. It had been subjected to such powerful lateral forces that it had been pushed up in the centre and looked like one side of the kind of tricorn hat favoured by late eighteenth-century dignitaries. Not surprisingly, the spot was known as *Chapeau de Gendarme*, or 'policeman's hat'. Clearly, this was not a world created in under a week six thousand years ago by a lonely god in need of an audience. Though he was not an impious man, my father had no time for literal interpretations of stone-age texts and for the obscurantism these encourage. Evidence was key, he insisted, and evidence was all around us. And he was very good at showing us where to look.

*

Maps were a major part of my educational journey. When children my age were drawing pictures of people and animals, I drew maps. Inspired by my father's impressive collection of Michelin maps, I learned to colour-code: mountains were brown, forested areas green, and oceans, lakes, and rivers blue. As I grew older and my map-making skills improved, I added refinements such as cars on the roads, houses by the roadside, happy children watching the cars and less happy children creeping unwillingly to school, people on bikes, and horse-drawn carts and haystacks and other significant features of the contemporary landscape. If I had any room left and all the right colour crayons, I added a steam train struggling up a gradient or an ocean-going liner sailing into port. Scale and perspective were not concepts I handled well. Gradually, my maps lost their *verité* and became increasingly abstract as shaded areas began to replace pictures of houses as representations of urbanisation. I loved maps, and I still do. And to my mind, maps do not get any better than the Michelin variety. Next to a Michelin map, a Google map is a cheap parody.

For those unlucky students who did not have a geography teacher as a father, conventional instruction had to do. Classrooms were not exactly filled with sources of visual stimulation. They consisted of four walls, a door, a couple of ill-fitting windows, a motley set of ancient desks and chairs, a blackboard at the front, and a stove in a corner. Decorative touches consisted mostly of damp patches in the ceiling and cracks in the walls. No attempts were made to paper over the cracks, not even with lists of the seven largest cities in France, the absurd lyrics of *La Marseillaise,* the phonetic chart of the sounds of English, or the dates of Napoleon's victories, let alone model student essays. We had walls, four of them, which was several more than children had in their own schools in France's African colonies, we were informed, and for that we should be grateful to the French State and not even think about defacing the walls with our juvenile creations. French education did not do creativity and from everything I hear it still does not.

The only classroom that had anything worth looking

at on its walls was my father's because that was where the school's map collection was housed. The collection, seven or eight strong at best, hung on two rusty hooks to one side of the blackboard. Getting at a map at the back meant lifting all the maps at the front and hanging them all back up again, a task for which my father enlisted expert assistance from a pair of students who, in addition to being among the tallest in the class, had been carefully screened for unfailing hand-to-eye coordination and a low propensity for goofing off and raising a laugh by dropping the maps on each other's head.

In primary school, things had been much simpler. Each classroom had one map: the map of France. French classrooms did not go in for flags or official portraits of the President of the Republic with his hand on his heart, and certainly not for crucifixes. Instead, the map of France had pride of place. Every now and then, the teacher grabbed a ruler and instructed us in the finer points of French geography as laid down by the Ministry of Education.

The maps had lost their edges to vermin and the ravages of time. But this did not matter because the edges were where foreigners lived and foreigners were not important, especially the Belgians. What mattered apart from learning the exact location of the seven largest cities in France was the endlessly-repeated fantasy that France was exquisitely shaped and fitted snugly inside a six-sided polygon, otherwise known as a hexagon. Watch the news or the weather forecast on French television and you will often hear the country referred to as *l'hexagone*. In hindsight, the whole point of the metaphor was to foster national pride through constructed aesthetics as if a country's borders were evidence of its people's genius and not the chaotic outcome of tectonic shifts or where a war had happened to come to an end. Never mind that the French and the Germans had settled once again where their common border should be only a decade earlier or that France and Italy had signed a treaty finally resolving their last border dispute even more recently. France's borders were eternal, we were meant to infer. School was succeeding in one of its major aims: to manufacture consent over national identity among the young, hopefully for life.

As long as I did not look too closely, some French borders did parallel one side of the hexagon reasonably neatly, give or take the odd kink: from Dunkerque in the north to Strasbourg in the east, for example, or from the Atlantic to the Mediterranean along the Pyrenees. But when I was first introduced to the *hexagone* concept in primary school, I could see that the claim made no sense. Anyone pretending that the Mediterranean coast from the Italian to the Spanish borders follows a straight line or that the Cotentin peninsula in Normandy does not stick out miles into the ocean or that the eastern side of the *hexagone* does not appropriate almost half of Switzerland is in effect a charlatan. There had to be a subtext, which was of course that the borders of less happier lands were not as aesthetically pleasing as those of France and that we were therefore lucky to be French. France was made to look elegant so it followed that there must be something elegant and therefore superior about anyone living within them. France was a country shaped not by accident but by destiny, a sacred truth that Americans, among others, will recognise.

*

It is tempting to look back in anger at this educational pantomime and rail against the blind transmission of unquestioned knowledge, the lack of imagination displayed by many of those involved, and the tedium generated by the experience. I was hardly alone in going through this and many had – and are still having – a far worse time of it. But it still puzzles me how an educational system that wasted no opportunity to remind students that they had been born in the finest country on earth, where culture, the arts, and intellectual pursuits of every kind were as natural as breathing could show so little interest in anything beyond rigid adherence to the curriculum.

French education as I knew it had no extra-curricular activities. We listened, we read, we memorised, we regurgitated, we passed. The curriculum had no creative writing component apart from learning to pen vacuous disquisitions on the human condition in our final-year philosophy classes. There was no school magazine in which we might hone our writing skills, share learning tips and jokes, gain a sense of audience, or learn to vent responsibly. There were no debating contests. Apart from games of marbles in the coal dust by the stinking outhouse for the boys and endless rounds of hopscotch for the girls, there were no team sports. There were no art classes, no film club, no drama club, no club of any kind, in fact. There was no performance of any sort unless I include mechanical recitations of Corneille and Racine. The only performance we knew was self-generated and took the form of the pranks we devised to relieve the tedium.

Even more amazingly for a culture that likes to believe it raised literature to heights unimaginable to speakers of other languages, our secondary school had no library. Perhaps our old school had no funds or space for such a luxury. But when with great fanfare, a brand new and much larger *lycée* opened its doors on the edge of town in the early 1960s, that had no library either. The idea that students might bury themselves in books of their own choosing and potentially emerge with unpredictable and potentially subversive insights was anathema to French education.

Looking back, French secular education was a carbon copy of Catholic knowledge transmission but with the God component left out. French secularism could not shake off its roots. It rested on blind faith in canonical content and the rejection of any reflection that might lead to the unorthodox. What constituted valuable knowledge was determined on high and passed on down by a pliant teaching profession kept on side by an expectation of the secular equivalent of eternal life: life-long job security followed by a gilt-edged pension. And as I was soon to discover, French university education was no different.

CHAPTER SIX: SPEAKING IN TONGUES

They have been at a great feast of languages, and stolen the scraps.

William Shakespeare (1564-1616)

A prominent French colonial figure once remarked: 'Remember that you are a Frenchman and have consequently won first prize in the lottery of life'.

Actually, I paraphrased this. The author of the original was in fact English-born Cecil Rhodes, the epitome of self-perceived British superiority and of the Victorian conviction that Great Britain had not only a right but a duty to rule the waves, colonise the world, and spread its self-evidently superior values across the globe for the benefit of lesser tribes.

When he wrote this, Rhodes was creating a paean to all things British. But any number of national identities could be substituted, as no doubt they are. In fact, most if not all nationalities are lauded in similar terms by their overlords through the national myths they construct for the purpose and promote through the schools, which they use to convince the young of their inherent exceptionalism, the superiority of their culture, and the State's right to uphold these at any cost.

A key tool in the myth-maker's box is language. Language is attractive because it can be represented in the popular imagination as endowed with attributes, such as being 'richly descriptive', for example, which are so subjective that no evidence could possibly be adduced to buttress belief in their veracity. To paraphrase Rhodes once again, it is enough to believe that by virtue of having been born in country A, B, or C, you have won first prize in the lottery of language.

Just as your country had exceptionalism thrust upon it by destiny, so did your language and by implication so did you. The notion is so woolly that it cannot be shown to be false by means of rational argument. Yet the blandishment is seductive and trusting students fall for it in country after country, generation after generation.

*

My grandmother, for one, was no exception. To her, a woman who knew her own mind and never shrank from speaking it in the interest of the intellectual and spiritual development of her grandchildren, only three languages mattered: French, Italian, and German. Each had its assigned function. As she explained it, French was for speaking to God, Italian to birds, and German to horses.

My grandmother was French so French came first, naturally. But her sense of the pre-eminence of French owed not only to what her schooling might have encouraged her to believe but also to her Catholicism. To French Catholics, France was the 'eldest daughter of the Church' so it followed that French must be God's own language or something very close to it. It was never clear to me what evidence this claim for France's superior status was based on. Italy, being where Catholicism has its corporate headquarters, seemed to me to have the better claim. But to French Catholics, France's primacy in this matter was gospel truth.

Italian was important because many saints had spoken it, including Saint Francis of Assisi, a perennial favourite among Catholics and for some reason the object of great devotion on the part of my grandmother and several of her widowed church-going acquaintances. Saint Francis was the 12th-century *bon-*

vivant turned ascetic proselytiser who founded the Franciscan monastic order and earned the devotion of generations of believers in his capacity of patron saint of animals (though he has now been rebranded as patron saint of the environment). Never mind that in the real world, anyone who went around trying to tame wolves and preaching to birds would be dismissed as the village idiot instead of being venerated as a miracle worker. But in matters of which saints should be venerated and why, rationality does not matter much. And of course, Italian was the language of the Pope and of most of his *coterie* of cardinals, some of whom were rumoured to be *papabili* and therefore to have the quasi-divine potential to become infallible overnight should the incumbent fall under a bus.

Italian was also important because it was the language of opera. My grandmother, then a starry-eyed ten-year-old and her slightly older sister Eugénie had been taken by their father from their rural base near Nancy to Paris to visit the 1889 *Exposition Universelle*, which featured among other wonders a very tall purpose-build steel structure that came to be known as the *Tour Eiffel*. Apparently, this odd-looking creation was regarded as a monstrosity by most contemporary commentators, who knew a fine building when they saw one and hoped that the moment the exhibition closed its doors the tower would be unbolted and melted down for canons and replaced by something really useful: a railway station, perhaps, or a government ministry or even a cathedral.

One evening while in Paris, my great-grandfather took his two daughters to see one of Puccini's operas: *La Bohème*, I think it was. The show made such an impression on the young girl that was to become my grandmother that she still talked about it in her eighties and used her considerable authority to shush us noisy children whenever an aria from the opera was played on the family radio.

Then there was German. My grandmother was not keen on things German, linguistic or otherwise. She was born just eight years after the end of the 1870-71 Franco-Prussian war, which had seen a victorious Germany annex almost all of Alsace and a large chunk of northern Lorraine and pushed the new border to within a few kilometres of the family home. She had lived through World War I and just two decades later, history had repeated itself. She and those of her generation had learnt to detest the *Boche* at mother's knee and she was determined to pass on her world view to the next generation and ensure its perpetuation.

Even though I was growing up little more than a decade after the end of World War II, mocking was easy because until I began to study history more closely in secondary school, I simply could not imagine armies on the prowl, large-scale destruction, food shortages, and especially the bodies of husbands, fathers, brothers, and sons coming home in wooden boxes. At the time, my grandmother's jeremiads about the tormentors from over the Rhine sounded like the carping of a tiresome old woman unwilling to let go of the past. But looking at it from her angle today, for reasons not entirely unrelated to German expansionism, she had known fear, disruption, hardship, and loneliness. She might have been expected to forgive but hardly to forget.

Unfortunately, the process of passing on her anti-*Boche* perspective was regularly undermined by my mother, who on Sundays when the winter cold ruled out the much-loved afternoon drive entertained us with her stock of World War II stories, which put an entirely different complexion on this calamitous episode in history.

Many of her yarns painted a picture of the French as

honest country folk coming to terms with adversity as best they could. One of our favourite tales described excited residents of nearby villages a few weeks after the 1944 Allied landings in Normandy springing to the stirrup and riding their bikes like the wind to bring their neighbours in the next village news of the imminent arrival of the American liberators. Church bells rang and crowds filled the streets, cheering loudly and hugging and kissing each other until another emissary came riding into town a few hours later to report that rumours of the death of German expansionism had been greatly exaggerated and that the Americans would be a while yet. Church bells fell silent, the rejoicing turned to gloom, and the waiting resumed.

So indirectly though perhaps not unwittingly, my mother succeeded in sabotaging her own mother's best efforts to inculcate in her grandchildren the dislike of the Hun that had been a feature of her entire life. The result was that we failed to grow up with this historical resentment in our hearts. For me in particular, the upshot was a hunger to hop on a train and go and find out, by studying their language if necessary, what those mythical Germans and especially those of my own age were really like.

*

But this was for the future. At the time in Lure, Haute-Saône, only one language mattered: French. Unless German and English as school subjects but also Latin as both a school subject and the language of church were included, no other language had any active presence in my family or in most people's lives as far as I was aware. Since we lived only about fifty kilometres from French-speaking Switzerland, we were easily persuaded by our schooling that the glories of the

French language brightened even the lives of nearby wretches who had drawn the short straw in the lottery of life and had been born something other than French. Luckily for these people, accidents of birth had placed them close to the source of all things bright and beautiful and had therefore made it possible for them to lead fulfilling lives after all by virtue of speaking French. But the way French was taught in school could not have been more off-putting.

In large part, classroom French meant studying and then memorising long chunks of classical poetry. Traditional French poetry favours the alexandrine verse, with lines of twelve syllables and a short pause in the middle. Lovers of poetry of the metronomic and unadventurous kind will love the French alexandrine. Unlike their English counterparts, French syllables receive roughly equal stress regardless of meaning. So especially when alexandrines are being recited by students with no interest whatsoever in the content, the effect is – at best – soporific.

Towards the end of the nineteenth century, subversive types such as Baudelaire and Verlaine experimented with other patterns, even – perish the thought – with lines consisting of odd numbers of syllables. Reading their poems in school felt like coming up for air. But for the most part, their writing was dismissed by French teachers as the decadent scribblings of disreputable versifiers and just as detrimental to public morality as the rampant alcoholism and deviant sexuality that went with it. After all, weren't absinthe-addled Verlaine and Rimbaud lovers at one time? And didn't that lead to attempted murder? Compared to the licentiousness that went hand in hand with these literary experiments, there was safety in the alexandrine. And in memorising alexandrines for homework and reciting them to teachers in the morning, what mattered was not sentiment or expressiveness but whether or not we had every line and every pause halfway through every line pat.

Obviously, professional actors are not schoolchildren, and every competent French thespian knows how to get around the rigidity of the alexandrine by modulating the lines so that meaning is foregrounded and structure recedes. But even if they were aware of this, our teachers never encouraged performance, not even when we were younger and learning La Fontaine's delightful fables about the human-like preferences of improvident insects that spend their summers making merry and then find the larder bare when the weather turns. Teachers were expected to assess memorisation of the canon, not subjective notions of expressiveness or audience awareness and they stuck to that teaching objective like glue. Our job was to stand and recite.

My classmates and I dreaded being summoned to perform at the front of the class, where the risk of ridicule was highest. Being asked to recite from our seat was intimidating but much less traumatic. It could even be fun. By observing older and wiser role models, I quickly learned that it was possible to prop up the textbook against the back of a cooperative classmate in front and read from the printed page, usually against a promise to return the favour at some future date. Of course, classmates sycophantic enough to sit in the front row did not have that advantage, but they made up for the handicap by being nauseatingly studious to boot and therefore in no need of educational shortcuts. But for dunces of the male persuasion such as myself, an additional bonus was that if the back's owner happened to be a girl, the strategy offered me a chance to cop a quick feel of her bra as I manoeuvred the book into position against her back. For a boy burbling with teenage hormones in provincial France at the time, this was quite a thrill!

But because the stratagem was so furtive and successful performance so dependent on the goodwill of classmates of demonstrated propensity to goof off at every opportunity, it was fraught with perils. On a good day, when called, I stood up, looked down soulfully as if deeply immersed in poetic subtleties, and read straight off the page. The risk was that the back's owner might suddenly turn uncooperative or simply shift in her seat and cause the book to slip and slam shut. This left me high and dry halfway through a tricky alexandrine I was pretending to have memorised.

Often, though, the shift was intentional. I vividly recall finding myself about midway through a particularly turgid passage of Corneille – *Le Cid*, I think it was – when the fiend sitting next to me suddenly reached for the book and turned over the page. I stopped in my tracks. I could see that the text at the top of the new page began in mid-sentence, so there was no way in which I could convincingly continue. Once the giggling had subsided, with a presence of mind that must have impressed even my severest critics among my classmates, I blamed a power cut at home the night before for preventing me from memorising the entire passage.

As the giggling resumed, I began to notice that conspiratorial glances were being exchanged, and it struck me that this disaster was not the result of a moment of boredom on the part of my immediate neighbour, which he had suddenly decided to relieve by engineering this hilarious jape. Clearly, I had been set up! But, although the victim, I quickly saw the funny side of it and joined in the mirth, as did the teacher, who had been looking out of the window pretending not to be aware of the real cause of my hitherto unnoticed interest in Corneille and my new-found fluency in reciting it. Evidently, not all French teachers in Lure, Haute-Saône were as convinced as the Ministry of Education supremos in Paris of the character-forming value of memorising that particular versifier's dreary output.

*

Occasionally, languages other than French, German, English, or Latin made a fleeting appearance in our lives. Every now and then, an itinerant peddler of North African origin – Morocco, it was said – shuffled into town with a pile of rugs on one shoulder and went door to door in search of a housewife in need of something colourful with which to adorn her living room floor. I never saw this hard-working man make a sale, but he was a regular visitor, and a friendly one too. But I rebuffed his cheerful greetings whenever our paths crossed and instead made merciless fun of his appearance, his darker skin, and especially the mix of French and what I took to be Arabic that he used when he tried to strike up a conversation.

On occasional visits to the homes of classmates of exotic ancestry, I ran into ancient relatives, mostly women dressed from head to toe in shades of grey even darker than those favoured by my grandmother. These women seemed to spend their days standing at the stove stirring strange-smelling concoctions. Most had reached France a few decades earlier after escaping the deprivations of Southern Italy or the brutality of fascist Spain. These women were friendly but remote and they spoke incomprehensible tongues, so I ignored them just as they ignored me.

One winter morning, diversity came to our primary

classroom in the form of a skittish, tongue-tied new classmate. His name was Paul, as it happens. He was introduced by our teacher as the child of a family from a far-away country called Hungary. A few weeks earlier, my siblings and I had watched from a living room window as a lorry was being driven slowly along our street and we had run downstairs at our mother's behest to add bundles of discarded clothes to the pile it was collecting. Apparently, the people of this far-away land had been very unlucky and they had to leave their homes suddenly and find refuge wherever they could including in places as unlikely as our little town, where they knew no one. I was about nine at the time so the Soviet invasion that had led to the Hungarians' plight was beyond my comprehension. But these people's distress was so palpable, it made sense to me that we should help them.

With a child's uncanny ability to adapt to almost any situation, Paul quickly went from silent as the grave to relatively garrulous in French, his new language, and he and I became friends. My mother, as was her instinct and through church connections, took his family under her wing and my siblings and I occasionally dropped by their house with more donations from the stash she collected from neighbours. And on these occasions, unfamiliar sounds were heard once again. But how was it that I understood Paul but not his parents, I asked my father. Paul could speak two languages, he replied, French and Hungarian. I puzzled over this. How was this possible since like the rest of us Paul only had one head and one mouth?

When I was a few years older, I started connecting foreign languages with communication and especially with travel by reading the notices attached to the window sills of French trains. These warned the passengers on the northbound, for example, not to stick their head out for an invigorating lungful of soot or run the risk of being decapitated by the southbound. These notices addressed all those passengers that mattered to the mighty *SNCF*: the French, of course (*Ne pas se pencher par la fenêtre*) but also eccentric tourists from over the Channel (*Do not lean out of the window*), impoverished immigrants from the Italian *Mezzogiorno* (*E pericoloso sporgersi*), and persistent invaders from over the Rhine (*Nicht hinauslehnen*). Those words opened up such exciting visions of discovery that I remember them to this day.

*

Dreams of escape aside, languages meant study. I started Latin when I was barely ten. From the very start, memorisation was central to learning: nouns and their classes, genders, number, cases, and of course verbs and their many tenses and moods. Studying Latin means learning to differentiate, for example, between *rosa* and *rosam* depending on whether the speaker is talking to the rose or giving it to a girl he hopes to impress. But if he is talking to several roses at the same time or if he judges that nothing short of the full dozen will persuade the girl to see things his way, the endings change to *rosae* and *rosas*, respectively. Romans used to spend a lot of time talking to roses, it seems. Nothing wrong with that, of course: Prince Charles talks to his plants all the time, apparently.

The learning process was so mindless that it was entirely possible to recite a Latin declension or conjugation to anyone in a position of authority regardless of whether they understood a word of it or even saw any purpose in it. A mother, quite unschooled in the ways of Latin and in the middle of cooking dinner would do since she could always prop the book against the back of the stove as we recited and she stirred. Or a grandmother, who would put down her crochet, take up the book, listen attentively, frown a good deal, and pronounce the declension memorised or more frequently, not.

Latin was tough at times. But what made it palatable was the fact that for some reason, I was fascinated by Roman history. The period was presented by our textbook as the last recorded flowering of human civilisation until France emerged in the seventeenth century as the replacement the world was waiting for. So I read the textbook from cover to cover and then moved on to French translations of Spartacus and the bravery of gladiators and later Suetonius' strangely titillating accounts of imperial depravity.

But what made the period especially attractive was that it bridged three school subjects: history, geography, and Latin. For the first time, I realised that school subjects were connected, an insight that seemed not to have dawn on the curriculum designers themselves. Suddenly, life was school and school was life. Finally, school made sense to me and I started to enjoy studying.

Caesar was my favourite Latin author. He was a soldier and he had a soldier's mind. This meant that he went straight to the heart of things without stopping at the subtleties unlike impenetrable bores such as Cicero or Virgil. His style was direct and his sentences were short. As far as I could tell, Caesar would not have known a subordinating conjunction from a hole in the ground.

Another reason I liked Caesar was that his journal was little more than a log, which he probably wrote at the end of each marching day as he sipped the pre-dinner cocktail in his tent. Keeping logs was what leaders of men did and still do. There must have been many more of these journals written by conquering Roman generals, with the difference that Caesar eventually climbed to the top of the slippery pole, so the writings of such an important man survived. But I doubt if even the most sycophantic of his courtiers saw them at the time as anything more than field notes or that Caesar himself dreamed that schoolchildren two millennia later would devote so much time and effort to poring over his daily scratchings.

But the real beauty of Caesar's writing was that because of what he did for a living, which was – in a nutshell – to march his men to the top of hills and then march them down again and in the process conquer as much of other people's land as possible day in and day out, he repeated himself a lot. This made translating him relatively easy and it is also the reason why I can still quote snippets of his prose in the original Latin. Since to be invincible soldiers have to get a good night's sleep, at the end of the day's land grab Caesar brought his horse to a halt, stood upon a peak, scanned the neighbourhood, picked a spot, and instructed his men to drop their *impedimenta* and built *castrum sub proximum collem* (a camp at the foot of the nearest hill).

I loved his descriptions of the area where we lived and in particular of the mighty Rhine River, *qui agrum Helvetium a Germanis dividit* (which divides Helvetic from Germanic lands) just as I knew it did from looking at maps or catching a glimpse of both countries on family excursions. And I warmed to his evocations of *monte Iura altissimo* (the very high Jura mountains), which I could just about make out through our living room windows on a clear day.

Caesar never mentioned Lure, Haute-Saône, of course. The place did not emerge until a full six centuries later. But he described familiar locations, especially *Vesontio*, which I knew as Besançon, the seat of our local archbishop. As long as we stuck to Caesar, Latin was fun. But if studying Caesar's Latin was supposed to help us develop higher cognitive faculties and appreciate abstraction, that particular curricular aim clearly failed. There was nothing abstract about Caesar.

Still, we chafed. What was the point of memorising Latin declensions and conjugations and grappling with Cicero and Virgil, we asked Monsieur Thaury, our Latin teacher, in one of his more relaxed moments. The answer came in two parts. The first and most frequently invoked justification was that studying Latin, with its complex endings and the predictable relationships between them, helped us to develop the analytical skills we needed. To do what, we asked? Why, to learn French, of course! What higher educational purpose could there be? And since French was in a sense a boiled down version of Latin, knowing the one probably did help us to figure out the intricacies of the other. But as reluctant adolescents, we needed more persuasive arguments, a greater sense of immediacy, and higher hopes of reward to leap into action where tedious declensions and conjugations were concerned.

We made this known to Monsieur Thaury. This kindly, humorous man was not without his share of troubles. His marital life, it was rumoured, was no bed of *rosarum* and when he escaped that to go to work he had to suffer our puerile jibes over his baldness. But he was willing to engage us in debate. Latin is difficult, we complained. What is the point of studying it since no one speaks it any more except priests? Well, that is precisely the point, Monsieur Thaury countered. Knowing Latin makes travelling in other countries much easier. When you get there, all you have to do is locate the local priest. That's easy. Priests officiate in churches and churches are big, conspicuous places. So find a church, go in, take off your hat, greet the man of God in your best Latin, drop a small coin in the collection plate, and enlist his services as tour guide and translator. What could be simpler? Your Latin may not be up to debating the exact nature of the holy trinity or the finer points of transubstantiation with him but it will get you a square meal, a bed for the night, and a cup of coffee in the morning.

The flaw in the logic was glaring. Even our small-town upbringing could not hide from us that there was more to travel destinations than Catholic countries. When we pressed Monsieur Thaury on his personal experience of talking to priests in Latin on his travels, he confessed that he had never left France in his life, not even at the invitation of the German authorities as he was too young to have served in World War II and been carted off to a POW camp. In any case, he added with a glint in his eyes, it would take more than the prospect of spending a night in a foreign doorway on an empty stomach for him to walk into a church and be civil to a priest.

*

If any of the descendants of those patriots who had fled Alsace after it came under German rule some eight decades earlier and settled in Lure, Haute-Saône still spoke German, it must have been confined to their homes because I never heard it. Its only presence was in the classroom.

At first, this was a happy experience. German vocabulary covered what I knew of life: family, home, school, the outdoors, animals, travel. There were songs too, then an educational innovation. We sang the German alphabet to Mozart's perennial tune. I delighted in the tale of the fox that stole a goose (*Fuchs, du hast die Ganz gestohlen...*) and I chuckled at the thought of the comeuppance the thief was about to receive at the hands of the hunter.

Monsieur Getz, our teacher seemed to have an inexhaustible stock of nursery rhymes and poems. It was part of his culture. Born in French-controlled Alsace but raised to speak German before French, he had been drafted as a very young man and newly-anointed German citizen into Hitler's army toward the end of World War II as it struggled to buttress its tottering defences on the Russian front. His culture was German culture, imbibed naturally, not learned from textbooks. What he brought of it into the classroom gave his lessons freshness and authenticity, qualities few second language teachers ever achieve.

After just two years of introductory German, I was moved by some of Goethe's marvellously concise and surprisingly accessible poems. Memorising them required little effort and reading them today remains pure pleasure: *Kennst du das Land, wo die Zitronen blühn?* (Do you know the land where lemons grow?) and especially the heart-rending tale of the doting father who tries in vain to save his dying child: *Wer reitet so spät durch Nacht und Wind?* (Who rides so late through night and wind?). The harrowing simplicity of the last line: *In seinen Armen, das Kind war tot* (In his arms, the child was dead) still brings a lump to my throat.

But within a year or two, the syllabus veered into pedagogical insanity and mythological burlesque as it turned its attention to the ancient Germanic tales that had inspired Wagner to compose those interminable operas that later so fascinated Hitler. Surprisingly, Monsieur Getz seemed as comfortable with this nonsense as he was with foxes, geese, and hunters: he must have picked it all up at mother's knee.

We learned, in German and sometimes by having to decipher the Gothic script, about the exploits of residents of the Valhalla, the mythical abode of Norse and Germanic warriors who had died in battle: Wotan, Thor, the Valkyries, male and female giants, and assorted scaremongers. I was twelve or thirteen at the time and interested in the real world, not in outlandish fabrications from the Stone Age. The predictable result was that I and most of my classmates were instantly turned off studying German. Looking back, perhaps this was a covert plot by reactionary forces in the Ministry of Education to make sure that we would go through life detesting all things German. If so, my grandmother, had she known, would have approved.

*

Astonishingly given the extent to which today's world speaks English and the vast sums that are spent globally on teaching and studying it, English played no part in our lives except as a school subject and therefore for many as one more source of agony. We were required to study two foreign languages. In eastern France, German invariably came first, English second so classroom exposure to German started at the age of eleven and to English two years later. In my case, because I was a year ahead of my cohort, this meant the ages of ten and twelve, respectively.

How alien English was to the life of Lure, Haute-Saône and its residents was brought home to us one day when our English lesson was interrupted by a knock on the door and the unexpected appearance of Monsieur Fronçaix, our Principal. He beckoned to Monsieur Messener, our English teacher, to join him in the hallway where the two conferred in hushed tones. Then without a word, Monsieur Messener came back in, gathered his papers and books, and left the classroom. In short order, one of the enforcers from the dreaded *étude* appeared and was put in charge until the start of the next lesson.

The following day, it transpired that there had been a horrific car accident at a railway crossing just outside the town involving a family of British tourists who had driven in thick fog and at full speed into the heavy metal barrier that had been lowered to let through an approaching train. Both parents, sitting in the front, had been killed instantly, one of them decapitated, it was said. Their teenage daughter, who was sitting in the back, survived and was lying in the local hospital in critical condition but just about capable of communicating with doctors and nurses.

The problem was that no one in the hospital, not even the doctors who were trying to save her life, spoke enough English to make sense of a non-French speaking patient at death's door. So they sent for Monsieur Messener, at the time the only English teacher in town and probably the only reasonably fluent English speaker for miles around.

From those dreary *lycée* days, when time stood still and grades were low, Monsieur Messener deserves credit for single-handedly teaching me the rudiments of English and putting in place the foundations on which I was to build later. But I now wish that at the time I had made a more generous contribution to his sense of accomplishment as a pedagogue.

Compared to most of our teachers, Monsieur Messener was relatively young. He had recently returned to his home town armed with a rare qualification: a degree in English. He was a strict disciplinarian but an effective communicator so he was always clear not only about what he expected us to do but more importantly why he expected us to do it. Unlike so many of our teachers, who saw their mission as passing on knowledge straight out of the textbooks, he exuded a sense of having given serious thought to his subject as well as his methods.

One of the innovations he introduced was the phonetic alphabet, which, unlike the hopelessly unsuitable Latin alphabet, matches each sound of English with a single symbol and vice versa. That said, knowledge of this code is obviously no panacea. My siblings all studied English under Monsieur Messener and yet offer living proof that there is no automatic link between the ability to analyse the phonetic structure of English and speaking it without the kind of accent that would do Maurice Chevalier proud or, for some of them, speaking it at all.

Monsieur Messener did not just know English and how to teach it. He lived it. In my final year in secondary school, he introduced yet another revolutionary practice into his classes. This consisted of bringing in his personal record player, playing one of his own recordings of excerpts from Shakespeare's plays, and guiding us through the finer points of John Gielgud's rendition of Hamlet's soliloquies, for example, as compared to Lawrence Olivier's. These are not easy texts under any circumstances. But the discovery that someone else, however fictional, had long ago seen 'the uses of this world' as 'weary, stale, flat, and unprofitable' struck a chord in the angst-ridden teenager that I had become. To me, even Hamlet's depressive meditations provided a welcome antidote to the tortured musings of the French philosophers we were expected to study in depth and regard as being of far greater consequence than mere foreign languages or even foreign literature.

One of Monsieur Messener's most durable legacies

was to show me that it was not only possible but in fact laudable to feel passionately about language. Sadly, at exam time, I rarely did better than average and often not even that. But at least, I felt broadly positive about the subject, and I harboured towards it nothing like the animus I reserved for chemistry, biology, and especially maths. I cannot blame Monsieur Messener for my educational shortcomings except in one respect.

At the start of my second year of English, Monsieur Messener made a rare pedagogical blunder: he assigned me a seat immediately behind the first girl in the class to wear a bra. I was growing up among four sisters, two of whom were already of bra-wearing age. I had seen bras drying on laundry lines and of course in the window of the lingerie shop in the middle of town. But this was different.

On warm days especially, the bra's owner, a tall, friendly girl named Isabelle, wore the kind of plain white shirt favoured by many of her peers with neither the inclination nor the means to turn themselves into fashion models. But perhaps because Isabelle was growing faster than her parents could afford to satisfy her need for ever larger clothes, her shirt seemed to my alert eye to fit her rather tightly. Whenever she leaned back in her seat, to peer at something important on the blackboard or to relax by gazing out of the window, the shirt hung loosely and the bra faded from view. But when she leaned forward over her desk because she needed to write something down or study the textbook closely, the shirt tightened again and the outline of the bra was restored to its full glory.

These were hardly ideal conditions for focused reflection on the complexities of the English language. But what was I supposed to do? My choice between looking down and concentrating on the difference between 'been' and 'being' or 'may' and 'might' or looking up at the thin white shirt in front of my nose and gazing in rapture. I chose the latter, and my school English suffered in consequence.

*

Today, my early fixation with bras and my command of English have both matured somewhat. But after more than four decades of living as a kind of renegade Frenchman and working almost exclusively through English, my mastery of French has remained stagnant and perhaps even regressed and I can hardly claim to be an expert on the modern language. But what of views on French and its speakers among informed observers? Are the French really as inflexible in the matter of their language as they are reputed to be?

I recall reading an essay on language by the British novelist and polymath Anthony Burgess, who had made his home on the French Riviera. Among other pithy observations about his host country, its culture, and its language, Burgess noted that even French prostitutes spoke elegant French. Quite what research methodology had led him to this conclusion was not specified. But he was an eminent linguist in the sense of knowing both linguistics *and* languages, including Malay, in which he was fluent. So whatever his sources, I am inclined to trust in his conclusions.

Today, the French elite routinely produces elegies on the death of elegant French and even of French *tout court*. In reality, France is as wired as any First World nation and the Internet offers ample evidence not of linguistic defensiveness but of liberation and creativity on the part of millions of French-speaking users. Perhaps French speakers are at last shedding the linguistic prissiness nurtured over the centuries by the *Académie Française* through its persnickety rulings over arcane points of grammar and spelling and its sniffy reluctance to sanction terms that passed into popular parlance long ago, as in looking for *un parking* before doing *le shopping* during *le weekend*. Or perhaps this was the stuff of legend all along and the French were never truly fooled by this retentive, condescending flim-flam and will continue to ignore it?

Yet not all French speakers are evolving at the same pace. My Canadian friend Esther, who speaks passable French and lived in Paris not long ago, tells the story of how she once pushed a note under the door of her *concierge* informing the lady that she was going on a business trip and indicating when she might be expected back. On her return, instead of praising Esther for her thoughtfulness and congratulating her on the clarity of the message, the *concierge*, who had probably left school at fourteen, if that, saw it as her educational duty to remonstrate with Esther over the fact that she had put the wrong accent over the wrong *e* in *arrivée*. And to compound the felony, she appeared not to know that this particular grammatical context required not the noun *arrivée* but the verb *arriver* anyway. This learned *concierge* would have made any *Académie Française* member proud.

CHAPTER SEVEN: RULE OF LAW

I have never let my schooling interfere with my education.

Mark Twain (1835-1910)

Given my passion for geography and the fact that studying it had never presented the slightest difficulty, why did I not choose that as my college major when I finally left Lure, Haute-Saône at the age of sixteen and headed north to the university city of Nancy, its gleaming spires, and its coffee bars filled with chattering students?

Flexibility has never been the strong suit of French education. Throughout primary and secondary school, the Ministry of Education sets the curriculum centrally and sees to it that it is taught uniformly in every classroom across the land. Periodically, the curriculum is tweaked, the result is handed down to textbook publishers, and instructions on how to implement the changes are sent out to schools. The overriding aim is that strict equivalence should apply across all schools at all times.

Periodically, the world of French education is racked by public agonising over plans to shave forty-five minutes a week of chemistry, for example, in a particular grade level or recalibrate the relative emphasis given in the history curriculum to Europe, Japan, and the United States during World War II in another grade. The media buzzes. The teaching unions denounce a lack of consultation and call for additional funding, smaller classes, and higher salaries. The teachers go on strike and stage vast street demonstrations and students barely in their teens join them. Depending on the vehemence of the popular reaction and the date of the next election, the proposed tweak is then watered down or, more often than not, dropped altogether.

For older students, broad options are available but they must be taken as a set, not *à la carte*. To the educational authorities, it is inconceivable that mere students should be allowed to exercise judgment in creating a personalised program of study that might suit their tastes, their scholastic record, or their aspirations.

The method behind this apparent madness has its roots in the *républicain* ethos and in particular in the generally commendable principle that all citizens should enjoy equal educational opportunities. Sweep away the mandatory, centrally-controlled curriculum and allow creativity to flourish and some schools or even individual teachers will shine where others struggle, thereby threatening the sacrosanct equivalence across schools. Obviously, a degree of unavoidable variation is to be expected. But to plan for variation would not only be unfair: it would not be *républicain*.

Clearly, in some circumstances, uniformity and predictability have their merits. In general terms, the French approach to meeting challenges combines rigorous analysis of each issue, meticulous attention to detail, and the systematic application of organising principles. This approach has resulted not only in those admirable Michelin maps but also in a generally competent and effective public administration. In map-making just as in governance, improvisation and inconsistency are largely detrimental. But in education, students come in many flavours and with many aspirations. If all students are to flourish, idiosyncrasies must be accommodated. Experienced teachers sense this in their bones and allow for these to the extent they are permitted. But in France, neither the culture nor the system that perpetuates it can be seen to concede the point publicly, so the rigidities remain.

At its heart, French culture tends to be unyielding and inelastic. It sees variation as irrational and tolerance of it as a weakness. Inevitably, persisting with the cosy myth of equal opportunity for all inevitably leads to subterfuge. In higher education, this mindset perpetuates a collection of identical but largely mediocre universities open to the *hoi polloi* at nominal cost while *la crème* is shunted off to prestigious institutions, the *Grandes Ecoles*, which cater for a tiny intellectual elite that invariably goes on to determine how the country is run, from politics through business and finance to public administration. For the rest, those with little hope of acceding to these educational heights, this preoccupation with uniformity at all costs stifles creativity and innovation and ensures that those who do not fit the pattern will fail, or pass but have a miserable time of it.

*

For some reason, a major tenet of French educational thinking has long been that like horse and carriage, history and geography are irrevocably joined. There is even a label for the pairing: *histoire-géo*. The label was in existence when my father studied the combination eight decades ago, and it is still used today. It is simply not possible to study history without studying geography or vice versa. Moreover, history must be the major and geography the minor. Students cannot show up at registration time and announce that they love geography but do not much care for history so would it be acceptable if they combined geography with politics, for example, and maybe a foreign language or two? Or better still, how about geography with environmental studies and anthropology? No, history first and geography second it is decreed and forever must be.

162

In truth, the teaching of both history and geography has moved on and is now much more data-based than I remember it. But at the time, I had to give up on my passion for geography because I feared being forced to focus on history and the memorisation it entailed (all kings and battles and popes and alliances and royal marriages of convenience and their respective dates), which was hardly what motivated me to study.

By then, I had moved on from my father's textbooks and I was becoming increasingly interested in international affairs, which I saw as a natural extension of history and especially of geography but with the focus on how modern societies arranged their affairs and dealt with their conflicts and aspirations. Luckily, I did not want for sources of information as I had daily access to radio news and especially my father's copy of *Le Monde*.

Radio news was a central feature of home folklore. We had no television but we lived close to Switzerland so Swiss radio stations broadcasting in French could be picked up clearly. These were always my father's first choice because he saw state-controlled French radio as nothing more than a propaganda tool wielded by the de Gaulle regime for its own self-aggrandising ends.

French commercial radio offered alternatives but these combined abrasive advertising with streams of inane chatter and this made my father livid. Swiss radio suited him because it was commercial-free and so kept information strictly separate from considerations of lucre, which in his view was exactly how information should be handled. So lunch and dinner were eaten to a background of oompah and yodelling regularly interrupted by discussions of whether the French might finally let go of Algeria and how growing American involvement in Vietnam might affect Kennedy's chances of re-election. In response, I asked questions, which my father was happy to answer.

But for more insightful analysis, nothing beats reading so like every other aspiring French intellectual, I turned to *Le Monde*. This was a tough read but the paper's international coverage was broad and its analytical thrust impressive as far as I could judge. Once *Le Monde* was done with global issues and the minutiae of French political shenanigans, it devoted vast acreage to reviews of books I could not imagine anyone but the reviewers themselves reading and none at all to sport. It consisted of nothing but solid text, with discreet headlines, no advertising, no photos, not even political cartoons. As a diffident teenager, reading a little of *Le Monde* each day made me feel taller. None of my classmates had ever looked inside – or even at – a copy of *Le Monde*. I may be younger and shorter, I said to myself, but I belong to a club that would not have them as members.

As a result of this growing interest in international affairs, it gradually dawned on me that I might become a journalist. Since I liked to read all about it, writing about it seemed a natural progression. I had no reason to believe that I had any writing talent but I assumed that an understanding of the issues and a willingness to ask questions about them came first and that writing ability would somehow follow.

The trouble was that for those interested in journalism, the Ministry of Education had decreed, as might be expected, a single, immutable route, which consisted of a college degree in law followed by political science at graduate level. Why law was the prerequisite was not clear to me. Law, or what I knew of it, seemed to involve tedious things like contracts and litigation and wills and testaments and codicils and utterly tedious things of that nature. Apart from the prospect of studying a subject that seemed about as appealing as maths, chemistry, and biology rolled into one, I could not see what any of this had to do with international affairs, politics, or journalism, and especially with learning to write.

From the moment I floated my plan, I faced scepticism from my father. He was keenly aware of my less than stellar record at memorising facts and he openly questioned my chances in a field that required almost nothing else. But the strongest opposition came from my mother. She had been traumatised by her father's bankruptcy and saw the legal profession as consisting mostly of bailiffs brandishing court orders and picking through family heirlooms to be sent to auction. My mother detested anything and anyone remotely connected with the law. But to their credit, my parents encouraged me to test my ability to make sensible choices and to deal with the consequences. So law it was to be. Armed with a pipe and a pouch of tobacco that helped to make me look a little older, I headed north to the *Université de Nancy*, three hours away by train.

In a more flexible educational system, a sensible route to journalism might have combined French, obviously, with history, geography, international affairs, perhaps English, and of course expository writing. I might even have been able to dispense with university altogether and got a job with *Les Affiches de la Haute-Saône* writing up car accidents and municipal council meetings before, hopefully, trading up to *L'Est Républicain* and one day perhaps, even *Le Monde*.

But not in France. French education could be fatal to the unconventional. And for me, so it proved.

*

Not long after I started attending law classes, my

165

parents' predictions came true. As they had warned, the subject was deadly dull. The curriculum included a class in constitutional law, which just about met my interest in French politics. Another introduced me to the highly relevant and potentially interesting subject of economics. But this class was taught by Professor Gendrôme, a man with a knack for turning students off, deliberately, it seemed. His practice was to sweep on-stage in one of those billowing black gowns still favoured by French law professors at the time and to read his elegantly scripted text, chuckling all the while at what we assumed were jokes. On the stroke of the hour, he stopped soliloquising, gathered up his notes, and swept off-stage just as theatrically as he had come. My fellow students and I soon discovered that his script had not changed in years. We knew this because refusal to take hints from our alarm clocks occasionally forced one of us to borrow lecture notes from students a year ahead, who had themselves often borrowed them from students a year ahead of them. On close inspection, the two generations of lecture notes dovetailed perfectly. Where Professor Gendrôme had ended on the stroke of the hour in a given week was exactly where he had ended on the stroke of the hour in the corresponding week the previous year, and the year before that, *ad infinitum*.

One of our instructors, Professor Clonballe, stood out. His specialty was family law: wills, testaments, codicils, that sort of thing, who got what in divorce cases and whether the legal status of illegitimate children as regards inheritance differed from that of the offspring of the righteous. On paper, this had the potential to make maths, chemistry, and biology seem exciting. But this man was the kind of born educator that could teach a class in watching paint dry and make the experience compelling. Like all his colleagues, he officiated in a cavernous lecture theatre that held hundreds of students. But he peppered his lectures with questions that encouraged reflection. He gave us time to ponder before eliciting our reactions and then gave every sign of genuinely listening to our answers. Being listened to by a professor made me feel valued so I responded by taking an interest. He never objected to being collared outside the lecture theatre by a student with follow-up questions. If anything, he seemed to relish them. But even for his classes, we were never required or even encouraged to use the library. I assume there was one somewhere on university premises but I never once set foot in it. Just as in secondary school, there was no need to look beyond the textbooks.

*

What made university life enjoyable was the company of friends. None of my old classmates had followed me to Nancy but had instead headed south to the *Université de Besançon*, much closer to home. This included best friend Daniel, whom I missed at first and reported to regularly. But as old friends faded out, new friends faded in. What we now had in common was no longer geographical origin but our field of study. My new friends came from all over eastern France, towns and cities I knew only by name and that in combination gave my new social circle an almost cosmopolitan feel.

At class time, we met outside the lecture theatre, shuffled in, took notes, and swapped gossip and jokes. When class was over, we shuffled across the street for lunch in the university cafeteria. As university tradition required, we picked up ancient customs such as fighting like ferrets in a sack to get ahead in the line, throwing bread at neighbouring tables, rattling our knives on the side of our plates each time someone sent a glass crashing to the floor, and complaining about the food. Lunch was followed by a single cup of coffee in a nearby *café littéraire* before we ambled back to the lecture theatre in anticipation of further enlightenment regarding the French Commercial Code or the obvious deficiencies of precedent as the central pillar of the despised English common law.

We never had to plan our meetings. The curriculum was so rigid that every student in each yearly cohort took exactly the same classes at exactly the same time. Besides, none of us had access to a phone where we roomed and with email and texting still several decades away, social practices were set early, and they stayed set. In fact, part of the charm of student life was its very predictability at least as far as its social side was concerned. Predictability in lecture content and eventually in failing grades was another matter.

Since we were not only college students but also French, the ritual cup of coffee was the occasion for lively discussions of what ailed the world and especially the *bourgeoisie* and its handmaiden, multinational capitalism. If we needed support for our views, my very own copy of the day's *Le Monde* was at hand. In fact, the daily newspaper and cup of coffee were two of the trinity of indulgences I allowed myself. The third was pipe tobacco. Evidently, nothing much had changed since my father's own undergraduate days. Pipe tobacco ran to serious cash. But for me, to be discussing what ailed the *bourgeoisie* in a *café littéraire* in a French university town and not be smoking a pipe would have amounted to an admission of intellectual inadequacy.

Where university life did not change much from my secondary school days was that girls played only a marginal part in the proceedings. Law was man's business, and girls were to be found, it was said, in the company of male students of delicate appearance and demeanour in departments of modern languages and sociology and other subjects of equally limited virile appeal. So girls would have to wait. Or as they probably saw it, we would.

Among my new friends was Bernard, a pimply, intense, highly articulate youth with unruly hair and geeky round glasses. Bernard and I walked the streets of Nancy for hours, discussing what ailed the *bourgeoisie* and multinational capitalism and how we might set both to right. Bernard was the product of a rigidly Catholic education and his idea of hitting back at the priests was to advertise himself widely and loudly as a committed Marxist and a passionate atheist. For me, this was both riveting and shocking. I was all for challenging received wisdom and upsetting the establishment and it had by then occurred to me that the Catholic Church and its teachings were not all they were cracked up to be. But atheism! Wasn't that going a bit far? Still, we talked, or rather Bernard talked. I nodded, occasionally venturing a comment or a question, which only egged him on and made his line of argument ever more taut and logical and his conclusions ever more inescapable, namely that God was dead and buried and Marx was alive and kicking, or words to that effect.

I ran into Bernard again after the long summer break following our first year in Nancy. At some point during the holidays, he had renounced Marxism and found Jesus all over again. Perhaps he had been struck by lightning and thrown off a horse. That year, our long walks across the length and breadth of Nancy were devoted to knocking holes through Marxist logic and bemoaning the changes to Catholic practice the recent Vatican Council had introduced, the nature of which

169

Bernard seemed to have studied in depth and committed to memory. I lost touch with him after that year. My guess is that he probably went on to dabble in Hinduism and headed for Kathmandu. Or perhaps he became a priest and spent his ecclesiastical career insisting on saying the Latin mass in a black soutane and biretta and ignoring injunctions from his bishop to fall into line, turn his altar around, learn to play the tambourine, and hug his parishioners. Or perhaps he flipped again and went off to Bolivia to fight along *El Che,* and if he survived, joined Al Qaeda and is now living in discreet retirement in a leafy suburb of Islamabad. Bernard was a tad mercurial, but he was very convincing no matter what ideology he happened to be promoting.

Just about everything we did was coloured by our politics. True to the mid-1960s mindset, we despised – or affected to despise – private property. No one I knew had a car, most of us could not afford the bus fare, and although Nancy was mostly flat, bikes were considered *infra dig,* so we walked. But it rained often enough so it was advisable not to stray too far from an umbrella. The question was whose umbrella. When neophytes first arrived in Nancy as freshmen, a rite of passage consisted of contributing an umbrella to the student pool. It did not have to be a fancy item bought in a glitzy department store. A humble, all-black model would do. The rationale was that with hundreds of students rushing to leave a lecture theatre or the university cafeteria at the same time on rainy days, there was no way of reliably determining which black umbrella belonged to whom. So we simply helped ourselves to one, any one, and went off singing in the rain. As long as everyone had been honest and contributed an umbrella at the start, the process was maximally efficient as well as ideologically sound. In these acquisitive times in which we now live, I imagine that the practice has gone the way of easy rides in a VW microbus shared with complete strangers with flowers in their hair.

True to the *Zeitgeist*, a major arrow in our ideological quiver consisted of publicly displaying an intense dislike of America for the terrible things it was doing not only in Vietnam but also closer to home, namely daring to operate military bases on French soil, including in north-eastern France close to the German border. Until de Gaulle tempestuously pulled France out of NATO and sent its bureaucracy packing to Brussels in 1966, American cars the size of adolescent whales were a common sight on the streets of Nancy, especially at night when their owners came into town in search of proper food and perhaps a little Rest & Recreation.

I must confess that I still feel occasional pangs of guilt about our puerile reaction to their presence. We marauded in small gangs at night in areas of the city where American cars were likely to be parked, and when one was spotted, two of us strolled past it casually, one on each side, and scratched the paintwork along its entire length with a key or some other sharp object. Our interventions were so surreptitious and brief and the risk of getting caught so minimal that they did not even bring on an adrenaline rush. Besides, this was no time for cheap thrills: the cause was too lofty for that. Anti-Americanism was rife on French campuses as elsewhere in the student world and we felt entirely justified in taking the retaliatory action that we did.

If you were in the US military and stationed near Nancy in the mid-1960s and you remember finding the paintwork on your Studebaker Cruiser scratched from end to end as you staggered out of a bar one night, it could well have been me or one of my equally immature friends.

*

For me and my ideologically-driven band of friends, reduced as we were to having fun on no money, another favourite prank consisted of annoying the French *bourgeoisie* at a time when it was least receptive to being challenged and least equipped to respond, namely, in the middle of the night.

Finding lots of French *bourgeois* to annoy in a single spot was not difficult since they tended to live one above the other in the kinds of residential buildings commonly seen in the swankier parts of French cities. Each vertical set of flats shared a front door with a bank of bells to one side, each one neatly labelled according to residents' names. For us, a crucial feature of these doorbells was that they consisted not of the flimsy recessed plastic buttons seen today but of solid ceramic buttons that stuck out from their base in the door frame.

The problem for resident *bourgeois* was that this arrangement turned them into sitting ducks for politically motivated pranksters with nothing to wake up for in the morning but law classes they did not much care to attend. The idea was to press all the bells and rouse all the *bourgeois* from their slumbers simultaneously. But since there were a great many bells and we had a limited supply of fingers, our *modus operandi* consisted of scouring nearby building sites and rubbish tips for two simple props: a flat piece of wood, perhaps a short plank or a section of floorboard, and a stick about as long as the targeted doorway was wide. We then sneaked up to the building, stood by the door a while trying to look casual to fool any law-abiding citizens that might still be about at the dead of night, and then set to work.

172

Like scratching the paintwork of American cars, the nigh-time bell-ringing was best done in pairs. One the co-conspirators held the plank vertically as close as possible to the bells, careful not to press them accidentally. Then his accomplice positioned the stick horizontally between the plank and the opposing door jamb before jamming it down sharply, at which point all the doorbells started ringing simultaneously and all hell was let loose.

Obviously, the strategic mistake on our part would have been to run off and implicitly admit guilt to accidental observers. But we seasoned pranksters knew better. The moment the ringing started, we strolled away from the scene of the crime as casually as we had come, stood on the nearest street corner, and watched the lights come on one by one in the targeted building.

Before long, the front door opened and a *bourgeois* in slumberwear appeared, stood there for a while looking confused, stared at the stick barring access to the outside world, scratched his or her scalp to assist night-time cognition, and visibly struggled to make a mental connection between the stick, the plank jammed against the doorbells, and the fact that all the doorbells in that section of the building were buzzing as one. Finally, the *bourgeois* unjammed the stick, which sent the plank crashing onto the pavement and put an immediate end to the cacophony, and finally picked up plank and stick, flung both into the street, and slammed the door shut.

Now, as every French intellectual knew, a defining characteristic of the *bourgeois* class was that its members were not very bright, which was precisely why the revolution could not fail. To us analysts of the French *bourgeoisie* and what ailed it, it was obvious that dumping plank and stick into the street was not a good move. A worker, a peasant, or an intellectual would surely have hung on to both as evidence of malfeasance and immediately alerted the *gendarmerie*, from our point of view a consummation most devoutly not to be wished. But no, with plank and stick now lying invitingly in the middle of the street, all we had to do was bide our time until all the lights had gone out in the building, add fifteen minutes or so to allow the *bourgeoisie* time to go back to sleep, and then sneak up to the building and go through the procedure all over again.

It was cold, it was windy, perhaps it was raining or even snowing. But this beat sitting up half the night reading law books and lecture notes.

*

At the end of my first year, to no one's surprise, I failed all my exams. This meant that the following year, I had to sit through the same lectures given by the same professors reading the same lecture notes in the same lecture theatre on the same day of the week. Some of my friends had managed to scrape through to the second year so my social circle thinned a little. But this had the advantage of giving me a chance to ease off on the critique of the *bourgeoisie* and multinational capitalism and explore alternative career options instead.

By then, three things had become obvious. First, I detested law as intensely as my parents had predicted and I had no realistic prospect of turning the situation around. Second, I was spending less and less time studying law and more and more studying German and English on my own. Against all expectations, I was beginning to realise something that had eluded me in secondary school, namely that I enjoyed studying foreign languages and I was quite good at it. Third, I was not made for the rigidities of French education. An escape route would have to be found and foreign languages might provide just that route.

During my second year in Nancy, I started taking part in government-sponsored gatherings of mostly French and German students, usually held on German soil presumably because the French were supplying the rhetoric, which was free, while the Germans were footing the bill. Only twenty years after the end of World War II, these get-togethers were daringly innovative and a far cry from the horror stories I had heard from my grandmother about how the Germans kept invading France because they had no good wines or cheeses of their own, both of which France had practically invented and had in abundance. When I finally travelled to Germany to have a look for myself, I saw better-dressed people driving better cars on better roads and amply provided with all the wines and cheeses they could possibly consume, not to mention vastly better beer. The Germans seemed a reasonably happy breed of men and women. My grandmother had been wrong. Whatever their main motivation for building empires that would last a thousand years, it could never have been getting their hands on perquisites of civilised living such as French wines and cheeses.

I liked Germany for its neatness, its beauty, and the hospitality of its people. As my grandmother never tired of repeating, their language could be harsh on the ear. But as far as I could tell, there was nothing very wrong with the Germans. As long as I remembered not to mention the war, I was treated with faultless courtesy. The Germans were good people.

As the field expanded, other nationalities joined our gatherings. On one of these occasions, I conceived a burning passion for a flaxen-haired seventeen-year-old

Norwegian siren named Karin, who, judging by the *blasé* manner in which she dealt with the technicalities of kissing, seemed to have been at it from a suspiciously young age. Perhaps, like Marilyn Monroe in *Some Like It Hot*, she sold kisses for the milk fund. I was hardly an authority on the subject but as far as I could tell, she kissed by the book. But learning took place in other directions too, most notably in the area of English, which, when they were not busy kissing, the Scandinavians in particular already spoke much more fluently than they spoke German or French, though there were exceptions.

On one of these jamborees, set in Provence this time, the group included a Polish youth and a Danish girl. Their names were Jerzy and Mia, if memory serves. Both were about eighteen. I do not know how Jerzy had managed to travel to the West at the height of the Cold War, but there he was. He spoke Polish and German, Mia spoke Danish and English. Neither spoke a word of French. They met, they walked by moonlight, they fell in love. Judging by the inordinate amount of time they spent entirely out of sight, we assumed that their romantic activities went beyond roaming in the gloaming and even kissing, but obviously none of us was invited to verify the speculation. Some of their yearnings must have been transparent and required no words. But at times, the lovers seemed to feel the urge to use their articulatory organs for something other than kissing and a cross-cultural communication problem arose.

By then, I had acquired modest communicative ability in both German and English and I spoke French, of course, so my services were often enlisted as interpreter. And since I was the only participant who could communicate with Jerzy and Mia as well as with our *Provençal* hosts, duty called. I borrowed a bike, rode into the local town, located the one and only bookshop in it, and bought two dictionaries: one English-French, the other German-French. A town that small in deepest Provence was not likely to offer the Danish-French or Polish-French combinations, let alone Danish-Polish.

It worked. For the rest of the time we all spent together, the lovers went around with fingers entwined and carrying their respective dictionary in their free hand, occasionally pausing to gaze at each other and sigh under a shady bower. The procedure was simple. Jerzy thought of a Polish word, translated it into German in his head, opened his German-French dictionary, leafed through it for the French equivalent, and pointed to the French word. Mia then looked up the French word in her French-English dictionary and translated the English equivalent into Danish in her head. Or vice versa if Mia felt moved to find speech first. Never before was greater linguistic effort expanded in the interest of true love.

I got back to Nancy from these jaunts not only marvelling at the niceness of foreigners and of Norwegian girls in particular but also at the potential for intellectual and emotional development a knowledge of foreign languages afforded. So I studied German on my own from textbooks, reviewing familiar grammar rules and creating illustrative sentences that seemed to make sense and be grammatically correct as far as I could tell. English grammar was easier. Perhaps my linguistic preferences were beginning to set. But English classes were also easier to come by. From a notice on a lamp post, I learned about free classes given in a stuffy room above a *café* and immediately joined.

The teacher was a toothy young American named Larry, who turned out to be a Mormon missionary fishing for converts, hence the free lessons. But whatever Larry's spiritual agenda, I had never heard so much intelligible and meaningful English in a classroom before. I recall how on one occasion, we came across the verb 'to singe' in an article he had taken from the *International Herald Tribune*, a daily recently made cool by the scrumptious Jean Seberg who earned a living by selling it on the streets of Paris in Godard's 1960 film *A Bout de Souffle*. Looking back, Larry must have been a born teacher or he would not have known how to explain to a class of French speakers a word as abstruse as 'to singe' without benefit of translation and make it meaningful and even memorable. I hope that this talented man took up language teaching as a profession and left the reaping of souls to amateurs.

The shameful part of this otherwise encouraging episode in my educational career is that I never had the courage to tell my parents that I was in effect dropping out of college. I was attending fewer and fewer of my law classes, and I did not even bother to take the final exams. On the day the results were announced, I came home with the startling news that much to my consternation I had failed once again. Why I stuck with this shabby deceit, I am not sure. It should have been obvious that despite the waste of time and expense, my father and my mother would probably welcome my decision since they had achieved their aim of not interfering in my life while letting me work things out for myself. The good news was that I was in a position to announce that I had at last found my way and that this would involve studying foreign languages.

The question was how to combine this newly-discovered interest and a chance of a job later. Over the months I spent studying German and English, I had convinced myself that if I spent a year immersed in each language, I would become more or less trilingual and therefore equipped for a job, preferably in something involving travel. My choice was between Germany and England. I knew each language equally well (or badly). I had never had a strong desire to visit England, a place roundly condemned in France for its foul weather and its even worse food, and England seemed very far from eastern France whereas Germany was a short train ride away. I had already visited Germany on several occasions and I liked the country and its people. But at the age of eighteen, this would be quite an adventure and I would need assistance in navigating the unfamiliar waters of either country. I knew no one well enough in Germany I could ask. But my older sister Bernadette had a friend named Jacqueline who was spending a year in England teaching French in a school near London and who agreed to help. So England it would be.

But before I get to that move and its long-term consequences, there is a lot more to be said about growing up in Lure, Haute-Saône, starting with the topic that rarely fails to engage readers, namely sex.

CHAPTER EIGHT: SUGAR AND SPICE

The voice of Love seemed to call to me, but it was a wrong number.

PG Wodehouse (1881-1975)

When it comes to making up stories about where babies come from, parents cannot be faulted for lack of imagination. In the Germanic tradition, babies are airlifted in by storks, bundled up snugly in a long piece of cloth suspended from the end of the bird's beak. But for children growing up in France, even in Alsace, where real-life storks remain part of the urban landscape, the dominant myth is that babies are discovered in cabbage patches. In the imagination of French children, babies are found accidentally not stiff with ground frost, spitting out slugs, and screaming their little lungs out as might reasonably be expected but gurgling and babbling merrily as if they have not a care in the world and are letting it be known that they fully expect the rest of their days to be just as merry as their first.

Why cabbage patches as opposed to any number of alternative locations is not clear. The airport or in 1950s France, the railway station would make more sense. At least, it would suggest a plausible method of delivery. The baby wasn't here before, now it is. It arrived on the 2:35 am *Paris-Bâle*, see? Simple. Problem solved.

By global standards, the cabbage patch theory is not all that cockeyed. Thai children, for example, are told that babies come from the moon, a revelation that must prompt every Thai child with an IQ of five and above to ask how the babies actually get from there to here and then wonder at the fantastical answers. By comparison, beliefs in storks as the transporters of choice or wind-swept cabbage patches as ideal landing sites seem almost scientific.

*

By the time I was eleven or twelve and on the cusp of pre-pubescence, I had become vaguely aware that there was more to babies than cabbage patches. But uncovering solid information on the matter was not easy. Especially when seen from today's perspective, at a time when images of more or less overt sexuality are on display everywhere, provincial Lure, Haute-Saône offered very little information about sex.

One factor must have been culturally inherited reticence on my parents' part, especially my father's, to discuss the topic at all, and behind that must have been the heavy hand of the Catholic Church and its phobia about matters of the flesh.

Yet even if the willingness to answer questions openly and truthfully was missing among those in the know, as founding members of the baby-boomer generation, we were surrounded by evidence. In the 1950s and 1960s, there were babies everywhere and working out their genesis should not have been rocket science. For my mother and father, it was a matter of precise recollection as well as deep fondness that after World War II officially ended on May 8, 1945, my father returned home from the POW camp where he had spent the previous five years on June 8. And on March 9, 1946 and not a day later, my mother gave birth to a bouncing baby girl, my older sister Bernadette.

In truth, at least until early adolescence, little of this mattered to me especially compared to whether my bike needed cleaning or how I was going to reveal to my father that I had come last in a maths test yet again.

The awakening came out of the blue one afternoon when I was about twelve. My mother ushered me into the parental bedroom with the air of one with pivotal information to impart. She opened the massive oak *armoire*, a family heirloom I had studied in some depth because this was where my parents stored Christmas and birthday presents ahead of time. Some additions to my Meccano set, perhaps, or extra lengths of track for my train set, or even the latest in foot-holders for my bike? And apart from purely selfish interest, if I picked my moment and managed a comprehensive review of the stash, advance information on what treats were in store for my siblings could always be traded against a promise to put a sock in it as opposed to turning witness for the prosecution on the occasion of my next *peccadillo*, which given my contemporary record, would not be long in coming.

The *armoire* was massive. It seemed to fill half the room and towered menacingly over me as I approached it on one my fact-finding missions. In colour, it was a rich mix of browns. Its filigreed iron lock and key were works of art. It exuded historical continuity. It had lived through three Franco-German wars and seemed ready to look several more in the eye. In smell, it blended ancient oak and dried lavender, freshly laundered linen, and the beeswax that filled the cracks in its geriatric architecture. As I opened the huge doors while on a data-gathering operation, the clunky metal lock and the whining hinges set off the kind of adrenaline rush that Ikea flat-pack furniture will never match. This *armoire* was a thing of majesty: it inspired awe and reverence, like an elephant in a zoo or a vintage locomotive in a museum.

But on that occasion, the treasure the *armoire* was about to reveal went far beyond Meccano, train sets, or bikes. My mother opened the mighty doors, rooted around among pillow cases and socks, and produced a book I had somehow managed to miss during my earlier investigations. Little did I know that the content of that book was about to change my entire perception of life and especially of how it came about at each iteration. In a candid, matter-of-fact way, my mother gave me the scoop: daddies, mummies, babies, familiar appendages and unfamiliar cavities and their variegated uses: in brief, all the variables with the exception of cabbage patches and storks plus the complex interplay between them, complete with user-friendly diagrams. And all conveniently packaged in an attractive volume of which I was now the proud owner.

Naturally, my mother, a devout Catholic homemaker and a credit to the Church, would not have dreamt of putting into the hands of one of her children a book on such a delicate topic if it had not received the Vatican's *imprimatur*, an important detail clearly stated at the front of the book. So there it all was, about as explicit as it was possible to make it without encouraging voyeurism among the faithful and framed within the context of Catholic matrimony as the sole condition under which the book's central motif might apply.

The focus of the book was a girl named Claire. She was beautiful, poised, confident of a higher destiny: very much, in fact, as I imagined the Virgin Mary would have looked if she had been born two thousand years later in Neuilly-sur-Seine instead of Nazareth and had worn slightly shorter dresses. Claire had a fiancé named Philippe. He was tall as Frenchmen go, handsome, quietly self-assured, clean living. At a time when nicotine was known to be good for you and every self-respecting Frenchman indulged, he did not seem to smoke. It was not difficult to see why Claire would feel comfortable contemplating Christian procreation with Philippe and Philippe with Claire, after they were married, of course.

The title of the book was *Claire et Philippe*. Not very imaginative, I concede, but snappier than 'What you've always wanted to know about sex but were afraid to ask', among competing alternatives. The book's genius was to combine text and subtext in one appealing whole. The underlying message was clear: this is how wonderful your life will be if you follow the script, but don't even think about trying any of this at home before you are married!

This was no fire and brimstone pamphlet. There were no lofty exhortations backed by dark threats in the Catholic tradition and none was needed. The tone was friendly, helpful, upbeat. Like those self-improvement guides so beloved of American book buyers, it focused solely on the positive. Clearly, editorial policy had been to avoid negative advertising and not dwell on the punishments that awaited young readers should they transgress. Instead, the book offered what marketers call a 'teaser', a glimpse of the good life to come if the shopper plumps for the product and gives the competition a miss.

Given prevailing conditions in the matter of information about sex, this book clearly did some good. It provided me with much-needed and factually accurate information. And by explaining that sexuality could be – should be – dealt with as part of a larger social and emotional picture, it made a crucial point while helping to dispel confusion up in the head by putting the nascent fires down below into context. I was lucky that my mother had the courage to deal with sexuality in the relatively open way that she did and that a book of this type was available. For this, I have to thank a committee of Catholic bishops for giving careful thought to adolescent sexuality, of the heterosexual kind and at a distance, for once.

How my mother guessed that this was the time to make her move, I will never know. Perhaps she consulted my father, who advised based on experience that it was now or never. Or perhaps between them, they had detected signs of growing curiosity on my part: an indirect question or a peek at a sister's expanding chest? The remarkable thing was that my mother did it at all.

My mother's timing was impeccable. For some time, I had been asking myself precisely the kinds of questions the *tête-à-tête* by the *armoire* had at last begun to answer. I had long rejected the hypothesis that babies were found in cabbage patches as too implausible to warrant further consideration and instead conjectured that their emergence must have something to do with a meeting of body parts, presumably one male and the other female. But quite how that meeting took place and precisely what body parts the meeting entailed remained shrouded in unknowingness. My initial post-cabbage patch hypothesis was that it might have something to do with fluids. But the only major fluid I knew to be common to both genders, apart from blood, was urine so I soon dismissed that option as implausible as well as off-putting. But I was getting warm. Clearly, I had the general geography of the thing right even if I was a bit off on the details.

As often happens when we become aware of something new, we begin to notice it everywhere: a new word in a language or a fashionable item everyone seems to be wearing that year. Once the feature has been brought to our attention, it pops up all over the landscape. And so it was for me with sex. Post-

armoire, I began to realise that the world was full of sex or at least of sex-related phenomena. Suddenly, Lure, Haute-Saône seemed to have been invaded by pregnant women. They were everywhere, shoulders pushed back and bulge to the fore. How could I have missed it?

I was almost seven when my youngest sister Marie-Jeanne was born but I have no recollection of any change in my mother's appearance or behaviour during or immediately after her pregnancy. All I remember is that she went missing one day and was promptly found lying in a hospital bed with an unfamiliar baby by her side. Just as memorable if not more so was the fact that my father had hired a woman from the town to come in each day to cook and clean in her absence. So for a few days, we got to do things a little differently and we ate slightly different food, which because of the novelty tasted much better than the regular fare.

And how did I manage to grow up with two older sisters without becoming aware that girls have to deal with peculiar physiological phenomena on a monthly basis? Had I noticed, my mother asked as we stood before the *armoire,* how my two older sisters occasionally sneaked into what passed for a bathroom in our ill-appointed flat, made discreet washing noises, and then emerged clutching something they did not want us boys to see? Sanitary towels, these items were called, apparently: the reusable kind at the time.

No, I had not noticed.

All of this had been going on month after month and the entire ritual had totally passed me by. Where did my sisters hang those towels to dry? I have no idea. How could this be? What planet had I been living on?

*

Sex was never mentioned, not even implicitly, in or out of the home. For many of us growing up in Lure, Haute-Saône, life firmly rested on three pillars, socially and emotionally: family, church, and school. The family setting was good at providing comforts of many kinds but frank and open discussions of sex were not on the menu. And how could a church that employed (supposedly) celibate priests to peddle the preposterous notion of the virgin birth be in a position to inform pre-adolescents about the facts of life? In school, there was the usual silliness among my male classmates about who sported the longest member, bizarrely referred to by French boys as *lune*, or 'moon'. But that had to do with the frustrations of powerlessness and expectations of manliness, not intelligent inquiry into the origins of life and the mechanics of procreation. Any suggestions by older boys claiming to be in the know of a connection between *lunes*, girls, and babies were treated not as information but as entertainment.

Sex education in school, primary or secondary, was not on the syllabus. This left independent research as the only route to enlightenment. My earliest attempt at uncovering the occult involved Josiane, the quiet, gentle, younger sister of bossy Françoise, our next door neighbours and frequent playmates. Josiane and I were both about eight at the time. To this day, I can point to the exact fir tree opposite our house behind which I helped Josiane pull up her pink dress over her head and reveal herself in nothing but her panties. I was transfixed. In return, I favoured her with a quick flash of my young manhood. It is never easy to read a woman's mind but as far as I could tell, she was unimpressed. At that point, whether from pressure of circumstances, information overload, or fear of divine retribution, we both deemed it wise to bring the controlled experiment to an end and restore our respective clothing to the default configuration.

In secondary school, sexual reproduction was slipped in obliquely in the biology textbook we were reading when I was already about thirteen. In their wisdom, the curriculum designers seemed to have determined that by that age we were just about mature enough to handle the delicate matter of reproduction in mammals. Not humans, mind you, just mammals, and very small mammals at that.

The biology textbook covered the entire topic of sexuality in half-a-page on the reproductive apparatus of the mouse, complete with a grainy black and white photo of some hapless female rodent spread-eagled and nailed to a board of some kind, with her belly slit up and most of her innards ripped out, leaving only her reproductive organs in place. By then, even I knew that there were daddy mice and mummy mice and that it took a meeting of the two to produce a baby mouse (or a dozen). But none of this was mentioned in the textbook. In fact, for all the coverage it received, the reproductive equipment of the male mouse might as well have been a state secret. That said, this did not stop me from reading the description over and over again just in case I had missed something important in earlier readings.

In the world in which I was growing up, much as a glimpse of a lady's ankle could trigger smouldering passions in a buttoned-up Victorian male, the fact that so little was being revealed only served to inflame the imagination. In the event, we never even studied that section of the biology textbook in class. Somehow, our biology teacher, Mademoiselle Simard, a dour, humourless little woman who would not have known a smouldering passion if it bit her in the *derrière*, simply skipped the section. Perhaps she felt that we probably knew plenty already and there was nothing new she could possibly teach us. Or she felt certain that the topic would never come up in any exam, the be-all and end-all of French education at the time, so why bother? But to give the textbook its due, it equipped me with a few useful concepts such as ovaries and uteruses, for example, along with the novel notion that eggs could be associated with girls and not just with chickens.

*

Even after my mother provided in the form of the *Claire et Philippe* volume, a key source of supplementary information on the subject of sex consisted of my father's personal library. My father combined a love of books with the habit of never throwing away anything that had been painstakingly and expensively accumulated. He spent much of his time at home in the semi-private space at the end of the hallway he called his 'study', where he could insulate himself to a degree from family squabbles. Pride of place in this *sanctum sanctorum* went to his desk, an impressive affair with a stack of drawers at each end and a large sheet of pink blotting paper on top that he later replaced with a laminated map of the world when nibs and ink gave way to the technological wonder that was the ballpoint pen. Next to the desk was another *armoire,* for ours was a generously-*armoired* home. This *armoire* was smaller and less awe-inspiring than the one in the parental bedroom but it was filled with a lifetime's worth of books, atlases, dictionaries, and encyclopaedias.

Tucked away at the back were some well-thumbed copies of the kind of magazines that would have played in the late 1920s the educational role the likes of *Penthouse* came to play – or so I am told – for the next generation of knowledge-deprived adolescents. A particular object of fascination on my part was a selection of tales from the *One Thousand and One Nights*. My favourite saga chronicled in relatively explicit details the escapades of a busty princess and her many male escorts including slaves, none of whom she could possibly have been married to, while her lord and master the Emir or the Vizir or something was away doing God's work and bumping off infidels. The men in the illustrations seemed implausibly muscular. But what stuck in my mind as was surely the illustrator's intention was the lady's pointy breasts as well as the look on her face, which I later learned to recognise as lascivious. As for the rest of her, some sort of translucent fabric covered what little of her nether regions she chose not to display directly. The effect was hypnotic.

Sensing that discretion was the better part of self-instructional valour, I timed my fact-finding safaris to coincide with moments when my father was out of the house or talking to my mother in the kitchen while she prepared the evening meal. To get at the magazines at the back of the *armoire*, I had to burrow behind a leather-bound encyclopaedia in multiple volumes, each weighing about a ton. Once I had my fill of the translucent fabric and the pointy Arabian breasts, it dawned on me that if I could cope with the weight, the forbidding cover, and the turgid prose, the encyclopaedia might contain just the kind of information I was after. For the most part, entries covered esoteric topics such as Socratic dialectic, how to tell a crayfish from a lobster, or the history of France's colonial conquests in chronological order of acquisition.

But I persevered and eventually got to entries about art. Artists, I quickly learned, have long been fascinated by the female form preferably in its naked manifestations. Perhaps this is because in a world that combined public repression of sexuality and the near-absolute power among the wealthy to do whatever they liked, there was always going to be a market for private representations of the forbidden among moneyed individuals with reputations to protect: bankers, aristocrats, cardinals, popes even. And for an artist on the verge of penury, it helped to have mastered the art of blending nudity and innocence against a mythological background that spoke of the erudition wealthy patrons pretended to be infused with. This made prurience respectable. And nobody could do this better than Botticelli, to whose work my father's encyclopaedia devoted substantial acreage.

To my keen eye, the Birth of Venus was a treat. There was a full frontal image of a beautiful young woman with not a stitch on, half-heartedly covering her modesty with her long flowing hair and trying her best to look as if she did not quite know what she was doing there and was really motivated by a higher purpose. As with all great art, especially when it hints at sexuality, the result was bewitching.

And if that failed to satisfy my aesthetic urgings, there on the opposite page was *La Primavera*, which offered not one but four near-naked women, all acting just as startled as Venus in her shell and utterly perplexed at how standing around wearing nothing but see-through robes could possibly motivate passing satyrs to reach out and grope.

*

Given the effort involved in taking a peek at pointy breasts or pert buttocks in grainy reproductions of ancient myths, readers might conclude that I was growing up in a wholesome prelapsarian Eden, where the depth of moral turpitude consisted of coveting a sibling's toys or second slice of birthday cake.

Readers would be wrong. For a hormone-fuelled adolescent, even one growing up in an environment shaped more by Catholic piety than by candid discussions of the properties of testosterone, Lure, Haute-Saône was a veritable den of iniquity, Haute-Saône's answer to Sodom and Gomorrah, almost. By the standards of place and time, opportunities for sinning – in the heart, at least – lurked on every street corner.

Even as I went about the mundane business of getting from one end of the town to the other, I risked damning my soul at every turn of my bike's wheels. If I took the route that took me past the railway station, I faced hints of whatever military depravity might be going on inside the *café* that served as Rest & Recreation headquarters for the local soldiery. But this route was the more circuitous and in any case the less scenic of my two options so it made sense to go for speed and convenience as well as depravity-avoidance and head straight down the *Grand Rue* instead. But even there, the Devil lay in wait in the window of the only lingerie shop in town. There for all to see were photos of women in bras, girdles, and even – I shudder at the recollection! – girdle-free panties.

Growing up in a small Catholic town quickly teaches that it is not just God who sees everything but everyone else too. Everywhere I went, curtains twitched in windows, front doors opened and promptly shut, and suspiciously frequent sorties were made by the citizenry to take weather checks, sweep dead leaves from their front steps, or give the brass door-bell another shine. The principal malefactors in this respect were two older ladies of some standing, one never married, the other a widow, who could be glimpsed at opposing windows overlooking the *Grand Rue,* noting every twist below through binoculars and then meeting on alternate sides of the street each evening to compare notes.

To say that I lived in constant fear would be an overstatement. But in truth, I never quite knew where the next informer was likely to spring from. But sooner or later, someone was bound to report to my parents or one of my older sisters that I had been spotted dawdling by the lingerie shop and ogling the bras and panties in the window. Or so it seemed at the time. Looking back, I doubt that my parents would have been surprised or bothered in the slightest. But Catholic guilt is burdensome and it weighed on my young mind.

Of particular concern in this respect was the Coop grocery shop, which in an aberrant moment divine providence had placed immediately across the street from the lingerie shop. My mother did most of her grocery shopping there so my siblings and I were known to Madame Prideaux, the austere owner, for often coming in with a handful of coins to pick up sugar or baking powder or whatever essential substance my mother was about to run out of. Madame Prideaux saw her role as being both provider of household necessities to the citizenry and custodian of small-town morality. In this latter role, she was ably assisted by the covey of gossipmongers and self-selected guardians of Catholic righteousness that gathered on her premises on their mission to nip evil in the bud. What was a teenage boy hungering after knowledge to do?

As I explained, we were boxed in by the topography of the town: it was either the high road and the lingerie shop and its grinning bras and panties in the window or the low road and the army men jumping out of their Jeeps and intent on serious depravity, whatever that might mean in practice. After protracted experimentation, I reached the conclusion that I could stick to the high road as long as whenever I had to pass the lingerie shop on its own side of the street, I got off my bike just short of it, crossed the street, rode past the Coop on the wrong side of the road, and then crossed back and continued on my travels. Had he been coping with hormonal surges in Lure, Haute-Saône instead of Nazareth, Galilee and had he owned a bike, this is what Jesus would have done, I reasoned. The thought pacified me, for a while at least.

And if that did not work, there was always confession. In my view, confession is the finest contribution ever made by the Catholic Church to alleviating the human condition because it provides a mechanism for reconciling self-indulgence today with salvation tomorrow. Curiously, this is a rationalisation no other major religion has ever shown any interest in emulating despite the availability of a large market for such a sensible approach to sin. But even so, bras were bras and panties were panties. Both had to be faced on a daily basis and I knew that if I patronised the confessional too often, I would be suspected by the priest in attendance of faking it, of not having true contrition. Growing up Catholic was not meant to be easy.

*

The photos of bras and panties in the lingerie shop remained part of my mental map throughout my formative years. And as if this was not enough of a spiritual challenge, the Devil had added further hurdles on the road to eternal life in the shape of one of the town's only two cinemas. One, the *Rex*, was located right in the middle of the *Grand Rue* and therefore as difficult to bypass as the lingerie shop. The other, the *Commerce*, was close to the railway station, almost opposite the army Rest & Recreation headquarters. Inexplicably, the one in the *louche* part of town showed only the humdrum output of the French studios: tales of daring involving moustachioed musketeers and their unconvincingly virginal *protégées* or inane comedies about traffic cops falling off bridges into the Seine or crashing into each other on the Champs Elysées. I was thrilled, of course, or I laughed. But my imagination quickly drifted back to the *Rex* and its more *risqué* offerings since as every teenage boy knew, it specialised in showing the French cinema's best attempts at poking a finger in the eye of middle-class morality.

The cinematic routine is shop-worn: *un homme* and *une femme*, each married to someone else, sneak into some no-tell hotel in Pigalle in the middle of the afternoon, leap up the stairs, and then thrash about between the sheets for an hour or so, pausing only to light another *Gauloise* and compare notes on the meaninglessness of it all. And judging by the lurid coverage she received, no one seemed to do cinematic sexual *ennui* better than the fabled Brigitte Bardot. Not that any of us had ever seen one of her films. Strict ratings applied and we knew that the *Rex* would never sell teenage boys a ticket. For me, interest was further whipped up by the Catholic magazines my parents subscribed to and the fulminations they printed against Satanic conspiracies designed to weaken the moral fibre of the nation and in particular against Brigitte Bardot and her central role in these schemes. Brigitte Bardot, I could only conclude, must be something pretty special! So inevitably, I went in search of confirmation.

But testing this hypothesis on the basis of solid evidence was not going to be easy. Luckily, the manager of the *Rex*, a man who must once have been a teenager himself and who has surely been awarded the *Légion d'Honneur* by now, obliged through the selection of stills he displayed by the front door of his cinema. In fact, the location of the display showed exceptional public-spiritedness as well as positional nous on his part because it allowed me to make repeated calls and leer at stills of Brigitte Bardot's divine *derrière* for as long as I liked without having to get off my bike. If danger was espied, it was easy for me to make a quick escape and claim I was never there. And what made contemplation even safer was the fact that the *Rex* was slightly set back from the street and tucked away between a noisy *café* and a motorbike repair shop, in neither of which widowed pillars of the Church, devotees of the confessional, and self-appointed guardians of middle-class morality were likely to be roosting.

When I was a little older, I discovered that the largest newsagent in town, the *Maison de la Presse*, stocked all kinds of publications aimed at the discerning French intellectual. This included a number of magazines specialising in film reviews written in the existential gobbledygook so beloved of the French thinking classes, then as now. But what I lingered over on my regular visits to this providential establishment was not the film reviews themselves but the photos of the main protagonists that accompanied them and that in a good week might include starlets photographed at the Cannes Festival, frolicking on the beach in various states of undress and pouting provocatively at the camera. But a sense of proportion was of the essence and I quickly grew eyes at the back of my head for signs that the shop owner was getting restless. After twenty or thirty minutes of my silent presence in the same corner of his establishment, he was bound to conclude sooner or later that this was not his lucky day and he was never going to make a sale. Eventually, he intervened. I'd seen quite enough for one day, thank you very much, he commented loudly from behind his counter, and didn't I have a home to go to and some homework to get on with? But for the most part, thanks to this grouchy but tolerant man, as soon as I was old enough to outgrow *Tintin en Amérique*, getting my weekly leer was not a problem.

*

What was and for quite a while remained a problem was moving on from the furtive thrills this data gathering provided to the next stage in my enlightenment. At the time, the next step on the road to manhood consisted entirely of fantasy, only much more graphic than what it supplanted.

One willing contributor to my store of mental images was friend and classmate Pascal, a key member of my social group. One of the youngest students in the class, Pascal was especially gifted at maths but also something of a snob, who never missed a chance to remind us that he was only living in lowly Lure, Haute-Saône because of his father's job. The family's spiritual home was Paris.

One summer, Pascal did something so daring, so sophisticated that we all gaped in disbelief when we heard: he went off not just to far-away Paris but to England to study in one of the many language schools the were springing up on the south coast in and around Brighton. On his return, he held us in thrall with lurid tales of boys kissing girls and girls kissing boys under the pier at night, and especially of one boy who – he had it on good authority, though we strongly suspected he was referring to himself all along – had even got his hand inside a Swedish girl's bra..., with the Swedish girl still in it. She had to be Swedish, the naughty nationality at the time, or the story would not have been credible.

And then there was Henri, the wastrel son of an ancient Catholic family that had somehow survived successive revolutions with its double-barrelled name and most of its acres intact. Henri surfaced in my final year of secondary school because he had been declared *persona non grata* by every Catholic institution of learning within a 100-kilometre radius and the only option left to him if he were to complete his secondary education was the local *lycée,* a proudly demotic and secular institution and therefore an affront to aristocratic sensibilities but better than nothing. Having repeated so many classes, Henri was several years older than any of us in the class and therefore nearly an adult. He was also a man of the world. Not only could he drive, he even owned a car. His notoriety derived from the fact – or at least the claim – that at the conclusion of a particularly cheery evening, he had driven his *Deux-chevaux* into a lake just for the fun of it. And of course, he did not just know someone who had got to third base with a girl. He actively encouraged speculation that he himself was a paid-up member of that exclusive club.

*

Around that time, rumours were beginning to reach even Lure, Haute-Saône that sex had been invented. This was a remarkable breakthrough and for an inquisitive teenager, a very timely one. The exact genesis of the event remains unclear but the early 1960s is generally believed to have been the time and

Swinging London the place. In fact, English poet Philip Larkin playfully claimed to have pinned down the exact date to 1963. Larkin described the event as the moment when 'sexual intercourse began'. But to observers and chroniclers, the phrase 'sex was invented' must have sounded snappier, or as George Orwell might have put it, more 'euphonious', so it is that wording that stuck.

It is now agreed that the 1960s witnessed an uncommon surge of human creativity that resulted in the simultaneous emergence of – in ascending order of importance – the laser, space flight, the Beatles, the Mini, the miniskirt, and an England football team that could win the World Cup. But the invention of the decade, far outshining all others in terms of vision and potential to contribute to human happiness and the one that will surely outlive them all was sex.

Needless to say, the so-called invention of sex was a figurative way of describing what was essentially a change in social mores. What was really invented in the 1960s was recreational sex, in part as a result of the growing use of the contraceptive pill but also of a general relaxation of private and public attitudes towards sexuality. But given the repression and ignorance that had long characterised these attitudes, it seemed that all of sex, not just recreational sex, had been invented. So a second reason why the phrase took roots was because it was apt. It captured the *Zeitgeist*.

In practice, what the invention of sex really meant was that there was now a sense in the air that an important shift was taking place. Everyone knew that sex had been invented because there seemed to be more of it about. In practice, this could have meant anything. Perhaps more people were having sex. Or the same number of people were having more sex. Or fewer people were having a lot more sex and then bragged about it in the media. Or perhaps it was simply becoming easier to talk about sex. Whatever the facts, a line seemed to have been crossed.

But for most of us teenage boys and especially those with a year or two of secondary school still ahead and no access to a *Deux-chevaux* with which to impress girls and in which to entertain them in style, the invention of sex led to little more than a perfunctory meeting of lips or perhaps a furtive squeeze during a slow dance. But what sustained us lovers of tomorrow through these challenging times was the increasingly realistic hope that we would eventually have sex. Not just one day when we were married and certainly not this weekend or even this year but before too long and sooner than we had ever thought possible. But for the time being, sex remained a spectator sport, a blend of impressions, aspirations, and interpretations.

By a stroke of luck, my last year in secondary school was graced by the appearance among us of a jet-haired girl named Eveline. It was the familiar story. For some reason, her father had been banished from Paris to the far-eastern French *gulag* by his employer. And as was the way of all Parisians parachuted into Lure, Haute-Saône against their better judgment, Eveline was unsparing in her critique of everything the town stood for. The contest was unequal. Her self-assured Parisian ways, even her accent made her seem as worldly-wise and sophisticated in my eyes as I must have seemed clumsy and uncouth in hers. But because she was uncommonly beautiful, she was used to attention and she loved an audience. And on occasion, it was my personal good fortune to be tapped by fate for that role.

Eveline lived not far from our house at the far end of town so I knew that if I timed by move right, there was a chance I might accompany her for most of the way home after school. This would mean walking along at her pace and pushing my bike, a risky position to be in since it might suggest to jealous rivals that my bike was broken and I was not man enough to know how to fix it. But the risk was worth taking.

So there we were one afternoon, on our way home, chatting of this and that. I forget the conversational trajectory but at some point Eveline and I found ourselves discussing sex. For me, being there and not in a classroom or at home and in the exclusive company of a beautiful girl suggested liberation on an intoxicating scale. And to be talking about sex, of all subjects, a topic I had never discussed quite so openly before not even with trusted male friends, was like having been beamed to another galaxy.

Eventually, Eveline and I got on to the sub-topic of sex education. I mentioned the *armoire* in the parental bedroom, the *Claire et Philippe* book, and the grainy photo of the eviscerated mouse in the biology textbook. Being from Paris, Eveline had seen it all before and she had no difficulty in going one better. She related how she had received what she called her 'sexual education' not from her mother but from her French literature teacher – a man, she mentioned in passing – the previous year in Paris.

I tried to imagine the scene: the two of them staying behind after class, he drawing helpful diagrams on the blackboard and guiding her through her personal copy of *Claire et Philippe*, she questioning dubious hypotheses about cabbage patches and storks and asking girlish questions about alternative scenarios. I was moved by the man's dedication to duty. I marvelled at the goodness of heart of the finest among the French teaching profession. I said as much. She stopped, so I stopped. She turned and eyed me quizzically, then smiled enigmatically, seemingly pondering whether I was being serious. The smile turned from enigmatic to pitying. Then she started giggling and finally burst out laughing. Her Parisian notions about *la province* and its rough-hewn residents were entirely justified, she seemed to have concluded.

Clearly, the invention of sex had affected some more profoundly than others. I had a long way to go.

CHAPTER NINE: GOD ALMIGHTY

It must be remembered that we have only heard one side of the case. God has written all the books.

Samuel Butler (1835-1902)

By the early 1960s, the French economy was growing steadily and car ownership was expanding fast. But even on the eastern fringes of the country where we lived, cross-border traffic was rare and anyone driving along a French road was assumed to be French and therefore most probably Catholic and on Sundays in need of spiritual maintenance. Suddenly, a new kind of sign went up on roads leading into towns and villages.

The signs were cross-shaped for easy recognition. Against a light blue background was a list of starting times for all the Sunday services available locally. Mornings offered as many masses as could be squeezed in: early morning mass, a couple more for late risers, high mass, an evening mass, even vespers. In nearby Alsace, where those perfidious Germans had spread the heretical variant of Christianity known as Protestantism, Sunday travellers were spoiled for choice as they could pick from not one but two cross-shaped signs, one per variant. For the Catholic Church, staffing this spiritual cornucopia was no problem as the seminaries were still turning out priests in droves.

Today, all this has largely gone. Most of the cross-shaped signs have been engulfed by vegetation, the Catholic ministry has shrunk to a rump, and even substantial towns have trouble finding a priest to say just one mass in just one of its remaining churches each Sunday.

*

Seen from the modest hill at the northern end of Lure, Haute-Saône, the most prominent feature of the urban vista below is a clutch of brownish houses with red roofs arranged in a circle a few hundred metres across. This is the medieval heart of the town. And right in the centre of the circle is the tallest building in town: the parish church.

The church is dedicated to Saint Martin, patron saint of soldiers. Over the centuries, the saint proved a somewhat unreliable protector as invader after invader marched through the town and left it in tatters. But by the time I was learning to don soutane and surplice and serve as an altar boy, the Catholic fascination with saints was beginning to wane and Saint Martin's supposed role in guiding human affairs was no longer of much interest.

The church was built during the second half of the eighteenth century. In outline, it follows the standard baroque model but in wealth of decoration, by baroque standards, it looks almost austere. The building is vaulted but whether as a result of error in calculating weight distributions or natural subsidence, the walls are visibly further apart at the top than at the bottom. Nothing short of divine intervention must be keeping the building upright. Above the altar is a large painting of a crucifixion scene designed to instil guilt in the most hard-boiled. Set against this is the altar, a shiny concoction of marble and ormolu and as splendid a piece of over-the-top rococo as any. But there the excess stops. Perhaps aristocratic patrons in grander, wealthier places were not willing to release the artistic talent in their pay and send it to such an outpost for long. Or perhaps the money ran out.

In the nineteenth century, serious effort went into brightening up the building. Both sides of the nave have brightly coloured stained glass windows representing scenes from Gospel lore: Mary's visitation by the Archangel Gabriel, the flight into Egypt, and of course the Crucifixion in case parishioners missed the painting above the altar and are feeling intolerably guilt-free that day. Below each window is a brief description of the scene, presumably intended to inspire the faithful and guide their devotions. But curiously, these are in Latin. Perhaps the aim was to elevate by mystifying, to encourage the congregation to feel its religion rather than to understand it. I spent many a sermon gazing at these figures and trying to apply my nascent knowledge of Latin to the inscriptions below them. As I stared up, I recognised the stories and since French and Latin share many cognates, putting two and two together was not all that difficult. I owe some of my relative prowess in Latin to the selfless craftsmen who created these windows.

Except for the altarpiece and the stained glass windows, the church has a slightly forbidding feel. Stone steps lead up from the street, the *Grand Rue*, to a pair of massive oak doors. In my days, these were left unlocked all day. With daily morning mass, confessions, the occasional funeral, and frequent visits by parishioners and passers-by seeking solace, a steady stream of the devout passed through those doors even on weekdays. If the church had possessed priceless art, with so many witnesses about, it would have been a difficult place to ransack with impunity.

The church is built on the conventional cross configuration. Along each side of the nave and below each stained glass window are full-size statues of major saints, gazing heavenward as they wobble on their earthly pedestal. Each transept houses a small chapel featuring a more subdued version of the central altarpiece. In my time, demand was brisk and mass was sometimes being said in both chapels even as a major service was underway at the main altar. Dividing the congregation from the choir and its splendid altarpiece is a barrier of black wrought iron. In my days, this divide could be crossed only by men and altar boys, not even by nuns.

At the opposite end, high above the nave, is the organ loft. The organ is the original eighteenth-century instrument, much patched up and tinkered with. Restored and cleaned up, its baroque design now looks almost as effervescent as the altarpiece. Tucked away in strategic spots by the main doors are the confessionals: dark, chilling wooden boxes oozing guilt and fear, with a squeaky door in the centre and purple curtains on each side to shield the penitent from voyeurs and gossipmongers.

In my days, the congregation sat in row upon row of wooden chairs with seats made of straw. These were relatively easy on the *derrière* even if some of the straw broke up into unruly strands that stuck out in unpredictable places and pricked the thighs of young parishioners in short trousers. But the chairs were upscale compared to the rough-hewn pews congregations in neighbouring villages had to endure. Free seating allowed families to cluster together. Only at funerals was decorum restored: the men sat on the left, the women on the right.

One side of the church was bordered by a narrow alleyway where the faithful parked their bikes by day. But as nightfall descended on this discreet spot, it was taken over by an unholy alliance of courting couples and those among the inebriated who could not quite make it to the *pissoir* behind the church.

The *pissoir* stood a few metres from the back door that gave access to the church vestry, the only remnant of the sixteenth-century church the baroque edifice had replaced. It was made of cast iron that had once been a pleasant shade of black but that had been exposed to the rigours of the climate and the miscalculations of the inebriated for so long that its walls were thick with yellowish streaks. A desperate male, especially during an exceptionally long sermon, had no choice but to tiptoe in, take up position, hold his nose with his free hand, and then run out as fast as he could. Female worshippers, I presume, stayed seated with their legs crossed or planned ahead or abstained from fluids for a week or so.

The place was abominable. The town was not rich and funds available for beautification were scarce. But rubbish was collected regularly and disposed of efficiently and the streets and all public buildings were kept clean. The *pissoir* was exceptional because it was a political *pissoir* and the mover and shaker behind municipal *pissoir* policy was Monsieur Pégnerot, our duly elected mayor.

Monsieur Pégnerot was a dapper little man in his fifties who liked to walk the streets of his fief, stopping here and there to gaze upon his handiwork and seeing that it was good, smiled benevolently on his electorate and raised his hat to the more influential among them. Crucially, Monsieur Pégnerot was a staunch *laïc*, a secularist, one of a school of French politicians for whom all issues were framed in terms of the titanic struggle between Church and State. His political affiliation was *radical*, a term roughly equivalent in the eyes of the Catholic hierarchy to the label 'communist' in American politics at the time. Not only was it out of the question that a *radical* mayor worth his salt might favour the Church. It was his solemn duty to do everything in his power to obstruct it at every turn.

This included making access to the church as problematic as possible. Short of taking the law in his own hands and mining the alleyway that ran along it, thereby relinquishing the votes of the amorous and the inebriated in one fell swoop, Monsieur Pégnerot's best option was to make the area at the back of the church so unwholesome, so noxious, so repulsive that only the olfactorily-challenged would brave it on their way to their devotions. The squeamish, Monsieur Pégnerot must have calculated, would turn back and go home or walk into a nearby *café* and order a strong restorative. Being as parsimonious as he was strategically savvy, Monsieur Pégnerot achieved his aim through the simple expedient of expressly forbidding his cleaning crews from going anywhere near the *pissoir* with buckets, mops, and disinfectant, an edict for which the cleaning crews if not the parishioners must have been profoundly grateful.

*

A few nuns played discreet but important roles in the day-to-day life of the parish. A group of them lived and taught at Sainte Anne, the Catholic school where I took my first confident steps on the road to educational under-achievement. Another religious community staffed a small dispensary where the sick could receive free primary care and from where the nuns fanned out on their bikes or on foot each day to tend to the unwell at home for free.

A key member of this selfless group of women was Soeur Marie-Chantal, a substantial lady who went about her errands of mercy with a permanent smile on her face and whose timely ministrations helped to save my youngest sister Marie-Jeanne from almost certain death from diphtheria as a baby. But this being Catholic territory, the church itself had to be staffed by priests and with the seminaries bursting at the seams, there was no shortage of them. The parish never had fewer than four or five. On my frequent visits to the elegant vicarage on urgent altar boy business, the place was jumping with ecclesiastical bustle. Taking care of worldly matters were two greying women, unmarried of course, who served as full-time housekeepers and cooks.

For many years, *primus inter pares* among the priests was Chanoine Bolletand. He was a man of late middle age, confident in his social position, which he understood to be that of spiritual guide to the middle class and up. Most afternoons, once pressing parish matters had been attended to, he went on long walks about town, tipping his ecclesiastical hat to the well-to-do and casting avuncular smiles in every direction like a monarch showering blessings on the multitude. Chanoine Bolletand radiated cheerfulness and optimism. If he was aware that the Catholic Church and the parish in his care in particular faced difficulties, he never allowed this to cloud his disposition.

Though I could not have been more committed to my duties as altar boy, I was a little young to debate theology with so eminent a figure. But in the more tangible matters of liturgy, there was little to investigate. Chanoine Bolletand was a man who knew what he liked and his views could not have been more transparent: he was a staunch traditionalist. Had he been an Anglican, he would have been High Church, and then some. He lived for pageantry. No vestments were too ornate, no music too splendid, no high mass celebrated by as many as three priests and aided by a platoon of altar boys too wasteful of resources. The smell of incense was like food to him. On major church holidays, the main altar heaved with floral displays, the creation of which he supervised personally. Once I was tall enough to reach the electric switch in the vestry that got the church bells going, I was instructed to let the tinkling go on a little longer than required by Church edicts simply because it sounded so joyful. To Chanoine Bolletand, heading the parish of Saint Martin in Lure, Haute-Saône must have seemed like the best of all possible worlds: an intimation in this life of what heaven would surely look, sound, and smell like in the next.

Chanoine Bolletand was a generous man within his means. After late mass on New Year's Day, he gathered his crew of altar boys in the vestry, formally offered his best wishes to us and our families, and then delved into the recesses of his soutane, extracted his wallet, and dispensed *largesse*. At first, I was shocked to learn that priests concerned themselves with money and that they even owned a wallet. But I soon overcame my spiritual concerns and learned to welcome this bounty.

An unfortunate side-effect of Chanoine Bolletand's munificence was that it motivated the venal element, boys from tepidly religious families who donned soutane and surplice only when begged to make up the numbers and usually in the hope of lucre. On New Year's Day, the line of volunteers seemed to go around the church three times. Their mercenary instincts would be punished at the Last Trump, I reasoned. And since these were often the very same boys who had recently got me into trouble with a teacher by launching another riotous prank and blamed it on me, they deserved what was coming to them.

The counterpoint to Chanoine Bolletand's sunny outlook was provided by Abbé Poirier. The most immediately noticeable thing about this priest was that he had a bad leg, probably a prosthesis. Even his heavy soutane could not hide a pronounced limp. He went about his duties around town on a specially adapted bike, with a pedal hinged in such a way that it stayed permanently down and on which he rested his bad leg while he pedalled with his good leg. He even managed to control the bike with one hand while clutching his missal in the other.

A mournful air clouded his face permanently. No one knew or said what misfortune had befallen him earlier in life but like the master he served, Abbé Poirier was a man of sorrow and acquainted with grief. He was also a man of great courage. Lure, Haute-Saône was hardly the high Andes, but there were a few tricky inclines here and there. Abbé Poirier negotiated them all in weather fair or foul as though he were a teenager showing off his new bike. His qualities were also intellectual. He was reputed to be the theological brain behind the parish and according to the *cognoscenti*, he preached a mean sermon.

From about the time I turned twelve, every Sunday morning at 8:00 am sharp, Abbé Poirier and I met at the front gate of the town's gaol opposite the pond that was home to the pair of sharp-beaked swans. His duty was to say mass for the benefit of the inmates, mine was to assist him. The gaol was no ordinary cop shop, housing the night's crop of drunks until they sobered up. It was home to a sizeable group of men convicted of violent assault, armed robbery, even – it was whispered – murder.

On arrival, the priest and I exchanged greetings and propped our bikes against the gaol wall and Abbé Poirier rang the bell. The tinkling of keys was heard within. The small flap in the thick metal door was lifted, a narrow-eyed turnkey took a suspicious look at us, and, deciding that we posed no security risk, unlocked the door with a great flourish of keys held on a ring the size of a steering wheel. We made our way to the tiny chapel deep inside the gaol along sterile hallways through a succession of gates that had to be unlocked and locked again one by one.

Sunday morning mass in the gaol was a sombre affair. Invariably, the chapel was full though whether the worshippers assembled in hope of remission for good behaviour in this life or the next was impossible to tell. The inmates sat in rows in their dark brown uniforms. Abbé Poirier went through the liturgy, I rang my bell at strategic moments, and the inmates intoned the appropriate responses in booming voices and perfect unison, and somewhat incongruously for armed robbers and murderers, in faultless Latin.

The tiny altar was separated from the congregation by a set of thick bars and there was no interaction between the two sides beyond the exchange of the prescribed Latin verses. When it was all over, perhaps because he felt bad about dragging a twelve-year-old into a world so devoid of cheer, the turnkey invariably presented me with a slab of chocolate. In the spirit of Christian charity in which it had been acquired, I shared the chocolate with my siblings after Sunday lunch. The week's disputes were instantly forgotten and I was declared exactly the kind of brother they had always wanted to have as long as I kept getting up at the crack of dawn every Sunday morning, biked over to the gaol, witnessed quiet desperation among the inmates, and biked back, bearing gifts.

Another memorable figure among the priests though for entirely different reasons was Abbé Vergnand. In appearance, he was as favoured by the gods as Abbé Poirier had been penalised. He was tall and elegant, with a full head of black hair. Where Abbé Poirier had the air of one for whom life would always be a struggle, Abbé Vergnand looked confident that it would always be a breeze. Among the more *outré* of his female flock, he was known as *le bel abbé*, the 'handsome priest'. What could have motivated such a good-looking man to take vows of celibacy, they tittered. What a waste!

The answer, it turned out, was that he had not..., at least not quite.

On the positive side of this open-mindedness, Abbé Vergnand was always ready to engage me and my church-going friends in debate over matters of Catholic faith, especially in relation to those religions we had been taught to denounce as mere idolatry. I welcomed the intellectual openness this encouraged. As I saw it, this was a huge improvement on the relentless promotion of a single belief system and the ceaseless denigration of all the others. Today, this approach has become commonplace as the comparative study of religions. But at the time, it was nothing short of *avant-guarde*. Set against the emotional variety of Catholicism favoured by Chanoine Bolletand, the contrast could not have been starker. Sadly, Abbé Vergnand's *penchant* for considering all sides of each question resulted in his undoing because it led him to consider all sides of celibacy too.

Not long after I left town to go to college in Nancy, rumours reached me that Abbé Vergnand had gone a tad beyond his pastoral duties as they pertained to a seventeen-year-old girl still in secondary school. Nor, apparently, was the pair particularly discreet about it. Suspicions were confirmed, I was reliably informed, during a church trip to Rome. With privacy in short supply and a busload of gossipy teenagers alert to everyone's moves, no one in the party could have failed to notice and then report the fact that Abbé Vergnand and the girl had sat together on the bus all the way there and back.

Soon after his return, Abbé Vergnand was summoned by his archbishop. Following traditional Catholic practice in these matters, he was informed that he was not being dismissed from the priesthood but simply transferred to a wretched village close to the episcopal seat in Besançon, where temptations of all kinds would be in short supply and the archbishop and his posse of informers would have little difficulty spotting and then pouncing on any further transgression.

*

As Chanoine Bolletand knew, pre-Vatican Council Catholicism spoke to the heart, not to the head. It combined choreography, music, colour, language in both prose and verse, and carefully controlled audience participation. At its flamboyant best, it was one of the major performing arts of its time. And for sheer spectacle, no event in the Catholic calendar could rival Easter.

At the conclusion of the evening service on Maundy Thursday, or Holy Thursday in Catholic parlance, the church was readied for three days of uncharacteristic sobriety to mark the grisly death of its central figure and remind the faithful that, however indirectly, his demise was their fault.

The altar was stripped of ornaments, purple shrouds were thrown over its baroque opulence as well as the statues of the saints on each side of the nave, and the organ fell silent. As the last parishioner left, the church was plunged into darkness. Next day, the Holy Friday service took place in the fading light of late afternoon, with austere Gregorian chant replacing the magnificence of polyphony. On the Saturday afternoon, a crew of volunteers set to work and built a bonfire on the pavement in front of the main church doors. This was to be the centrepiece in the elaborate staging of the shift from darkness to light, from despair to hope that the Resurrection symbolised. Lengths of leftover timber and bits of broken furniture generously contributed by parishioners were piled high. In the heyday of muscular Catholicism, a brace of heretics or a covey of witches might have been added to the stack to save on fuel. But by then, the Church had moved on. Shortly before the start of the midnight service, the bonfire was drowned in kerosene and set alight as transfixed worshippers watched, with nothing to shield the passing traffic from the soaring flames and swirling cinders. Try getting that scenario past the fire regulators today.

Then the pageantry began. The congregation was invited to enter the darkened church and take their seats. Chanoine Bolletand picked up the heavy Paschal candle that was to spread light where there had been darkness and lit it directly from the bonfire. He then passed it to his second in command, usually Abbé Vergnand, who led the altar boys and the rest of the priests in procession up the steps, through the heavy oak doors, and into the church. As he reached the assigned spot under the organ loft, Abbé Vergnand paused and intoned the first call of *Lumen Christi*. He then repeated the chant twice, each time pitching it a couple of tones higher. The musical device was crude but hugely effective in delivering the welcome message that darkness was at an end and light was dawning. Seasoned altar boys ducked to avoid being scalded by falling blobs of molten wax as Abbé Vergnand lowered the Paschal candle towards the much smaller candle held by the member of the congregation standing closest to the aisle on each side of the nave. Audience participation did the rest. Candle lit candle, first along each row and then forward towards the choir until the church was ablaze with light. At this point, a trusted altar boy with in-depth understanding of church wiring went into the vestry and switched on every light in the building. The sudden re-emergence of organ and church bells added sound to colour. The stage managing was impeccable, the display compelling, and the effect deeply moving.

*

For sheer spectacle and audience participation, only one other event in the Catholic calendar could give Easter a run for its money: the yearly celebration of *Communion Solennelle*.

Around the age of thirteen, Catholic boys and girls were deemed to have reached a sufficient level of maturity to be capable of making an informed choice of religious faith and a life-long commitment to it in full cognisance of the theological niceties this implied. All that remained was for them to proclaim their choice before the world and seal the bargain by receiving communion.

Later in my teens and increasingly influenced by the comparative study of religions promoted by Abbé Vergnand, it dawned on me that the premise was absurd. In putting teenagers through this pretence of choice based on reflection, the Catholic Church was being about as fair and balanced as Fox News is today. Clearly, this was about control. Professing no religion was unthinkable or regarded as an unmistakable sign that the offender was a communist, perhaps even a *radical*. Hinduism and Buddhism were off the radar and the competing religions of the book were routinely ignored if not demonised or simply ridiculed. Protestantism was close enough to Catholicism for its adherents to be pitied rather than censored for having made a wrong theological turn. Islam was considered a misfortune that afflicted darker-skinned residents of North-African French colonies who longed to be relieved of it by French missionaries. And as everyone knew, the Jews had put Jesus to death. In practice, religious doctrine was Catholic doctrine, with the threat of excommunication and everlasting torments keeping the intellectually adventurous in line. In brief, there was no choice.

On the appointed Sunday, a date common to all churches in the archdiocese of Besançon, after painstaking rehearsal, several dozen bewildered-looking adolescents shuffled into the church in two neat columns, ready to take their vows of life-long Catholic observance before God and the Church. In large part, the *Communion Solennelle* was a rite of passage, a chance to be inducted into the ways of grown-ups and to hear the club rules spelt out. The public drama was there to make sure that the rules stuck.

For the communicants, the raiment of the day consisted of a commendably unisex white robe of a monastic design, supplemented by a rough rope around the waist and a plain wooden cross around the neck. The choice of colour was no accident: it symbolised purity. Exactly what the wearers were expected to be pure about at the age of thirteen was unspecified. But since the ceremony coincided with the onset of puberty, the subtext must have been self-abuse avoidance for the boys and for the girls the perpetuation of that blessed state that, since for the majority immaculate conception was a long shot, would end only on the first night of a Catholic marriage. As with the edict that priests remain celibate, despite occasional signs such as the *Claire et Philippe* primer that enlightenment might be dawning, the age-old Catholic refusal to deal with sexuality and an obsession with virginity permeated many of the Church's practices, including *Communion Solennelle*.

The yearly *Communion Solennelle* was a major event in the parish calendar. Support for the young

217

communicants in their hour of spiritual need came from every family member able-bodied enough to squeeze into a car or board a train. For a couple of days each year, traffic in the *Grand Rue* increased noticeably and exotic car number plates were seen everywhere. Cramming the multitude into the church was a logistical challenge. Family members, close relatives, and assorted well-wishers filled the aisles, even the space at the back by the gloomy confessionals under the organ loft. Others pushed against the wrought iron barrier that divided the nave from the choir like rock fans pressing against the stage at a concert.

At the conclusion of the service, the newly-inducted communicants stood outside to have their photos taken and the congregation dispersed. Lunch beckoned. But by late afternoon, everyone was back for vespers, the crowd now swollen with the addition of stragglers, relatives from distant outposts who had underestimated travelling time, missed a train connection, or suffered a flat tyre and had missed the main event.

Post-prandial proceedings were shorter and more light-hearted. Patting their full stomachs and mollified by generous transfusions of rare vintages, members of the congregation gave the distinct impression that they were beginning to discern the lighter side to Catholicism. Jollity was in the air. In a social rather than religious sense, *Communion Solennelle* was a celebration of French provincial life and of the role the extended family played on major occasions in the calendar.

Today, the Catholic Church is withering and mass is often said if a priest can be found to say it at all before congregations of half a dozen or less. Few in post-religious France will bemoan this loss of Catholic control. But the festive spirit and the chance for families to re-unite these occasions created will be missed.

If the *Communion Solennelle* ritual was conceived and executed on a grand scale, christenings were discreet, private affairs squeezed between the end of Sunday high mass and lunch. As soon as the service was over, one of the priests, flanked by an altar boy or two, stayed behind to welcome the beaming parents, the grouchy new-born, and the godfather and godmother by the baptismal font just inside the church doors. Although the ceremony was brief, the star of the show invariably failed to get into the spirit of things and screamed blue murder from start to finish. For altar boys, the main attraction of these events was the unwritten rule that the proud godfather should mark the occasion by producing his wallet and bestowing alms. And as always when cash was involved, this led to improbity. Once again, the lure of lucre was such that although the duties of the altar boys were light, the chance to add to my savings had to be shared with at least one of the very same fair-weather friends who disgraced themselves every New Year's Day by circling Chanoine Bolletand's wallet like hyenas at the kill and who volunteered in droves for the honour of assisting in the induction of a new-born into the Catholic faith. Some altar boys have no shame!

Perversely, Catholic death rituals were as elaborate as birth rituals were furtive. Despite the celebration of hope and redemption so much in evidence at Easter, it could not have been more transparent which, of life or death, was more central to the Catholic mindset.

Catholic funerals were wonders of choreographed morbidity. Regardless of whether the reaper's victim had breathed his last in his own bed or in the local hospital, his remains were displayed in the family living room for all to see and commiserate over. The coffin rested on trestles, mourners stood with heads bowed, and speech turned to murmur. In the kitchen, the women toiled to keep the living fed. About an hour before the church service was due to begin, priest and altar boy, both turned out in black soutane and white surplice, set off on foot from the church in the direction of the house. Even when school was in recess, altar boys were in short supply for these melancholy occasions. Respect for the departed precluded a monetary dimension and with no prospect of a post-burial tip only the selfless volunteered. An additional requirement was that the altar boy be the hardy type. Apart from having to deal emotionally with the gloom, trudging through the streets in all weathers holding a heavy crucifix aloft was not for the faint-hearted. Predictably, the fair-weather contingent cited prior engagements, which left the field wide open to weatherproof individuals such as myself.

Once the appropriate rites had been read out by the priest, the coffin lid was lowered into position and nailed down to a background of weeping and blowing of noses. The coffin was carried out of the house and lifted onto the hearse and the *cortège* set off through the streets towards the church, altar boy in the lead. Traffic gave way. Even known secularists going about their Satanic errands stopped in their tracks, held their hat to their chest, and bowed. Death was indiscriminate and reaped kings and beggars, pillars of the Church and fire-breathing members of the *radical* party with equal fervour so respect was due to all.

Once the coffin had been lifted out of the hearse and carried into the church, a funeral service of variable length and elaborateness began. For the moneyed classes, nothing short of a full sung mass would do. But for the majority, a short service was considered more appropriate. On some occasions, the mourners were visibly so unfamiliar with church procedures, when to sit or stand or how and in what sequence to cross themselves, that they looked around for role models among the recognisably pious, who presumably had it pat and could be relied upon to provide a blueprint. Clearly, on these occasions, the decision to go for a church service had flowed from social pressure, a belief that paying lip service to Catholic rites was a prudent bet on the nature of the hereafter, or a combination of both.

At the end of the service, Monsieur Marchand, the town's undertaker, a known freethinker and suspected philanderer to boot, put on his most unctuous face, perfunctorily sprinkled holy water over the coffin, and invited the mourners to file out of the church. The coffin was reloaded onto the hearse and the stately procession resumed along the *Grand Rue* and up the hill to the town's cemetery. By then, the crowd of mourners had thinned as interment was felt to be a private event so a much more intimate gathering witnessed the final rites being performed and the coffin being lowered into the cold earth.

But the drama did not always end there. Even in death, there was no escaping the perennial struggle between the Church and the forces of secularism. In some cases, the fault line divided the bereaved family, which controlled the event and had opted for a religious ceremony, and close friends and colleagues who knew full well that the deceased had hated the Church and all it stood for with a vengeance. Although power resided with the family, dissenters had one last chance to publicise their views along with those of the deceased and snub their noses at what they saw as hypocritical posturing. The method was simple but highly symbolic and deliberately public. Once the coffin had been lowered into the grave, one of the mourners with secular leanings pulled a red carnation out of one of the wreaths and tossed it into the grave. As everyone knew, red signified a left-wing and therefore anti-clerical bend, perhaps even communist sympathies. The family glowered, friends in the know repressed a smile, the priest looked heavenward, and the altar boy watched and wondered at the malice in men's souls.

Like life itself, funeral services varied in pathos. Luckily, I was spared the traumatic experience of officiating at a child's funeral and having to get my young head around the perverse rationalisations that attempt to reconcile such tragedy with a supposedly loving god who seems to take pleasure in inflicting extreme pain while keeping believers in the dark over his motives for such cruelty. But with the Algerian war in full swing, even a community as small as Lure, Haute-Saône occasionally had to deal with the death of one of its sons in that vicious and pointless conflict. On these occasions, there was no doubting that the tears were genuine. No amount of suavity on Monsieur Marchand's part, not even Abbé Poirier's legendary rhetorical skills, seemed to be able to reconcile the bereaved to their loss and to the ghastly injustice of it all. Perhaps the devout and the secularists had more in common than they realised. French politicians may be less capricious than this cruel god but they were just as callous.

*

Given how much time I spent in the company of priests, I should be in a position to divulge outrageous tales of sacerdotal misbehaviour, especially in relation to altar boys. In fact, I have none to report. True, I was hardly a picture of juvenile pulchritude but such design flaws on nature's part have never been known to give pause to a lecherous cleric. How the priests I served dealt with the self-inflicted rigours of celibacy, I cannot say except for the one case that led to Abbé Vergnand being banished to the outback, where adventurous schoolgirls would be few and far between. What I can say is that the priests invariably treated me with courtesy and gratitude for the help I gave them in carrying out their duties.

That said, even a place as sedate as Lure, Haute-Saône was not entirely free of sexual chicanery. Not long after the affair of the heart involving Abbé Vergnand and the schoolgirl surfaced, an even greater scandal erupted. Though the commotion had ramifications for the parish, it did not in fact involve a priest but a well-known figure in the town, Monsieur Touriez, a highly respected individual and devoted family man. In the interest of lawsuit avoidance, I will not dwell on what Monsieur Touriez did for a living. Suffice it to say that it had to do with helping to keep the French State solvent by taking a periodic look at the content of citizens' wallets and relieving them of any surplus.

On Holy Thursday, Christians of many hues celebrate the last supper Jesus shared with his disciples before being put to death. The ceremony includes the ritual washing of the feet, a re-enactment of Jesus' display of humility and affection towards his followers. Each year in the parish of Saint Martin, twelve good men and true and of unquestioned piety were invited to represent the disciples. Clad in white robes, they took their seats in two facing rows in front of the altar. This was a major occasion, so Chanoine Bolletand officiated. Resplendent in his ceremonial vestments, he went down on his elderly knees, dipped a white cloth in tepid water, dabbed and then kissed the first pair of feet in the line, and then scooted sideways to face the next disciple impersonator. Not a man to make do with one priest when two would do, he insisted on being shadowed. Obviously, Abbé Poirier, with his bad leg, could not be expected to stoop to floor level and rise again twelve symbolic dabbings later so Abbé Vergnand or one of the other priests in residence assisted. For an altar boy, to be chosen for the role of carrier of the basin or custodian of the cloth was the ultimate accolade. The day I heard I had been tapped for the part, I knew I had made it at last.

Evidently, the supply of good men and true and of unquestioned piety must have been finite in Lure, Haute-Saône because year after year, the chorus line remained exactly the same. Even the seating arrangement was fixed and the event never had to be rehearsed. The identities of these men have faded from memory, except for two. One was André, the rosary-telling adult son of our reviled landlady Madame Brossard. The other was Monsieur Touriez, the respected civil servant with a professional interest in other people's stash.

Curiously, given that his professional activities must have involved confronting evasiveness and downright mendacity on a daily basis, Monsieur Touriez was the most jovial person I had ever met. In disposition, he came in somewhere between sunny and ebullient. He did not just smile, he laughed. Framing the rictus was a crimson face crowned with a shock of unruly white hair. His eyes twinkled with *joie de vivre* and the anticipation of a chance to slip in a *bon mot* and have his audience in stitches. Being in church was no impediment. On Holy Thursday, as he donned his white robe in the vestry, he was in cracking form, ready to entertain. This was a solemn occasion, but Monsieur

Touriez did not do solemnity. For him, there was no time like the present for having a laugh.

His *modus operandi* during the ceremony was to sit stiffly on his chair and replace the Cheshire cat grin with an air of profound devotion. To us altar boys, this was unnerving. Monsieur Touriez did not do devotion any more than he did solemnity. The comedian in him must be up to something. When it was his turn to have his feet dabbed and Chanoine Bolletand turned his attention to his proffered extremities, he started twiddling his toes until the altar boy in charge of the water basin broke into uncontrollable giggles and the rest of his colleagues dissolved into hysterics. How the priests kept a straight face was a mystery. Perhaps they teach classes in dealing with buffoonery in the workplace in Catholic seminaries.

Though already a grandfather, Monsieur Touriez was a man of boundless energy, who extended goodwill in all directions. One of these involved the local troupe of Boy Scouts, which he and other volunteers took on sorties into the woods and on occasional camping trips. This was a closed book to me. The world of merit badges and colour-coded scarves was out of bounds because my father detested anything that smacked of regimentation and especially of the unholy alliance between regimentation and piety. But these expeditions were wildly popular and on each occasion, Monsieur Touriez was reportedly the life and soul of the party.

One day, out of the blue, the citizenry of Lure, Haute-Saône was rocked by the revelation that Monsieur Touriez was being investigated by the local constabulary for taking his pastoral responsibilities a tad too far and showing undue interest in some of the scouts in his charge. The good burghers of Lure, Haute-Saône had become resigned to Monsieur Touriez taking an interest in the content of their wallets. But they had not expected him to pay equally close attention to the content of their sons' y-fronts.

To no one's surprise, the affair was quickly hushed. Even good men and true, pillars of the Church, and doting grandfathers erred on occasion. To deny and then suppress under guise of forgiveness was the standard Church response and to allow the machinery of government to whirr on as normal was the standard State response. In fact, mastery of the art of ignoring anything that might upset the apple cart was a talent common to both. In effect, the two were all of a piece: dogmatic, bossy, obsessed with uniformity, prone to denial, and largely unaccountable. They were mirror images of each other, each recognising its own failings in the other and denouncing these publicly and loudly the better to conceal their own version of them. Ostensibly, the two were sworn enemies but each depended on the representation of the other as evil to justify and perpetuate its own power. Choosing between the two was pointless. Luckily, there was a way out, namely leaving this sinister pair to their mutually reinforcing, ritualistic skirmishes, which I did at the earliest opportunity.

*

Even before Abbé Vergnand's introduction to the merits of theological competition, I knew that Catholicism did not have it all its own way. In Lure, Haute-Saône just as anywhere else in France, it was impossible to ignore the perennial rivalry between the Catholic Church and secularism, of which the vile *pissoir* behind the parish church was the most obvious symbol. But religious alternatives had a hard time of it. If it was mentioned at all, Islam was dismissed as an aberration or as geographically too remote to warrant

226

consideration. Modern industries and services were coming to the region slowly and the required workforce could easily be recruited from long-term residents who were being shed by dying trades, and substantial immigration from North Africa and Turkey was not yet under way. If there was a Muslim community, it was all but invisible.

Jews had a small presence mostly among business owners or civil servants parachuted into Lure, Haute-Saône from far-flung parts of the country. But there was no synagogue. Jewish rituals were presumably observed in some homes but public observance would have involved a drive or a train journey to the nearest place of Jewish worship, thirty kilometres away in Belfort, a trip most Jews seemed unwilling to undertake each week. There had been synagogues in some local towns but all had closed — or been forced to close — by the middle of the nineteenth century. Obviously, World War II had done nothing to revive their fortunes. With minimal Jewish numbers came minimal anti-Semitism, at least on the surface. Perhaps the country was in a state of amnesia over French collusion in the rounding up and deportation of Jews during World War II and the topic was taboo. Or the small town context, in which everyone met almost everyone else on a daily basis made it difficult to single out any one minority for special treatment, whether of the considerate or the antagonistic kind. In practice, what little religious counterbalance to Catholicism there was came from Protestantism.

During my last two years of secondary school, I came to know Antoine, the son of the minister who had just been posted to the town to attend to the small Protestant community. Antoine was tall and lanky. Like Washington Irving's Ichabod Crane, his appearance suggested 'the genius of famine descended upon the earth'. But he made up in intellectual heft what he lacked in brawn. He was a consummate debater and his tastes were eclectic. Every topic was game: contemporary politics, social issues, Vietnam and Algeria, and of course religion. At an age when grappling with abstractions was beginning to look more rewarding than devising the next prank or listening to the *braggadocio* of my more frivolous friends about their alleged female conquests, I was ready for friendship with someone of Antoine's calibre.

Antoine and his family lived next to the Protestant church his father served, a short walk from the Catholic church, in fact, or a slighter longer one for those wishing to bypass the stinking *pissoir*. Sundays were busy days for both persuasions. But on weekdays, if classes ended early or getting home a little later than usual was not likely to lead to confrontation, I sometimes joined Antoine in his family's living room, where I was warmly welcomed by his parents and where I had a chance to gaze at his equally tall and lanky but hauntingly beautiful younger sister Monique.

When they were not busy, Antoine's parents and on occasion Monique joined in the conversation. When they did, there was no discernible change in Antoine's attitude. There was no sense that his parents' participation was constraining the discussion or that Antoine or Monique were being patronised. Clearly, debating major issues *en famille* was entirely natural to them. Even his father's professional and spiritual status did not permit him to pontificate — so to speak. This was a debate of peers. And the fact that equal treatment was extended to a daughter and sister was especially eye-opening. In more familiar worlds, girls could be beautiful or feisty but not both. In Antoine's family, those restrictions were for the birds.

To be fair, my own family was no stranger to

debate. But the range of topics was narrower, the tone more didactic, and female participation more limited. If all Protestant families were like Antoine's, I mused, there was a lot to be said for Protestantism. Perhaps I should build on the intellectual foundations laid by Abbé Vergnand, explore, and fearlessly critique the Catholic certainties I had internalised. Yet throughout the two years of my friendship with Antoine, I did not once set foot inside his father's church. On several occasions, I had seen my grandmother tying herself in knots at the thought of attending the funeral of a Protestant friend or even sending her condolences in writing and then rushing to confession as fast as her arthritic legs could carry her. And despite the growing sense of intellectual release I was experiencing, the denunciations of alternative viewpoints as the work of the devil and threats of excommunication in this world and eternal damnation in the next were still ringing in my ears.

As a child, being not only a witness but a participant in Catholic pageantry was enchanting. But leaving the fairy tales behind and eventually joining the ranks of the rational was hard work. The trouble with religions is that they must keep the faithful in a perpetual state of infantilism because this is key to ensuring the perpetuation of irrational beliefs. The effect is powerful and very long-lasting. For those seeking liberation, it can take a lifetime to shake off an ideology as tenacious as it is delusional.

CHAPTER TEN: SAY CHEESE

It's so beautifully arranged on the plate, you know someone's fingers have been all over it.

Julia Child (1912-2004)

There cannot be much about France and food that has not already been said. So before I contribute my two *centimes'* worth, let me make an important distinction clear. There is French food and there is food in France. And on reflection, this distinction neatly parallels the one between French kissing and kissing in France because both French food and French kissing can easily be idealised to the point where it becomes very difficult to tell reality from fantasy. Let me explain.

In general terms, French kissing is regarded as a good thing by those who give it a shot, in France or anywhere else. But even seasoned practitioners have off days and the experience can go from volcanic to anaemic from one attempt to the next. French kissing is invariably volcanic only in the fantasies of those who for one reason or another do not avail themselves of the option. Similarly, French food can range from superb to deadly dull depending on circumstances. French food is invariably superb only in the fantasies of those who wish they could afford to eat in places that serve tiny helpings of underdone meat parked next to a dollop of some mushy vegetable on an oversized octagonal plate brought to the table with a theatrical flourish.

Now consider kissing in France. Today, even in France, shower gels and deodorants have largely replaced *eau de cologne* as the primary means of making oneself fragrant and welcome in polite society, at least among the younger generation. But this has also had the unfortunate side-effect of turning kissing into a free-for-all and the obligatory method for greeting friends and utter strangers alike upon meeting and again at parting. This is hard work, especially for the hapless residents of Brittany where the standard requirement is for no fewer than four consecutive kisses. In recent years, the practice has even crossed borders so that it is now a common sight to see politicians known for their loathing of each other kissing like fast friends as the television cameras roll. But overall, it would be churlish to deny that kissing one and all indiscriminately is a vast improvement on yesteryear's moist handshakes, stiff bows, and starchy how-do-you-dos.

In less expansive days, kissing in France was restricted to family members. The process involved getting uncomfortably close to relatives with a questionable record of personal hygiene, including some – mostly though not exclusively males – with views on shaving that favoured infrequency. To children, kissing in France was a chore, something that had to be done to oil the wheels of social intercourse and avoid getting smacked. By comparison, the modern French kiss-fest is a happy development, but it has very little to do with French kissing.

And so it is with French food. Historically, for many outsiders, French food was little more than a concept and a negative one at that: horse and rabbit meat, frog's legs, tripe, garlic, rich sauces, smelly cheeses, that sort of thing. Even if for their sins the outsiders happened to find themselves in France, French food was best avoided. This belief long influenced the eating habits of (among others) those British families glimpsed as they picnicked by the side of poplar-lined French roads in summers of yore. Just like the campers they travelled in and the tea pots they refreshed themselves from, the food they ate could not have been less French. They loved the setting but they trusted French food no further than they trusted the French themselves so they filled their campers with tins of baked beans and bottles of HP sauce and lived on that for weeks. They would have nothing to do with French food. For a privileged minority, French food represented the sublime, the ideal. For the rest, it was detestable.

A substantial contingent of foreign admirers of French food has long consisted of those whose gastronomic proclivities are influenced primarily by nostalgia. This includes generations of visiting romantics with fond memories of breaking bread with a lover on a park bench after a *nuit de passion* in a one-star hotel in Montmartre followed in the morning by a trip to the *épicerie*. But is it the *baguette*, the *saucisson*, the *Côtes du Rhône*, or even the verdant setting or simply the afterglow of the *nuit de passion* that led to the idealisation of French food in the lovers' minds? As always with rigorous investigation, it is fiendishly difficult to disentangle the variables.

For many, whether French or otherwise, the harsh reality is that just as with kissing in France, the daily experience of food in France often falls short of the fantasy. True, compared to Scottish or Russian food, to name but two, French food is more than palatable. But compared to the exuberant offerings available on every street corner in Mexico, India, or Thailand, French food can be a little dull and all the more disappointing for generating such high expectations among diners and so much pretentious nonsense in the output of food critics.

In day-to-day practice, except for those who can afford to dispatch a *domestique* to the *boulangerie* around the corner at the crack of dawn, the smell of a fragrant *croissant* wafting into the bedroom along with the *café au lait* is a fantasy. Similarly, lunch is rarely the fabled three-hour food-fest washed down by a selection of vintages precisely calibrated to match each course. All too often, lunch consists of a slab of leathery steak, a couple of spoonfuls of some pulped vegetable, a green salad tossed in any dressing as long as it is *vinaigrette*, the same three runny cheeses that appeared on the table every day that week, and finally fruit provided the diner is partial to apples, pears, and perhaps oranges. Reasonably healthy, I concede, but not exactly *gastronomique*, let alone innovative.

Unless I missed it, nothing much seems to have changed in this respect. Some may like it hot, but not the French. According to French culinary scripture, salt and pepper are good for you but most herbs and all spices are best left to foreigners, preferably in their own countries. Add to that the unshakeable belief, shared in equal measure by the populace, the elite, and the media and given regular boosts by fawning foreigners convinced of the inherent peerlessness of French food, and the result of this culinary *hauteur* and reluctance to be inspired and refreshed by outsiders is – *quelle horreur!* – cultural invasion. Today, French *cuisine* has left itself wide open to nimble providers who offer something French tradition has never condescended to concern itself with, namely a sharper focus on consumers than on providers and the readiness to adapt to changing lifestyles. Step forward McDonald's, or *Macdo* as the French call the franchise, and its hugely successful expansion across France in recent years. Had it not been so self-absorbed and self-satisfied, French *cuisine* would have seen it coming and responded accordingly.

*

In a family consisting of six children, two parents, and a grandmother, all needing to be fed on a schoolteacher's salary, a combination of thrift and culinary flair was key. Luckily, my mother possessed both in abundance.

With the very first supermarket making its appearance in Lure, Haute-Saône only the year I left to go to college, the diet of my childhood was dictated in large part by market day. Each Tuesday morning, itinerant merchants converged on the town and set up their stalls on what had been the fairground. The cattle market was long gone and the modern market included most of the products available in the town's shops, only at lower prices: food, clothing and shoes, electrical appliances, tools, and all manner of household goods. The stalls were set up on either side of a long central path. At peak trading hours, it took children an eternity to get from one end of this crowded arrangement to the other in part as a result of protracted contemplations of the displays of plastic toys that lined the route.

Every Tuesday morning, soon after dispatching the last of her children to school, my mother gathered her shopping bags, hopped on her bike, and headed for the market. She patronised mainly the food stalls, where over the years she had developed friendly relations with the vendors. At stall after stall, she filled her bags and then carried them over to the stall where she bought her fruit. The vendors were a friendly couple from a nearby village who had earned a reputation for two rare qualities in those of their calling. One was a disdain for the time-honoured practice of placing their best fruit at the front of the display and serving the customers from the wizened rejects at the back. The other was their ability to spot really ripe fruit, especially melons. They rarely missed and their trustworthiness and expertise were rewarded with my mother's repeat business.

Another advantage of the warm relations between my mother and this couple was that they acted as custodians of her purchases. With a large family to feed for a week, she had far too many heavy bags to carry home on her bike so she left them at the back of the fruit stall for later collection. For the rest of the family, the Tuesday market routine involved my father, who normally walked to work and back, getting the car out, picking us up as we came out of our classes, driving over to the market, and parking as close to the fruit stall as possible. Our orders were to jump out, collect the bags, lift them into the back of the car, and jump in with a glowing sense of mission accomplished and the anticipation of a juicy peach or a slice of ripe melon for dessert.

*

By tradition, the Tuesday lunchtime treat was horse meat. No butcher in town sold this delicacy, at least not openly. But one butcher in the market did and Tuesday lunch invariably featured ground horse meat cooked much like beef burgers but served without buns. Who knows what overworked equine wretch we were helping to recycle, but my siblings and I could not get enough of the stuff. One thing that cannot be said of horse meat is that it tastes just like chicken. It is as pungent as lamb, but in consistency and chewiness, it is closer to coarse ground beef. Once minced, shaped into a patty and fried on both sides until the centre is cooked and the last sign that it was once animal muscle has gone, it looks, smells, and tastes very much like the low-quality offerings of one of the less reputable hamburger chains. But somehow, somewhere, my siblings and I had picked up the information that horse meat was considered *infra dig* by discerning diners so we kept our tastes to ourselves in case some of our classmates were also privy to this information and decided to use it against us in the interest of hilarity.

Another immutable practice was the weekly appearance on the lunch table of fish, this time on Fridays. One of many issues on which Catholic doctrine was somewhat conflicted was the role of fish in its rituals. Second only to the cross, the fish is a major symbol of Christian belief, having initially functioned as a clue to mutual recognition at a time when the nascent faith was actively persecuted and coming out as a follower of this bizarre cult could mean death. More recently, the oblong shape of the symbol has been put to use by those who see value in reducing an entire belief system to the single word 'Jesus', fitting it inside the outline of a fish, and displaying the result on the back of cars and trucks, a fact that has not escaped those Americans who love Jesus as much as they love their automobiles – and that is a lot of Americans!

The problem for the Catholic Church was that the uplifting symbolism of the fish had to be reconciled with the fact that Friday was the day when Jesus was crucified, and it was the duty of the Church to make sure that the faithful felt eternally guilty about this deplorable turn of events. In other words, they had to suffer. And a good way for the Church to generate a lot of soul-cleansing, guilt-assuaging suffering was to mandate the consumption of the nastiest, trickiest, smelliest food it could think of, namely fish. So we suffered. How we suffered! If God has not forgiven humanity or at least my siblings and I by now, I cannot imagine what will swing it.

Fish was unpopular not only because of the treacherous bones and the slimy skin but especially because of the foul smell. Fish was purchased and brought home in shallow wooden boxes in which it languished unappetisingly in what was left of the ice in which it had travelled the length and breadth of the

236

country to get to eastern France from the nearest fishing port. What reached market in Lure, Haute-Saône and eventually our Friday lunch plates was not exactly fresh, to say the least. My siblings and I dreaded Fridays because we dreaded the fish Fridays brought into our diet. My mother and grandmother, both steeped in Catholicism from youth, ate their fish dutifully if not enthusiastically, as did my father, who perhaps because of the relatively recent deprivations he had suffered as a POW, was happy to eat almost anything. But we children put up fierce though futile resistance.

As soon as the fish appeared on the table, the whining started. When that failed, we tried pleading. We pledged irreproachable future behaviour in return for being allowed to pass on the fish. When it became clear that our entreaties were falling on deaf parental ears, we switched to pathos. Tears were shed that streamed down our cheeks and cascaded into the fish. But the torrent had no more effect on my parents than any of the strategies we had tried in succession. The combination of Catholic doctrine and family law was inflexible. The fish would have to be eaten. So it was, Friday after Friday. We hated fish. We hated Fridays. I suspect some of us hated Catholic doctrine too, but that would have been between ourselves and our confessor.

*

Our diet was as varied as my mother could make it in the circumstances. But children like routines so innovation was not expected. We ate meat every day but only at lunchtime. Dishes followed each other in an immutable sequence: starter, vegetables, meat, salad, cheese, and dessert. Vegetables and meat were served as separate dishes, never jointly. Permutations in the

237

sequence or a degree of experimentation, serving meat and vegetables together, for example, or reversing the salad-cheese sequence or even combining the two was not so much prohibited as simply unimaginable.

Of our three daily meals, breakfast was the least varied. It consisted of a thick slice of the previous day's *baguette* made palatable by a generous coating of margarine. Cereal was unheard of. The breakfast drink was hot milk served in a bowl held cupped in both hands. To the milk were added sugar and a teaspoonful of chicory, a coffee substitute that harked back to the shortages of World War II. Chicory also performed an important function as a marker of maturity because the breakfast drink of the younger members of the family consisted of milk and sugar only. Chicory also had the advantage of not adding the effect of caffeine to schoolchildren's natural effervescence and inability to focus. As French tradition required, the slice of bread was dunked into the hot milk, which left yellowish pools of melted margarine floating on the surface. Endless entertainment sadly accompanied by stern reminders that we would be late for school could be derived from blowing the fatty pools around the surface of the milk and rearranging them in infinitely varied patterns.

At lunchtime, an enduring family favourite was spinach. The fact that so many modern children seemed to loathe spinach suggests that their national *cuisine* has yet to crack the subtle art of turning this rough greenery into a mouth-watering delicacy. True, looking at spinach puréed into submission by a French cook, it is hard not to notice an uncanny resemblance with fresh cow pats. But perked up with a little horse meat gravy and some grated *gruyère*, it is a dish fit for a king. Most vegetables emerging from a French kitchen amount to little more than baby food. But few children enjoy choking on stringy beans or pulling strands of celery from between their teeth. For them, the mushier the better.

The meat dish was often pork in the form of sausages (another favourite) but never lamb, which my parents detested. Less popular than pork though not nearly as penitential as fish were the inexpensive cuts of chewy beef that reached the table in stews.

Salad was almost always lettuce, with minor variants in season. But variation never extended to the dressing, in our home or anywhere else, as far as I could tell. From occasional visits to the homes of relatives, I quickly learned that, just as in my family, the canonical salad dressing must consist of the same five ingredients: oil, vinegar, mustard, pepper, and salt, in set proportions and regardless of taste or circumstances.

All of us loved cheese: the fattier the better. A concession to local taste was the presence on the table of *cancoillotte*, a runny, almost liquid cheese specific to eastern France, which is scooped out of a pot with a large spoon. To me, in fragrance and consistency, *cancoillotte* suggests last week's *camembert* left to ripen in the midday sun and then diluted with superglue. It is an acquired taste. Most of the family gave the stuff a wide berth but my brother Pierre practically lived on it and still does. Importantly, the cheese was the one part of the meal where a degree of choice was permitted. Everyone had to eat some cheese but there was always a small selection so individual taste could be accommodated. In all other areas, we all ate what everyone else ate. And individual preferences certainly did not extend to how much we ate. We ate what was on our plate: all of it. Break that rule and you got none of what came next, including dessert. The simple idea, unfortunately slipping away in this consumer age, was that food was precious and should never be wasted or thrown away.

A positive aspect of this practice was that it forced us from a young age to gauge how hungry we were and discouraged us from asking for more than we could reasonably eat. If we had underestimated our potential and more was available, we could always ask for a little extra. But overestimating was costly since every last morsel on our plate had to be eaten. Luckily for my parents, we were kept in line by the ghastly prospect of having to spend the rest of the meal staring at our half-eaten stew or crying into our fish while the rest of the family were tucking into dessert.

Even today, the habit of eating every last *soupçon* of food on my plate can land me in diplomatic trouble. On the rare occasions I am invited to dine at the rich man's table, I have to remind myself that leaving nothing at all on my plate signals to my host that I enjoyed the food but that I have room for more. So more will immediately be offered if it is available. But if not, I will have embarrassed my host by suggesting that I was underfed. To this day, when I dine in style, I have to remember, however reluctantly, to leave a little pile of something perfectly edible on the side of my plate. Perhaps the rich man's *majordomo* keeps a pig at the back of his master's mansion to feed all those leftovers to.

*

Long before I learned to send uneaten food back to the the rich man's kitchens against my better judgment, my family and I ate a largely standard French diet. A central component of every meal was bread: 'God's food', as my grandmother called it. By tradition, the *baguette* was sliced up by my father in the kitchen and brought to the centre of the table in a small wicker basket. By default, one slice was placed next to each plate and more could always be requested. In fact, not requiring more bread was considered somewhat deviant and pressure was applied early to encourage consumption. Bread fulfilled two simultaneous functions: one was to fill up the hungry on the cheap. The other was that in large families at least in which dishwashing was a major logistical concern and had to be kept manageable, it allowed all of us to ready our plate for the next dish so that at the end of the meal only one plate per family member went back to the kitchen as opposed to four or five.

For the uninitiated, learning this detergent-saving technique requires careful observation and assiduous practice. Each diner breaks off a small chunk of bread from his assigned slice, munches on part of it, and then uses what is left to push a small amount of food onto the fork in the time-honoured lower-middle-class manner. The diner then chews on some more of the bread, pushes some more food onto the fork, and when all the munching, pushing, and eating is done he uses what is left of the bread to mop up all traces of food left on the plate. Once the knack has been acquired, the plate is so clean at the end of each course that it could almost be put away unwashed in readiness for the next meal. In my family, even dessert was served on the plate that had just played host to the meat-vegetable-salad-cheese sequence.

Dessert was light. On most days, it consisted of fruit, usually apples or pears and in season grapes or perhaps strawberries or plums. Cherries were a huge hit with us children because eating them involved digging around in the dish for pairs joined up at the stalk. Lucky finds were immediately and loudly publicised and turned into priceless jewellery that we wore as earrings regardless of gender. My parents did not normally allow food to be toyed with but this was a scene they found entertaining so an exception was made. Apart from oranges and bananas, no exotic fruit was ever seen in the house. It would be many years before I had my first taste of fresh pineapple let alone mango or papaya. Out of season, some of the fruit we ate came out of a tin. Lower-quality fruit could be cooked and stewed pears and especially stewed prunes came close to fish in the penitential stakes.

The universal drink was *kefir*, which my father saw as a health drink and made himself. This is a slightly sour concoction made not from fermented milk as is the case in the drink's birthplace in the Caucasus but from figs. For my father but never anyone else, a post-lunch ritual consisted of a glass of wine: always one, never more and always red, never white. Once we were through with the cheese, my father got up, went to the kitchen, got the coffee going, and returned with the bottle of *vin ordinaire*. A bottle lasted about a week. For the grown-ups, this was followed by coffee, which my father drank boiling hot and in one gulp. No one ever fathomed how he did it.

Dinner was a modest affair, invariably starting with soup regardless of weather conditions. Piping hot soup is a treat in winter but an ordeal in summer, but as always, the option to pass was not available. This was often followed by pasta or rice jazzed up with a generous squirt of tomato concentrate from a tube. Everyone in the family liked pasta and rice, but for us children, the squirting was the best part. No meat or cheese was served and the meal usually ended with a slice of homemade cake or fruit pie. A special dinnertime treat was the humble potato, which my mother cooked in all sorts of delicious ways. Best of all was when the potatoes were boiled then sliced up, quick-fried, and served with grated cheese. Pizza was unknown but our favourite potato dish gave us a chance to experiment with the elastic properties of melted cheese and we delighted in impromptu competitions for the longest cheese thread. As with cherries transmogrified as earrings, my parents found these games amusing and tolerated them despite their obvious potential for serious mayhem.

*

It may seem startling today, but a lunchtime treat was chicken, which was rarely bought. Most often, it came as a gift after a visit to rural relations. As we said our goodbyes, a plump and unsuspecting target was lured closer with the traditional cry that announced feeding time and called for all chickens to gather around and tuck in. Despite its protestations, the chicken was then trussed up and thrown into the back of the car for the drive home. Occasionally, the appearance of chicken on the lunch table could be traced back to the parents of a young rustic in one of my father's history or geography classes, a student with a firmer grasp of the intricacies of poultry rearing than with those of the War of the Spanish Succession and whom my father had tried to help with a little free coaching. On these occasions, a grateful parent drove into town in the mud-splattered family *Deux-chevaux*, asked for directions to our house, rang the bell, and delivered a flapping, clucking chicken into the apprehensive arms of whichever one of us came to the door.

Converting the chicken from alive-and-kicking to dead-as-a-doorknob involved the messy business of putting the beast to death by hand, a skill my mother had perfected during World War II, when in rural environments at least, virtually all food was home-produced. Sensibly, she timed the bloodletting so we would all be in school and unable to take a gory interest in the proceedings. When it reached the table, the chicken was invariably preceded by green peas of the delicate, slightly sweet *petit pois* variety: first the peas, then the chicken, never together. Except in high summer, when my father's small vegetable garden yielded a few consumables, the peas came out of a tin. As I got older, being asked to help and entrusted with the tin opener in the kitchen was part of the appeal.

A rare dinnertime treat was pancakes, the thin, light type known as *crèpes*. The default method for serving the pancakes was to daub them with jam. The amount of jam going on each pancake was closely monitored by our parents, but then came the best part: the opportunity to roll up the pancake by hand and eat it as a wrap. The rolling mattered almost as much as the eating because being allowed to handle our food with our fingers was a rare privilege.

A variant on the wrap idea was for my mother to first stack all the pancakes together with thin slices of ham and cheese alternating between them. The result was a kind of 'pancake cake' that was then sliced up into wedges and eaten just like an ordinary cake. On pancake nights, my siblings and I squeezed into the kitchen and watched my mother toss each pancake and – usually – catch it on its way down. When we were older, we were allowed to toss a pancake or two. But this required extraordinary control and more often than not, earth-bound pancakes landed up half in the pan and half over the edge, or worse. But this did not make them any less edible. As I said, no food was ever wasted, especially not pancakes.

Except for salt and a little pepper, spices played no part in our food. Onion and garlic went into stews but they were so overcooked that they were barely recognisable. Even if fragments could occasionally be identified, so little taste was left in them that they could easily be put past spice-averse children.

Though I was vaguely aware of their existence, vegetables from warmer climates, such as green peppers, courgettes, or aubergines, were regarded as dangerously alien: Italian, probably, or even Provençal, which was not much better. Tradition was key. Though some the magazines my mother subscribed to featured recipes, cooking skills were supposed to have been acquired by women early in life and experimentation was regarded as aberrant. If she needed a recipe to guide the preparation of a dish she cooked too rarely to have memorised the moves, my mother consulted one of her most treasured possessions: an ancient cookbook she had inherited from her mother as her mother had inherited it from her own mother decades earlier, with additions gleaned from friends and relations lovingly written in long-hand and kept on loose sheets inserted between the yellowing pages of the cookbook. The result was that the diet was self-perpetuating, a quality we warmly welcomed because like all children, we were valued predictability.

*

Overall, my mother's cooking was reliable and – except for the Friday fish – pleasant but unadventurous. She enjoyed cooking but rarely tried anything for which the ingredients were not readily available, preferably regionally. We never ate seafood but since my siblings and I assumed it smelled and tasted much like fish, we never asked to be given a chance. My mother only occasionally attempted true culinary fireworks such as *soufflés*. But she excelled at *charcuterie*, including *patés* and especially meat pies, tasty combinations of cuts marinated in white wine, parsley, and onion. The result was exquisite. Consumer opinion differed on whether her meat pies tasted better when they were still warm and soft as they emerged from the oven or cold and firm later in the week. Either way, they went down a treat.

Her *forte* was desserts. She loved baking and she was very good at it. To me, the true glory of French food is its desserts.

The beauty of these confections is that they are so light. The dough is airy and fluffy. There is just enough sugar to make the dessert pleasant to the taste but not so much that it becomes nauseating. There is variation in the range of chocolates, fruit, and even alcohol types that can be used. A French dessert is exactly what a dessert should be: an insubstantial complement to a meal, not a dense lump of starch that has to be hacked apart before it can be eaten and differs little in consistency from the meat and potatoes that preceded it. A French dessert requires no effort to squeeze into an already full stomach.

Luckily for our family, my mother never tired of creating desserts. She produced flans, tarts, pies, and cakes of every description. Pretexts to serve one of her mouth-watering confections were generously provided by family events and the Catholic calendar: birthdays, but also patron saint's days and major holidays such as Christmas, Easter, Ascension Day, or simply the fact that it was Sunday. Sometimes, she just felt like baking. My siblings and I were often invited to state our preferences and no reasonable requests were turned down. Birthday boys and girls had first pick but no one ever dissented and refused to eat a sibling's choice of dessert. We did not know a dessert we did not like and my mother did not know a dessert she could not bake to perfection. As she neared the end of her life, she cooked increasingly simple fares for herself and eventually stopped cooking altogether when she no longer had the energy. But the last thing to go was dessert making, even if her trademark walnut cake had to be eaten with caution because as she still cracked the nuts by hand, her failing eyesight and shaking fingers made it increasingly difficult for her to pick out the tiny shell fragments, which found their way into the mix.

Among desserts, the only rival to my mother's baking in the family's affections was ice cream. This time, my father had top billing. On the morning of a special occasion, he got the car out and collected a slab of ice from his friend and fellow-POW Monsieur Sagret, the wine merchant up the road. He then took down from a kitchen shelf the ancient ice cream maker, a family heirloom that had outlived two world wars. This contraption consisted of a rotating metal container built into a wooden cask with a metal handle fitted into the cranking mechanism in the lid. My father went down on his knees on the unpaved floor of the gloomy basement of our house, surrounded by parked bikes and every pair of young eyes in the family. He hacked away at the ice with hammer and chisel and arranged the chunks around the container. Then he poured in the batter my mother had just made and entrusted to whichever one of us she deemed least likely to trip on the way down and send the stuff flying. My father then spent what seemed an eternity and a lot of sweat cranking away until he judged that the batter had become proper ice cream that could be carried back upstairs. He did this by raising the lid and dipping a finger into the mix. Naturally, there was no shortage of offers of second opinions. But this was a special occasion and the standard prohibition against dipping fingers into food was temporarily relaxed. Sadly, the technological marvel that was the ice cream maker was eventually consigned to the scrapheap and replaced by an electric version that simply whirred away discreetly inside the refrigerator. Homemade ice cream never tasted quite as good again.

In general, my father took little part in food preparation. His role was to bring the ingredients home from the Tuesday market in his car and pay for it all, which he did generously. His one regular involvement went like clockwork.

Every evening on the stroke of half past six, he folded up the copy of *Le Monde* he had been reading while keeping a wary eye on us as we got on with our homework and went into the kitchen, where my mother was getting dinner ready. Supervision of our homework then transferred tacitly to my grandmother, who made up in sharpness of hearing what she lacked in mobility and missed none of our juvenile capers and was always ready to quash them with a single word. Besides, we knew that any misdemeanour on our part would bring the majesty of the law down upon our heads and that the mandatory sentence was no dessert, and this did wonders for concentrating restless young minds. Once in the kitchen, my father contributed by keeping an eye on anything that might boil over or stirring anything that might go lumpy. Meanwhile, the two of them reviewed the events of the day, in and out of the home. This was grown-up talk and largely private, though I guessed that school reports probably formed a substantial part of the discussion along with incentives and rewards and, in my case especially, appropriate forms and degrees of retribution.

Meal times were set in stone. Breakfast time was dictated by the school day or attendance at Sunday mass. Even school holidays offered little variation. Eating was something we did at meal times, never in between. There was no question of shuffling over to the refrigerator and helping ourselves to a snack as the mood took us. To their credit, the French are not impulsive eaters. They do not do snacks: they do meals. Lunch was served at noon and dinner at seven, precisely. This remained true for my parents throughout the rest of their lives. Even on family travels, a packed lunch was produced at precisely those times, at which point my father parked the car in a convenient spot by the roadside and the family picnicked on the grassy verge. Travel plans were made with meal times in mind and departure and arrival times were set so as to pose as little risk as possible to the sacrosanct meal schedule.

Lunch and dinner were eaten communally, and with nine people sitting at the long dining room table, conversation was lively despite competition from Swiss radio news. The chatter was interrupted only by requests for silence from my father so that he could focus on announcements of missile crises in Cuba and the imminent start of World War III or some such topic of utter irrelevance to children.

Meals taken at friends' homes on occasions such as birthdays varied little from what I knew at home. Meat was a little more plentiful, perhaps, and the cheese selection a little wider. But the beef was just as chewy and unappetising. Best of all, since most of my friends came from less religious families than ours, even if the visit took place on a Friday when school was in recess, there was little risk of having fish foisted upon me.

In every one of those homes, all the basic ingredients of the traditional French fare were present: the salad dressing was *vinaigrette* and spices were beyond the pale. Even travel to relatively alien Germany offered few surprises except for the black bread, which my siblings and I instantly dismissed as inedible. Very few travelled to England or had ever tasted English food but everyone in France learned at mother's knee that it was an abomination. When it was time for me to pack my bags and take the night train to London at the age of eighteen at the start of my adventure in studying English and much else besides, a major source of collective anguish among family and friends was how I would feed myself. Like every other self-respecting French person, I would of course reject English food. But what other options would there be? Would I starve and come running back and beg for some of my mother's stewed prunes or even some of that hated Friday fish? Or would I end up eating Spam a lot until I got used to it and thought it tasty? Only time would tell. But for concerned parents, siblings, and friends, these were anxious moments.

CHAPTER ELEVEN: ON YOUR MARKS

Other forms of transport grow daily more nightmarish. Only the bicycle remains pure in heart.

Iris Murdoch (1919-1999)

For children of all ages and backgrounds, a major aim in life is to find ways of dispersing surplus energy. Children rarely lack inventiveness or spontaneity and they can generally be relied upon to devise their own entertainment while staying fit and learning social skills at the same time. In some cultures, school steps in early and takes control by promoting selected sports, especially team sports. But not in all cultures.

When I was growing up in Lure, Haute-Saône, primary school offered no organised sport. But students did not want for exercise. Since lunch meant eating at home and nowhere else, we all walked to school and back twice a day. In school, time not spent in the classroom was spent in the schoolyard, with teachers taking no part in the proceedings. The pedagogical reasoning seemed to be that since children had plenty of excess energy, they could be left to their own devices and release it as they saw fit, within reason. Given enough space, they would burn off that energy and come back to the classroom ready for more memorisation. As they paced up and down the schoolyard in pairs throughout the breaks, all the teachers had to do was keep a wary eye on the bustle and be ready to jump in and break up the odd *mêlée*.

Surprisingly perhaps, the girls were the hyperactive ones. They spent their breaks skipping ropes, throwing balls at walls and at each other, and drawing mysterious squares in the dust with a stick and then hopping from square to square on one foot, carrying on elaborate conversations as they skipped, threw, drew, or hopped.

By contrast, boys' games were competitive, largely silent, and highly energy-efficient. Unless it was raining and we were confined to the sheltered section of a building that had once been the cloisters of the monastery before it became a school, my friends and I congregated at break times by the smelly outhouse at the far end of the schoolyard, crouched in the coal dust, and played marbles. There we honed our skills at strategic thinking, hand-to-eye coordination, and the subtle art of haggling over the value of marbles we might trade. Compared to the girls, the amount of physical energy we boys expended was very small. And if we had any left over, it would soon be dissipated on the long trek home. Pocket money was unknown, home-cooked food reasonably healthy, fast food unheard of, and computer games decades away so there was little risk of any of us turning into tubs of lard prematurely regardless of whether school offered physical education or not.

Things changed in secondary school but only sporadically. Depending on the vagaries of hirings by the Ministry of Education in Paris, students learned on the first day of each school year whether or not there would be physical education. In most years, there was none. But no one saw this as pedagogical or administrative failure. In those years when physical education was added to the timetable, it consisted almost exclusively of choreographed drills in the dusty schoolyard. For me, this was a poor substitute for afternoons spent racing down country lanes and exploring forest trails on two wheels.

When I was about twelve or thirteen, my classmates and I learned at the start of one academic year that a physical education teacher had landed in Lure, Haute-

Saône. I cannot recall his name so this will save me the trouble of masking it to spare him the public shaming he so richly deserves. From the start, we hated this man.

He was massive, with a military crew cut and a touch of the bovine in his appearance. Throughout the term, he wore the same track suit a shade of green the French call *caca d'oie*, or 'goose shit'. Twice a week, we were ordered out of the classroom and made to stand in rows in the schoolyard. Whatever their moral defects, the French are not prudish so physical education mixed the sexes, at least up to a point: the boys stood at the front, the girls at the back. So with the teacher facing us and modelling the moves, we jumped up and down, landing with our feet apart or together alternately while raising our arms in the air and swinging them back down again. Over and over and over.

Not surprisingly, tedium set in and whether out of absent-mindedness, wilful mischief-making, or sheer bad luck, one of us soon broke ranks and landed instead of soaring or raised arms instead of swinging them down. This brought the teacher's instant ire upon the miscreant, invariably a boy. The teacher's approach to restoring order in the ranks was to call the guilty party to the front, make him turn around, and kick his backside violently. As long as they themselves were not the guilty party on that occasion, a few classmates found this mildly funny. But most of us felt sorry for the victim and rallied around at the end of the lesson with words of comfort and shared the insults we wished we could have aimed directly at the teacher. Some parents were said to have complained to the Principal but parents had negligible influence over what went on in schools and teachers were not to be questioned.

Why this cruel man reserved his unusual tastes in

punishment for boys was not clear. Perhaps he had unexpected delicacy of feeling towards the gentler sex. Or girls were always less likely to break ranks and rebel. Or quite simply, they were screened from view by the boys at the front and the teacher could not see what they were up to at the back. Or perhaps the practice had to do with a fascination on his part with boys' rear ends. Over the years, most of our teachers ranged from excellent to effective but uninspiring. A few were downright incompetent and one or two had personalities and methods that bordered on the unpleasant. But this man was the only true sadist among them.

*

Towards the end of my secondary school years, the municipality of Lure, Haute-Saône managed to lay its hands on some funding and built a new stadium on the edge of town. It consisted of a running track with a football pitch in the centre, a modest stand, and an area to one side devoted to the latest advances in physical education. At the appointed hour, we were marched over from the school building and made to run around the track. We wore no sports clothing or running shoes and we received no instruction of any kind. Presumably, the thinking was that running as fast as possible was something that came naturally to teenagers so firing the starting gun and shouting sarcastic abuse at the stragglers was all the pedagogy that was required. Needless to say, the bovine man in the goose-shit track suit, who had somehow managed to get himself re-appointed for another year, excelled at it.

Birds of a feather flock together, they say. Like me, three of my friends, Philippe, Pascal, and Jean were several months younger than the average for our cohort and therefore shorter and thinner than most. None of us was remotely athletic (except on a bike), and all shared a conviction that the way to girls' affections when the time came would be through displays of brains, not brawn. So as the gun was fired, we ambled onto the track and quickly lost sight first of the leaders and not much later of the middle orders too. If cramp did not lay us low first, we feigned it and tumbled onto the grass at the first opportunity and rolled around just enough to look convincing but not too much or too long so as not to attract undue attention.

Once the pointlessness of this charade became obvious even to the teacher, we were ordered over to the climbing frame that stood in a corner of the stadium. The frame included two vertical ladders, one at each end. The upper part of the structure consisted of a slightly wobbly metal platform about a foot wide. On the underside were hooks to which were attached fraying, rain-sodden ropes. We lined up at the foot of the frame and took turns to shinny up one of the ropes. Few of us ever made it much above ground level and predictably, those who came first on the track also reached the top of the slippery rope to a mix of admiring gasps and sneering comments on the part of the less physically developed and those who prided in being nerdy. Presumably, there was a skill to rope climbing and like all skills, it could probably be taught. But once again, no instruction was offered. Like running around a track, knowing how to shinny up a rope was presumed to be part of our genetic makeup.

Having shamed ourselves at rope climbing, it was now time to have terror added to humiliation. Along one side of the platform at the top of the frame was a flimsy chain hung so low on thin uprights that we practically had to crouch to reach down and grab it. On the other side was a gaping chasm. *Terra firma* was four metres below, about thirteen feet. First we had to climb up the vertical ladder. Once at the top, we hauled ourselves onto the platform, grabbed the thin upright, and tried to stand. If a fear of heights did not have the better of us and we did not lie down on our belly simpering, we inched our way forward, holding onto the chain for moral support and trying hard not to look down. Once we made it to the other end, things got even worse. First, we had to turn on a sixpence with nothing but the upright to hold on to, lie flat on our belly again, and then start backing into the void with only our feet as our guides as we searched for the top rung in the ladder. Once down, some walked away nonchalantly, some laughed hysterically, others burst into tears. I will not reveal in which category I belonged. Had this sado-masochistic travesty of physical education been tried in an American school, there would have been a line of tort lawyers waiting at the bottom of the ladder fighting for the students' signatures on writs.

During those academic years when the school payroll ran to a physical education teacher, I was occasionally able to give the misery a miss by way of a doctor's certificate stating that upon careful examination, the physician had concluded that in his professional opinion, my feeble constitution was not up to physical exertion on this scale. Over the years, I learned two different approaches to securing that blessed end. At a younger age, the strategy consisted of simply pleading with my parents to be removed from physical education. I knew that if I kept up the whining long enough, there was a fair chance that they might relent and make an appointment for me to see Docteur Magraix, the trusted family physician. But as I grew in age as well as in understanding of what motivated my father, I developed a more Machiavellian approach. I knew that my father placed supreme importance on education so I argued – however implausibly – that I too valued education above all else and that time spent on the track or at the climbing frame was time not spent studying and therefore wasted. This did the trick. Given my scholastic record, my father must have had his doubts about my true motivations. But he was hardly in a position to contradict me without disavowing one of his most dearly-held beliefs.

But sooner or later, Monsieur Françaix, our Principal, stepped in and spoiled my stratagem by hinting to my father, his colleague and friend, that there were only so many doctor's certificates he could put past his overseers in the Ministry of Education and that questions would soon be asked about what he was proposing to do to help keep alive what looked like the sickliest boy in the entire school. My father had no option but to concede and the ordeal resumed for another term.

*

Football played a very small part in the lives of residents of Lure, Haute-Saône, in or out of school. Even when there was a physical education teacher in residence, there were no team sports of any kind. The town had a football team of sorts, which we glimpsed in action as we headed out on Sunday afternoon family drives. But no one I knew took any interest in its fortunes.

When I was about ten, stories went around that France had distinguished itself in the World Cup, played in Sweden and at which a 17-year-old Brazilian teenager named Pelé had shone. The names of the French stars – Kopa, Fontaine, Piantoni – were briefly lauded and quickly forgotten. Football was a minority interest even among boys. If on our annual camping trip my brother and I made friends with boys who owned a ball and invited us to join their games, it quickly became obvious that we were clueless and we were soon demoted to observer status. My father mentioned having played during his POW years and occasionally offered technical advice but he never encouraged participation by my brother or myself. As for my sisters and their friends, the notion that girls might play football never crossed anyone's mind.

Without question, the sport of choice was cycling. For most residents of Lure, Haute-Saône, pedalling was a natural extension of walking, only faster. Except for very young children, the elderly, the town's few plutocrats, and the army contingent who roared around in their Jeeps, just about everybody in town owned a bike and used it. Biking was not so much a sport as a way of life. For me, Christmas or a birthday might add a shiny new accessory to my bike and cause universal admiration tinged with envy among my friends. But for sheer excitement, nothing could beat the *Tour de France*.

Each year as they have done since the turn of the twentieth century, the organisers of the *Tour* pick a route that over three weeks follows the contours of the *hexagone*, more or less, and takes in the mountain climbs that sort the men from the boys and provide most of the drama. For some reason, during all of my childhood and adolescence years, the organisers never once put Lure, Haute-Saône on the itinerary. But in lucky years, they routed the race through a corner of eastern France my brother Pierre and I could just about reach on our own bikes.

Planning was feverish and highly detailed. My father's legendary map-reading skills were enlisted, and my brother and I debated at length the ideal vantage point along the route from which we might view the race and the best way to get there at the right time. Get there too soon and we would have to stand in the hot sun for hours. But underestimate the challenge and get there too late and we would be turned away as the *gendarmerie* closed road after road as the race neared. So on the long-awaited morning, we made our way there on our bikes, picked a spot, and waited, the excitement level surging.

The arrival of the race itself was preceded by the *caravanne publicitaire*, a long line of cars promoting the wares that went a long way towards financing this otherwise free show: soft drinks, cosmetics, magazine subscriptions, cars, even those wonders of the modern age: televisions. The procession snaked through village after village, stopping briefly where small crowds gathered by the roadside. Pretty girls jumped out, smiling alluringly, and pressed brochures and samples on ecstatic spectators. Then, the pretty girls jumped back in and the *caravanne* moved on to maintain the required distance between the last car in the line and the front runners.

Among the crowd, a few of the spectators were the objects of even greater attention than the pretty girls because they had brought with them another wonder of the age: a portable transistor radio. If we could sneak close enough to the owner of one of these instruments, we could follow the race as it happened and construct in our minds images of steely determination, boundless endeavour, and pouring sweat long before seeing it for ourselves. We had every intention of reliving the drama by listening to radio reports at home that night and reading all about it in the newspaper in the morning. But for those brave enough to face the tiring bike ride and the long wait, to be there in person and witnessing on a glorious summer morning one of the greatest sporting events in the world with the aid of the latest gadgetry was an inebriating experience and one that would provide bragging material for weeks to come. Surely, this was worth the gruelling trip and the uncomfortable wait even if when it finally came, the main event lasted for mere seconds and amounted to little more than a blur as the *peloton*, the tightly bunched pack of riders, whooshed past at lightning speed, giving spectators barely a chance to pick out the *maillot jaune*, the current leader's yellow jersey.

*

From debates my brother and I held with our sisters, girls seemed to see bikes as convenient means of getting from here to there. But to boys, a bike was what a car is for many today: a symbolic extension of its owner, a source of personal pride, and an object of veneration. We were well aware that our public image depended not only on having a bike but on knowing how to use it to best advantage and especially on how to keep it shipshape. By the time I was eight or nine, I could put a wayward chain back on its sprocket in an instant. Next came learning to mend a flat tyre and before long, I was replacing worn brake pads and cables and tweaking the mechanism to perfection as to the manner born. Even a complex *dérailleur* could be taken apart, cleaned, and put back together again between breakfast and lunchtime. Most of this expertise was acquired on the job through trial and error. But expert tutelage was available too.

Next to the railway crossing in the middle of town was one of many bike repair shops that catered to this mass market. It was run by two partners of recent Alsatian extraction, Monsieur Muller and Monsieur Klein. The partners looked like Haute-Saône's answer to Laurel and Hardy. Monsieur Muller was overweight and permanently grumpy. Perhaps he was born grumpy or maybe he resented my frequent presence on his premises and especially the fact that I only paid for the few repairs I could not carry out myself and never for the use of his tools or the professional advice he reluctantly offered. Meanwhile, Monsieur Klein was thin and jovial and always ready to welcome me with a wave and a smile as he spotted me getting off my bike outside his shop. This man was one of my heroes. True, his heavy German accent made communication difficult, but I learned mostly from observation. As long as I could sit unobtrusively and watch him at work, there was little need for words.

But observation soon led to experimentation, often using specialised tools I was allowed to borrow but could never hope to own. In no time, the care of the bike in sickness and in health had yielded all its secrets. At first, I worked on my own bike. Later came the ultimate accolade: being invited to lend one of the partners a hand, here loosening a recalcitrant nut, there locating a pinprick in an inner tube by holding it under water and watching for tiny bubbles. When business was slow and my own bike had received all the attention it required, I sat outside and watched the trains and the passing traffic and went back to dreaming of one day exploring further than my bike and my spindly legs could carry me.

Those were halcyon days. Immune as I still was to the complexities girls were soon to introduce into my life, bike cleaning was a regular ritual. Nothing went uncleaned. The bike was tipped upside down and every nook and cranny was subjected to my ministrations. Spokes were scoured and then lovingly polished. Brakes were taken apart and restored to prime condition. Even ball-bearing units were taken out of their casings and scrubbed free of the oily grime they had accumulated over the weeks.

My stock in trade consisted of just two items: a rag, easily obtainable from a mother whom the Great Depression and the deprivations of World War II had taught never to throw anything away, and some petrol as the cleaning agent. This too was readily available. There was a filling station at the end of the road and all I needed was a few coins and an empty bottle. The filling station attendant was happy to oblige. He measured the half-litre I asked for, relieved me of my coins, and scouted around for a used cork. If none was available, he stuffed a piece of rag into the neck of the bottle and I biked home confident in the knowledge that no bike-disfiguring grime was safe.

*

Once the bike had been restored to factory condition, it was time to think up imaginative ways to put it to good use. That was never difficult. For my inner circle of friends and myself, the finest product of our creative instincts was the game of *poursuite*. Given the penury that afflicted us all, the game was not just fun, it was also free. All that was needed was three friends with one bike each, a sunny summer morning ahead of us and no obvious reason to spend it at home, and plenty of energy.

As soon as I could make a discreet exit from the breakfast table without giving the impression I thought I was staying in a hotel or my entire family had caught the plague, I joined my three friends at an agreed spot. The manpower usually consisted of best friend Daniel, classmates Jean and Pascal, and myself, though depending on the vagaries of family circumstances and the occasional bout of sickness, the human resources could vary.

Once the customary handshakes had been exchanged, two pairs were formed. One pair rode off with a five-minute head start, the other gave chase all over town. The ground rules were simple. The pursued could go anywhere as long as they remained within city limits. But they could not get off their bikes and they had to be fully visible at all times. This was no infantile game of hide and seek. The moment the pursued were spotted by the pursuers, the game was up, roles switched around, and another chase got under way.

For the pursued, a cunning ploy was to follow what I now know as the *Purloined Letter* principle and take up position in the most conspicuous spot imaginable – right in front of the Post Office, the railway station, or the parish church, where pursuers suspecting wily strategies on the part of the pursued would never dream of looking.

Exactly what constituted city limits had to be negotiated. The inner urban core of Lure, Haute-Saône did not extend very far so we soon found ourselves in a kind of *rus in urbe* consisting of lush meadows seen through increasingly wide gaps between the houses. But consensus was easily reached. In any case, it was never in the interest of the pursued to go as far as the very last house on any street leading out of town since this left them with no escape route if they spotted their pursuers before the pursuers spotted them. Since the rule book prohibited participants from riding out of town, the last turnoff was the obvious place to stop, lean against a wall, and talk of this and that while scanning the horizon for approaching friends on bikes.

The game helped work up an appetite. My mother could have put some dog food or even some leftover Friday fish on my lunch plate and I would have wolfed it down as though it were her finest *paté en croûte*. My

263

friends and I should have had the game patented. Perhaps there is still time.

*

Another approach to spending as little time as possible at home subjected to family strictures was to head for the open spaces beyond city limits. High summer was haymaking time. The romantic potential of hay was as yet undiscovered but haystacks offered a chance to goof off, explore our daredevil side, and test the limits of bike technology all at once.

This time, there were no rules. The idea consisted of gathering a band of energetic, fun-loving friends with a taste for silliness. We met, agreed a destination and the best way to get there, and set off. As we pedalled along country lanes, it was not long before one of us spotted a convenient haystack by the roadside. One after the other, each rider allowed enough distance to provide plenty of momentum in the run-up and then aimed straight for the haystack at top speed. As the front wheel of the bike came into abrupt contact with the haystack, the rider then somersaulted over the handlebar and dived headfirst into the hay. At least, that was the plan. The problem was that from a distance, one haystack looked much like any other and the exact capacity of each stack to absorb impacts was difficult to predict. On a good day, we landed in the hay while the bike crumbled to the ground some distance away. More often than not, we landed on top of the bike or the bike landed on top of us. But taking knocks was an inherent part of the game, which was designed in large part to impress competing alpha males in my social circle, not to display delicacy of feeling.

When my friends and I turned thirteen or fourteen and had become strong enough and sufficiently independent, we were ready to tackle the next challenge on the list: the long-distance bike ride.

A popular destination was the Swiss border just past the small town of Delle, about three hours' hard biking each way and just about manageable in one afternoon. For me especially, a major attraction of the ride was a chance to peer into another country and imagine future travel. For all of us, the main draw was the line of shops on the then cheaper Swiss side and their mouth-watering displays of chocolate. At a time when border checks within Europe were taken seriously and every foray into a neighbouring country and back could add four more stamps to a passport, the Swiss border guards watched us as we abandoned our bikes on the French side and walked the remaining few metres to the border post, where the guards waved us through without as much as a look at our French identity cards. Once on Swiss soil, we wandered up and down the line of shops and selected the largest slab of chocolate we could afford, preferably the nutty kind. After a final glance at the foreign and the exotic, we headed back across the border, recovered our unguarded, unlocked bikes, and pedalled homeward.

Once I had developed the stomach for true heroics rather than mere chocolate, my next step was the all-day bike ride. Most of my friends were the fun-loving type and regarded the single-mindedness needed to plan and execute these expeditions as too close to masochism for comfort, so an all-day ride was usually a solo effort. It was also an ambitious proposition, with real risk involved if something went wrong so detailed planning was of the essence. Out came the trusty Michelin map once again and I picked a route on the basis in part of novelty but mostly of length and especially of difficulty in terms of gradients. Provisions for the day consisted of a ham and cheese sandwich and a plastic bottle filled with lemon tea. After a hearty breakfast, no other sustenance would be needed all day and the bottle could be refilled again and again at the public fountain that still graced every French village and that was used to water homebound cattle and feed the stone washtubs where, with near-universal ownership of washing machines still well into the future, village women did their laundry. I took a little money in case of emergencies and the Michelin map completed the kit.

The ride started soon after dawn. Even on what promised to be a hot summer day, I wore a light jacket at first to ward off the early morning chill. I took very few breaks because it was generally better to keep going steadily than to relax and then face the morale-sapping task of rebuilding momentum after a snooze in the clover.

As long as I planned these rides well, I stuck to the route, and the weather cooperated, mishaps were rare but not entirely unknown. On one otherwise uneventful ramble along the bucolic byways of Haute-Saône, I had a flat tyre. This was par for the course. French country roads were roughly surfaced so this was not unexpected. And of course I knew all about bike maintenance. I had patched up enough inner tubes to feel confident there was nothing a French country road could throw at my tyres that I could not deal with. I was wrong.

I got off, upended the bike by the roadside, and set to work. Minutes later, I was off only for the tyre to go flat again, and again, four or five times until the early evening darkness threatened and it began to look as though I might have to face facts and summon help.

I pushed my bike to the nearest village and went into a *café*. Public phones were unheard of back then. Even a relatively urban place such as Lure, Haute-

Saône was entirely free of them. If for some reason you needed to make a phone call, you went to the post office, gave the operator the number, and waited until the respondent came through and you were directed to one of the numbered cabins. The alternative was to walk into a *café*, have the one and only phone in the place pushed in your direction across the zinc counter, carry on a conversation over a crackly line and to a background of clinking glasses and shouted orders, and then hand over three or four times the real cost of the call.

To add to the challenge I and my ailing bike were now facing in that remote spot, phone ownership was still a gleam in my parents' eyes. So I called Monsieur Gagney, our friendly neighbour and the lucky owner of the only phone in the entire street. As was routine on such occasions, a son or daughter with nothing better to do was dispatched to our house and my father eventually came on. I explained my predicament, gave my coordinates, and stood outside the *café* awaiting his arrival in his car.

The rescue operation then began. With considerable difficulty, we squeezed the bike into a family car hardly designed for rescue missions of this type, I took my place in the car next to my father and we drove in pitch darkness, getting home, to my mother's consternation, well past the sacrosanct dinner hour.

Following humiliation on such a scale, I knew that restoring my bike to health would require expert advice. So next morning, as early as possible to avoid detection by mockers, I pushed my ailing steed all the way to the bike repair shop by the railway crossing, where I consulted with Monsieur Klein at length. I then upended the bike on the pavement in front of the shop and, armed with the required tools, I extracted the offending inner tube. I pumped it up and held it under water as per normal procedure. Immediately, a multitude of tiny bubbles began burbling up to the surface from countless tiny holes in an entire section of the tube. I could not imagine what might have penetrated the tube as I rode my bike along some innocuous country road the previous afternoon. Most probably, it had died of natural causes after a lifetime of self-effacing service.

Clearly, the tube was beyond redemption. A brand new one would have to be purchased. I handed Monsieur Klein a handful of coins, installed a shiny, fragrant new tube, pumped it up, and rode off. All that remained was to test the efficacy of the repair and the likelihood that unlike the previous afternoon, it would last. An extended tour of the town over what was left of the morning took care of that. I had been successful at last.

That day lives on in infamy in my mind. But I still pride in my personal record for an all-day ride: a 210-kilometre jaunt into the Jura Mountains and back, longer than most stages of the *Tour de France* itself. Once he was old enough and up to the challenge, my brother Pierre became an occasional biking companion. One summer, we went off together on a week-long ramble across the German border and up and down the Black Forest. In the process, we learned how to make German Youth Hostel beds in the approved manner or suffer the indignity of being named and shamed on the public address system and ordered to go back and do it again and do it properly.

For me, these long bike rides were a crucial part of growing up because they taught me resilience and the importance of taking the long-term view, which involved not only planning carefully but also conserving energy as opposed to indulging in a mad dash whenever the mood took me. Catapulting myself into haystacks had undeniable charms but it belonged to the realm of childish things, which eventually and regrettably, would have to be left behind.

*

If my bike was my main means of escape and exploration during summer holidays, during the school year, it was the most sensible way to get to my classes and back. And in secondary school, any student – the vast majority, in fact – who rode a bike to school had to negotiate the fact that having been a monastery, the building had no bike shelter. The monastic ethos did not encourage mobility, it seemed.

When we reached the school, we jumped off, leaned our bikes against the wall, and ran inside. For the studious and the toadying, early arrival earned approving smirks from teachers. But it also meant that those students' bikes were first against the wall, to be joined later by those of the idle and the rebellious, who had ambled along the byways, swapped gossip with friends, and reached school at the eleventh hour. So at the end of the school day, the studious and the toadying had to wait until the last of the idle and the rebellious had taken their bikes off the front and they, the studious and the toadying, could get at theirs at the back. This served them right, of course. But the true beauty of the system was the honour code that regulated it. Bike locks were unknown, yet in all my years in secondary school in Lure, Haute-Saône, I never once heard of a bike being stolen. It was not that kind of town.

A few years later, once government munificence had equipped the town with a purpose-built secondary school, the picture changed though the honour code endured. The new school came with a dedicated bike shelter. This consisted of an elegant concrete structure with a roof that sloped inward from both sides so that the centre of the roof was lower than the outer edges, with the inevitable result that in driving rain the roof provided no shelter at all and the bikes got soaking wet. Admittedly, the bikes had got just as soaking wet when they were parked ten deep against the old school wall. But at least that arrangement had cost the tax payer nothing.

In fact, money evidently being no object, the State had provided not one but two bike shelters: one for the boys at one end of the school and one for the girls at the other. Each shelter was vast and capacity was not an issue. Perhaps the State feared that the sexes would intermingle at bike retrieval time and indulge in questionable practices that would bring shame to the school, the town, and by implication all of French education. In reality, being about fourteen or fifteen when the school was built, I knew all the secluded spots where, in theory at least, the wages of sin could be earned after hours in the form of a furtive kiss or a tentative squeeze. I for one was never likely to attempt anything so brazen in the middle of the day and in public especially with teachers looking on. Perhaps the Ministry of Education contractor was left with some spare concrete and, like any *fonctionnaire* worth his salt, he calculated that if he did not use it, he would be given less next time around.

*

At a time when American teenagers were cruising along Main Street in hand-me-down Chevys or parking at the far end of drive-in theatres and smooching in the back seat instead of watching the film, the go-getting element in Lure, Haute-Saône dreamed of owning a Solex.

A Solex was a kind of motorised bike that only a combination of war-time scarcity and French ingenuity could have dreamt up. It consisted of a heavy frame with a two-stroke engine mounted on the front, limited at first to 45cc but later rising to a dizzying 49cc. It came in any colour as long as it was black. But it featured a snazzy square headlight, at the time a radical departure from conventional designs.

To get the thing going, the rider jumped on and pedalled furiously until sufficient momentum had been gathered. The rider then grabbed the vertical lever above the engine block and pushed it down hard until the ceramic roller below the engine came into contact with the front tyre and the rotating wheel fired up the engine. In fact, the process was similar to convincing a recalcitrant car to start on a particularly cold morning. As long as the car owner was wise enough to opt for manual rather than automatic transmission and does not live in Iowa or Holland, he or she can always let the car roll down the hill and then let in the clutch until the momentum kick-starts the engine and the problem is solved.

That, in effect, was the Solex principle. Obviously, the front tyre had to be extra thick to take all that friction from the roller and this plus the weight of the engine mounted so high up added to the notorious instability of these beasts. The exhaust system consisted of a short pipe seemingly designed to pump low-grade petrol fumes straight up the rider's nostrils. But low-grade petrol fumes smelled good because they denoted modernity and relative wealth as well as freedom of movement. Besides, the Solex was not originally designed to safeguard public health or impress gawkers but to get French farmers to their fields at minimal cost, and it did that brilliantly.

Though there may have been an element of sour

grapes involved, the sudden appearance of a Solex within my social circle invariably led to a sense of betrayal of the bike cause in part because it suggested laziness but also because this ostentatious display of wealth seemed unseemly in such a tightly-knit, egalitarian society. As to the vexed question of whether going around on a Solex could be considered manly, the majority view was that it could, not only because of the considerable amount of pedal power needed to fire the thing up but also of the degree of skill needed to keep such an unbalanced contraption upright and steering it safely through tight spaces.

One of the best features of the Solex was its broad, luxurious saddle, which sank about six inches as the rider sat on it, or rather *in* it. By contrast, the saddle on my bike consisted of a sliver of rock-hard leather so thin that it threatened to rend the *derrière* far beyond what God intended. Worse, the part of the saddle that stuck out between my upper thighs at the front was so unforgiving that if I rode my bike for more than an hour or so, I lost all sensation in the scrotal region and all appendages attached thereto, just as if you sit on one leg for too long, you will fall over if you try to get up because your lower body now seems to consist of just one leg instead of the two you remember owning. If I was out riding my bike and my bladder started hinting that it was time for a pit stop, I had to stand around and pretend to be admiring the landscape for several minutes before normal sensory functions returned and I could locate, identify, and operate the equipment as per normal procedure. As some long-forgotten observer once remarked, if the world were a rational place, it is men not women who ought to ride side-saddled.

*

By a generous definition of sport, Lure, Haute-Saône provided plenty of opportunities for healthy outdoor fun. The key was a bike, some map-reading skills, imagination, and a few good friends with the willingness to explore and the determination to keep pedalling when all strength seemed spent. Above all, it took healthy scepticism towards the rigid ways of school sport and especially towards those charged with enforcing them, by kicking our backsides if necessary.

It has been said that the invention of the bicycle had a greater liberating effect on both urban and rural populations and especially on women than any other technological breakthrough, before or since. I cannot speak for the many who experienced that liberation at the dawn of the bicycle age. But I cannot imagine growing up in Lure, Haute-Saône without a bike.

CHAPTER TWELVE: MUSIC FOR A WHILE

The sound of a harpsichord: two skeletons copulating on a tin roof during a thunderstorm.

Thomas Beecham (1879-1961)

If sport played only a bit part in our school life, the fine arts figured even less prominently. At primary school age, painting was something children were expected to do spontaneously in their spare time, not a serious subject to be added to the curriculum. From my seven years of secondary school, I vaguely recall that we had an arts teacher for just one year. But apart from the faint recollection that this person was tall, lanky, and female, I have not the slightest memory of what we did in class.

Music fared little better.

In primary school, musical interludes consisted largely of belting out *La Marseillaise* once or twice a week. In secondary school, we had no music rooms, no instruments, not even tutors hired from outside to teach those with an interest in learning an instrument. Obviously, there was no school orchestra, no school band, not even a school choir. If anyone in the Ministry of Education in Paris gave music any thought, it must have been regarded as an effete distraction from proper study.

In all of those seven years, we had a music teacher for just one year when I was about fourteen or fifteen. Even if her name now escapes me, she at least figures clearly in my recollections, unlike the hapless lady who may or may not have taught me something about the visual arts.

Her mission was to induct us into the wonders of

274

classical music. As she stood almost apologetically before us, this admirable lady seemed so out of place in this barren environment that she looked as if she had got off the train in Lure, Haute-Saône by mistake. She was the only teacher in the school without a dedicated classroom and she had no piano or even a guitar on which she might demonstrate a musical point or invite one of us to try out an interesting musical trick. Beside the standard issue blackboard and stick of chalk, the only teaching aids at her disposal were the sole record player in the entire school and a modest stack of records. The coverage was patchy but the basics were there: a Mozart symphony or two, Beethoven's Fifth, some Schubert string quartets, Tchaikovsky's Swan Lake, and as a nod to the cradle of civilisation, Berlioz' *Symphonie Fantastique*. In between, she read from a book on the lives of The Greats and answered rare questions all the while trying her best to dissuade the peasants in the room from brandishing their pitchforks and rioting.

This teacher's heroic attempt at injecting a little high-end culture into our provincial lives was lost on virtually all of my classmates. A few came from homes where at least one parent had a musical background of sorts and some had access to a record player and even a classical record or two. But most of my friends' parents seemed to regard Maurice Chevalier as the epitome of musical sophistication and every one of my friends was convinced that the *yé-yé* genre, France's answer to the Beatles' *ya ya*, and in particular the repertoire of a very young Johnny Hallyday were about as high as the human creative genius could soar.

For better or worse, I was at the time beginning to imbibe Vivaldi, Bach, Haydn, and Mozart (on which more later) at home. To me, the music lessons that year offered not only relief from the pretensions of French literature and the frustrations of maths and chemistry but also confirmation that my bizarre musical tastes were shared by at least one other human being. Through my questions and comments and at considerable risk of being ostracised by my classmates as teacher's pet, I made it clear to the teacher that I was genuinely interested in what she had to say and that she had at least one friend in this harsh world. I do not think that I was flattering myself when I caught her casting hopeful glances in my direction as if seeking moral support: 'I know *you* understand', her pleading eyes seem to be saying. I missed her badly when she failed to show up at the start of the following school year but I did not blame her for absconding.

*

Initially, music making at home consisted exclusively of singing. Once most of my siblings and I were past the *Frère Jacques* and *Au Clair de la Lune* stage, the repertoire moved on to the all-time Catholic favourites, starting with a simple *Ave Maria* response to prayers read by my mother and eventually graduating to the much more challenging *Tantum Ergo*, whatever that meant. This took place *en famille* following our nightly ablutions, such as they were. The singing was led by my mother, who had a fine soprano voice.

During the weeks leading up to Christmas and until Twelfth Night, known to Catholics as Epiphany, we gathered around the nativity scene that we jointly unpacked each year from the shoe box in which it was kept and lovingly recreated in a corner of the living room on the first day of Advent as excitement over Christmas began to mount. All the key protagonists were there even if many of the plaster figures were a little chipped: Mary, Joseph, the baby Jesus, an ox, an ass, an angel hovering above from a nail in the wall, a contingent of sheep and a shepherd, and a trio of richly-robed, extravagantly-turbaned, luxuriantly-bearded Magi. Only one camel, though. Since scripture makes no mention of the three Magi sharing one animal, to save on fuel after splurging on gold, frankincense, and myrrh or to minimise their dung footprint, perhaps, I can only suppose that the nativity scene had lost two of its original camel figurines as they were dropped by a child over-eager to help with setting up the arrangement. A few years on, to an increasingly sceptical teenager surveying the nativity scene, the plaster figures betrayed not only naive tackiness but also questionable historicity. But at a younger age, what mattered was the overall effect, and the overall effect was magical.

All through the four long weeks of Advent, as the agonising wait for Christmas dragged on, the musical highlight of each evening was the communal singing of *Venez, Divin Messie* (Come, Divine Messiah), ostensibly a plea to the deity's envoy to get his skates on and come down and sort out the mess humans had made of their affairs. But for us children, the song expressed more immediate concerns with Christmas and its plenty as well as the frustrations of the inexorable wait. Still, the countdown was on and unlike seekers after Messiahs, we would not be disappointed.

On Christmas Eve, when the wait was over at last, the repertoire switched to the French classics: *Il est né le divin enfant* (Born Is He, Little Child Divine), *Les anges dans nos campagnes* (Angels O'er The Fields Were Singing), and of course *Douce Nuit* (Silent Night), a lovely melody that I initially assumed was French but was slightly disappointed to learn later was in fact Austrian. But this discovery turned out useful because it enabled me to dissuade my grandmother from expunging it from our repertoire on the grounds that it was German and therefore had no place in a French home. The carols were rendered with zeal. But *Petit Papa Noël* was banned on account of its irreligious references to rooftops and toys in their thousands and especially to the theologically unsound notion that in between errands, every child's favourite fat Finn dwelled in heaven and not, as everyone knew, at the North Pole.

Twelve nights later, Epiphany rounded off the Christmas celebrations with a flourish. This was a bitter-sweet moment. A year is a long time in the life of a child and the following Christmas seemed an eternity away. But the mood was soon lightened by the appearance at the end of lunch of the much-awaited Epiphany cake, which by tradition contains a lone dry bean slipped in by the baker and invisible to lunchers unless they lift the cake and look underneath for the tell-tale patch in the pastry. The idea is that the lucky finder of the bean becomes king or queen for the day and gets to wear a paper crown. The practice, common in French-speaking Europe but also in Spain and in parts of Latin America, stems from an ancient association between Epiphany and the Magi, often referred to in those cultures as 'kings' as indeed they are in the popular American carol 'We Three Kings of Orient Are'.

Family tradition required that the cake be cut by my father. Each of us then bit gingerly into our share to avoid losing a tooth to the bean if it happened to be lurking in our own slice. Once the bean had been located and triumphantly displayed and the hollering had died down, the winner had the paper crown deposited on his or her head with mock solemnity by my father and then spent the afternoon playfully bossing around less fortunate siblings. As I grew older, it puzzled me that since we all shared the same cake, the draw invariably favoured one of the six children in the family and never one of the adults. Only later, once we were old enough not to be shocked by the revelation of the sleight of hand to which my parents jointly descended, did my mother confess that she tipped off my father by making a discreet mark on the visible side of the cake and that he made sure that the three adults in the family helped themselves first from a safely bean-free section of the cake.

Next morning, the nativity scene was dismantled and the figurines returned to their shoe box and stored away for another eleven months.

*

Like school, home was entirely without musical instruments. My father was said by some of his relations to have had some ability on the piano but he always denied it. Perhaps he had been forced to take piano lessons and had hated the experience so much that he had no wish to recall the ordeal. On the rare occasions we were admitted to the drawing-rooms of the well-to-do, each featuring the obligatory upright piano standing in a corner and groaning under framed photographs of fierce-looking ancestors, my father never gave the slightest impression that he was itching to go over and tickle the ivories.

My mother, always more voluble than my father about most subjects and about family anecdotes in particular, recounted having had to take violin lessons and not having relished the experience in the slightest. She dealt with the imposition by asking to be allowed to practice in the benevolent presence of her father, typically putting bow to strings just as her more disciplinarian mother was about to go out on some errand. The terms of the accord were that as long as she practiced a little, he would let her off the hook soon after his wife had rounded the corner.

In our case, a privately-financed musical education for six children was out of the question. Musical talent was thin on the ground in Lure, Haute-Saône so private lessons meant a train journey to a nearby metropolis, most likely Belfort, where the arts supposedly flourished and music teachers were said to line the streets. To my parents, this would have been far too great an expense. Besides, basic education came first. Musical talent, if any, got no one a coveted government job. It would have to take care of itself.

My first chance to explore music independently came when I was about ten and I won a harmonica in a raffle. The harmonica was the diatonic type, with just ten holes and designed to play in just one key. Playing the harmonica is largely a matter of breathing in and out more or less normally through your mouth while sliding the thing from side to side and trying not to let the sharp edges cut your lips to shreds. Most of the time, you breathe in on one note and breathe out on the next and most simple tunes consist largely of a series of alternations between breathing in and breathing out. Provided that you do not become prematurely fixated on hexachordal combinatoriality and it is not your ambition to perform a five-part motet single-handedly, it does not take very long to produce a recognisable tune on the harmonica: *Frère Jacques*, say, or *Au Clair de la Lune,* if you prefer.

Later, as my lungs expanded and my mouth-to-ears coordination improved, I requested as a Christmas present a deluxe model, the chromatic type, this time. This marvel had fully sixteen holes and a button to one side that made semitones possible and therefore allowed the performer to play in more than one key. So

I gradually moved on from nursery rhymes to more ambitious compositions including *La Marseillaise*, with its fiendish key change in the middle but, mercifully, without its fatuous lyrics. I mention the lung issue because doing justice to serious music on a chromatic harmonica goes far beyond the normal breathing routine. Take that tricky passage in the middle of *La Marseillaise*, for example. The tune does not simply lurch into a key most composers don't even know exists. Just as you are psyching yourself up for the shift and the extensive use of the side button this is about to entail, you have to negotiate the bugle effect by breathing out on no fewer than nine consecutive notes, each of which has to be held for what feels like an hour and a half and with absolutely no chance of catching your breath in between. If you are French but lack strong lungs, it is simply not possible to play the chromatic harmonica and swell with patriotic pride simultaneously.

*

Beyond Christmas carols and my humble harmonica, the main source of live music in my early life was church. Only the almost furtive *messe basse* had no sung component. Targeted at the early-rising segment of the market, this service was designed to combine sleepy devotion and speed, and mumbling served the purpose admirably. But each Sunday, the *pièce de résistance* was the *grand messe*, a resonant affair with organ and choir in full flight and plenty of back and forth between priest and congregation: all in Latin, naturally.

As Sunday high mass was about to start, choir members gathered, climbed the creaky stairs that led to the organ loft at the back of the church, and positioned themselves on either side of the instrument. Recruitment to the choir was gently selective and its efforts were not without merit. The forces consisted of the usual mix of ages and genders, with the unmarried daughters of middle-class families providing a sizeable contingent. This included the choir leader, Mademoiselle Seguin, a respected *notaire*, and her two equally unmarried sisters. The organist, Mademoiselle Caucheresse, was another. All were hard-working, spirited women who toiled in the dusty recesses of the baroque building while the priests basked in the limelight below. The choir suffered from the dearth of tenors familiar to choir leaders the world over but a brace of solid baritones knew how to make themselves heard. An over-ambitious choice of repertoire, a Palestrina motet picked to mark a major holiday, for example, was always liable to disintegrate halfway through. But the standard offerings and in particular the canonical sequence of *Kyrie, Gloria, Credo, Sanctus*, and *Agnus Dei* went smoothly every time.

For the choir, the time to shine was Christmas. The Puritanical notion that music is somehow ungodly and a distraction from proper devotion could not have been more foreign to the version of Catholicism I grew up with. Church services and especially Christmas services without music would have been unthinkable.

True to Catholic tradition, the devotional sequence kicked off with midnight mass, followed by a full-blown sung mass in the morning. Coming on the heels of Advent and its deliberately thin musical offerings, the opening blast of the organ just before midnight sent a tingle down my spine: Christmas festivities had truly begun. In a family where children were in bed by nine and parents by ten, staying up so late for the once-a-year event was exhilarating enough, but the music pitched the excitement level even higher.

The highlight of midnight mass was the rendering of *Minuit Chrétiens*, a seasonal favourite known to English-speaking carol singers as 'O Holy Night'. This is the work of Frenchman Adolphe Adam, the prolific early nineteenth-century composer of a string of long-forgotten operas and one enduring ballet, *Giselle*. Although the lyrics are soppy as they come, the melody is a minor masterpiece. But it is very hard to sing because it goes from 'Swing Low, Sweet Chariot' range one minute to 'Queen of the Night' territory the next. This was not a feat Mademoiselle Seguin and her well-meaning crew of warblers had any hope of doing justice to unaided. To pull off the trick, they needed expert assistance. This came in the form of the dashing Monsieur Lambert.

If Lure, Haute-Saône had been possessed of boulevards, Monsieur Lambert would have been best described as a *boulevardier*. In effect, he was a fop. A natty dresser, he went about his errands on sunny days in white slacks, white shoes, and striped blazer, with a boater atop is immaculate *coiffure* and a silk scarf around his slender neck. He was not a regular member of the church choir. In fact, he was never seen in church except once a year during midnight mass. His reputation as a tenor of distinction meant that he was much in demand at the musical *soirées* held by the town's better class of housewives for the entertainment and edification of their peers. He sang in the reedy, slightly pinched tones favoured by French tenors and he enjoyed the adulation of one and all and especially of the choir members, who regarded him as God's gift to music..., just as he regarded himself.

Now and again, rumours went around that Monsieur Lambert was paid for his contribution to Christmas worship. To me, this was shocking. How could this man accept pieces of silver for what he apparently considered a mere date in the artistic calendar but everyone else including myself saw as a matter of everlasting life?

More shocking still at least for the older altar boys, who shared this tidbit once they deemed me mature enough to be taken into their confidence, was the rumour that Monsieur Lambert was occasionally invited by one or two of the town's better class of housewives to grace more than their drawing room. But even if I had more than the vaguest notion of what this rumour meant in practice, with Christmas, divine service, the prospect of a midnight feast closely followed by the opening of Christmas presents, and especially Monsieur Lambert's celebrated interpretation of *Minuit Chrétiens* to focus on, who cared about what the town's housewives got up to in between musical *soirées*?

At the start, Monsieur Lambert's performance of *Minuit Chrétiens* was uneventful. For the first few lines, the melody hovers dangerously close to the lower reaches of his range but he invariably managed it. It then rises in illustration of words suggesting hope and redemption and finally soars in a heart-stopping leap on the cry of *Noël, Noël* before returning to earth and ending on a trill, suggesting that joy has indeed come to the world. For the singer, the problem is negotiating the leap of a full octave on the final *Noël, Noël*. Regular Christmas worshipers and, not least, altar boys knew what to expect. Fun was about to be had.

Among the altar boys, the tittering started as soon as Monsieur Lambert started belting out *Peuple debout, Chante ta délivrance!* (People Arise! Sing Of Your Deliverance!). The suspense was unbearable. He sailed through the first *Noël, Noël* with the melody largely unscathed. But when he reached the final *Noël, Noël*, Monsieur Lambert invariably undershot the high note by about three quarter tones and emitted a sound halfway between a rasp and a croak.

At this point, the tittering intensified then turned to giggling and finally to out-loud laughter. We exploded. We elbowed each other and covered our mouths to hide our guffaws from the priests as best we could. From year to year, we longed to hear Monsieur Lambert's singing again and we mimicked the more idiosyncratic aspects of his interpretation gleefully. The eleven-month wait followed by the four lean weeks of Advent seemed endless, but the anticipation of Monsieur Lambert's cameo performance at midnight mass made the long wait worthwhile.

*

So much for live music, but what about the canned variety? Lure, Haute-Saône was hardly at the vanguard of technological advances, but everyone I knew had a radio: one per home, rarely more.

In our home, the radio receiver was a thing of substance. About the size of an average modern television, it came with a switch for choosing from long-, medium-, and short-wave modes, a large knob for selecting stations, and an even larger knob for adjusting the volume. The loudspeaker was covered with a sheet of loose fabric that vibrated in concert with the disembodied voice beyond. The front of the radio consisted of a sheet of glass on which were written the locations of major transmitters. Behind that was a vertical needle, which slid sideways at every twiddle of the large knob. So in my idle moments, whenever my father did not require the exclusive use of the radio for informational or instructional purposes, I twiddled and I felt that I was getting to know the world a little better. If the needle came to rest on a spot marked Hilversum, for example, I heard a language that my father, who seemed to know where every place was in the world, announced was Dutch. If the needle settled on Droitwich, the language must be English. Not that I could tell the difference.

The radio sat in splendour in a prominent section of our living room. In many of the other homes I had occasional access to, the top of the family radio featured a selection of photos, often flanked by a plastic flower in a thin vase for aesthetic balance. In our home, at the conclusion of lunch, once he was free to give casualty counts in Algeria or Vietnam his undivided attention, my father stood by the radio, leaning slightly towards it as if lending an attentive ear to a close friend imparting sensitive information.

Later, when I was about twelve or thirteen, came a technological breakthrough that astonished the world, or at least Lure, Haute-Saône: the transistor radio. I had – and still have – not the slightest idea what a transistor is or how it does what it does. But I remember that the result was revolutionary. Suddenly, listeners could take their music and their news with them everywhere they went including any vantage point they elected to occupy along the route of the *Tour de France*. Transistor radios must have been livening up Fourth of July barbecues, high teas on English lawns, and boating parties on the Seine for years. Lure, Haute-Saône could hardly have been the first destination targeted by transistor radio marketers. But when it came, it was a sensation, in our home at least.

The upheaval in our listening habits came one day when Patrick, a classmate, invited me and my inner core of friends to spend a summer afternoon at his house. Patrick was a relative loner who flitted in and out of our social group. But the mid-afternoon snacks at his house were tasty and our Monopoly games in his yard lively and fun. Invitations from Patrick were rare, so they were never turned down. When one came, we guessed that Patrick had something important to discuss with us or, most likely, to show us.

Patrick lived at the top of the hill at the northern end of town high above the urban hubbub, such as it was. The house had been a farm not so long ago and it still betrayed its origins in appearance as much as in location. Next to it was a large semi-rural space that combined untended grass, fruit trees, and a wooden table and benches. In one direction was the town, in the other the great open spaces. At the back was a converted barn, which housed the family Renault and Patrick's father's workshop.

Patrick was an only child who had been raised by a mother and a grandmother who doted on him. His father was a shadowy figure who lived on the edge of the family group and was rarely seen inside the house. He spent his days in his workshop, sawing and hammering and eventually turning out furniture of unimaginative design and questionable durability. Like our school *concierge*, he invariably wore faded working-class dungarees and he had a thin cigarette permanently hanging from a corner of his mouth. Every couple of hours or so, the door of the workshop creaked open and he came out of hiding to breathe God's air. He shuffled about the yard, looking disgruntled and running a critical eye over his son's choice of friends. He then leaned against the wall of his workshop, rolled himself a fresh cigarette, and enjoyed an invigorating puff before shuffling back into his lair, and the sawing and hammering resumed.

I mention Patrick's father because this partially house-trained caricature of a grumpy Frenchman did not seem the type that would go scurrying after every technological innovation, chequebook in hand, unless it was the latest in handsaws or a revolutionary new kind of nail, perhaps. If Patrick had got us up to his hilltop retreat, it must be because he planned to dazzle us with an acquisition he himself had lobbied for.

And so it was. As we gathered around the wooden table in the yard that afternoon, Patrick proudly unveiled the first transistor radio any of us had ever seen.

It was about the size of a large brick. Compared to the heavy, immovable radios we were familiar with, it looked like a toy. Instead of the standard dark brown most radios came in, this one was bright blue. It had a nifty on/off switch, a sliding volume control, a collapsible antenna, a rotary dial, and most startling of all, a carrying handle. What would they think of next!

Patrick revelled in his moment of triumph as he patted the blue radio with one hand and changed stations with the other. We sat, transfixed, and begged to be allowed to touch the thing and maybe twiddle a bit, just once.

The fly in the ointment was that in common with all my friends, Patrick's musical tastes ran exclusively to French *yé-yé*, Johnny Hallyday included. But Patrick controlled the rotary dial so *yé-yé* it was, all afternoon. Respite came from commercials, often extolling the magical powers of mineral water and its uncanny ability to set even a French liver right in minutes regardless of how much *foie gras* a diner had put away the night before. Linking *yé-yé* to commercials and back again was a stream of cheerfully inane patter designed to encourage the masses to look on the bright side of French life while never learning anything of consequence about it. In French radio talk as in much of French discourse, it is not what is said that matters so much as *how* it is said.

Patrick was good company. He cultivated an air of

detached nonchalance as if nothing really mattered except having fun out of school but especially *in* school and preferably at one of his classmates' expense. He was a notorious prankster who specialised in launching outrageous schemes calculated to bring school discipline to its knees and then sat back and watched others take the blame.

But there was more to Patrick than met the eye. With just two more years of secondary school to go, entirely out of the blue, he announced that he was hereby renouncing all pranks and abjuring all japes and would henceforth devote his days and the best part of his nights to studying. I liked Patrick because he had always been unstinting in his efforts to subvert school and all it stood for and inject some spark into the tedium. For as long as I could remember, he had been a stalwart supporter of the confederacy of dunces of which Principal's son and best friend Daniel, physics and chemistry teacher's son Philippe, and I were committed members. But Patrick meant what he said. He went on to ace all the exams we resolutely kept failing and later sailed through university in record time. We of the true faith never quite forgave him for this act of betrayal. His just deserts came in the form of decades of academic drudgery as professor of French literature along with endless tribulations at the hands of successive wives, who never quite managed to live up to the doting for which his mother and grandmother had set the standard.

*

For music lovers such as myself, who knew that there was more to the harmony of the spheres than Maurice Chevalier, *yé-yé*, and Johnny Hallyday, *France Musique* was the radio station of choice. The difficulty was that it was only available in the FM waveband. For my friends, this was not a problem. They never listened to anything other than commercial stations and these broadcast in long wave, which every French radio receiver catered for. The upside of long-wave was that French radio fans were never far from a fix since it reached into every corner of the *hexagone* and even beyond. The downside was that the fare was strong on *yé-yé*, mineral water commercials, and cheerfully inane patter but weak on Mozart.

In all matters cultural, my father ruled the roost and listening choices in the home were his alone to make. These were guided by two core beliefs. One was that information supplied by anyone determined to sell you something you did not know you needed was inherently suspect and therefore to be shunned. This put commercial radio of all stripes beyond the pale. The second was that except for the occasional strain of Swiss oompah and yodelling, music meant classical music, which for my father meant Mozart, mostly.

I never discovered where my father's love of Mozart originated. The rural setting in which he grew up during and immediately after World War I could hardly have provided the inspiration let alone the means. As far as he was willing to reveal, nothing in his schooling or in the environment provided by the priests who taught him predicted his musical tastes. In occasional references to his first teaching job with the Jesuits, he mentioned that the school boasted a gramophone player and a stack of classical music records and that the long winter evenings were often spent among colleagues, chatting, smoking, and listening to music. I can only surmise that Mozart must have figured prominently in these men's listening habits.

When I began to feast on classical music as a young teenager, *France Musique* offered an eclectic fare as long as listeners were partial to the syrupy (think Brahms), the soporific (think Mahler), the jarring (think Prokoviev), or the plain loud (think Brahms, Mahler, or Prokoviev). But now and again, the *France Musique* programmers managed to squeeze in some Mozart, a little Haydn, and even an occasional baroque piece, mostly by Vivaldi or Bach but sometimes even by Handel.

Before dinner, except for some inevitable bickering, the recitation of Latin declensions, and occasional sighs of despair at the pointlessness of algebra, our homework took place in quasi-monastic silence. But after dinner, the mood changed. Siblings went to their nightly ablutions in an immutable sequence: the younger the earlier, while the older and later ablutionists awaited their turn by giving Latin grammar and the pointlessness of algebra further consideration. By then, in a home blessedly free of television, the family living room was alive with the sound of *France Musique*, which provided much-needed relief from the school-related gloom.

*

How a preference for one type of music over another emerges is mysterious. But like language, music goes in through the ears and it requires no formal deconstruction to be internalised, especially early in life.

By the time I was about fourteen, despite having no theoretical grounding in music and no practical experience of music making beyond what my modest skills on the harmonica permitted, I could tell Mozart from Haydn after just a few bars, followed soon after by the almost unerring ability to tell Bach from Handel and Vivaldi from everyone else.

Over the years, I tried – I honestly tried – to add the syrupy, the soporific, the jarring, and the plain loud to my listening range but to no avail. With due respect to Brahms, Mahler, and Prokoviev and their many devotees but also to Johnny Hallyday, the Beatles, Abba, Bruce Springsteen, Michael Jackson, Lady Gaga, and every rapper – dead or alive – that ever mouthed an obscenity, my tastes have remained anchored in music composed before about 1800, with a special place in my affections for compositions from the baroque era, including those of Couperin and especially Purcell.

What led to this predilection initially was my father's inspired decision to splurge on an FM radio receiver. In this respect, he was an innovator as this was the very first FM radio Monsieur Tiétard, the local dealer, had ever managed to sell in Lure, Haute-Saône.

The FM radio was a thing of beauty. It was massive, so large that fully half of the vast dresser on which it was to sit had to be cleared of books and family mementoes to make room for it. To the inexpert eye, nothing apart from its bulk distinguished it from its predecessors. It had just as many knobs and the dial had Hilversum and Droitwich and all the other familiar stations on it. The difference was that it had the capability to bring *France Musique* to discerning ears.

The problem with the FM radio was that ,as with most wonders of modern science especially at the trial stage, the beast was prone to sudden swoons. When this happened, my father dropped by Monsieur Tiétard's workshop on his way home from work, informed him of the latest dereliction of duty on the part of the FM radio, and requested after-sales service as soon as was convenient. Quite when this would be was always a little vague. Monsieur Tiétard was no mere radio repair man: he was an *artiste* of the listening world, who followed his heart, not the condition of his bank account or the dictates of his appointment book, assuming that he had one. He was not strong on schedules. But he would not rest until he had the FM radio buzzing again.

On a day and at a time of his choosing, Monsieur Tiétard shut up shop and rode his bike over to our house. Once in the family living room, he opened his toolbox and set to work. If my siblings and I were at home on these occasions, we watched in awe as he turned the radio back to front and revealed a mysterious world of bulbs, coils, cables, and wires. He took his screwdriver to everything that could be screwed or unscrewed, here testing a bulb, there tightening a cable, and meandering between wave lengths and stations to check on what was working and what was not.

Monsieur Tiétard was the kind of radio technician that would leave no cable untightened, no bulb untested, and no knob unturned until he had *France Musique* back on the air. This could take a very long time indeed. If the technological challenge meant that he had to pass on the sacrosanct French lunch, so be it. Always attentive to the hungry, my mother kept him alive and on task by diverting a little sustenance from our own lunch in his direction. But if the technical problem was especially baffling, my siblings and I had to leave the lunch table and head back to school for our afternoon classes while he still had his head inside the radio and was still screwing and unscrewing like a deranged scientist tinkering with a malfunctioning Frankenstein. Time did not matter to this most dedicated of men. Only results counted. Besides, the likelihood that a resident of Lure, Haute-Saône might walk into his shop that afternoon and ask to see the latest offerings in FM radios was remote: better spend it toiling in the service of music in a customer's living room than sitting in his deserted workshop bemoaning the public's enduring love affair with long-wave radio, *yé-yé*, Johnny Hallyday, commercials for mineral water, and cheerfully inane patter. They do not make FM radio technicians like Monsieur Tiétard anymore.

*

Even when the bulbs, coils, cables, and wires deep inside the family FM radio went out of alignment and the contraption fell silent, there was another way to keep music alive. The top of the radio consisted of a heavy lid that concealed the latest in record player technology. All that was needed to provide the musical background to an evening of memorising Latin declensions and pondering the pointlessness of algebra was a record collection, which my Mozart-loving father went about assembling in his usual methodical manner.

As soon as the family finances allowed, he signed up to a record club modelled on the then ubiquitous book clubs. The rules required that subscribers buy one record each month. The catalogue was surprisingly eclectic. It was strong on the syrupy, the soporific, the jarring, and the plain loud. But it also made room for Vivaldi, Bach, Handel, Haydn, and of course Mozart. Over time, my father showed far greater openness of mind than I would have done in his position or have done ever since, and a substantial dose of Beethoven, Schubert, Chopin, Verdi, even Dvorak was added to the collection.

To start off the collection, the record club presented new subscribers with a compilation of all-time favourites. Buried in the middle of one side of our very first record was Vivaldi's concerto for two trumpets in C, a gem I played so often that it is a wonder the track did not wear out. To the uninitiated especially, the piece is immediately seductive because it combines

294

pulsating energy with harmonic simplicity, colour, and virtuosity. If music this exuberant does not all your cares beguile, nothing will.

As I listened, sleeve notes provided the human dimension so often lacking in recorded music and even in live performances. Bach complained about being paid late and being overcharged for his beer, and he had trouble controlling his numerous children and in particular his teenage daughters. Handel had to navigate the temper tantrums of prima donna *castrati* as well as the vagaries of the economic climate if his productions were to succeed. Mozart conducted a cheerfully scatological correspondence with his beloved sister Nannerl and later wrote letters filled with sexual innuendos to his wife Constanze, switching to (surprisingly good) French whenever the content threatened to embarrass even him. Vivaldi was a man of parts. He earned his crust as a priest but fooled his ecclesiastical employers into believing that he suffered from asthma so that he could sneak behind the altar while saying mass and fake coughing fits as he jotted down the musical idea that had just come into his head before he forgot how it went.

I never read the sleeve notes on Brahms, Mahler, or Prokoviev. Compared to the earlier composers and their musical fireworks and especially to Mozart and his preternatural combination of endless creativity, boundless energy, and earthy normality, the lives of composers who knowingly catered to the lachrymose, the catatonic, and the hard-of-hearing would almost certainly have been an anticlimax. The risk was not worth taking.

Later in life, I graduated from the harmonica to the recorder, the guitar, even the lute. Quite what my audiences thought of my skills is not for me to say. But my earliest encounters with classical music were formative as well as hugely enjoyable. And for that, I am grateful to my parents for their willingness to put up with my juvenile efforts on the harmonica and later for making it possible for me to graduate to the chromatic model. Above all, I am grateful to my father for his decision to invest in the FM radio and the record collection.

Like all fathers, mine made a few questionable decisions about how he ran family affairs. But the day he brought *France Musique* into our living room and then signed up to the record club were two of his truly inspired moments.

CHAPTER THIRTEEN: COUNTRY ROAD

To my mind, the only possible pet is a cow. Cows love you. They will listen to your problems and never ask a thing in return.

Bill Bryson (1951-)

Except in the depth of winter, for parents and children alike, the Sunday afternoon drive was the highlight of the week. Like dogs wagging their tails at the prospect of a trip to the shops in the back of the pickup truck, my siblings and I could not wait for Sunday lunch to be over and for the signal to be given that it was time to jump into the family car. But the excitement was nothing compared to the buzz that built up over several weeks as the time approached for an all-day trip to Champdôtre, my father's ancestral village.

Children are easily puzzled, so they like explanations, preferably simple ones. If none is offered, they make one up. In my mind, Champdôtre was aptly named: it was a place of *champs*, or 'fields', and fields meant boundless spaces and the freedom to range through their riches.

Champdôtre was tiny. The village sat at the eastern edge of Burgundy, which consists of a featureless expanse that stretches from the sloping vineyards where world-renowned *Bourgogne* vintages are produced to the lazily sinuous Saône River. The landscape is flat as can be.

The village clustered around the intersection of two rural roads leading nowhere in particular except to even more nondescript villages. Almost all the buildings were farmhouses. Each one was home to a family operation consisting of an middle-aged couple, a son or two and their respective wives, and a smattering of offspring. Most farms featured a herd of cows, perhaps a few rabbits, and lots of chickens. The village boasted a primary school, a post office, and a municipal hall, all of which doubled as meeting places where crop prices, weather forecasts, and village gossip could be traded. Railway tracks still ran past the village and steam trains had once taken the villagers to Auxonne, the local market town, and beyond to the bright lights of Dijon, the regional metropolis. But in my day, the trains no longer ran and the little railway station stood shuttered up at one particularly forlorn end of the village.

Near the intersection of the two roads stood the village church, a squat building of attractive pink sandstone. In a dusty open space at the intersection itself was a small war memorial. For such a small place, Champdôtre had managed to send a surprising number of its sons to the World War I slaughter, one or two of whom shared our family name and would have lengthened the roster of required social calls had they lived. On Sunday afternoons, the space around the war memorial was aroused from its week-long torpor by noisy games of *pétanque* as farmers relaxed under ancient plane trees and their heavy steel bowls landed with a thud that sent up a cloud of dust. Opposite was the village *café* and next to that the butcher and the baker. No candlemaker – at least not anymore.

The church and the *café* eyed each other suspiciously across the hallowed *pétanque* ground. Each building was the nexus of one of the two opposing belief systems, Catholicism and secularism, which in Champdôtre as in Lure, Haute-Saône as well as in all of France had defined much of social life for as long as anyone could remember. Both schools of thought and their respective rites involved wine, but there the resemblance ended. The function of each one

298

was clear: those who patronised the one shunned the other, and vice versa, except for a clutch of prudent farmers who modelled their theology on Pascal's, hedged their bets, and attended mass but sat out the sermon in the warm embrace of the *café* in winter or over a quick game of *pétanque* in summer.

*

One of my father's rare yarns from his childhood linked church and *café* in a highly incongruous manner. During his rare stays in the village when his boarding school was on holiday, my father was regularly pressed into service as an altar boy. This gave him a chance to witness major village rituals from which most children were normally excluded or chose to exclude themselves. The population of the village was still substantial even after the carnage of World War I so church functions were frequent, including funerals.

On these melancholy occasions, by convention, the hearse was pulled by a wheezy nag well past its shelf life but considered ideally suited to the task since a funeral *cortège* is best conducted at a stately pace. Of all the horses in Champdôtre, that horse was the least likely to exceed the speed limit and go cantering off over the horizon just for the fun of it.

But on one occasion, fate decreed that an ancient farmer and the horse that was supposed to ferry him to his final resting place should both join the Choir Invisible on the same day. This was harvest time and no spare horse could be had for love or money, until someone remembered Monsieur Linôve.

A distant relative of my father's, Monsieur Linôve was a farmer. In Champdôtre, neither characteristic was going to get him noticed. But Monsieur Linôve was different because he was a strong believer in a positive

299

correlation between alcohol consumption and agricultural yields. Each weekday morning, he harnessed his horse, loaded a generous supply of *vin ordinaire* into the cart, clambered onto the driving seat, and pointed the horse field-ward. By sundown, Monsieur Linôve was no longer capable of telling an agricultural yield from a hole in the ground, but through assiduous practice over the years, the horse had memorised its moves. As horse and cart were not uncoupled all day, as soon as Monsieur Linôve managed to haul himself on board, the horse went on automatic pilot and headed homeward. Indirectly, that is.

One of the key factors the horse could be relied upon to remember was that the route from field to farmhouse passed first the church and then the *café,* where the horse came to a lumbering halt, Monsieur Linôve clambered down from the cart in the most dignified manner he could muster under the circumstances and staggered inside. There he remained until festivities were declared over for the night. But before the assembled farmers could make their way back to their loved ones, their final duty consisted of carrying Monsieur Linôve out of the *café*, hoisting him onto his cart, and giving the horse a slap on the rump to send it, the cart, and Monsieur Linôve on their way before bidding each other good night. The horse then trundled through the darkened village entirely unaided and, without fail, delivered Monsieur Linôve to his doorstep and into the arms of the long-suffering Madame Linôve.

On the day of the funeral in question, as the search for a spare horse to harness to the hearse was becoming increasingly frantic, a perspicacious neighbour reported that as he passed Monsieur Linôve's house that morning, he had noticed his cart standing idle in the farmyard. This was peak harvesting time, when farmer and horse should have been making hay and not wallowing in the matrimonial bed or on the thick layer of straw, respectively, into which each would presumably have collapsed on their return to base the night before.

Polite inquiries with Madame Linôve revealed that Monsieur Linôve had done himself exceptionally well in the *café* the night before and had been quite unable to bestir himself and head for the fields that morning. This being the case, the perspicacious neighbour reasoned, his horse must be available. Once a suitable financial arrangement was reached, the horse was persuaded to cooperate and leave the comfort of the stable, where it must have been thanking its lucky star that its owner was shiftless, drunken Monsieur Linôve and not some masochistic type who believed in toiling from dawn to dusk and never touched anything stronger than *café au lait*.

So the horse was led to the hearse and harnessed to it. At the conclusion of the funeral service, my father as head altar boy, priest, horse, hearse, grieving relatives, and friends of the family, in that order, began their doleful journey to the cemetery at the far end of the village. But what no one had considered was that the very first building the *cortège* would pass as it left the church would be the *café*. And once there, the horse reverted to default mode and made its customary pit stop outside the *café*, there to reflect, one imagines, upon the uncanny parallels between the equine and the human conditions and the transitory nature of earthly life for all.

And there the horse remained, lost in its reveries, from which nothing could budge it.

The villagers tried everything: they commanded, they shouted, they pulled, they pushed, they slapped, they whipped, they entreated, they cajoled, they blandished: nothing worked. The horse stayed put as if tethered not to the hearse but to the *café* itself. It was as if the horse was impersonating a mule.

With the bereaved getting restless and muffled tittering beginning to ripple through the ranks, it occurred to one of the mourners that since the stick approach had failed, the carrot alternative might be worth a shot. If, this strategist reasoned, a bucketful of oats were to be placed in front of the horse and then moved forward little by little once the horse took the bait, this might uproot it and induce it to put its best hoof forward at last. The reasoning had been sound: the horse took a nibble, seemed to be considering its options, and finally decided to go with the majority view, bring the mule impersonation to an end, and proceed with the sad business of ferrying the deceased through the village and across the Styx.

Posterity does not record how the succession for the honour of pulling the village hearse went. Presumably, a more pliant nag was head-hunted and offered a permanent contract until some multinational firm of funeral arrangers or other acquired the rights to handle the entire process, from the closing of the eyes and the plugging of orifices to throwing in the last shovelful of earth and erecting the gravestone. As years went by, government regulations ballooned and village rites for the disposal of the departed became about as full of surprises as a commute on a Swiss train or Election Night in Singapore.

*

At the time of our visits to the village, my father's family seemed little better than dirt poor. But earlier generations must have enjoyed relative wealth because

302

my father's two surviving aunts lived in what was still the largest house in the village. Appropriately named *Grand Cour*, the compound consists of buildings that occupied three sides of what was literally a 'large yard'. Clearly, the house had once been *grand* in both the English and the French senses of the word. The construction date was proclaimed in black tiles that stood out against the red-tiled roof: 1805. By the front door was the farm's only source of fresh water, a deep well kept safe – more or less – by four vertical stone slabs that propped each other up and formed a precarious barrier to youthful inquisitiveness.

When water was needed, it was hauled up in a tin bucket hanging on a long chain and then poured into cooking pots and, more rarely, washbasins. On a lucky day, free entertainment sprung up when loud clangs followed by a splashing sound and, depending on the gender of the water-gatherer, a high-pitched wail or a stream of blasphemous oaths signalled that the bucket had come off its moorings and dropped to the bottom of the well. Restoring the water supply was then a simple matter of fishing the bucket back up by catching it with a hook lowered down the well at the end a long rope. These were dramatic moments in the life of the *Grand Cour* and all its residents.

Facing the house on the far side of the yard was a barn of magnificent proportions and filled with wondrous smells: onions, the main local crop, and hay, but also apples and potatoes. To children confined to exiguous homes for most of the year, the building seemed vast, with dark corners and mysterious spaces scattered almost randomly around the structure and at various levels, each one awaiting exploration. With a selection of our cousins from among the fifteen on the paternal side often in attendance and a multitude of village children permanently in search of playmates, my siblings and I did not lack for company and explorations invariably took place in groups. Besides, such a cavernous building would have felt far too spooky for a visiting child to explore alone. Diversions involved pretending to be operating long-abandoned farming machinery, including a horse-drawn mechanical harvester on which pairs of explorers took turns at being farmer or horse and then swapped roles, and climbing rickety wooden steps to a higher level and jumping into the hay below.

One end of the barn was occupied by the stable that was home to the farm's only remaining working horse. Partitioned off – just – from the stable was the outhouse, which consisted of a large wooden box with a hole in the top plugged by a wooden cover that did what it could to keep the place relatively salubrious. Impaled on a rusty nail in the wall was a sheaf of square pieces of paper cut from recent issues of *Le Bien Public*, 'The Public Good', the aptly named local newspaper. In winter, the place was frigid. But in all seasons, trips to the outhouse meant lifting the heavy cover, ignoring the fetid pile below, and for children, and then sitting precariously on the edge of a hole designed for much larger bottoms to a background of rattling noises from the horse next door as it fed or shifted in its sleep. If the combination did not induce instant constipation in the chronically diarrhetic, nothing would.

Facing the street on the other side of the farmhouse was a large vegetable garden that yielded all the prerequisites of a French country diet: peas, green beans, tomatoes, lettuce, leeks, potatoes. Next to the barn was an orchard. The trees were no longer cared for but they still managed to yield a wide variety of fruit: apples, pears, cherries, plums, even quinces. An early lesson for visiting children was to beware of fallen plums. Juicy as they were, by the time we got at them, most had been burrowed into by wasps, which did not take kindly to seeing their feast interrupted and took their revenge by stinging the offender on the inside of the mouth. Any produce that could not be enjoyed on the spot was turned into jams and preserves for the winter months. Beyond the orchard were fields that stretched to the horizon, with the church tower in the next village just visible in the distance, much in fact as in Millais' moving paintings of 'The Gleaners' or 'The Angelus', with their featureless, parched rural landscapes in which the artist placed the figures of simple country folk at their work or their devotions. To naturally effervescent children, the scene seemed lifeless, with the tedium it induced dispelled only by the occasional shrieks of a mother struggling to control her own children in a nearby farmhouse. But to adults seeking solace from the vicissitudes of daily life, the serenity of the sight, the twitter of birds, and the regular peal of church bells must have seemed idyllic.

*

My father's living relatives consisted of two aunts and two uncles on his mother's side. When they addressed us or the rare outsiders who ventured into the village, they spoke a strongly accented but comprehensible form of French. But among themselves, they switched to the *Bourguignon* dialect, which put their conversations beyond our reach and made them sound remote and mysterious. Although my father was clearly able to follow these exchanges, I sensed early that it would not be wise to ask if he could speak the dialect because he seemed to feel uncomfortable about revealing too much of his humble origins.

'Soul of the house', as Spanish speakers would say,

was Tante Constance. As one of my father's aunts, she was technically a great-aunt to us. But she was known to everyone in the village as Tante Constance, so that was good enough for us. Although she could not have been much more than seventy when we started making regular visits to the village in the mid-1950s, she looked very old, with a wispy body, an emaciated face, and thin grey hair permanently tied in a bun. She wore a grey overall she never seemed to take off except to go to church on Sundays. She was praised throughout the village for her meat pies, fragrant concoctions of chicken or pork marinated in white wine and stored in a dark larder deep inside the house, which to children made hungry by working off surplus energy in the open air all day, suggested gastronomic paradise. Her other claim to fame was her encyclopaedic knowledge of significant dates in the lives of every villager, alive or dead, a subject on which she was frequently consulted by forgetful neighbours in need of a refresher on local demographics.

Tante Constance had an inexhaustible store of patience with children, perhaps because she had never married and had never had any children of her own. Nothing in Champdôtre happened fast, but Tante Constance was especially adept at slowing the action even further to suit the pace of the youngest child in her presence. In more favourable circumstances, this good and deserving aunt would have made a fine pre-school teacher.

Her specialty was introducing young visitors to the mysterious world of chickens. One of the highlights of visits to Champdôtre was egg collection. At night, Tante Constance's chickens were corralled in a coop, a loathsome cubicle where even curious children feared to tread and where the chickens roosted in staggered vertical rows, like an audience at the opera. During the day, they had the freedom of the farmyard, and they wandered and pecked at gravel to their hearts' content. No doubt, the eggs they delivered – and eventually the chickens themselves – tasted the better for it. But first, the eggs had to be located.

A few unadventurous hens never seemed to venture beyond the safety of the coop, so if the egg-collector could cope with the stink, the place always yielded a few eggs. But the majority of the hens regarded the entire *Grand Cour* compound as their oyster, so to speak, and they laid their eggs wherever they could find a soft surface on which to settle and deliver. This usually meant hay so the barn offered rich hunting grounds including each end of the wooden manger from which the horse drew its feed.

The daily egg hunt was keenly anticipated. At the peak of the clucking that signalled *mission accomplie* on the part of the hens, every child in attendance that day was given a small wicker basket and Tante Constance presided over team formation and routes, which were designed to ensure that no likely spot was overlooked or searched more than once. Then the quest began, with the younger searchers tugging at Tante Constance's apron strings while the older and more independent element set off in search parties of two or three. Upon discovery, each egg was lifted out of its hiding place and delicately deposited into the wicker basket, which we were instructed to put down in a safe spot to avoid mishaps as we searched. When the harvest seemed to be in and hope of further finds abandoned for the day, we each picked up our basket and carried it back tremulously to the house in anticipation of an aromatic omelette for dinner that night and of the next day's hunt.

Instruction in the care of the chicken in sickness and in health came from assisting in the daily feeding ritual.

Twice a day, Tante Constance broke off from whatever was keeping her busy at the time and announced that feeding time was upon us. Joy unconfined! She picked up the large wicker basket in which she stored the feed and led us into the farmyard. Then she emitted her high-pitched signature call that signalled to the chickens that it was lunchtime, at which point they congregated from every direction at top speed. At first, we listened and then practiced until we had the call pat. Then we tried our hand at scattering the feed. This is a subtle art form, which involves hand-to-eye control of the highest order. The trick is to grab a handful of feed and scatter it in front of the chickens in a gentle, semi-circular sweep as opposed to hurling it at them.

If one of the hens happened to have a brood in tow, the ultimate thrill consisted of picking up a chick and cuddling it. Chicks are made for children's hands, though the chicks may beg to differ if only they could be consulted in the matter. Holding one for a few seconds and learning to calibrate one's strength to the size and vulnerability of the chick should be part of every child's education. I suppose this is why the more enlightened among schools introduce pets into young classrooms. Perhaps some schools have chicks too, at least until some of them become roosters and start throwing their weight around, as Tante Constance's roosters invariably did.

The Champdôtre chickens were an endless source of entertainment but also of education. As I explained earlier, this was a world in which information on the origins of the species was tightly withheld by those in the know. But sooner or later, a visit to Champdôtre delivered useful hints through the strange displays of some of God's creatures, great or small. Invariably, the roosters obliged, or rather, one particular alpha rooster obliged.

Now, a rooster's approach to seduction departs entirely from the procedure I was later to learn is considered good manners among my own species and which I have tended to follow, with varying degrees of success. A rooster entertaining thoughts of dalliance seems to know that its advances are going to be turned down flat by the object of its desire, so it does not bother to make any. Instead of introducing itself and exchanging civilities with the hen, swapping farmyard gossip, perhaps, or discussing the weather or the toothsomeness of the gravel, your ardent rooster simply jumps to it, literally. Key to success is to sneak up on the target from behind as it is pecking at things right and left, leap about six feet in the air, and land on top of it like a chopper touching down on a helipad.

What follows is several seconds of incensed squawking and flapping of wings on the part of the hen, gravity-defying attempts by the rooster to keep its balance, and much shedding of feathers and churning of farmyard dust by both. And as suddenly as the rooster jumped on, it jumps off again, rearranges what is left of its plumage with a show of male superciliousness, and struts off in search of the next target with its crest up high, looking as pleased with itself as if it had just cracked Fermat's last theorem or discovered a cure for cancer. I asked Tante Constance what the purpose of these bizarre commotions might be, but her account was cryptic and unconvincing. But this was not a problem: what mattered to me was the spectacle, not the motivation for it.

*

Another popular resident of the Champdôtre household was Tante Constance's only surviving sister. Curiously, she did not seem to have ever had a name but was known simply as *Petite Marraine*, or 'Little Godmother', though no one seemed to know whose godmother she may once have been. She never offered an opinion on any subject but simply bustled about all day as she attended to the needs of others. Residents and visitors alike tended to treat her as a silent but useful fixture and no one ever seemed to consider the possibility that she might have a point of view to contribute or even a wish to express. A tiny mouse of a woman, she bore her subservient fate with good grace. If she felt put upon, she never gave any hint of it. Instead, she went about her chores with a benign smile on her face as if she could imagine no more fulfilling existence than one spent waiting on others hand and foot. When her work was done, she slept on a tumble-down cot in a dark corner of the vast kitchen that was her principal domain in readiness for another day of quiet service.

Every lunch time brought a regular visitor to the house, or more precisely to the dining room, in the person of Oncle Alphonse. As lunch was about to be served, Oncle Alphonse pedalled into the farmyard, rested his bicycle on one side of the well by the front door, pushed his way through the set of multicoloured plastic strips that was supposed to act as a door screen and keep flies at bay, shuffled into the house, and sat down at the dining table. Oncle Alphonse liked his food, but he especially liked not to have to cook it himself or even take his plate back to the kitchen, let alone offer to wash it up. That was what sisters had been invented for especially as modest sums occasionally changed hands for this service. Oncle Alphonse was a charmer, in a slightly muddy kind of way. He was a genial soul, but his was a personality best enjoyed from a distance as he obviously believed that shaving more than once a week was a waste of precious lather and parsimonious use of soap and even toothpaste was a virtue. But this being France, an arm-length approach to ablutions had not stopped him from acquiring a reputation as something of a *roué*. Looking back, I do not recall ever seeing him in the company of a woman or even hearing of one specifically linked to him, though this may have been due to the unmentionable fact that he was never married to any of them.

His main claim to fame and the justification for the attention he clearly felt was due to him was that he had spent the best part of World War I in Greece and Turkey. In early twentieth-century Champdôtre, this must have seemed beyond exotic. At a time when few villagers ever ventured beyond Dijon and many still walked to the weekly market in Auxonne to save the train fare, having sailed the length the Mediterranean, fought valiantly (or so he said), and sailed back in one piece made him, in his own eyes at least, Burgundy's answer to Ulysses. He claimed to have fought in the Dardanelles. To hear him tell it, it was only the doltishness of the combined French and British top brass that had prevented him from single-handedly defeating the Turks at the Battle of Gallipoli. Very little of this was true, my father let it be known privately. But Oncle Alphonse had clearly enjoyed his time away from the village. Apart from the price of onions, he talked of nothing else. At the first signs that he felt a story coming on, my siblings and I exchanged glances across the dining table before our eyes rolled ceiling-ward. I knew what everyone else around the dining table except Oncle Alphonse was thinking: Oh, no! Not Gallipoli again!

Oncle Alphonse could be a bore but at least he was a jovial bore, which is more than could be said of his slightly younger brother, Oncle Edouard. A dour, grumpy kind of bore, Oncle Edouard lived in splendid isolation in a small house inside the *Grand Cour* compound next to the main farmhouse. Greeting anyone and in particular visiting children seemed to cause him intense personal pain. During school holidays, a friendly girl named Christiane, who was said to be his daughter, appeared out of nowhere and shared our games. She seemed never to have had a mother. This struck me as odd, but as in the matter of roosters landing on hens, I soon learned that some aspects of life were beyond probing. Some things were better left unsaid.

In a pleasant cottage between the *Grand Cour* and the church lived René, the village wheelwright, and his sister Annie. Both figured in the long list of village folks who had never managed to find a marriage partner and they shared the task of caring for their ageing mother. There was nothing Annie did not know about a sewing machine and its uses, and she helped with household expenses by adjusting a hemline here, taking in a baggy overcoat there, even dying entire wardrobes black within hours whenever the Reaper claimed another villager. Meanwhile, René toiled in his workshop, where I spent many afternoons watching wood shavings fly off his machines as he shaped replacements for worn-out cart parts and even the odd coffin. Death holds no special fears for children, who believe that they will live forever and dying is something other people do. And fresh sawdust smells wonderful!

*

With only the seriously wealthy owning phones, visits to Champdôtre were arranged in writing. My parents picked a convenient Sunday and my father took up his pen and wrote a courteous letter to Tante Constance suggesting a family visit. She never went anywhere except to church, the butcher's and the baker's in the middle of the village, and occasionally the cemetery, so the reply invariably came back positive and excitement began to build up. On the appointed day, we piled into the family car and headed southwest.

Excluded from these trips was my eldest sister Odile, who stayed behind in Lure, Haute-Saône and kept my grandmother company for the day because my parents feared that one of her epileptic fits might strike at any moment and would be very difficult to cope with, especially if it hit while we were on the road. Did she feel slighted at the sight of the packed family car disappearing around the corner for a day of country pursuits, or did she welcome the chance of spending the day free of parental supervision? On the rare occasions I gave it any thought, I had no way of knowing.

The drive took just two hours, but to children anticipating a reunion with popular aunts and another look at the antics of hyperactive roosters, those two hours ground exceeding slow. The route took us through deepest Haute-Saône, which meant a succession of villages with names that suggested bucolic bliss. I can still rattle off the names by heart: Grandvelle, Frétigney, Velleclaire, Chaumercenne, and many more. Memorising that list was pure pleasure. Had I been allowed to substitute the list of all the villages between Lure, Haute-Saône and Champdôtre for the list of irregular plurals, I would have aced primary school.

It being Sunday in Catholic France, we attended early mass and then immediately drove off. The drive was timed so that arrival would coincide with the sacrosanct lunch hour of twelve noon, precisely. Greetings were exchanged to the sucking sounds of

French-style kissing, children were praised for having grown so much since their last visit, questions about school were asked and evasive answers given, and the extended family sat down to the serious business of eating.

As with everything else about the household, the menu was set by Tante Constance. A special favourite was tapioca soup. For some reason, this humble dish had failed to make it into my mother's recipe book so it met with loud approval whenever it was announced. Rabbit stews were a common fare, as were Tante Constance's renowned meat pies. Occasionally, the very alpha rooster we had watched a few months earlier getting his harem into the family way reappeared, though in subdued mood, on the lunch table. No doubt its genes were alive and kicking somewhere in the farmyard.

All of this tasted heavenly. But two things made those lunches special. One was the cheese dish. To call it a dish is perhaps an overstatement. What really happened was that a small selection of cheeses was brought to the table on a plate. In a house with only a larder and no means of refrigeration, the offerings were not easy on the nose. But what we all lived for was the moment when Oncle Alphonse, having wiped his plate clean with a chunk of bread, turned it over and declared himself ready for his cheese. At this point, whichever adult was seated next to him cut off a piece of cheese almost as pungent as Oncle Alphonse himself and plopped it on his upturned plate. This was beyond cool! We begged to be allowed to eat our cheese off the back of our plates just like Oncle Alphonse. But even on these joyful occasions, my parents never relented. Parents can be so obtuse at times! How they are allowed to rule unrestrained over entire families is something children will never understand.

The other treat was the ritual introduction of older children to wine, the staple drink (as might be expected) in a Burgundy household. But Champdôtre was no Montrachet or Clos Vougeot territory but onion country and instead of a *grand cru*, the best lunchers could hope for was some of the cheapest, lowest grade, most *ordinaire* wine on offer when the itinerant grocery van passed through the village one afternoon each week. But what mattered to us children was that when we reached the advanced age of twelve, we were introduced to wine with full parental approval. This was serious growing up!

Even at such a gullible age, we knew that what we were drinking and what the adults had in their glasses shared little more than a name. Our tipple consisted of one finger, if that, of wine at the bottom of a tall glass, topped up with water and made palatable by a generous dose of sugar. The resulting drink was an attractive shade of pale pink and tasted delicious. Looking back, this was sensible policy on the part of the adults because it introduced children soon to be teenagers to sensible alcohol consumption as a normal part of social intercourse and lowered the risk that they would end up associating it with secrecy and guilt and eventually excess.

But all good things must come to an end and by mid-afternoon, my father started twiddling his car keys and issuing warnings that under no circumstances would he be caught up in what came to be known in family lore as *l'heure des vaches*, or 'cow time'. Most travellers have traffic jams to factor into their plans; my father had cow jams. If he allowed us to extend our games just a little too long, we would hit Chaumercenne, Velleclaire, Frétigney, and Grandvelle just as every cow in Haute-Saône – and that was a lot of cows! – was being herded back to base in the gloaming for milking and an early night after a busy day chewing the cud *al fresco*. But cows are not sheep in disposition and they are a lot bigger. In any homebound herd of cows, there are always two or three that will meander from side to side in search of a grassy spot they missed on their way out in the morning. Experienced from the inside of a car, being scrutinised by an inquisitive cow staring through the windows and dribbling from the corner of its vast mouth is an exquisite thrill. But my father was not interested in thrills, however exquisite. What concerned him was what a stray horn might do to his paintwork and his insurance premium in a close encounter with a cow. So our departure time was precisely calibrated and absolutely not open to negotiation.

*

Parting was sweet sorrow, but there was always the summer to look forward to. Each August, as soon as my father had discharged his annual duties at the funfair he helped organise in support of the local POW association and with almost a month to go till it was time to creep unwillingly back to school, we headed for Champdôtre once again. The difference was that this consisted not of an all-too-brief afternoon jaunt but of several weeks of rustic delights. Once my parents had entrusted us and our few belongings to the capable hands of aunts, they loaded some home-grown vittles into the car and headed back to Lure, Haute-Saône. For them, this was a chance to recharge their batteries, read good books, and in the first half of the 1950s at least, procreate some more. For us, there were two huge positives to this policy. One was that no one in the village had pursued book learning assiduously enough to have any credibility as a tutor so our summers were entirely free of homework and our waking hours could be devoted fully to country pastimes. The other was a chance to be spoiled rotten by Tante Marthe.

Tante Marthe was my father's eldest sister and therefore our real aunt, and a dream of an aunt at that: cheerful, kindly, patient, resourceful, and very fond of children. In the family photo I mentioned earlier, she comes across as a poised, beautiful young woman. But God's ways are mysterious and she too missed out on marriage and became a nun instead. Her religious order was an open one, which favoured engagement with the world. So she picked up basic nursing skills and returned to the village of her birth where she devoted her life to providing free primary health care and in summer to indulging those of her twenty-one nephews and nieces who happened to be in residence on any given day.

We spent our days making our own entertainment around the *Grand Cour* compound. But at night, we retired to the much smaller house where she lived at the far end of the village, where farmhouses thinned out and eventually gave way to the two rows of poplars that lined the road to Auxonne and that remain a distinguishing feature of the French rural landscape to this day. Occasionally, we accompanied Tante Marthe on her errands of mercy around the village, which sometimes meant going into houses even more modest than her own. But the welcome was warm and offers of a cool drink and a slice of freshly-baked fruit tart were gratefully received. If the visit took place in the early evening, an additional treat consisted of being ushered into the stable to watch the milking. This was done by hand and the more fearless of the young visitors joined in, tugging ineffectually at the unfortunate animal's teats until the volunteers were lifted off their three-legged stools and replaced by a more competent handler. I was not among the fearless. As I said earlier, cows are very large creatures and although their moves are more predictable and less jerky than those of horses, the underside of a cow is a scary place for a three-foot tall person to be.

On weekdays, we headed outdoors immediately after breakfast. But on Sundays, church beckoned and Tante Marthe's duty was to supervise our weekly *toilette*. The house had the luxury of a hand pump just outside the front door so the oldest and most able-bodied cousin in residence led the water-gathering mission, with younger siblings and cousins taking turns at the pump when the previous incumbent tired. Back inside, brothers, sisters, and cousins stood around a large enamel basin at the centre of the kitchen table and scrubbed away: face, neck, hands, and if it had been a particularly hot week, perhaps feet. But nothing in between, ever. No soap, please: we are French!

At the end of the month, the reappearance of my parents was bitter-sweet. There was one last country lunch to savour. My father paid for our upkeep by pressing some money on Tante Marthe, which she made a well-rehearsed show of refusing until she finally pushed the money into one of the pockets of her vast apron. We loaded plums, pears, one or two of Tante Constance's meat pies, and perhaps a live chicken or rabbit into the car and headed back to Lure, Haute-Saône and the dire prospect of school.

*

Today, Champdôtre has been spruced up. The manure heaps are gone. There is efficient street lighting and even a stop sign where the two roads intersect by the *café*. But the village feels as lethargic as ever because the young have migrated to the cities and left little

318

more than a geriatric rump behind. Very few new houses have been built and some of the older ones have crumbled. But newly-prosperous visitors to the remaining residents park as many cars in front of the farmhouses as can be seen in any American suburban driveway.

Clearly, the Champdôtre of horse carts, straying cows, and lecherous roosters is gone. To catch a glimpse of it, watch René Clément's 1952 film *Jeux Interdits*, or 'Forbidden Games'. It was shot about the time my father acquired his very first car and we started paying regular visits to our rural relatives. The farmhouses, the furniture, the clothes, the farmyard animals, even the meals are exactly as I remember them. The two children in the film even play our games including giving dead birds Christian burials and fashioning crosses out of twigs to mark the spot. The atmosphere is there too, good and bad. At best, rural simplicity means a warm welcome, a bowl of hot soup, a slice of home-baked pie, an entertaining yarn, and words of comfort in times of affliction. But rural poverty can also bring out the worst in adults and breed petty disputes, selfishness, and if necessary, the betrayal of children and all the good they represent. At the end of the film, the little girl's anguished cry as she searches the orphanage to which she has just been banished for the friend viewers know she will never see again is truly heart-rending. The soundtrack is hauntingly beautiful. To me and not only because it speaks to cherished childhood memories, *Jeux Interdits* is one of the greatest French films of all time.

CHAPTER FOURTEEN: GRAND TOUR

Tourists don't know where they've been, travellers don't know where they're going.

Paul Theroux (1941-)

Sunday afternoon drives and day-long trips to Champdôtre, doting aunts, clownish uncles, and amorous roosters were treasured highlights of family life. But when it came to the sheer joy of getting in the car and staying in it for as long as possible, the ultimate treat was the annual camping trip.

Toward the end of each school year in June, my father gathered the family around the dining room table and produced a selection from his vast stock of Michelin maps and unfolded each one. With evident pleasure at holding his audience spellbound, he then announced a fully worked-out route. This was to be no consultation session, meant to sound us out over where we might like to go that year. Instead, he revealed the route with the authority of one handing down an eternal truth. Additional details were provided in the form of a sheet of paper listing in his neat script all the significant towns we would pass along the way. To the right of the list was the distance between each town down to the last half-kilometre, with a running total to the right of that and a grand total at the bottom, all carefully calculated from those wonderfully precise Michelin maps.

He then took us in imagination through each stage of the trip: exactly where we would go, how long we would stay in each place, and what there was to see and do along the way. My siblings and I cheered locations we liked the sound of and moaned playfully at the mention of the ones that, for no very clear reason, struck us as boring. Neither reaction had any effect on my father. He had given the matter long and careful consideration and his mind was made up: this would be the camping trip that summer.

The route was chosen to take in as many of the sights as possible provided these were not in or near towns much larger than Lure, Haute-Saône. My father detested cities and especially driving through them so he stuck to the sylvan byways. This took no special skill on his part as French roads consisted almost entirely of sylvan byways, with bypasses, overpasses, and especially a German-style *Autobahn* network still little more than a vertiginous dream in the planners' minds.

The delays involved in navigating unfamiliar towns, the rough state of many French roads, and the limitations of the car into which we squeezed ourselves and our camping gear meant that each leg of the trip had to be kept short. My father was in the uncomfortable position of having to reconcile a love of travel with a modest income and a large family. This left him with few options when it came to choosing what car to buy. Even for the wealthy, the choices were limited. As watching any French film from the late 1950s or the early 1960s will confirm, virtually all the cars on French roads were of French make. Once in a while, a Volkswagen, an Austin, or a Fiat and even more rarely an American import the size of three French cars and with fins sticking out in every direction could be seen. But for the vast majority of right-thinking Frenchmen – and much more rarely Frenchwomen – a car meant a French car.

Just five manufacturers obliged. Three of them, today's survivors, made two models each: Renault, Citroën, and Peugeot, our local champion and mass employer. Two more, now defunct, offered just one model each: Simca and Panhard, the latter being the august firm that had started car manufacturing in France at the end of the nineteenth century. The Panhard option appealed to my father because, like Volkswagen and Fiat, the company specialised in inexpensive 'people's cars'. My father's very first car, a small Panhard he bought in 1951, had a 600-cc engine and came in either dark green or dark blue. His second, a few years and several children later, was powered by a mighty 850-cc unit and came in light grey or light green. But its main advantage was that it was a full-size family car. And with the annual camping trip and much else by way of driving on my father's mind, an inexpensive but spacious family car was exactly what he was in the market for.

Anyone who has ever driven a car will appreciate that wrapping a full-size family car around an 850-cc engine and encouraging the owner to fill the result with a large family and a month's supply of camping gear is going to present technical difficulties. So much so that the challenge had clearly defeated the cunning of the Panhard engineers and the car was seriously underpowered. The model was named Dyna, presumably short for *dynamique*, though it was anything but.

Even on a good day, lightly loaded, with a favourable tail wind, and on a straight stretch of road across flat country, the Panhard struggled to reach one hundred kilometres per hour, and an average speed of sixty kilometres per hour over extended journeys was a realistic ambition. This placed the car close to the bottom of the performance scale, just above the notoriously anaemic *Deux-chevaux*. In fact, a frequent subject of debate among my classmates was whether our respective dads' car could *faire du cent*, or 'do one hundred'. Since my father was a prominent schoolteacher in a small town and just about everyone knew him, everyone also knew what car he drove. So there was no way I could conceal that my own dad's car had no hope of *faire du cent*, especially with the family inside. But my father was not concerned with impressing his children's friends and he was absolutely fine with taking three or four days to cover the six or seven hundred kilometres to the nearest beach and a welcoming camping site close to it. For him, a Panhard was just the ticket.

Like American cars of the time, which were designed to be commodious above all else, the Panhard had the gear stick mounted on the steering column as opposed to the floor so it would not waste precious cargo space and lower the number of passengers that could be squeezed in. Seating in both front and rear was on bench-like seats that reached from side to side and that welcomed as many family members as were willing to sit in close proximity for hours on end without coming to blows. Add the miserly fuel bills and the chance this arrangement gave families to spend entire summers outdoors, why would a sensible householder with a passion for the great open spaces and a large family want to drive anything else?

*

As I got older and my map reading skills improved and even impressed, I was put in charge of navigation. The seating arrangement was simple: the men sat in the front, the women in the back. My job was to scan the horizon for upcoming turnoffs, often indicated by a rusty sign half hidden in tall summer grass, while keeping the other eye on the Michelin map in my lap. In moments of respite, my brother Pierre and I competed to see which of us could spot the most exotic number plates, especially those from obscure *départements* such as Deux-Sèvres (79) or Lot-et-Garonne (47) and of course Haute-Saône (70), with my brother keeping meticulous records. The problem was that this created frequent distractions from my map-reading duties and I occasionally failed to warn my father of imminent turnoffs. My father hated wasting a drop of petrol on unnecessary journeys. On a lucky day, given a wide road, accommodating verges, and little traffic in either direction, he was able to turn around and get back on track almost immediately and dereliction of duty on my part cost me little more than a mild rebuke. But if he found himself on a narrow winding road or a very busy one and he had to drive some distance in the wrong direction, the mild rebuke turned into an angry diatribe often supplemented by a smack on the side of my head he could reach without endangering life and limb while at the wheel. Thus are the navigating skills that distinguish globe-trotters from mere tourists acquired.

My siblings and I never had reason to regret my father's selection of destinations. We loved those camping trips. But first, the equipment had to be assembled. My father took care of the basic hardware: tent, folding table and seats, and inflatable beds and bedding while my mother attended to portable gas stove, cooking pots, plates and cups, cutlery, and the staples that would keep hungry children sated after a day working up an appetite on the beach: pasta and rice, mostly. The rest was bought locally including local types of *saucisson* and *paté* noticeably fattier than what we normally ate at home. Regional differences in eating habits were still apparent and with distribution systems unsophisticated and slow, gastronomic specialties remained largely restricted to the area where were produced. Today, these differences have been largely homogenised by the ubiquitous presence of vast supermarkets and endure only in the dearly-held myth that every French person is linked almost mystically to a small patch of *France profonde*, where specific foods are uniquely found.

At the time, regional differences were particularly in evidence in the availability of cheeses. But experiencing this variation was ruled out by the logistics of camping. Cheese was eaten over several days and could not be kept in a tent with no means of refrigeration or carted around on hot summer days in a packed non-air-conditioned car. So my mother shunned normally popular but potentially malodorous cheeses such as *camembert, munster, bleu,* and especially the infamous *cancoillotte* my brother practically lived on. Instead, she opted for firm varieties such as *cantal*, a deliciously tangy cheese from the Massif Central region, and especially *gruyère*, which, the moment it appeared on the folding dinner table, generated alarming speculations over mice running around the tent at night among younger siblings and absurdist debates over which tasted better, the *gruyère* or the holes, among older ones. And as always when food is eaten outdoors, even the familiar pasta or rice spiced up with a squirt of tomato concentrate was declared vastly superior to the exact same dish when eaten at home.

Like all children of school age, we counted the days to the end of the school year, the start of the long summer break, and especially the family camping trip that began a few days later. The night before our departure, my father assembled camping equipment, bags, and food supplies next to the car. He stood for a while contemplating the heap and working out the logistics of getting it all on board, paying special attention to the size, shape, and consistency of each item. He then loaded – and when we were old enough, enlisted our assistance in loading – item after item into the car. Not a cubic centimetre of space was wasted. My father had an uncanny sense of what would fit in, in what corner, and in what sequence. Everything he and my mother planned to take on the trip went in. Nothing ever had to be left behind and returned to storage. Then he stood back, wiped the sweat off his brow, surveyed his handiwork with evident satisfaction, and slammed down the boot. In the morning, he added wife and children to the mix and off we went, leaving my grandmother to hold the fort, once again assisted by my older sister Odile on the grounds that if one of her recurrent epileptic fits struck, it was bound to make the camping trip very difficult. Curiously, I reflected later, Odile never seemed to have these fits when she was at home with my grandmother and no longer under the direct supervision of my parents. Looking back, there must have been a strong psychosomatic component in her condition. Unless I chose not to notice it, she did not seem especially aggrieved at seeing us go. On our return, she seemed in rude health and glowing with optimism. I suspect she had thoroughly enjoyed her new-found freedom.

*

Our first camping trip took place less than a decade after the end of World War II, when improvisation was everything. Understandably, the French authorities had given priority not to dotting the landscape with rest areas along the highways and camping sites at the end of each one but to rebuilding or replacing the housing stock, bridges, schools, and hospitals. So we pottered along all day, stopping wherever my father spotted a grassy surface on which he could park the car and give

326

the family a chance to share a picnic lunch and weak-bladdered children an opportunity to answer calls of nature facing a tree or crouching behind a bush.

By mid-afternoon, my father started giving his undivided attention to what might constitute a suitable *bivouac* for the night. The strategy consisted of identifying a suitable farmhouse, drive up to the front door, and park the car some distance from the manure heap that still graced many French rural residences at the time. My father got out of the car and knocked on the door. In fact, most often, he was spared that formality as the farmer, his wife, a representative sample of their children, and the family dog had long spotted us driving up from the main road and had already formed a welcoming committee.

Negotiations presented few difficulties. Leisure travel was beginning to pick up and farmers were alert to the needs of travelling families, the dearth of facilities in which they might be accommodated, and the chance to earn a *franc* or two by offering assistance. So a suitable spot was indicated at the back of the farmhouse where the tent might be pitched. We were shown the well, or if the farm was thoroughly modern, the water pump. The family outhouse was placed at the disposal of all that might need it and were brave enough to use it. A little money changed hands, my father rewarding the family for its hospitality while my mother purchased a few necessities for that evening's dinner and the next day's breakfast: a loaf of homemade bread, a little local cheese, a selection of fruit, and invariably a generous quantity of milk still warm from having come off the production line only minutes earlier. If we were lucky and the farmer's family was especially welcoming, we were taken on a tour of the shed where the cows were being milked. More intimidating was watching the horse as it was freed from harness and being invited to add handfuls of hay to its manger as it fed.

That was the routine, unless the weather turned against us. On one memorable night deep in the heart of the Champagne region, just as a suitable farm location was spotted on the horizon, a storm of exceptional power hit. The heavens opened, thunder roared, lightening lit up the sky. The tent would not be pitched and dinner would not be cooked outdoors that night. So the obliging farmer *du jour* offered us shelter in his barn. We shared a meal at the farmer's table and I recall lying down on a luxurious bed of fragrant hay and trying to go to sleep to the ominous sound, just as in the Champdôtre barn, of the horse next door rattling its bridle against the manger as it chomped through its dinner or dreamed equine dreams.

We lived in the landlocked eastern reaches of France so a major summer treat was to spend time at the seaside. My parents were not keen on hot weather so they tended to shun the Mediterranean in favour of the Atlantic and even the English Channel. Normandy was a particular favourite in part because of its temperate climate but also because my father, as both a history teacher and a relatively recent POW, yearned to visit the sites of the 1944 Allied landings and pay his respects to the fallen among those who had come to set him and his comrades free.

The white cliffs overlooking the beaches were lined with German-built concrete bunkers that we explored gingerly because they evinced an undefinable sense of menace but also quickly because of the stink left behind by visitors who saw them not as witnesses to a major historical event but as convenient latrines.

Once in secondary school and old enough to study my father's history textbooks, I had seen photos of half-submerged landing barges and the bodies of dead soldiers littering the beaches. Fifteen years later, the landing barges had been cleared and the bodies laid to rest in vast military cemeteries a short walk inland from the edge of the cliff, where they lay in countless rows under perfectly aligned white crosses amidst immaculately kept lawns. From the brutality and the chaos had emerged a neatly ordered world, so aesthetically pleasing that I recall an unexpected sense of inner peace instead of the revulsion that would have been an appropriate reaction to human tragedy on such a scale.

One summer in the late 1950s, my father's route planning took us to the pine forests, the golden beaches, and the sandy dunes of the Landes region south of Bordeaux. There we frolicked all afternoon, building castles in the sand, flooding them, and then building them all over again. In the camping sites that were rapidly becoming the norm, we mixed with children our own age, often from distant parts of the country and so speaking French with problematic accents. On occasion, we had as neighbours the ultimate in exoticism: a British family, complete with their strange-sounding language, the odd-looking camper they travelled in, a large tea pot, and the curious habit of frying up eggs, sausages, and bacon for breakfast instead of dunking chunks of stale bread in hot milk as all civilised human beings were known to do.

Over the long months of the school year, we amused ourselves at the dinner table with countless retellings of scenes from the Landes beaches. On one of those idyllic afternoons, uproar suddenly erupted in a group of holiday-makers nearby. Family members started gesticulating and uttering strange oaths as they bent over and scoured the sand for something one of them had obviously lost. The object of the search, it turned out, was the dental brace a daughter had dropped in the sand and into which it had promptly sunk without trace.

Dental braces were expensive items that adorned only the overindulged mouths of the children of the seriously vain among the well-to-do. This exclusive set did not include my siblings or myself even though some genetic malfunction on the paternal side had left us all with gaps between our teeth and especially between mine. But possession of a brace had the potential to land forgetful or clumsy owners of these adornments in serious trouble, as our young neighbour on the beach was to find out that afternoon. As the unfortunate girl was subjected to torrents of parental abuse over her carelessness, the frantic search for the elusive brace went on until the cause was declared lost and the device given up to a sandy grave thanks in part to every family member having jumped up and down on the very spot for half an hour, burying it deeper still. The hapless girl was loudly informed that the cost of a replacement would come out of her pocket money for as long as it took. Bitter tears ensued, which broke our young hearts because we knew all too well how it felt to cross a short-fused, money-conscious parent.

*

The family quickly learned to love the pine forests, the dunes, and the beaches of the Landes and we returned to them three summers in a row. But for sheer drama, we had to look further north. In my experience, nothing could beat the sight of a transatlantic liner docking at Cherbourg, the customary port of call on crossings from Southampton to New York and back again.

My first visit to Cherbourg – and my first sighting of the sea – took place when I was about five and these ships were by far the largest artefacts I had ever set eyes upon. The audience was large, too. The arrival and

330

a few hectic hours later the departure of one of these behemoths was big news. Liners took five days to cross the Atlantic and they carried thousands. Their comings and goings were major events, announced in the local newspaper days in advance as if Cherbourg was expecting the Queen of Sheba or the Second Coming. The names of celebrity passengers were listed too, but I had eyes only for the ships. On the appointed day, what seemed like the entire population of the town and of every camping site within driving distance was there, asking to be awed. And awed we duly were.

The fleet included pre-war relics such as the *Normandie* but also the then brand new *United States*, a sleek leviathan and current holder of the much-coveted Blue Ribbon, the prize awarded to the liner that had made the fastest crossing of the North Atlantic. When the plume of black smoke was spotted on the horizon, necks were craned as excitement built up on the quayside. Gradually, the plume became a large dot and the large dot became a ship. A team of diminutive tugboats went out to meet the beast, guide it into port, and edge it delicately against the quay. Docking involved an exchange of loud calls and theatrical gestures between sailors and port workers on the quayside. Thick ropes were tossed overboard, each one caught expertly by a thick-set man in blue trousers, dark blue sweater, and black *béret* and coiled around a massive bollard. Gangways were rolled along the quay toward the ship and then raised at one end by a tall crane. The decks were lined with waving passengers continuing to New York or Southampton or simply having arrived at their destination but in no hurry to end the fun prematurely. Everyone except the busy port workers waved back at this good-humoured crowd of total strangers. Before long, passengers began disembarking, warily treading the gangways and then falling into the arms of loved ones as they reached *terra firma*. Meanwhile, the tugboats sat patiently on the edges, waiting to swing back into action at the conclusion of operations and edge the ship back out.

The liners were impressive. But what captured my imagination was the sight of the tiny tugboats as against all odds they heaved and expertly guided a ship many times their size. To a five-year-old boy aspiring to manly deeds, the implausibility of some maritime David making a helpless Goliath safe was deeply inspiring. On that very first visit to Cherbourg, I resolved to be a tugboat pilot when I grew up.

The highlight of these dramatic visitations was being allowed to climb on board whichever titan of the sea had just docked and enjoy the freedom of the decks, which was implicitly extended to all as if everyone on the quayside was a VIP. Visitors wandered up and down, enraptured and often becoming disoriented in the immensity. But there were plenty of helpful attendants willing to guide stray visitors back to daylight and the search for the exit was a game like no game my siblings and I had ever played before.

But soon came the call for non-passengers to go ashore or risk finding themselves stranded in Southampton or Lower Manhattan. So the crowd re-assembled on the quayside, my siblings and I already clutching at memories and collectively rehearsing the stories we would tell our friends once we got home as we watched the ship being pushed back out by the tugboats as gently as it had been guided in and then heading out to open sea. If you missed the era of the great ocean liners, watch the embarkation scene in the 1953 film *Gentlemen Prefer Blondes*. That is exactly how it was.

Today, I am generally keen on modernity. I certainly would not want to go back to camping within sniffing distance of the manure heap outside a French farmhouse with a stinking outhouse and no running water. And before preoccupations with airport security made air travel an ordeal, I was thrilled at the mere thought of getting ready for a flight. But some gentle wistfulness is in order when it comes to the lost world of passenger liners. These ships were magnificent and their comings and goings were a sight to behold. True, today's crude carriers, container ships, and even cruise ships are even larger. But try getting your children through security at an oil terminal or a container port and requesting for them the freedom of the decks for an hour or two. Even if you succeeded, what would there be to marvel at beside banks of computer monitors?

Adding to the personal nostalgia is the fact that *United* and *States* (pronounced *you-nigh-ted-stets* in the approved French manner) were the first two words of English I ever heard my father utter. Depending on which liner was in port when we visited, he must also have contributed *Queen*, *Mary*, and *Elizabeth*, but that was about it. My father had been reared on Latin and Greek and had willy-nilly picked up some German during his enforced World War II sojourn in Austria. But he neither spoke nor understood English. I think he regretted it mainly out of a sense of gratitude toward the Americans and the fact that it was they and not, contrary to what our history textbooks claimed, de Gaulle's fearless *légions* that had restored him to freedom.

Come to think of it, my father's English lexicon included two more entries: *corned* and *beef*, pronounced *cor-ned-biff* because that is the way it looks to a French person reading the words on the side of a tin. This delicacy remained at the top of my father's personal list of favourite foods long after the Americans reached his camp and started feeding it to the POWs, who welcomed it as a nutritious alternative to the thin gruel their German hosts had been relying upon to keep their reluctant guests alive. Years later, he insisted that *cor-ned biff* still tasted as delicious as on the day of that first sampling.

*

One year, my father decided to be a little more adventurous so we headed further south all the way to the Pyrenees. We lived in hilly country and I was familiar with the *Vosges* and *Jura* mountains but nothing had prepared me for the magnificence of the Pyrenees. Needless to say, a visit to the region by a devout Catholic family had to include a stopover in Lourdes. The rampant commercialism of the place was already apparent even to a pre-adolescent who understood or cared little about profit. But the experience of joining thousands of pilgrims in night-time procession, each carrying a lit candle and singing *Ave Maria* in unison, creates an indelible memory especially in the mind of a dedicated altar boy growing up in the emotional atmosphere of contemporary Catholicism. The power of faith expressed and experienced collectively is awesome. It can be inspirational as long as it leads participants to behave benevolently especially toward those who do not share that faith. But given that it can also lead to hysterical antagonism toward all others and to the extent that these mass events rest on faith in miracles and therefore validate irrationality and even magic as legitimate ways of knowing, it is difficult to think of anything positive to say about them, unless of course you happen to be a hotelier or a candlemaker.

On the drives from one camping site to the next through southern France, we stopped at makeshift stalls along the road, where overripe fruit was sold to passing tourists: cantaloupes, apricots, huge tomatoes, peaches so enormous that they were difficult for children to bite into without ending up with pulp up their noses and juice running down their chins and onto their shoes. None of these wonders of nature grew in the less sun-kissed part of the country where we lived. For fruit to reach the markets of northerly places such as Lure, Haute-Saône in tradable condition, it had to be picked long before it was ripe. But this did not apply at source, where the gap between picking and selling was measured in minutes and that between purchase and consumption in seconds. The summer heat was oppressive and the arid camping sites of southern France could be hard to take but the fruit on display at those roadside stalls more than made up for it.

Another attraction of a camping trip through the south of France was a chance to leap into the warm waters of the Mediterranean. On our first visit to these shores, my siblings and I all learned to swim within days of each other, something the life-threatening surf of the Atlantic beaches had long prevented us from doing. And on the way from Lourdes to the beaches of *la grande bleue* was the little town of Mazamet, where Tante Marguerite, my father's second older sister lived. As is the way of families, the shenanigans she had reportedly engineered two decades earlier in an attempt to spoil my parents' wedding had been put aside and we felt warmly welcome in her home.

A major factor behind this transformation was that Tante Marguerite had eventually managed to tie the knot. She had married a local man whose first wife had borne him four children in quick succession and then died in childbirth on the fifth occasion. Thanks to the matchmaking skills of a Catholic organisation, the distraught father had married Tante Marguerite *en seconde noces*, thereby becoming our Oncle Alfred. She quickly added two more sons to the roster. Not one to shirk effort, Tante Marguerite toiled cheerfully as she raised this vast brood and the family's hospitality was boundless and heartfelt despite their modest means. Raising seven children on the wages Oncle Alfred earned from manual work in a local tannery cannot have been easy.

How the two of them communicated was a mystery. She never lost the heavy Burgundy accent that my father had largely shed or at least toned down. Meanwhile, Oncle Alfred spoke with the kind of *méridional* accent we knew about and had heard mocked in radio comedy shows but never experienced directly. Without simultaneous translation by Tante Marguerite or one of her two sons, our cousins Jacques and Michel, Oncle Alfred's questions and stories flew over our heads. Jacques and Michel were patient in their attempts to make us feel included as well as welcoming as they took us up and down the surrounding hills in search of wild berries and blissful escape from family gossip. With his neighbours, Oncle Alfred spoke a strange tongue we understood even less and that we were told was called Catalan.

Today, Catalan is heard everywhere on the *Catalunya* side of the Pyrenees. But on the *Pyrénées Orientales* side, it is rarely used even in local shops or markets. Everyone speaks French. Even the lilting *méridional* accent that had perplexed us so much on our visits to our southern relatives has been replaced by the flat *staccato* of imported standard French. Some road signs now have a Catalan equivalent such as *Benvinguts a Perpinyà* but below, not above the French version. And when local language activists wield their paint brushes at the dead of night, it is often the Catalan version they deface. In just a few decades, the French

State has done an extraordinarily efficient job of wiping out regional languages even in the most recondite corners of the *hexagone* including the Catalan borderlands. Today, the French State can afford to pay lip service to multilingualism and even preach it in the hallowed chambers of European Union institutions because it knows that it is far too late for what is left of these languages to pose a serious threat to the supremacy of French. Obsessive systematicity has been the winner, diversity the loser.

Back in Mazamet, Tante Marguerite outlived her husband by three decades, soldiering on alone in that modest house in a quiet corner of a humble Pyrenees town. Something in the mountain air must have agreed with her: she died a few weeks short of her one hundred and eighth birthday.

*

In his own unassuming way, my father was quite intrepid. One year when I was about fourteen, he conceived the audacious plan to take the annual camping road show in the astonishingly novel direction of Germany. Franco-German reconciliation was in the air and my father was not one to bear a grudge.

My grandmother was scandalised, perplexed, and fearful all at once. She was scandalised because Germany was where Germans lived. And Germans, as she never failed to remind all that would listen, had inconvenienced her repeatedly by taking away first her husband and then her son-in-law, demanded to see her *Ausweis* every time she went past her front door during World War II, even billeted themselves in her best bedrooms and emptied her wine cellar when it suited them. She was perplexed because she could not imagine what there could possibly be in Germany that could not be enjoyed, twice over, in France. She was fearful because she was the worrying type. To hear her tell it, even on a good day and within the relative safety of French borders, travel was fraught with perils and a trip rarely ended where it was supposed to and never on schedule. How could a *sortie* into Germany not bring calamities down upon our unwise heads? She might never see us alive again, she lamented as we jumped into the car and waved her and my sister Odile goodbye.

As I saw it, Germany was modern, easy to manage, and very beautiful. The camping sites were clearly marked, efficiently run, and immaculately kept, a far cry from the cheerful improvisation that characterised their French counterparts. Black Forest villages seemed more prosperous and better kept than those on the side of the Rhine I was familiar with. Mad Ludwig of Bavaria's Hohenschwanstein Castle combined to perfection the sublimity of the mountain backdrop and the ridiculous pretensions of men. And because they were too small and inconsequential to be worth bombing at the close of World War II, the small towns that dotted the roads were full of delightfully misshapen gingerbread houses that seemed straight out of the fairy tales of my childhood.

One day, my father decided to address modernity head on and treat the family to the thrill of driving on a stretch of Germany's fabled *Autobahn* network. As we headed north toward Frankfurt one afternoon, the traffic slowed, then picked up speed, then slowed again, until the driver of the car in front slammed on his brakes for no apparent reason. Perhaps my father was less alert than he should have been; or perhaps the family Panhard was overloaded; or perhaps it was a combination of both. But the upshot was that he could not stop in time and we rear-ended the car in front. We were not going fast or perhaps we were lucky because with seat belts – let alone air bags – still awaiting invention, we escaped with slight shock but with not a scratch on any of us. The car we had hit was some kind of armour-plated gas guzzler that unlike my father's flimsy Panhard had been built to last a thousand years and came out of the skirmish as unscathed as we were. But the bonnet of our car had twisted badly and had been forced over the windscreen. There would be no more camping that summer.

With one of only two lanes now blocked, the traffic on the *Autobahn* got steadily worse. A tow truck was summoned by some mysterious force and appeared from we knew not where, and the driver proceeded to lift the front of our car in preparation for the ignominious crawl into Frankfurt. The German couple in the car we had hit were the tall, blue-eyed, *Reich*-building, *Untermensch*-crushing type, just the sort my grandmother had warned us against. Had she been with us, she would have gloated: I *told* you! What struck me at the time was that despite our obvious predicament, this couple showed not the slightest sign of sympathy. In fact, they looked incensed. How inconsiderate of this scruffy French family to interrupt our trip and delay us in this manner!

Father and boys joined the tow truck driver in his cab and mother and daughters sat on the rear seat of the damaged family car. We drove through the grimy suburbs of Frankfurt and eventually reached a ramshackle garage, where negotiations began. Evidently, dealing with stranded French tourists was not something the garage owner did on a regular basis, so language quickly became an issue. My father's German was brought into service at first, but twenty years after his most recent foray into Germany, it had become rusty, assuming it had ever been good.

Eventually, my older sister Bernadette and I were called to duty and the two of us and the garage owner settled on a stripped-down version of English, the very first time I had a chance to speak the language outside the classroom. The outcome was that we would take with us the possessions we could carry and leave everything else in the car until vehicle and content could be shipped back to Lure, Haute-Saône. A taxi was called and we were driven to the railway station in Mercedes splendour. For my siblings and I, this was not just our first ride in a Mercedes: it was our first ride in a taxi. For me, the crackling of the two-way radio was straight from outer space. Germany seemed a very advanced nation indeed!

We sat for hours in the cavernous Frankfurt *Hauptbahnhof* waiting for our train south, eating *bratwurst* smeared with sugary mustard and drinking milk out of cartons. We had never seen cartons filled with milk before. Milk was supposed to come out of cows, not cartons! This was real travelling! This was exciting! We then stood all night on a series of overcrowded trains that eventually took us all the way back to Lure, Haute-Saône where another taxi, this time a modest Renault, got us home to a relieved but not entirely surprised grandmother and our sister Odile.

For several long weeks that summer, my father grumbled about insurance companies and their legalistic, *centime*-pinching ways. The family took up the practice of going on long walks around town on Sunday afternoons until one day the station master sent word that the family Panhard had somehow found its way back to Lure, Haute-Saône and was awaiting collection. I jumped on my bike to verify the scoop, and just as reported, there it was, all forlorn and tethered to a flatbed in a siding at the far end of the railway station.

The car was a sorry sight, rather like a much-loved family pet that has been run over and is being returned by a well-intentioned neighbour, still breathing but with several bones broken and chunks of fur missing. Seeing this treasured family possession in such pitiful condition and in full view of the entire town and its multitude of willing gossips was not just distressing, it was humiliating. A day or two later, the local Panhard dealer hauled the car off the flatbed and towed it into his garage, where he set to work on restoring it to prime condition. When his work was done and the car was duly returned to its rightful owners, we went through the possessions we had left behind in that seedy garage on the grimy edges of Frankfurt. Not a thing was missing. But whether this was due to the garage owner's honesty or, as my grandmother insisted, to the fact that our camping gear was in such pitiful condition that even naturally larcenous Germans would not steal it was debated around the dinner table for weeks.

This was an unhappy experience at the time but in the end we had every reason to feel pleased with ourselves. Under difficult conditions and with no help from the haughty German couple in the armour-plated gas guzzler we had rear-ended, we had done our bit for Franco-German *rapprochement*. If there is no monument or even a modest plaque recording our misfortunes and our contribution to cross-Rhine *entente cordiale* on the northbound side of that *Autobahn* about an hour south of Frankfurt, there should be.

CHAPTER FIFTEEN: LIVE AND LEARN

You can get anything you want, at Alice's restaurant.
                                        Arlo Guthrie (1947-)

Nostalgia is good clean fun late in life but at the age of eighteen it makes no sense. Idyllic summers spent feeding chickens and hunting for eggs, the spectacle of liners docking at Cherbourg, and bike rides along country lanes with good friends were blissful interludes between long months of classroom tedium and a deep sense of academic ineptitude made worse by even greater failure in university. Nostalgia was not an option. The way was forward and that meant facing the challenge of becoming fluent in English.

So one fateful evening, still three months short of nineteen, I said goodbye to my family. My father offered his good wishes and gave me some money, not a lot but enough to get me started until I found work. I went to bed and slept a little. I was woken up soon after midnight by my mother, who accompanied me to the door, looking a little tearful, I thought. My father did not reappear, which bothered me. But he had been kind to me the night before. I walked to the railway station through the deserted streets of Lure, Haute-Saône with my belongings on my back and jumped on the red-eye *Bâle-Paris* I had heard whistling through town during sleepless nights but never seen. In the morning, I found myself at the *Gare de l'Est*, catching my first glimpse of Paris. Few impressions remain. I was too busy negotiating the urban bustle and locating the *Gare du Nord* and my train to Calais, which would connect with the ferry to Dover and finally with another train to London.

As arranged, Jacqueline, my sister Bernadette's friend, was waiting for me at Victoria Station. From there, she took me on a succession of trains to Wickford, the small town deep in the Essex commuter belt where she was teaching French in the local secondary school and where she lodged with a local family, who extended their welcome to me for a few weeks in exchange for modest sums. To facilitate my investigations into the British way of life, I borrowed a bike and started exploring the town, concentrating exclusively at first on the logistics of keeping to the wrong side of the road.

On Sundays, a small crowd gathered for the obligatory family lunch. The house filled with the overpowering smell of roast beef, which appeared on the table surrounded by golden potatoes and plump Brussels sprouts. The beef was a little pungent for my taste and the sprouts had sat in boiling water a little too long but the roast potatoes were just as tasty as the French equivalent. If this was what English food was like, I recall commenting to Jacqueline, it did not seem nearly as bad as years of mental conditioning in France had led me to expect. There was no risk I might long for my mother's Friday fish.

For the rest of Sunday afternoons, the family gathered in front of the television. Most of what I watched went over my head in part because of the unfamiliar topics but largely because my English had a long way to go before it was up to deciphering those pesky idioms that make every language colourful but also difficult to understand. What was I to make, for example, of a show called 'Going for a Song', which consisted of old people milling around vast exhibition halls and gazing lovingly at old clocks, paintings, and furniture? What did this have to do with singing, I asked Jacqueline, whose command of English and of the more obscure features of the British way of life was of course far superior to mine. Nothing, she said. It's just an idiom. Learning English was going to take a lot longer than I had anticipated.

Just as puzzling though for different reasons was the family's devotion to another Sunday afternoon show entitled 'Songs of Praise'. This time, the show really was about singing and as soon as Jacqueline had explained the meaning of the word 'praise', it all made sense. The show was shot inside a church, not too dissimilar to the Catholic churches I was familiar with but not quite the same either. Anglicanism, it seemed, was a lot like Catholicism but with even more bells and, judging by the incessant swinging of thuribles and the incense vapours that swirled around the building, more smells, too. The parishioners seemed older and wealthier than those that filled the church of Saint Martin in Lure, Haute-Saône every Sunday but also more committed, more passionate about their singing and the good it seemed to be doing their souls: suspiciously so, in fact. To a former altar boy of my vast experience, nothing about hymn singing could possibly drive worshippers to such naked displays of spiritual elation. Could they be faking it, I recall wondering? Is it possible that television cameras encourage their subjects to feign emotions?

And why did this family, who never went to church and whose home was entirely devoid of religious symbols or practices of any kind, feel such allegiance to a television show devoted to the proposition that public displays of religiosity makes people visibly happier? Later, as I learned about the ability of institutions to survive long after they have lost all purpose, I concluded that this television show was there to make viewers feel good about the lingering presence of the Church of England on the edges of their lives, about the nation it was supposed to symbolise, and by implication, about themselves. As with all obsolete practices, it was enough to know that it was there not as an opportunity for active participation but simply as a feel-good show, like the Trooping of the Colour, the Oxford and Cambridge boat race, or a royal wedding.

*

Once I had found my footing in England and felt comfortable exploring the novelty on the wrong side of the road, I started venturing further from Jacqueline's base in Wickford and eventually taking daily trains into the heart of London in search of a job.

To my provincial eyes, London was a swirling multitude of faceless people rushing towards unfathomable destinations while trying to avoid crashing into each other by zigzagging along the thronged pavements. The counterpoint to this frenzy was provided by the stately procession of red double-decker buses with route numbers that went up not into the dozens, which I had seen, but into the hundreds, which seemed unthinkable. Destinations ranged from the intriguing (Crystal Palace, Elephant & Castle) through the famous (Wimbledon Park, Wembley Central) to the unexpectedly pastoral (Shepherd's Bush, Snaresbrook).

How did Londoners manage not to get hopelessly lost every time they went past their front door? And how was I going to make sense of this jostling vortex as I searched for shelter, employment, and English lessons? I had landed in what was still one of the world's largest cities from a universe where for any street I chose to ride my bike along I could predict with near-total accuracy depending on time of day which shops would be open or who I would see cycling home from school or to work, chatting on a doorstep, or watching the world go by from a window. Next to such provincial serenity, the complexities of London had my brain in a spin. But as I stood marvelling at Londoners' ability to see method in the madness, I also sensed that if I had the pluck to dive into the maelstrom, the patience to crack the puzzle, and the guts not to rush back to the small-town certainties I had just left, opportunities were there for the taking. But first, I would have to learn a lot more English.

*

Expertly tutored by Jacqueline, I learned to locate and scan the display that was a feature of every newsagent's in town for notices offering jobs of such an unambitious nature that they could only appeal to those with little English and, until Britain joined the (then) Common Market in 1973, no working visa and therefore no legal means of supporting themselves. This meant cleaning jobs, mostly: the offices of local businesses or the homes of the better-off. I was under pressure because the small amount of money my father had given me the night before my departure was dwindling alarmingly so anything would do as long as it enabled me to staunch the haemorrhage. And after two or three weeks of increasingly anxious search, I was offered both employment and shelter by an elderly Dutch couple, Mr and Mrs Bessevant, who lived in an elegant house within walking distance of Holland Park. The pay was low but the basement room they offered me was homely and the job required my presence all morning and part of the evening, which left plenty of time for studying English in the afternoon.

My next step was to look for an English class that would have a place for me with the tuition bill preferably sent to the British taxpayer as was the norm in those idealistic times. Soon, I learned that a branch of one of the largest public colleges of higher education in this part of the capital, West London College, might offer what I was looking for. In essence, West London College was a British version of what Americans would call a' community college'. One branch of the college, housed in an unprepossessing corner of South Kensington, specialised in teaching English as a second language and therefore in equipping wandering souls such as myself not only with new linguistic skills but also with a student visa and the all-important permission to stay in the country as well as the opportunity to earn a living, however illegally.

The building stood in a narrow side street close to Gloucester Road underground station. Until I was able to cobble together the £5 I needed to buy the red second-hand bike I had seen in a repair shop practically crying out for a doting owner to take it home and lavish TLC on it, underground access to everything mattered.

The branch of the college occupied the top floor of a dark Victorian school building. The climb was interminable because each floor had very high ceilings. The reason for this, my new classmates and I were told, was that Victorian architects, medical experts, and educators alike agreed that a plentiful supply of air was as essential to the intellectual development of London's children as multiplication tables and the list of the seven largest cities in England and that the best way to ensure educational success was to give children as many cubic feet of the stuff as possible. Apparently, they used a mathematical formula to calculate the space needed: so many square feet of floor space, so many children, so many cubic feet of God's air above them. The downside was that in winter, what little heat managed to radiate from the iron-age heating system soared ceiling-ward, leaving everyone in the room numb with cold. But in Victorian England, I later learned, this would have been regarded as sound educational policy since effort and comfort were regarded as antithetical and a little suffering was known to be good for the soul.

The branch consisted of two parallel rows of classrooms. At one end was the staircase, at the other the office, which also doubled as meeting room for the teaching staff. In the middle was a small cafeteria, where we spent our breaks acquiring the English passion for cups of tea and cheese and tomato sandwiches. Two friendly though incomprehensible Cockney ladies were in charge, brewing the tea, making the sandwiches, and washing cups and saucers. Valuable information about English was exchanged there but also about exotic lands: Sweden, Israel, Turkey, Colombia, Vietnam, even Belgium. The cafeteria was a microcosm of all that was good about London and it offered exactly what I had come to acquire: English but also friends from backgrounds as varied as those of the friends I had left behind in Lure, Haute-Saône had been uniform.

Classes were held in the afternoon: three hours a day, five days a week, which added up to the fifteen weekly hours required for a student visa. I spent eighteen months studying English at West London College. These were formative times, vividly recalled today.

Four teachers stood out. One was Miss Talbot, an older lady with an impish grin and a sense of fun that made everything she taught seem like play. She instructed us in writing including the skill of extracting meaning from a text and condensing it, an activity known at the time as *précis* and a priceless teaching and learning tool that seems to have vanished. Miss

Talbot did what very few of my teachers had done before: she spotted the positive and then encouraged it. She was the first to point out to me that my English was improving rapidly and to give me specific evidence to support her assessment. The effect was hugely motivating.

Another was Mr Enderby, the quintessential Englishman who introduced us to Somerset Maugham's *Ashenden*, an absorbing collection of World War I spy stories set in and around Switzerland and the very first book in English I ever read. Mr Enderby's other specialty consisted of delivering self-deprecating one-liners with a straight face. Many of his jokes went over my head but his lessons were a delight. Privately, it was rumoured, Mr Enderby had an eye for pretty girls, including a jet-haired French classmate named Geneviève whom I had timid hopes of impressing. Sagely assuming that the rumour was true and that the contest was unequal, I chose to focus on my studies instead.

A third was Mr McCluskey, a distinguished-looking white-haired gentleman who painstakingly took us in his Ulster accent through every imaginable syntactic transformation in the English language. Active to passive, as in: She kicked the cat – The cat was kicked by her. Or direct to indirect speech, as in: She asked me: 'Do you often kick the cat?' – She asked if I often kicked the cat. If English had it, we transformed it, page after page, class after class. Mr McCluskey was of the view that no one could legitimately claim to know English unless they had been through every syntactic transformation in the book. I believed him. How such a mechanical approach to teaching can lead to successful learning remains a mystery. In theory, it should turn everyone off studying. But Mr McCluskey had a way. Somehow, in his classes, it worked.

And finally, there was the lovely Miss Hutchinson, younger than the other three, fresh out of university, and said to be in possession not only of a master's degree but also of the latest in English language teaching methods, whatever those were. Curiously, I have no recollection of what she taught. I assume it was something significant and she probably played a major part in my linguistic development, for which I am grateful. But all I remember apart from her name are her figure and her smile, in that order. In the London *patois*, she was 'a bit of alright'. I spent her lessons gazing in rapture and wondering how it was possible for an English teacher to look so ravishing. I am sorry I do not have more to say about your pedagogic skills, Miss Hutchinson. But believe me, it is not because I did not think about you a lot.

Someone else who thought about Miss Hutchinson a lot was George, a classmate from Cyprus. He was older than most of us, large, and brimming with self-confidence. He had signed up for English classes not because a daily dose of syntactic transformations was essential to his intellectual development but because he needed a student visa in order to stay in the country and help an uncle run his Greek restaurant in Soho. George was jovial and good-hearted. He enjoyed an audience and most importantly, he was willing to subsidise it. He never seemed to want for money. While the fortunate among us went around on bikes and the truly destitute hoofed it everywhere to save the bus fare, George had full access to his uncle's Ford Zodiac, at the time one of the largest cars in England apart from the odd American import. On weekends, the five or six of us who formed his loyal entourage luxuriated in the Zodiac as he drove us all over London in search of excitement and for him fresh chances to spend money on nurturing our mutual friendship. And regardless of where he took us that day, the route invariably led to Soho and his uncle's restaurant before it opened for dinner, where he seated us around a table and fed us leftovers from lunch, all for free.

A favourite destination was Heathrow Airport, then a hugely glamorous location, where we went up to the observation deck and watched the jets come and go. Then George treated each one of us to a cup of coffee and a slice of something expensive while we stared at the jet-setters sauntering past, swinging their branded luggage and holding a *debonaire* cigarette at arms' length as if they were generously offering to share its health benefits with the sedentary proletariat.

A popular companion on these jaunts was Vuong, a classmate from Vietnam. Vuong was a slender, doll-like boy with dainty mannerisms, long, silky hair he kept rearranging with an elegant sweep of his delicate hand, and the kittenish smile of a young *coquette*. One afternoon after class, Vuong announced that he would like to have our little band of friends over at his place for a cup of tea. So George was instructed to point the Zodiac towards the southern end of Ladbroke Grove, an area where the imposing elegance of Holland Park gives way to the rougher edges of Notting Hill.

The house was vast, dark, and silent. While Vuong was attending to the kettle, we sat in the living room and puzzled at the largest collection of electric guitars any of us had ever seen under one roof. The other salient feature of the room was the inordinate number of ashtrays, each one overflowing with cigarette butts of a design I could not remember seeing in my father's ashtray back in Lure, Haute-Saône. Come to think of it, there was an unfamiliar smell in the air too. No room I had ever been in smelled quite like that. When Vuong returned with the brew, we asked about the guitars. Simple, he said: we were sitting in the living room of

Jimi Hendrix. A megastar musician, my classmates informed me as soon as they could get their breath back. Obviously, with Bach, Handel, and Mozart as my personal musical heroes, I had never heard of this 'Jimi Hendrix'. But I took their word for it and I have been bragging ever since about having once taken tea in the living room of the greatest rock guitarist the world has ever known.

Quite what Vuong's function might be in the Hendrix household – apart from making the tea – was not entirely clear. But even for an innocent abroad such as myself, it was not too difficult to think of one or two useful roles he might have played. Vuong exuded mystery and that was exciting! After all, why swap Lure, Haute-Saône for London and resist being drawn to the unexpected and the exotic?

One Sunday afternoon, Vuong took charge once again and announced that he had a new destination in mind for us. This time, George was instructed to park the Zodiac outside an old block of flats just off Oxford Street. Vuong led us up the stairs and produced from his pocket the key to yet another residence he seemed to have access to. This time, the lord of the manor was Johnny, a slightly older Scot with a broad, welcoming grin, a love of company, and a talent for making visitors feel at home. His cooking was superb, his coffee even better. But what made Johnny fascinating was not his Glaswegian accent, though that was exotic enough, but his homosexuality, which he flaunted as if was the only way for a man to live. Jamaican boys were his passion, he announced with a wink, with sylph-like southeast Asian boys a close second. Given that homosexuality had been decriminalised in England only months earlier, Johnny's public positioning of himself in such a way showed inordinate courage as well as rare self-confidence.

Johnny worked for a travel agency in ritzy Mayfair and he held us in thrall with tales of the fabulous places where his professional junkets had taken him: Barcelona, Beirut, even Las Vegas. In between travel anecdotes, Johnny introduced us to the airline pun genre. Aer Lingus was Aer Fungus and Air France Air Frowns. TWA stood for 'Try Walking Across' and BOAC for 'Better On A Camel'. The Philippines' PAL was 'Plane Always Late' while Portugal's TAP stood for 'Take Another Plane'. But to me, the runaway winner was QANTAS: 'Quick And Nasty, Typical Aussie Shit'.

As an up-and-coming student of English, I found this wordplay revealing as well as amusing. I was reaching the level of proficiency at which I could handle multiple meanings. I was becoming the older equivalent of a seven-year-old on whom it is dawning that the link between words and their meaning is arbitrary and can therefore be tampered with, especially for fun. The result is the pleasure the child takes in telling and retelling jokes about the boy who blushed when he opened the refrigerator because he saw the salad dressing or the scientist who installed a knocker on his front door because he wanted to win the no-bell prize.

But Johnny had another string to his bow. Next to boys, his other passion was classical and especially baroque music. Now I had someone to talk to about my musical interests! His stash of records was impressive: Bach, Vivaldi, Handel, Mozart. All the key names and numbers were there. But best of all was being introduced to the exquisite compositions of Henry Purcell, a composer I knew only by name. What with the cooking, the coffee, the airline puns, and the baroque repertoire at the drop of a gramophone needle, I was in heaven. Gradually, I found myself spending more time in Johnny's living room and less with my classmates in George's Zodiac. Jimi Hendrix was to them what Josef Haydn was to me. I ignored their taunts about being a Jamaican boy in disguise and we all agreed to differ.

*

But I digress. Back to George, our Cypriot benefactor, and the lovely Miss Hutchinson, MA. Being older, speaking better English, and practically minting his own money, George was pleased with the hand life had dealt him. Although somewhat corpulent and a tad greasy in appearance, George fancied himself a kind of motorised *boulevardier* and something of a ladies' man. In particular, he was convinced that he had what it took to bag the object of his open – and my secret – desire, the lovely Miss Hutchinson. I was realistic enough to sense that if anyone in the class could pull it off, it had to be George. I liked George and I wished him well. But I am sure that if his fantasy had come true, he would have bragged about it till the end of time. So it is safe to assume that his lustful ambitions went unrequited and the shapely Miss Hutchinson remained *inviolata* at least as far as anyone in my class was concerned.

I studied and passed a succession of increasingly challenging exams and my moment of academic glory finally came when West London College organised a public reading competition open to all its international students. To my intense pride, I was selected to represent first my class then the South Kensington branch and eventually going head to head with a German girl in the final to be held in the much larger building that served as the nerve centre of the college. The set text was from Forster's *Passage to India*. Luckily, my brush with academic destiny at West

354

London College was hugely facilitated by my employer, Mrs Bessevant, whose house in Holland Park I cleaned for a living.

Her husband, Mr Bessevant, was a former stockbroker with as easy-going an attitude to life as it was possible to imagine. His only interests seemed to be golf, port, and cigars. Where he had three passions, his wife, Mrs Bessevant, had just two. One was creating punishing work schedules for herself but also for anyone she paid to provide a service or run an errand on her behalf. The other consisted of conducting a personal crusade to make safe for posterity the self-evidently superior ways of what had been – or she claimed to have been – her aristocratic up-bringing in late nineteenth-century Holland.

She abhorred the title 'Mrs', which she regarded as insufferably common, and insisted on being addressed in all social contexts as 'Madame', which she spelt in the French manner and expected everyone to pronounce accordingly, with the stress on the second syllable and the tone rising slightly. She was also an indomitable motivator who could not see a piece of furniture that did not need polishing or a floor that did not need scrubbing. On a number of occasions, she even had me hosing down the front of the house in the pouring rain. Soap suds not blood coursed through her arteries. The lady was dictatorial to her fingertips but she had a heart of gold and she took me clueless and penniless as I was under her wing. Adding fearlessly to her long list of self-assigned missions, she resolved to help me win the West London College reading competition despite the fact that she spoke English with a rasping Dutch accent that even I could tell was hardly the ideal model. Day after day, she made me stand before her as she read from *A Passage to India* and then coached me until I had every word, every pause, and every twist in the intonation pat and all during the working hours she was paying for, bless her.

On the appointed day, the great and the good of West London College gathered in a marbled hall to listen to the two finalists as they went through their lines. I was good. The German girl was good. In fact, I thought we were so equally good that the five-guinea first prize and the one-guinea second prize would surely have to be combined and split equally. But the German girl won. The only explanation I could offer at the time for this blatant miscarriage of justice is that she was cute. How could this not have biased the mostly male jury? In the morning, I took my wounded pride and my one-guinea cheque, the first financial instrument I had ever seen with my name written on it, to the Midland Bank in Notting Hill and opened my very first bank account. In the world I was emerging from, cash was king as well as scarce. With teenage employment unknown and ATMs still awaiting invention, no one my own age had a bank account or felt the need for one, not even in college.

But what on earth was a guinea? Until the early 1970s, a pound was divided not into one hundred pence as it is now but into twenty shillings, each further divided not into ten but twelve pence. This may sound absurd. But in reality, the shilling and its twenty-to-one relationship to the pound was not the British eccentricity that may be imagined but a Roman concept with a long pedigree. In fact, as late as the 1960s, it was common to hear the older residents of Lure, Haute-Saône refer to a five-franc coin as *cent sous*, or five times twenty.

To complicate matters, a guinea was worth one pound and one shilling, or one pound plus one twentieth of a pound. In effect, the guinea was a cheap trick dreamt up by rapacious professionals – the usual suspects: lawyers, doctors, stockbrokers – to make their services look five per cent cheaper than they really were. An additional side effect of this sleight of hand was that it set them apart socially from grocers, milliners, haberdashers, and similar rabble who billed in mere pounds. In a sense, the guinea was a forerunner of the ploy since perfected by American stores where the sales tax is added to the bill only at the very end by a checkout operator with an indignant 'blame-the-government-not-me' look on his face. More recently, the baton of financial obfuscation has passed to airlines, which routinely offer to fly hopeful travellers across entire continents for £0.99 and only reveal as the customer is about to confirm payment that with airport taxes, airport security charges, fuel surcharges, checked baggage charges, in-flight meal charges, in-flight entertainment charges, and VAT plus a £5 online booking convenience fee, the damage to the privy purse is actually £499.99.

Initially, my plan had been to gain equal competence in English and German by spending a year in England and then another in Germany. Towards the end of my year in London and thanks in no small measure to Miss Talbot, Mr Enderby, Mr McCluskey, and the unforgettable Miss Hutchinson I sensed that my English was coming along rapidly. But even though I had demonstrated my growing competence by almost coming first in the West London College reading competition, I had not reached the level of proficiency I considered adequate. So I decided to stay on for one more year. Deep down and still largely unconsciously, I was sensing that London was becoming home to me and I was in no hurry to leave. So I stayed, and stayed, and I was lost to German philology and German philology to me, a turn of events I have had no reason to regret so far.

*

Ostensibly, swapping Lure, Haute-Saône for London was about learning English. But unconsciously at first and then increasingly plainly, it was really about growing up, or as it might be more appropriately called at the age of eighteen or nineteen, maturing. And among other things, maturing meant learning about work.

During my first hesitant year in London, my arrangement with Mr and Mrs Bessevant offered comfortable shelter and an adequate income. But as I grew increasingly confident about my ability to cope with the complexities of city life, I began to long for greater independence. So I moved into a small 'bedsit', a room with a washbasin in a corner and a crude bathroom on the landing below in a converted Victorian house on the eastern fringes of Notting Hill close to Paddington Station, where a semi-transitory population of immigrants and short-term residents mix in comforting anonymity. To pay the rent, I took what work I found: once again, cleaning homes, offices, and hotels. No one ever asked for documentation so the awkward question of my lack of a working visa was never raised. But over the months, I began to long for something more adventurous and the idea of earning a living by moving about London was looking increasingly attractive.

Ever since my brother Pierre and I started pushing our Dinky Toy cars around the sandy patch we had remodelled as a racetrack next to our house in Lure, Haute-Saône, we had been dreaming about cars. So once I found my footing in London and managed to save a little, I set about fulfilling the dream. I would learn to drive. This would incur serious expense especially for someone entirely dependent on house and office cleaning for survival. Luckily, a back street operator I found in the phone book, with an office of sorts at the top of a dingy staircase in a now defunct Victorian building on the dark side of Paddington Station, was happy to oblige at less than market rate.

On Day One, my instructor, a former policeman, took charge until we reached a quiet street somewhere in nearby Maida Vale where he pulled up and we swapped seats. He then launched me on my driving career through West London's leafy suburbs and, too soon for my taste, the hurly-burly of the Kilburn High Road. This involved sharing congested space with streams of buses and cars and vans and taxis and motorbikes and hundreds of scurrying shoppers who never seemed to know which side of the street they wanted to be on and who kept leaping into the road on a whim to see what bargains they might find on the other side.

My instructor was a man of few words but strong views on sound driving habits. He had low tolerance for being interrupted and in any case, my English was not always up to understanding what he was saying, so he had my full attention. And after just one course of lessons, this fine pedagogue declared me ready for the rigours of the British driving test, its tight three-point turn, tricky hill start, and hair-raising reverse parking manoeuvre. He had called it right. Under his expert guidance, I had become a fit and proper person to hold one of Her Majesty's red driving licenses.

Soon, I set about converting my new qualification into cash. I scoured the pages of the *Evening Standard*, the Holy Book of Londoners in need. With what was left of my savings, I bought my very first car, a venerable Austin A30 and I spent mornings before heading to my afternoon English classes at West

London College as well as every weekend driving what Londoners call a 'minicab'.

Everyone knows London's black taxis, their sputtering diesel engine, their impossibly tight turning circle, and their high door clearance, designed – legend has it – to allow a gentleman to climb in and out without having to take off his bowler hat. But the defining characteristic of a London taxi is not the vehicle itself but its driver and especially his permanent readiness to mouth off on every conceivable subject including the awfulness of the government and especially the celebrities he once had 'in the back of the cab'.

What is less well known and even less appreciated is the fact that aspiring taxi drivers first have to pass a fiendishly difficult test called the 'Knowledge'. On a typical day, the taxi drivers of tomorrow can be seen all over London preparing for the test on small motorbikes called 'mopeds'. On a clipboard in front of the rider is a route and a list of all the streets and all the public buildings passengers might ask to be driven to. The details include every one-way street, every no-right turn, and every other obstacle conscientious city planners saw fit to put in everyone's path. Needless to say, making this test as difficult as possible is also a cunning way to restrict the supply of taxis and keep fares absurdly high. But that is another story.

A minicab, by contrast, is an ordinary car driven by an ordinary 'bloke' who at least when I was giving it a shot was barely required to show proof of insurance and was never questioned on his – very rarely her – background let alone tested on his ability to tell north from south or asked to display his appreciation of the fact that Tower Bridge and London Bridge are not different names for the same bridge.

Minicabs were not metered so Londoners in a hurry

depended for financial survival on their negotiating skills. Minicabs were not marked either so they could not be hailed on the street, and they were not allowed to trawl for business. The upside of this arrangement was that minicab drivers were willing to take passengers anywhere unlike the drivers of black cabs who were notoriously picky about destinations especially if these involved the 'wrong side' of what Londoners affectionately call 'the river'. Conveniently, minicabs swarmed around large pubs late at night and popular clubs even later. Once a would-be passenger had the fare pinned down, all he or she had to do was get in, refrain from throwing up all over the back seat, and keep one eye on the street signs and the other on the trusty *London from A to Z* so that the driver could be given the directions he was obviously incapable of supplying himself. With black cabs, drivers took passengers to their destinations. With minicabs, it was the other way around. Simple, really, once you knew the rules.

The job was tailor-made for transient types and cultural vagabonds with no interest in anything as old-fashioned as a career plan and deep contempt for anyone with a career plan of their own. Minicab driving was ideal for optimistic, up-and-coming drifters, the kind of person major cities are uniquely equipped to attract, mould, and supply to prospective employers who see a lack of a working visa as no problem at all and a short-term outlook in an employee as a plus and not as a warning sign of a sociopath in the making.

For anyone who like me was averse to following a script imposed top down, minicab driving was a dream job because I never knew where the next call was going to take me. But on occasion, there was no escaping temporary collusion with the despised corporate world as lucrative contract work was dangled before my eyes.

Typically, these calls came from large companies in search of a drudge with a driving license and the willingness to cart around unglamorous company junk as opposed to glamorous company executives. A major client of the minicab company that employed me was Marks & Spencer, the department store chain, which was then pioneering the application to business management of a mysterious labour-saving device called the 'computer'. When the summons came, a crew of three of us working for the minicab company converged from our base in Soho onto M&S headquarters on Baker Street, a short hop from where Holmes and Watson had their supposed bachelor establishment.

My fellow drivers, two amiable English lads named Mike and Steve, were slightly older than me, equally averse to making career plans of any kind and just as dedicated to living for the day. Both were good company and the three of us became friends. Though the names Mike and Steve were entirely par for the course in late 1960s London, given the evasive answers they gave to my innocent questions about their professional backgrounds, I came to suspect that the names might in fact be made up. As I said, in the world of minicabs, no one ever checked, least of all Arthur (pronounced 'Ahffah'), the ruddy-nosed Cockney who owned the business and who sat in the office all day: chain smoking, taking bookings on one phone, and conducting interminable conversations on another with mysterious associates discussing business ventures that he assured us – protesting a little too much, I thought – were irreproachably 'legit', as he called it.

The reason Mike, Steve, and I had been head-hunted by Arthur for the M&S assignments was not our in-depth knowledge of the garment trade but the fact that we drove the three most ancient, most battered cars in the minicab agency's unimpressive fleet, and sending us out on archive storing duty lowered the risk that we might invite some corporate high-flier to sit in one of them. Once at M&S headquarters, Mike, Steve, and I descended into the depths of the corporate world and stood in awe before huge machines that reached to the ceiling and seemed to consist almost entirely of spools that spun one way for a while and then suddenly spun the other way for no obvious reason.

The storeroom held stacks of cardboard boxes filled with fanfold printouts of employee records, payroll calculations, and all manner of tedious information arranged in neat columns that only slaves to the corporate ethos could possibly have the patience to go through. We free spirits collected the boxes, crammed them into our jalopies until not another sheet of fanfold could be squeezed in, drove to a warehouse in a decidedly unglamorous corner of southeast London where M&S stored its archives, and returned to base to await payment. In between calls, we sat on a grubby sofa in the minicab company's office above a sandwich shop, talking of many things, comparing routes to key destinations, ogling passing miniskirts down below, and taking it in turns to fetch scotch eggs and cups of tea from our downstairs neighbours.

I loved the opportunities for exploration the job provided. But it could not last. With the freedom came unpredictable pay, which sat awkwardly with the inescapable thought that the rent was due once again. As financial worries crept in and became the norm, there was only so much emotional compensation I could derive from spending evenings in my cold bedsit calculating how many more coins I could afford to push into the voracious gas meter before the heater died and trying to keep my mind off financial worries by tearing the perforated edges off sheaves of classified M&S

archives accidentally left behind in the back of my car. So for a while at least, I reverted to being slave to the cleaning ethos instead.

*

Meanwhile, I was rapidly become fluent in English and I had learnt that I was capable of keeping body and soul together. But one area my small-town upbringing had left me with plenty to learn about still was sex. And where better to remedy this than in a hotel, an institution built around beds and the imaginative uses people devise for them. It all started with my semi-perpetual search for a better job, but this particular job was information-rich beyond expectations.

Armed once again with the day's copy of the *Evening Standard,* I presented myself at the portals of the Consulate Hotel, a peeling building at the Notting Hill end of Bayswater Road directly opposite the Czechoslovak Embassy and a stone's throw from the Soviet Embassy in Kensington Gardens. The Czechoslovak Embassy was rumoured to be the beating heart of Soviet intelligence gathering in London and the speculation was easy to verify simply by looking up at the forest of antennas that sprouted from the roof of the building, a forbidding-looking concrete structure that had risen on the bombed ruins of a row of Victorian family homes and whose monolithic design would have gladdened the heart of any Stalinist architect.

I was interviewed by Miss Petrie, the hotel manager, an unsmiling woman who reminded me strangely of Mademoiselle Simard, my detested biology teacher. I must have impressed her with my obvious readiness to do anything however menial because I was hired on the spot and immediately entrusted with the awesome responsibility of serving as assistant to Alf, the head dishwasher, in the hotel's cavernous kitchens.

Alf was a proletarian of the old school. He had served his country chasing Communist insurgents up and down the highlands of what he still called Malaya though it turned out on closer questioning that his strategic interventions had been confined to field catering. His chief claim to military fame was to have once been commended by top brass for the quality of his camp coffee, a noxious-sounding brew of chicory (for taste) and caramelised sugar (for colour) that according to Alf tasted just like real coffee – better, in fact.

Alf took his duties seriously. In his eyes, dishwashing was as noble a calling as any and fawning respect for any employer generous enough to pay a living wage was a requirement of every job. Alf lost no opportunity to admonish the entire kitchen staff over our tendency to focus on the funny side of life. In this, he had the implicit support of Miss Petrie, the hotel manager, a woman of Scottish descent whose Pict ancestors must have been hibernating the day God created the sense of humour. Hotel lore had it that the lady was not at all keen on male companionship. So jibes flew and Alf huffed and puffed at the impudence of the young and admonished some more.

To give him his due, Alf knew his dishwashing and under his stern gaze I learned every secret of the kitchen sink. In particular, I picked up the standard military technique for scooping several inches of congealed fat with bare hands from the bottom of enormous cooking pots before submitting them to standard military washing procedures involving torrents of scalding water and generous lashes of industrial grade detergent. Today, I remain a hopeless cook but I wash a mean dish. I do not even mind the chore. According to my younger sister Madeleine, I am the only person she knows who leaves her kitchen cleaner at the end of a visit than at the start.

Next to the man-hating Scottish manager in the hotel's pecking order was Jimmy, the Irish chef. Jimmy was still in his mid-twenties and immensely proud of having scaled the professional heights at such a young age. True to stereotype, he had a freckled face, flaming red hair, and an incandescent temper. I quickly learned to hold my counsel and stay out of the way when he embarked on one of his rants against the dastardly British and their repugnant perpetrations in Northern Ireland as the diatribe invariably concluded with Jimmy stabbing a chopping board or a door frame with his carving knife. In my eyes, young and eager to learn as I was, Jimmy's redeeming feature was not his deftness with a spatula or an egg whisk but his extensive collection of pornographic magazines. I knew I was accepted as a trusted member of the team when Jimmy invited me into his lair down the hallway during a break one morning and gave me the freedom of his library. The holdings were extensive. As far as I could tell, if people got naked to do it, Jimmy had a magazine about it. Under his expert tutelage, I learned even more about sexual combinations than I did about dishwashing under Alf's.

I vividly recall a publication entirely devoted to the specialised doings of a pretty young brunette who could have been the girl next door. On the cover of the magazine, this conscientious young lady was shown looking down at a hairy belly with her parted lips aiming straight at the tip of the erection that protruded from it, and the rest of the publication consisted of variations on that theme each expertly photographed from a wide variety of angles. Only really hot girls did that, Jimmy informed me with the air of one whose appeal to women was such that, like *Don Giovanni*'s, the extent of his conquests called for professional cataloguing.

For me, it was not so much the obvious eroticism of the scene that left me speechless but the discovery that it was done at all. I had no idea. It even had a name, apparently, or rather several. The conceptual leap from youthful contemplations of Brigitte Bardot's bare *derrière* outside the *Rex* cinema in Lure, Haute-Saône to this was substantial. Jimmy's cooking was unremarkable and his rages terrifying but my motivation for being in London was to come of age and I could not have come to a better place or wished for a better mentor.

One day, into this combustible mix was thrown the lovely Maria, a pretty Portuguese girl about my age who had come to London with a similar aim in mind and was paying for her English classes by working in the hotel as a chambermaid. Maria was vivacious, cheerful, and invariably good company. In short order, spurred on by daily perusals of some of Jimmy's magazines, I was consumed with yearning for Maria and I applied myself to winning her consent to a tryst. Nothing doing.

I attributed my failure to charm Maria to my inexperience and lack of self-confidence. So I decided to seek guidance from that expert on affairs of the heart and regions below, Jimmy the Irish chef. As man to man, Jimmy informed me, he too had tried and despite his exalted position near the top of the hotel's social pyramid, he too had failed. But neither of us, he added, should conclude that our failure had anything to do with a lack of manly attributes, especially in his case. No, the problem was that Miss Petrie, the man-hating hotel manager, had beaten us both to Maria's heart and had recruited her to her deviant sorority. This was not sour grapes, Jimmy assured me, as he thumbed through a particularly lurid offering from his library on that very subject for my educational benefit. He had proof. For one thing, despite repeated attempts on his part, Maria took not the slightest interest in the contents of his library. For another, anyone could see that everywhere that Maria went Miss Petrie was sure to go, loitering with Sapphic intent and bestowing her rare smiles on Maria and on Maria alone. Or so it seemed to Jimmy. Perhaps he was right. After all, he knew a lot more about these things than I did.

*

Though but a humble assistant dishwasher, my growing linguistic skills came in handy when communication up and down the hotel proved problematic. One morning, I was temporarily released from fat-scooping duties and summoned upstairs to help defuse a diplomatic incident involving an irate French guest who was loudly complaining of having been served salted butter with his breakfast toast and not the expected unsalted variety. The charge sheet also impugned New Zealand as a legitimate source of butter especially when contrasted with Normandy. So would I please hunt up and down the hotel and procure unsalted butter this instant so breakfast could proceed as nature intended.

I recall failing in my quest and gratefully leaving the matter in the man-averse but generally capable hands of Miss Petrie, the hotel manager. Next morning, the news percolated down to the kitchens that the French guest had packed his *valises* and checked out. Perhaps he had heard of another hotel somewhere in London known for serving unsalted Normandy butter at breakfast time. Or perhaps he had planned to leave that morning all along and had simply stuck to his original schedule. But given that Miss Petrie thought it important to inform me personally of this otherwise unremarkable event as she passed me on the stairs, I concluded that in her opinion it was all my fault.

Thanks to its geographical location, the Consulate was the hotel of choice for the Soviet Embassy. The Cold War was at its height and very few Soviet citizens were allowed out through the Iron Curtain. But even those who were granted exit permits never quite had the trust of Soviet officialdom since there was always the risk that they might hear capitalism's siren song and abscond unless watched night and day. So the Russians visitors were parked practically across the street from the Embassy inside the Consulate so that a watchful eye could be kept on them with minimal inconvenience and maximum efficacy.

At a time when the Soviet Union was represented in the media – not entirely without reason – as the heart of darkness, dealing face to face with real-life Russians provided a useful corrective. We toiled below stairs and except when called upon to mediate butter-related disputes in the dining room, we rarely met the guests. When we caught a glimpse of them, the Russians could be identified instantly from their frumpy appearance and the dowdy clothes they wore. But they were invariably charming. In particular, they had the endearing habit as they checked out of loudly proclaiming their appreciation for the warm welcome, the homely comforts, and Jimmy's culinary skills by making their way down to the kitchens and showering us with gifts. Female members of the kitchen staff got a set of roughly hewn Russian dolls, males a toy car made of crudely cut grey plastic. As befitted her status, Miss Petrie the hotel manager received a gift of vodka, which Jimmy the Irish chef accused her under his breath of pressing on Maria to get her in the mood for some unnatural hanky-panky. Everyone got broad smiles, slaps on the back, warm handshakes, hugs, even kisses. No other guests ever gave the kitchen staff a thought as they packed their bags. Perhaps these theatrical goodbyes were drilled as part of an image-boosting ploy by their Soviet minders, but I doubt it. The Russians were the friendliest, kindest guests we ever served. But this also made me wonder what standards must have been like in Soviet hotels if a short stay in a third-rate hostelry such as the Consulate could lead to such displays of heartfelt gratitude.

Another set of regular guests at the Consulate consisted of the Harlem Globetrotters. Quite what these comical basketball superstars were thinking when they – or their agent – chose the Consulate as their London base was a mystery. Perhaps as born entertainers they liked to surprise. And surprise they did.

Being much bigger than anyone else and trading on displays of boundless energy, they ate twice as much. Their breakfasts consisted of double rations: where mere mortals got two eggs, three sausages, and four rashers of bacon, the Globetrotters got four, six, and eight, respectively. Each athlete got two pots of coffee instead of one. Even the statutory ration of salted New Zealand butter was doubled. They thrived on the nutrition but also on the attention they were so good at generating.

As the astonished upstairs staff related it, their party piece consisted of getting up in the middle of breakfast and improvising a show, dancing jigs all over the dining room and bouncing basketballs around the tables and lobbing them over the guests. When the novelty palled, they headed out into the corridors and entertained passing chambermaids with their antics before bounding downstairs and repeating the performance for the benefit of the kitchen staff.

The Globetrotters only appeared at breakfast time.

They were out training all day and performing all evening. They relished their huge breakfast and the chance to impress an audience. But they missed out on the feature of the Consulate Hotel that so impressed visiting Russians: Jimmy's flagship lunches.

Jimmy had two arrows in his culinary quiver: the egg, sausage, and bacon combination, and stews. There may have been details of Jimmy's art my inexpert eye missed. Perhaps he was a dab hand at selecting fresh herbs and rare spices and combining them to produce subtle flavours. But as far as I could tell, his appreciation of condiments did not go beyond salt and perhaps pepper.

Every morning once breakfast was out of the way, Jimmy started by decanting into a pot the inch or two of beef suet I would later scoop out in congealed form at the dishwashing stage. Then in went potatoes, carrots, and onions followed by a measly allocation of stringy beef, an ingredient Miss Petrie the Scottish manager evidently regarded as a luxury and whose dispensation she regulated and watched over like a hawk. The result was palatable enough as long as guests did not expect the *cuisine* to be too *haute* or too *nouvelle*. In fact, Jimmy's stews bore a striking resemblance to my mother's humble lunchtime offerings. The taste was acceptable and the helpings generous. Most importantly in those cash-strapped times, it was all free. I, for one, never complained.

Nor for that matter did the Russians. And one aspect of their stay departing Russians invariably singled out for praise during their farewell rituals was the food.

The ultimate test of their sincerity and presumably of the abysmal standards of Soviet catering came one lunchtime when for some reason we were running late. Perhaps Jimmy had spent the morning mooning over Maria's treachery, studying newly-discovered sexual combinations in one of his magazines, or ranting about British bastards and stabbing his chopping board with his carving knife. With the lunch gong about to go, it became increasingly obvious that the guests would have to be kept waiting. Anyone familiar with the scene in *Fawlty Towers* where Polly and Manuel entertain the hungry diners with her singing and his guitar playing while Basil struggles against adversity to bring in the *canard à l'orange* specially ordered for Sybil's *gourmet* night will know exactly what we were up against.

As the lunch hour neared, came, and passed, Jimmy became so flustered that when he finally determined that the stew was done to perfection and ready to be ladled out, he picked up the huge pot with a violent jerk and dropped it and its entire contents on the kitchen floor.

I should add that however technically challenging and time-consuming my dishwashing responsibilities were, my duties also included mopping the kitchen floor at the conclusion of operations each afternoon before the night crew took over. This was done with a grubby mop I dunked into a dark brew of once soapy water and a week's worth of spilled cooking fat. I confess that in the rush to get home, I rarely bothered to change the water or rinse out the mop. But I felt confident that no one knew this. Besides, it was surely a matter of minutes before hungry guests started a riot upstairs. So Jimmy and I got down on all fours and coaxed most of the errant stew back into the pot with our bare hands to a background of much tut-tutting from Alf, who volunteered the view that such a disgrace would never have happened in the army.

Jimmy fired up his stove again, gave the stew a quick stir, and up it went to delight the palates of the assembled Russians. We knew it did because when their stay at the Consulate came to a much-lamented end next morning, there they were in the kitchens, standing on the exact spot where the stew had lain in ruins not twenty-four hours earlier, demanding to meet in person the *stewmeister* who had made their dining experience so memorable and pressing twice the usual number of grey plastic toy cars on him. Looking back, it is possible that these Russians had a rich sense of humour and that they were in fact 'taking the piss', as Londoners would say. But I doubt it. This was from the heart.

True to form, the CIA misread the signs. Instead, it spent years convincing the Pentagon, a string of incumbents in the White House, and the US public that the Sovs were about to take over the universe thanks to their superior technology and their fail-safe methods. Had they asked, our bumbling crew in the kitchens of a flaking hotel on the edge of Notting Hill could have told them as early as the mid-1960s not only that most Russians were in fact charming people but also that things were far worse in their country than their spooks were telling them. To mix metaphors, if the evil empire was not yet on its last legs, it was heading for the rocks. Anybody could see that.

*

I had come to London to learn English. But in the bargain I also learned about – in random order – unsalted butter, minicabs, fellatio, Henry Purcell, basketball, lesbianism, stews, Jamaican boys, Irish politics, and alternative takes on the Soviet menace. In the process, I added useful expressions to my growing English vocabulary: funeral ode, Aussie shit, camp coffee, camp behaviour, beef suet, British bastards, slam dunk, giving head. Though I could hardly have foreseen it at the start, it became increasingly clear to me this was exactly what I had left Lure, Haute-Saône for. Where else but in a vast, generous, serendipitous city such as London would this rich experience have been possible?

And speaking of experience, at about that time, up popped Maryse, as if on cue. She was a French classmate at West London College with whom I had been paired to present to the class our reading of one of the set books, Terence Rattigan's play *The Winslow Boy*, a tale of justice denied in an English 'public' school and a minor version of France's *Affaire Dreyfus*. Over long hours spent fathoming the play's meaning and discussing its literary merits, Maryse and I became more than friends. She insisted – somewhat implausibly – that she valued intellect in a man above all else and that my superior understanding of mid-twentieth-century British drama made her buckle at the knees. She was not shy, to put it mildly. Her central insight into the human condition was as memorable as it was simple: a kiss that tastes of *cognac* is preferable to one that tastes of toothpaste. Another of her many attributes was her record collection, which included the complete Simon and Garfunkel *oeuvre* to date, a body of work I warmly recommend as musical background to voyages of youthful discovery, especially those involving travelling companions as unabashed as Maryse. My education was nearing completion.

CHAPTER SIXTEEN: COMPARE AND CONTRAST

Eighty per cent of success is showing up.
                                    Woody Allen (1935-)

I journeyed from Lure, Haute-Saône to London at the age of eighteen to learn English. The gamble paid off and later provided me with a rich professional life, teaching in universities in places as diverse as California, Texas, Hong Kong, Singapore, and Thailand. The experience was personally fulfilling and I hope that I managed to make a positive contribution to the intellectual development of at least some of my students by encouraging them to throw the rule book out of the window and experiment with unfamiliar thoughts. I like to think that I had some success in California and perhaps in Texas and Hong Kong but I have my doubts about the impact my approach had in overly controlled Singapore or overly deferent Thailand.

But initially, English did not pay the rent on my humble flat on the unfashionable edges of Notting Hill. When I got home from the daily grind, dinner was a bowl of the same cereal I had for breakfast that morning and a mug of tea or perhaps a plate of egg, chips, and Spam in a greasy eatery. Often, home was a frigid bedsit with a wheezy gas heater with an insatiable appetite for coins, a grubby carpet, an unheated bathroom shared by half-a-dozen tenants up and down the building and, if we were lucky, a pay phone on the draughty landing. So why did I put up with it?

One factor was variety. London was wildly cosmopolitan: Indian store owners, Jamaican bus conductors, Italian waiters, African students, Japanese executives, Greek restaurateurs, American tourists, and everywhere a jabber of languages I had never heard before. To adapt a line from Robert Browning, London may not have been 'where waters gushed and fruit trees grew', but everything was indeed 'strange and new'. Another factor was freedom. London did not just suggest freedom, it served it up in fistfuls: freedom from immutable schedules, from petty discipline, from routines, from predictability, and from provincial certainties of all kinds.

Another factor was friends, in combinations of nationalities, backgrounds, and inclinations I could not have imagined before making the journey: larger-than-life, generous Cypriot George and his Zodiac; delicate, mysterious Vietnamese Vuong and his connections to musical mega-stars; jet-haired French Geneviève, who shared our laughs and our rides around London in George's car but who loved to tease us over whether or not she had responded to the supposed advances of Mr Enderby, our witty West London College English teacher; pretty Portuguese chambermaid Maria, whose romantic proclivities remained shrouded in mystery; gay Glaswegian Johnny and his retinue of Jamaican boys, his skill with a cooking pot, and especially his stock of baroque music records; fellow minicab drivers Mike and Steve and the speculations we shared about minicab agency owner Arthur and the exact nature of his business activities; even Jimmy the Irish *stewmeister*, though his tendency to fly off the handle at the slightest provocation made it a good idea to stick to the safe topic of pornography while in his company and turn down invitations to spend time with him anywhere that served alcoholic refreshment; and of course enchanting, audacious French Maryse and her willingness to share with me her considerable expertise on Simon and Garfunkel and much else besides. Over convivial curries and endlessly refilled pots of tea, we entertained and informed each other, discussing films we had seen or concerts we might afford to buy tickets for, recounting love affairs or engineering new ones, and creating a world in which this motley crew of young minds could thrive.

The gravitational pull of cities and the chances they offer the young and the restless, the inquisitive and the clueless have been noted for as long as cities have been in existence. But around the time I was diving into the London swirl, no one expressed this yearning for freedom and the willingness to have a go better than London-born Cat Stevens, singing in that marvellously sonorous voice of his to the twang of a slightly out-of-tune guitar:

If you want to live high, live high,
And if you want to live low, live low.
'Cause there's a million ways to go,
You know that there are.

For me, though the atmosphere was highly congenial, I had no choice but to live low. But I had tremendous fun doing it. The aim, which I perceived only hazily at the time, was to be in places where something improbable was always likely to happen and to be receptive to opportunities as they emerged. To do this, I had to be free of commitments to anything much beyond the next few weeks. I also had to be willing to sell my limited skills to anyone who would hand over enough cash for me to live on: pay the rent, feed myself, attend the occasional film or concert, and especially spend time with friends in pubs or sitting on each other's floor drinking tea and smoking, in my case my pipe – for, like Bill Clinton at Oxford, I never learned to inhale – and for others, something shared, more potent, and somewhat less legal. In between puffs, we challenged each other's theories of everything and we elaborated schemes for restructuring society along more benign lines.

If I could relive my late teens and early twenties, I would do exactly the same thing. Not in London perhaps, though I still think of the city as a kind of spiritual home. Retracing my steps would be bound to disappoint. Perhaps in New York for its vitality, or in Los Angeles for its friendliness and its openness, or in San Francisco for all of the above plus its extraordinary beauty, or even in Berlin or Sydney. But the list is short. Not many cities qualify.

*

The irony is that my presence in London and my chance to embrace its bounty resulted from an accident. Fate had played a hand. I had spent two frustrating undergraduate years trying to get my head around French law before concluding that French law and I were not made for each other. The solution was to study and later use foreign languages professionally. But of the two languages in contention, German and English, which should I go for first? In the event, English won the toss purely thanks to Jacqueline, my older sister Bernadette's school friend, and to her offer to help me settle in England where she happened to be teaching French. Had she been teaching French in a German school instead, I almost certainly would have gone there especially since Germany was much closer and I was already familiar with the country. My life would surely have taken a very different course.

But in truth, I doubt if I would have sustained the effort and come this far in my personal makeover. Unless Jacqueline or some other hypothetical friend of my sister's had been teaching French in a German

378

school near the Danish border or in the outpost that was West Berlin at the time, I would surely have been tempted to cut my losses and head back to Lure, Haute-Saône as soon as the going got tough and the money began to run low. But once in England, I did not have enough money for a train fare home so I had no choice but to stay put and, for good or bad, lie in the bed I had made for myself.

In retrospect, the good far outweighed the bad. The choice may have been accidental, but it turned out a good one. With the *insouciance* of youth, I never stopped to consider at the outset the thought that leaving home, family, friends, culture, and language at the age of eighteen might be a quixotic gamble. This was a leap of faith. That it paid off owes a great deal to chance. But is it also possible that London was exquisitely suited to providing the setting for the makeover I craved, consciously or otherwise.

In hindsight, my quest for English was merely the catalyst for a deep yearning for the unexpected. So in principle, any one of the cities I listed above could have provided the crucible I was looking for. In fact, had I grown up in Ludford, Herefordshire, for example, and not in Lure, Haute-Saône, I probably would have found the prospect of trying my luck in Paris hugely tempting. I would even have had the pretext of needing to learn French, still a major international language at the time. After all, I would have had plenty of predecessors, both illustrious and anonymous, as the roll call of those the City of Lights had welcomed, nurtured, and freed from oppression far worse than anything I knew was a long one. But when my chance to swap a humdrum provincial existence for big city life came, Paris was far more French than London was English and slotting comfortably into Paris society required – and still does – accepting French cultural norms lock, stock, and barrel. In France, even in Paris, there was no *à la carte* option: you were, felt, looked, sounded, and behaved French or you suffered the consequences. Not so in London. As Cat Stevens knew and celebrated, the city and its cultures offered a million ways to go. As far as I could tell, Paris offered just one.

*

Looking back, was I too harsh on France and in particular on Lure, Haute-Saône? Did I mock small-town values unjustly? Was I too damning of the French State, French education, and the Catholic Church? Did I grind my axe too mercilessly?

Get off the *Paris-Bâle* in Lure, Haute-Saône today, and the welcoming party will no longer consist of a couple of unshaven, moustachioed Frenchmen leaning on their battered Renault taxis, with a moth-eaten *béret* on their head and a *Gauloise* hanging from the corner of their mouth. Lure, Haute-Saône has moved on. In fact, it is quite possible that had I been born there two decades ago instead of six and grown up in a much less repressive atmosphere, I would feel quite content at the thought of spending my life there or in some other French town just like it instead of embarking on a quest for a linguistic, cultural, and emotional makeover.

The town has grown a little. It even has an air of quiet prosperity. Public buildings have been spruced up and herbaceous borders adorn street corners. The hospital where I was born has been upgraded and greatly expanded. The stinking *pissoir* behind the church is no more. A few traffic lights have appeared where they do least aesthetic damage. Meanwhile, passing traffic whizzes by on a sleek bypass that makes the town more invisible than ever. But for those who wish to linger, there is now a US-style motel offering free wifi and even, of all improbable amenities, a conference centre. Lure even has its own Japanese restaurant. But anticipating perhaps the limited appeal of that *cuisine* to local palates, the management thought it prudent to add Chinese and even Thai specialties to the menu. The old highway to Belfort to the east is lined on both sides with hypermarkets, fast food restaurants, and car dealerships. Evidently, Lure, Haute-Saône is no stranger to the French determination to transmogrify its urban landscape along American lines even as its elite knocks America and its people relentlessly for their poor taste and their crass commercialism.

There is now a proposal to have UNESCO confer World Heritage status on Le Corbusier's work, including the lovely church on the hill at Ronchamp. This is welcome, though I suspect it will take more than this grand gesture to put Haute-Saône on the tourist trail and turn Ronchamp into the Machu Picchu of eastern France. But the town now has its very own Wikipedia and Facebook pages in English, even if these remain work in progress and peter out after just a few lines. The lone photo on both webpages features the railway crossing of legend, where I watched all those steam trains whoosh past. This is now the very model of a modern railway crossing, with shiny plastic barriers lowered automatically at strategic moments with no apparent need for human intervention. The photo looks north into the heart of the town. Look closely on the left and you might spot the *Rex* cinema, where I flirted with eternal damnation by leering at photos of Brigitte Bardot *au naturel* on my way home from school and even – may the Lord have mercy! – from church.

In the photo, the small-town torpor is almost palpable. But for the visitor, the place has its charms. It is compact, restful, unpretentious. If you are looking for a quiet spot where to spend your next summer holidays, you could do worse than booking into one of the town's modest hotels and going walkabouts. When you tire of watching the trains at the railway crossing and walking the length of the *Grand Rue* and back again, drive north into the foothills of the Vosges mountains and around the patchwork of tiny lakes reached along twisting lanes so narrow that passing another car will involve death-defying manoeuvres that will test your driving skills to the limit. On the way, you will probably pass through Corravillers, my maternal grandfather's ancestral village. Once back in the comparative urban vortex, dine on *sashimi* or *paad thai*. Lure, Haute-Saône is a fine place for a week or so. But for anything longer, take a friend by the hand and walk him or her through the streets of London instead.